CAMELOT

BOOK 3 IN THE CHRONICLES OF ARTHUR

PETER GIBBONS

Boldwood

First published in Great Britain in 2025 by Boldwood Books Ltd.

Copyright © Peter Gibbons, 2025

Cover Design by Colin Thomas

Cover Images: Colin Thomas

Interior map: Irina Katsimon

The moral right of Peter Gibbons to be identified as the author of this work has been asserted in accordance with the Copyright, Designs and Patents Act 1988.

Every effort has been made to obtain the necessary permissions with reference to copyright material, both illustrative and quoted. We apologise for any omissions in this respect and will be pleased to make the appropriate acknowledgements in any future edition.

A CIP catalogue record for this book is available from the British Library.

Paperback ISBN 978-1-83518-260-4

Large Print ISBN 978-1-83518-261-1

Hardback ISBN 978-1-83518-259-8

Trade Paperback ISBN 978-1-80625-668-6

Ebook ISBN 978-1-83518-262-8

Kindle ISBN 978-1-83518-263-5

Audio CD ISBN 978-1-83518-254-3

MP3 CD ISBN 978-1-83518-255-0

Digital audio download ISBN 978-1-83518-258-1

This book is printed on certified sustainable paper. Boldwood Books is dedicated to putting sustainability at the heart of our business. For more information please visit https://www.boldwoodbooks.com/about-us/sustainability/

Boldwood Books Ltd, 23 Bowerdean Street, London, SW6 3TN

www.boldwoodbooks.com

For my family, as always.

Then to Hrothgar was granted glory in battle,
    Mastery of the field; so friends and kinsmen
    Gladly obeyed him, and his band increased
    To a great company. It came into his mind
    That he would command the construction
    of a huge mead hall, a house greater
    than men on earth had ever heard of.

> — FROM 'BEOWULF', AN OLD ENGLISH POEM
> WRITTEN IN THE NINTH CENTURY, SET IN
> THE SIXTH CENTURY

BRITAIN, C. 540

N

PICTLAND
DAL
RIATA
LOTHIAN

GODODDIN

BERNICIA

RHEGED

DEIRA

ELMET

SAXONS

GWYNEDD

POWYS

DEMETIA

GWENT

Kingdoms of

DUMNONIA

KERNOW

Dumnnonia

THE GREAT SIXTH-CENTURY KINGDOMS OF BRITAIN

After the collapse of the Roman Empire in 400AD, the legions left Britain to descend into a place of constant, brutal warfare. By the sixth century, the island is ruled by fierce kings from behind crumbling Roman strongholds and menacing hilltop fortresses. The south-east and western kingdoms have fallen to marauding Germanic invaders known as Saxons. The Saxons are a warlike people from across the sea, first invited to Britain by Vortigern, a weak king of a small kingdom, to aid him in his wars against the rival kings of Britain.

Rheged – Located close to Cumbria in modern-day England. Ruled by King Urien from his seat at the Bear Fort. Warriors of Rheged carry the bear sigil upon their shields.

Gododdin – A kingdom in Britain's north-east, close to modern-day Northumberland and East Lothian. Ruled by King Letan Luyddoc from his fortress Dunpendrylaw. Gododdin's warriors march under a stag banner.

Dal Riata – Kingdom on Scotland's west coast, covering what is now Argyll.

Dumnonia – Ruled by Arthur as steward for Prince Madoc ap Uther. Dumnonian warriors march to war with a dragon sigil upon their shields. Located in Britain's south-west, mainly in modern-day Devon, Somerset and Cornwall.

Gwynedd – Ruled by King Cadwallon Longhand. Located in north Wales and Anglesey.

Elmet – Ruled by King Gwallog. Located in the area around modern-day Leeds, reaching down south to the Midlands. Elmet's warriors wear the *lorica segmentata* armour and red cloaks of the Roman legions.

Bernicia – Lands lost to Ida, the Saxon conqueror. Covers what is now south Northumberland, Tyne and Wear, and Durham. Its warriors once fought beneath the proud banner of the fox.

Deira – Lands stretching along much of Britain's west coast, which fell to Saxon invaders in Vortigern's Great War.

Lothian – Ruled by King Lot, encompassing what is now south-east Scotland.

Powys – Ruled by King Brochvael the Fanged. A large and powerful kingdom in what is now central Wales.

Pictland – Lands occupied by the Picts in Scotland's north.

Demetia – Lands in the south-west of what is now Wales. Ruled by King Morholt and his Irish warriors who took the kingdom by force.

Gwent – A kingdom between the Rivers Wye and Usk, in what is now south Wales. Ruled by King Tewdrig.

Lyndsey – A Saxon kingdom lying between the River Humber and the Wash, ruled by King Cwichelm.

Benoic – A Brythonic kingdom on the borders of Armorican Brittany and Gaul, ruled by King Ban.

Cameliard – A Brythonic kingdom in Brittany, neighbour to Benoic. Ruled by King Leodegrance.

1

547AD, BRITAIN

The war for Britain raged. A time of blood, conquest and shield walls. A wolf age, a storm age, a time of spears, shields and swords. The age of Arthur.

The war for Britain raged. A time of blood, conquest and shield walls. A wolf age, a storm age, a time of spears, shields and swords. The age of Arthur.

Eight hundred Saxon warriors trampled across a field of soft heather. Wind shook the undergrowth about their heavy boots as they led wagons full of plunder westwards. Wooden wheels creaked and groaned beneath the weight of stolen ale barrels, hocks of ham and sides of beef, wood axes, iron spits, furs and rolled wool. They sang a rowing song in their coarse, brutal language, keeping time by clashing axe blades against iron shield rims. Purple flowers spotted the heather and fields flowed like the sea, blown by the same breeze that whipped away columns of smoke rising behind the Saxons as evidence of the destruction left in their wake.

Laughter and song drifted across the land as big men with long, braided hair and beards, hard-baked leather breastplates, spears, seaxes and fur about their necks and shoulders marched west towards Britain's heartland from the east coast south of Bernicia. Daring men and Saxon warriors who had rowed across the wild sea on shallow-draughted warships, braving ferocious storms and waves like mountains. They had rowed those clinker-built vessels across the grey-green surging whale road, the narrow sea which separated Britain from Armorica, Benoic, and the lands of Saxons, Jutes, Angles and Franks to bring their blades and their malice to a land already brutalised by raids and invasion. Such men risked their lives, surviving treacherous waters, placing their lives in the hands of their gods, Woden and Thuror, leaving behind farms, mothers, wives and children. They came for silver, women, land, reputation and glory, just as thousands of their countrymen had done before. The Britons called them all Saxons, but the men who came across the sea were also Angles and Jutes. Men from hard lands swept to ruin in the murderously lawless days after the collapse of Rome's vast empire.

'Is that a bird's wing?' asked Kai, his chestnut eyes squinting as he peered down into the valley at the marching Saxon column.

'An eagle's wing,' Arthur said.

A brute of a man with a tattooed face and arms like ale barrels strode before the Saxons carrying the eagle's wing on a long pole. It was their battle standard, a symbol of their commander's prestige.

'When did their ships arrive?'

'Two weeks ago, we think. They've already sacked three villages since then.' Arthur glanced up at the sky, and then at fallen leaves whipped across the land by a swirling wind. 'This should be the last of them. The swallows and swifts have gone, so no more ships will come until spring.'

'Are they aligned with any of the Saxon kings?'

'It doesn't matter.'

'Why not?'

'Because we are going to kill them anyway.'

Arthur stalked away from the hilltop hidden from the Saxons below, turning to where five hundred men in black cloaks awaited him, carrying shining leaf-shaped spears and shields scored by blades, their helmets dented, and their clothes stained and faded. Hard faces stared back at him, broken noses, men with missing fingers, and eyes like flints. They saw a tall man in a shining coat of chain-mail armour and a night-black cloak about his shoulders, a bright helmet topped with a plume of raven feathers and a sword belted in a red scabbard at his waist. The sword. A gift from Merlin the druid. Neit, god of war, named the blade Caledfwlch when she was forged in the distant mists of time. Ambrosius Aurelianus had wielded her glorious edge during the Great War when men called the sword Excalibur, and now she belonged to Arthur. He rolled his shoulder to soothe its constant ache, a gift left there by a Saxon spear point. Arthur locked eyes with his men, noticing how they lingered upon his face, torn and scarred by King Uther Pendragon's sword when they had fought beneath the great standing stones on Sorviodunum's sweeping plains. Arthur had killed Uther that day and become Pendragon himself. He was the *dux bellorum*, Britain's warlord, steward of Dumnonia, high king, warrior and killer of Saxons.

'Do we fight?' asked Dewi, the captain of Arthur's fiercely loyal black cloaks. He handed Arthur a heavy shield cut from linden-wood boards ringed and bossed with iron.

'We fight.'

Dewi grinned and hefted his own shield. 'Then do we go home?'

Arthur clapped him on the shoulder and glanced up at a shifting afternoon sky the colour of a burned cauldron. 'Do you miss your wife?'

'It's been five years, lord, since the battle of the River Dubglas, and I can count on one hand the weeks we've spent with our families since. Even in winter, we've stayed away from Dumnonia. Fighting cursed Saxons with ice in our beards.'

'After today, we'll go home. You have my word.'

What passed for a smile curled the corner of Dewi's mouth. The tall, lugubrious warrior nodded towards the men. 'A rest will do them good.'

'But not for long. You are right, it has been too long since we fought the Saxon hordes at the River Dubglas. Since then, we've penned the enemy back, and yet still Rheged, Gododdin and Lothian do not recognise me as Pendragon. There must be a reckoning in the north before long.'

'We've been too busy killing Saxons, lord.'

'And yet there are always more. Ready the men.'

Arthur left Dewi to bark and jostle the men. Spears clanked against shields, axes slid into belt loops as men drank the last of their ale and took a quick meal of cheese and black bread. Kai stood by his chestnut gelding and handed Arthur the reins to his own mount, Llamrei, a huge white stallion. Arthur stroked the horse's long nose, and it nuzzled his shoulder.

'It's time,' Arthur said to Kai, his foster brother.

'You're sure this will work?' Kai asked, his curly hair tousled as always about his broad face.

Arthur shrugged. War was about trickery, deception, manoeuvre and slaughter. It was risk, scouting unknown hills and valleys and luring an enemy into a fight on ground where he was unsure and then falling upon him with ruthless savagery. Arthur had learned those hard facts in a lifetime spent with sword in hand, fighting implacable enemies who surrounded Britain, encroaching like wolves upon the flock he was duty-bound to protect. 'It must work. Or my black cloaks and I will die in the valley. The Saxons will cut us to pieces and our corpses will rot in the field. Go to your men. You have two hundred warriors who must be ready, almost half our force. Make sure Idnerth, Orin and Einion are prepared.'

They both mounted, and Llamrei turned in a circle, stomping his powerful legs so that Arthur had to wrestle with the reins to keep the stallion still.

'I'll see you after,' said Kai, and he leaned forward to clasp Arthur's wrist in the warrior's grip. Black death-ring tattoos covered both men's forearms, and for a fleeting moment Arthur remembered how as boys at Caer Ligualid in the kingdom of Rheged, he and Kai had dreamt of earning a warrior's death ring, the thin tattooed ring warriors etched on one another's arms to signify a kill in battle. Those rings symbolised a warrior's reputation, the sign of a fighter's prowess, and one of the many ways of identifying a member of the elite warrior caste. Death rings had once seemed so important. Arthur and Kai had talked of them endlessly, running through the Caer's forests, fighting with stick swords as they slew imaginary enemies and earned the rings every young warrior yearned for. Both men's arms were now more tattooed rings than unmarked skin. Arthur and Kai had slain so many that they had stopped adding rings to mark their kills. The blood of their enemies dunged Britain's battlefields and there were always more enemies yet to fight.

Kai galloped off down the hillside and Arthur watched his brother and friend disappear beyond a copse of hazel trees. A fox darted from the trees, stared up at Arthur's black cloaks, and then darted back into the undergrowth. The fox was wise to seek cover, for soon those hills would ring with the din of war.

A bark made Arthur smile, and his dog Cavall came bounding from amongst the men and leapt playfully at Llamrei's flanks, which the horse dutifully ignored. Cavall had once been a Saxon war dog. He was an enormous beast with slathering jaws, powerful head and haunches, but was now Arthur's loyal dog who followed him everywhere, even onto blood-soaked hillsides where men screamed, and the war god rejoiced in the malevolent joy of violence.

'Today we face more Saxons,' Arthur called to his men. The black cloaks stood to attention at the sound of his voice. Spears stood straight; iron points dull against the grey sky. 'We face men come across the sea, following in the wake of those who have come before. Sea-wolves, slavers and murderers who seek to steal our land, kill our womenfolk and make our children their slaves. If they had heard of Arthur's black cloaks, perhaps they would have stayed at home with their goats and their wives. These are the last of this year's raiders. The rest of the Saxons hide behind their high walls, trembling at the thought of our black cloaks and our blades.'

The men chuckled and exchanged knowing glances. Llamrei whickered, and Arthur stroked his neck.

'We are the men who protect Britain from her enemies. We are the swords who keep our people safe. We are the spears who drive the invader back into the sea. We are the black cloaks! The victors of the River Glein and the Dubglas. We have soaked our blades in Saxon blood. We are the Saxon-killers!' Arthur drew Excalibur from her red scabbard and held the mighty blade aloft and the black cloaks roared and shook their spears in salute. 'If we do not stop this horde fresh from the dark seas, they will kill and rape their way across Britain until they find land to take for their own. Just as Octha, Ida, Hengist, Horsa and Cwichelm did before them. Kingdoms have fallen to such men. But not today. We are the protectors of Britain, and if these men wish to make our land their home, they must trample across our bones to do it. Who do you fight for?'

'Arthur! Arthur! Arthur!' five hundred voices called back to him.

'March then, you murderous whoresons!' Dewi barked at them, and they followed the captain down into the depths of the valley below. To reach that valley, the Saxons had to crest a rise which concealed Arthur's men from the west. Arthur wanted to lure them in to his trap. He had to bring the Saxons to the fight and lead them into the bowels between ancient British hills. He was east of the old kingdom of Lyndsey and south of Bernicia and Deira. Each were Saxon kingdoms occupying Britain's west coast and had belonged to the Saxons since their brutal warlords had thrown the Britons out with axe, seax, fire and conquest.

The Britons called the lands lost to the Saxons, Angles and Jutes: Lloegyr, the lost lands. Arthur had spent five years pushing the Saxons back, further and deeper into Lloegyr, penning them back into their coastal fortresses and securing the borders of his under kings to keep his people safe. But more Saxons came each summer, new ships with new warriors and Arthur must make an example of those who came across the sea. He must spread fear amongst their people, hoping that one day the boats might stop, and Britain could be at peace for the first time since the Roman legions had left it a desolate, lawless place at the mercy of warlords and warriors.

Arthur urged Llamrei into a canter and Cavall followed, the war dog's tongue lolling as he ran alongside the great stallion. Arthur reached the hill's crest and Llamrei reared on his hind legs, whinnying and raking the air with his forelegs. He wheeled the horse about and glowered down at the marching Saxons. Drops of rain pattered against Arthur's helmet and he let Llamrei prance amongst the heather, cutting an unmistakable figure beneath the dark sky. The Saxons shouted and pointed at him, their leather and fur clothes in dour hues of brown and grey, and their leader came forth to stand beside the big man with the eagle-wing standard. The leader was a squat, bandy-legged man with broad shoulders and a wolf's head perched atop his own and its fur draped down his back. He carried a wicked-bladed, long-handled war axe, and he pointed the weapon at Arthur.

Arthur ground his teeth and grinned mirthlessly. His heart pounded in his chest because it was almost time to fight, almost time for the thunderous clash of arms where men hewed and hacked at one another, lifted into a state of ecstasy by the exhilaration of danger as they fought in the gossamer-thin veil between this world and the next. A Saxon war horn blared, and eight hundred Saxon warriors quickened their pace in Arthur's direction, taking the bait. They saw a lord in his war finery, a man with a sword, helmet and chain mail, each of which marked him out as wealthy. Capture Arthur's mail or sword and a man would become instantly wealthy beyond his wildest dreams. He could buy his own ship, build a stout longhouse, roof it with thatch, and purchase four slaves to wait on his every need. All that man needed to do was cut Arthur down, kill a man who had cut the hand from King Ida of Bernicia, who had killed Uther Pendragon in single combat and slain Octha the Saxon warlord in a desperate riverside battle.

Arthur dug his right knee into Llamrei's flank and urged the horse down the hillside. He caught up with his men, who waited for him in the valley basin where a sickly thin brook twisted its way through peat and bracken. Arthur took a spear from Hywel, a trusted warrior who wore the Roman *lorica segmentata* armour of the men of Elmet and a blood-red cloak about his shoulders.

'Will they fight, lord?' Hywel asked, his hand resting on the hilt of his gladius, the short Roman sword he wore at his right hip.

'They'll fight,' Arthur replied, 'and they'll die.'

'Here they come.'

The big man with the eagle-wing standard was first over the western rise, and then hundreds of Saxons followed. They paused on the hill crest, staring down at Arthur and his five hundred warriors. They had the larger force but hesitated to face so many Britons. So far, they had fought only defenceless villagers and fishwives, and to face shields, spears, knives and axes was enough to give any man pause.

'Now we run,' Arthur said.

'Right, lads!' Dewi bellowed. 'Run for your miserable lives, and let the dogs see you do it.' He kicked a black cloak up the arse and the men set off at a run.

'Don't see why we are running from those shit-stinking curs,' complained one black cloak.

'It's them should be running from us,' said another.

'Just do as you're told,' Dewi said, lumbering into a run, his buckles, straps and weapons jangling. 'We run and then we kill. That's all you need to know.'

Arthur cantered ahead, turned his horse, galloped around his men and then rode ahead of them as though he fled for his life. The Saxon war horn blared, and the horde came streaming down the hill like a pack of wild animals, weapons waving, voices undulating and shouting their bloodlust. All hesitation fled from them like a tide at ebb. Men who had come to kill them ran away like frightened rabbits and the Saxons smelled blood.

Arthur led Llamrei over the next gentle rise and down into a stubbled grazing pasture, sat before a dense forest like a horse-shoe of green surrounded by sprawling oak, ash and elm trees stretching up and away to the east and north. Arthur leapt lithely from Llamrei's back and landed on the balls of his feet. He slapped the stallion's rump and Llamrei cantered off towards the treeline. Arthur unslung the shield from his back and readied his spear. He stood alone in that scrap of bramble and nettle and the forest creaked around him. Rain pounded the leaves and boughs like the sigh of the sea. He closed his eyes and breathed deeply, taking in the damp rain smell upon the earth, chest heaving as he let the soil, grass, trees, wind, rain and sky of Britain soak into his body, strengthening him for what must come next.

The black cloaks ran down the slope towards Arthur and formed loose ranks behind him.

'Do it badly, now,' Arthur ordered as his red-faced men came to a halt, puffing from the effort of running in leather and wool, carrying shields, long knives and spears. 'Ragged lines and poor order until I say otherwise.'

Hywel and Dewi took their places to Arthur's right and left, and the rain stopped as the Saxons crested the rise and hurtled down the ridge. Sunlight punched through the broiling clouds and golden shafts shone, glinting upon spears, helmets and cloak pins.

'Hold,' Dewi growled as the men shifted about Arthur, rest-less, spears held at odd angles, gathering in loose formation.

The Saxons came on, teeth bared and eyes wild at the prospect of slaughtering a war band of frightened Britons.

'Arawn and Maponos protect us,' said Hywel, calling upon

the gods through gritted teeth. Every black cloak stiffened, men touched amulets at their necks for luck and whispered to whichever god held their favour. Some men talked to themselves, urging their heart to stay strong and their weapon to strike hard. One warrior in the second rank vomited and more than one pissed where he stood so as not to break formation. Eight hundred Saxon killers hurtled towards them, intent on slaughter, their blades shining and their faces twisted with malevolent fury. It was time to stand and fight and show the Saxon sea-warriors the price of raiding Britain.

2

The Saxons spread out in a wild charge. No ranks or discipline, just a wild, baying horde. Arthur flexed his hand around his spear's ash shaft, palm sweating, mouth dry. Enemy boots pounded the earth, and Arthur could feel every thud beating in time with his heart. He took deep breaths, fighting to hold his nerve until the right time, until the perfect moment to strike at the enemy. At two hundred paces, he could make out men's flowing hair and the colours daubed upon their shields. At one hundred paces, he could see eyes, teeth and the iron trinkets braided into their beards. At fifty paces eight hundred men filled the shallow valley, and their charge was enough to make even the stoutest warrior consider retreat. At twenty paces downwind, the acrid stink of their sweat and the rank stench of their furs filled Arthur's nose, and he snarled.

'Shield wall!' Arthur bellowed.

The black cloaks gave a clipped roar in unison, and shields overlapped one another with loud clanks, unruly spears became a forest of slanted points resting on iron shield rims as the black cloaks formed three solid ranks of spears and shields, just as they had done so many times before.

The lead Saxons paused, realising that instead of an afraid, fleeing rabble, they instead faced organised ranks of well-armed, drilled and grim-faced warriors. As the leading men slowed, the Saxons behind them kept on coming, and Arthur braced himself, shoulder behind his shield, overlapped one side by Hywel, and Dewi on the other.

A long-faced Saxon with his beard woven into two ropes crashed into Arthur's shield. The force drove Arthur back half a pace. He braced his knee against the bottom of his shield just as the Saxon hooked his bearded axe over the top edge and tried to yank it down. Arthur's knee kept the shield in place, and so the spear thrust by the enemy behind the first Saxon, which should have ripped Arthur's throat out, instead found only stout shield boards.

Arthur shrugged the Saxon off the shield and punched its heavy boss into the man's face. He stabbed with his spear and the point tore through a Saxon's cheek. Arthur brought the weapon back and punched its blade into an enemy's chest. The first Saxon spat blood, his nose broken and mashed like a squashed turnip, and he beat at Arthur's shield with his axe. He crashed the axe blade down, catching Arthur's spear against his shield, breaking the weapon in two. Men pressed close, enemies heaving at one another, the Saxons held by the black cloaks' impenetrable shield wall. A warrior in the rank behind Arthur howled in pain, and another black cloak gurgled as a Saxon spear opened his throat. The iron stink of blood filled the air, weapons hacked and clanged, and Arthur held fast.

'They're getting around our flanks,' said Dewi, and then ducked as a spear flashed above his head.

'Hold,' Arthur said, grimacing as the axe continued to

thunder into his shield, its wielder shouting like a madman. The press of fighting men was too close to wield Excalibur's long blade, so instead Arthur reached to the small of his back and drew his seax. Its bone handle felt cool in his sweating palm as he held the weapon low. Its blade was as long as Arthur's forearm, with a single edge and a broken back tapering into a wicked point. Arthur stabbed the seax beneath his shield but found only fresh air. He grunted and stabbed again, and this time the seax met resistance, its point cutting into soft flesh. Arthur twisted the blade as the Saxon stopped battering Arthur's shield and instead howled in pain. Arthur drew the blade back and drove the Saxon down with his shield. He stamped down hard on the Saxon's throat and sliced his seax blade across another enemy's face.

Space opened up in front of him, and Arthur quickly glanced across the front line. Battle raged as eight hundred Saxon warriors surrounded his smaller force. If the fight continued, Arthur's men would surely die surrounded and outnumbered. He laughed, a mirthless laugh of war-joy because the Saxons had done what he'd hoped they would. They had charged at an enemy they perceived to be weak and in flight, and now they would die.

'Raise the dragon banner!' Arthur called above the din. 'Raise the banner.'

Dewi peeled away from the shield wall and another man took his place next to Arthur. Moments later, the Pendragon banner with its clawing dragon rose from the black cloaks' ranks high on a spear shaft. It waved in the sunlight and the black cloaks let out a single roar of approval. A sound peeled out from the forest, metallic, undulating and high-pitched like an iron beast.

'The carnyx,' said a black cloak in the second rank, and so it was. The carnyx was a war horn. A long, curved bronze tube the size and shape of a spear shaft, topped by a magnificent bronze wolf's head with its mouth agape and snarling. Arthur's war horn.

The forest around the battlefield shook as though a giant charged through its boughs, and hundreds of warriors raced from the woodland, shaking their ground with their war cries. Kai led his warriors from the south, Idnerth and his warriors of Elmet in their Roman plate armour came from the west, Orin led a hundred men of Gwynedd, Einion six score men from Powys, and Lancelot brought the warriors of Dumnonia to the fight. Hundreds of Britons, men of different kingdoms who had once warred amongst themselves over grazing rights, boundaries, access to rivers and cattle raids, all brought together beneath the Pendragon banner, fighting for Arthur, the high king of Britain.

The Saxons wailed, the sound of their despair like the groans of lost souls wandering in the underworld.

'Now kill them!' Arthur called to his men, his jaw set and eyes blazing. 'Kill them all!' The Saxons broke away from Arthur's shield wall, anger drained from them like water from a holed bucket. Warriors came from the forest on all sides and the Saxons, who had raced towards a fight with bloody slaughter in their hearts, now faced death themselves.

Arthur slid the seax back into its sheath at the small of his back, dropped his shield and drew Excalibur. He held the blade aloft and the black cloaks let out a roar to shake the very ground. The sword's leather-wrapped hilt felt comfortable, like the god-forged weapon was made to fit his hand. Strength flowed into him from the sword, the blade given to him by Merlin, with which Arthur was to restore Britain to its people. Sight of the sword imbued his men with confidence and strength and as the Saxons stepped away from the press of the shield wall, the fighting truly began.

Arthur brought Excalibur down hard, two hands on the grip, and the tip slashed through a Saxon's face, splashing hot blood across the next Saxon, staining his flaxen hair crimson. Arthur stepped forward and drove the sword's point into the guts of that man, twisted the blade and ripped it free. Hywel, Dewi and the black cloaks tore into the Saxons as their leader tried to jostle his men into some form of defensive battle order. Arthur saw him through the press, the squat man gesticulating wildly beside the enormous warrior holding the eagle-wing standard high.

Lancelot and Kai reached the enemy first. Lancelot was tall and broad-shouldered, his flat, broad face shouted in anger and his sword flashed. He crashed into the enemy with his shield, throwing two men from their feet, and Kai came with him, cutting and slashing with his deadly blade. Idnerth's warriors in their Roman armour, strange shields and short swords came not in a wild charge, but in an organised line, terrifying in its cold, inevitable precision.

'Gwynedd! Gwynedd!' roared Orin, the champion of that kingdom. He was a monstrous brute of a man, and his huge axe swung with such ferocity that it hacked a Saxon's head from his shoulders with its first strike.

Arthur parried an enemy spear thrust and ducked beneath a seax aimed at his face. He left those attackers to the black cloaks behind him, bounced off an enemy shield and twisted around a blue-eyed Saxon staring at the incredible sight of Roman soldiers advancing on him like warriors from legend. Arthur made for the Saxon leader and the squat man turned, saw the chain mail, helmet and sword and he grabbed the shoulder of his monstrous standard bearer and pointed towards

Arthur. The big man snarled and thrust the standard at another of the squat leader's champions. The big man drew his axe and seax and came towards Arthur with fury in his wild eyes.

A black cloak darted at the big Saxon, who swayed away from a spear thrust with the lightness of a dancer. He flicked his axe with a look of disgust on his face and opened the black cloak's throat with his axe's sharp edge. Arthur charged at him, lunging with Excalibur and forcing the big man to parry the sword with his axe. Arthur kept moving, feinting his body left, and then darting to the right around his foe's axe hand. He stamped down hard onto the Saxon's knee and kept moving as the man's seax slashed at his midriff but found only space. Arthur kicked the knee again and slashed Excalibur down hard onto the warrior's elbow, half severing his arm in a brutal cut. The big Saxon stared at Arthur, grimacing in pain, the shock of his terrible wound draining the colour from his face. Arthur killed him with a thrust of Excalibur's point. The sword punched through wolf fur and leather and into the man's broad chest. It met bone, and then found the Saxon's heart, piercing it and killing him instantly.

Arthur dragged his blade free and swung towards the Saxon leader, only to find him trading blows with Lancelot. The Saxon leader's wolf's pelt fell from his head to lie amongst the blood and piss of the field, churned to filthy, stinking mud by the madness of battle. The long axe swung at Lancelot, but he caught its haft with his left hand and slashed his sword down hard onto the leader's collarbone with an audible crack. Saxons fighting beside their lord wailed with impotent sorrow as Lancelot killed their leader with the ease of a father practising swordplay with his child.

'Well met,' said Lancelot as he caught Arthur's eye. He pulled the helmet from his head and grinned at Arthur, his

strange cuirass of gleaming fish scales unmarked, and his hair
and beard clipped close to his head.

'Well met, indeed.' Arthur took his arm in the warrior's grip,
and they watched together as the Saxons struggled and died
beneath the Britons' anger. Idnerth's soldiers cut through the
enemy like a wood saw, their short swords stabbing and cutting
at men and their shields battering them to the ground.

'Are they Saxons?' Lancelot asked.

Arthur wiped Excalibur's blade clean on the russet cloak of
a dead enemy and slid her back into the scabbard. 'Does it
matter?'

'I suppose not. They could be Jutes or Angles. All the same,
really.'

The battle was over, and, like all battles, the real killing
began when one side broke and ran, and now the Saxons tried
to flee from that field where they had dreamed of a great
slaughter but found only death.

'Dead men can't join forces with Ida, Aelle, or any of the
other Saxon kings.'

'So, is it peace, then, at last?'

'Perhaps, my friend.' Arthur clapped Lancelot on his wide
shoulder. 'For the winter, at least, until our enemies sharpen
their axes and seaxes in spring. An army can't march without
food in its belly or ale to drink. So, we won't see the Saxons
pushing north and west until spring. We have them, Lancelot.'
Arthur grabbed his friend's muscled shoulder. 'For the first
time, we actually have them. Ida and his sons haven't ventured
out from their high crag in Bernicia for two summers. Aelle
and Eormenric fight each other in the south. Warlords fight
for lordship of Lyndsey. The Saxons are in disarray. Come
spring, I shall rally the kingdoms and raise the largest army
Britain has seen since the Romans left, and we'll crush the

Saxons. We'll march east and south and wash the coast with their blood.'

'Can we really do it?'

'We have to. There will never be another chance like this. The enemy has never been so weak. All we must do is drive the blade home and cut the heart from the invaders' chests.'

'And then?'

'Peace. Wives. Children. The good things in life.'

Cavall appeared at Arthur's legs, his tail wagging and his tongue lolling. He bent and scratched the dog behind the ear. Arthur's eyes stung and his shoulders ached. Wounded men groaned and writhed on the ground around him and Arthur had the overwhelming urge to sit down, to rest, even though the carnage of battle still played out across the blood-soaked field.

They spared no Saxon lives that day, and Arthur ordered his men to strip the Saxon corpses of anything of value and leave them to rot on the battlefield. He kept four ale barrels and a wain of food for his men and sent four mounted scouts eastwards to seek survivors from the Saxons' raids. A dozen of his black cloaks followed, leading donkey-pulled wagons towards those people who would desperately need their stolen food, ale and goods returned.

Arthur's men camped that night in a clearing just inside the forest. Men made makeshift tents from cloaks and old sailcloth, and they made campfires over which flitches of pork and sides of beef turned on spits to fill the woodland with the mouthwatering smell of roasting meat. Dewi had a young warrior clean Arthur's armour and weapons, and as the sun set red over the treeline, Arthur sat upon a fallen log wearing only a woollen jerkin and trews.

'Here, lord,' said Hywel. He handed Arthur a trencher of hard bread stuffed with steaming meat. Arthur smiled and took the food. He sat before a small fire ringed with stones and he stretched the ache from his back and took a bite of roasted beef. The juices ran into his beard, and Arthur's stomach groaned with delight.

'Can I sit?' asked Kai. Hywel left, and Kai sat beside the fire.

'Of course, as long as you don't steal my food like you did when we were boys.'

'I swear I won't.' Kai placed a solemn hand on his chest. 'You used to tell Father whenever I took your sweet cakes. You were always his favourite.'

'What? Are you drunk already? Lunete was Ector's favourite, and you were always the best with practice swords and spears.'

Kai laughed and took a swig from an ale skin. 'They were good days, running around Caer Ligualid without a care in the world.'

Arthur thought of his spear-father, Ector, once the champion of all the Britons and the man who had raised Arthur like his own son. 'It almost seems like a different life.'

'I can still best you, even though you wield Merlin's magic sword.' Kai leaned in and nudged Arthur with his shoulder.

'I don't doubt it, brother. Just don't tell anyone.'

'Don't tell anyone what?' said Lancelot, taking a seat beside the fire with an ale skin in each hand.

'That Orin of Gwynedd and Einion of Powys fought better than you today,' said Kai.

'What? Have you lost your wits? Did you not see me cut down the Saxon leader?'

'I saw you flailing around whilst Orin and Einion fought with the hardiest of the enemy.'

'How could you not see? I was...' Lancelot was halfway to standing when he noticed the twinkle in Kai's eye and kicked him playfully in the shin. 'Bastard.'

Orin, Einion and Idnerth approached the fire, each of them rosy cheeked from drink.

'There's mead in one of those barrels,' said Orin, jerking a thumb over his shoulder.

'The last time I drank mead, I was sick for a week,' Kai replied.

'It's fine stuff; they could have brewed it with Gwynedd honey.'

'Nothing is brewed in Gwynedd but sour ale and pinch-faced women,' said Einion.

'The only mead or ale I've ever drunk from Powys tasted like cat's piss.'

'How do you know what cat's piss tastes like?'

The champions of Powys and Gwynedd turned and fixed one another with steel eyes and jutting chins.

'Alright,' said Arthur. He rose and stood between the two warriors, both outstanding fighters from neighbouring king-doms. 'It has been a long summer, and I thank you and your men for your service. We have recovered much of Lloegyr for our people. Tomorrow you can all march for home and spend the rest of this year with your families.'

'Truly?' said Orin. 'I thought the fighting would never end.'

It won't, Arthur thought. 'No more ships will come this late into the summer. We know the forces Ida and his son hold behind their high crag at Dun Guaroy in the north-east, and that rival leaders fight for Lyndsey's throne in the east. In the south, Eormenric rules Kent and his men are too busy defending his borders from his Saxon rivals to strike further into our lands.'

'Eormenric and Aelle are still at war?' asked Lancelot.

'So I hear. The south Saxons and the Saxons in Kent fight over Londinium and its river. It is all set up for us. The dice board swept clear, just waiting for the final throw. We shall take our chance in the spring.'

'When more ships will come across the narrow sea.'

'Hopefully, those men who look across the water with raiding and plunder in their hearts will hear of what happened today. Perhaps they will hear of a cousin or friend who sailed for Britain and met his end beside a deep forest on a distant battlefield. It might give them pause. That is my hope. That the scops and bards who tell stories to hungry young warriors of Britain's rich land and weak warriors might now also tell stories of our victories, of our champions and how many Saxons, Jutes and Angles we have killed these last years.'

'Too many to count,' said Einion.

'And yet still more come,' Idnerth added. His long, clean-shaven face had become lined and his short, close-cropped hair showed more silver than black.

'Return to your homes, then. With my thanks. But tell your lords that I shall call you to my banner in the spring, when we shall bring the fight to the Saxons once more.'

'My lord Brochvael might want his warriors to stay at home next year,' said Einion. 'Powys needs her sons.'

'Not whilst we fight in the borderlands, she doesn't. Remind King Brochvael that he has never known such peace as he has enjoyed these five years. No Saxon raids on Powys, no wars, no simple folk captured and enslaved. The only reason Brochvael wants his men to fight at home is to raid Gwynedd, Gwent and Elmet. But is there more glory in cattle raids against fellow Britons, or in fighting our enemies from across the sea?'

'Don't ask me, lord.' Einion raised his hands and blew out his cheeks. 'I fight where I'm told and kill who I'm told to kill. I'm just letting you know what he will say.'

'Which I appreciate. Enjoy the food and drink tonight and

celebrate our victory. Tomorrow, you march for home, as do we all.'

They cheered those last words, and Arthur took his seat. He ate and drank in silence as the champions boasted to each other about their deeds in battle. They talked of the Saxon warriors each had bested in the years since the battle at the River Dubglas. Arthur stared into the flames and thought of Ida, Aelle, Eormenric and his enemies looming behind their stout palisades, sharpening their seaxes and dreaming of conquering the rest of Britain.

After the food was gone, and the ale flowed too freely, Arthur left them to enjoy the victory. Exhaustion made his eyes feel full of grit and his limbs ached like he had pulled an ox team all day long. He retreated from the sound of men's laughter and loud stories and found his leather tent stretched between two trees.

'Arthur Pendragon,' said a deep voice, startling Arthur. He turned to see a tall man stood beneath the night-darkened boughs. He came closer and the hairs on Arthur's neck stood up and he shivered involuntarily. The man came barefoot, his feet crunching through leaf mulch and fallen twigs. He carried a black staff in his right hand, and he glowered at Arthur, his face drawn and wrinkled with a long, hooked nose above a cruel slash of a mouth. The man wore a black tunic and a cloak of purest white hung about his shoulders. Two great wolfhounds padded out of the gloom and sat beside him, sniffing the night air and licking their whiskers at the smell of meat.

'Lord Kadvuz,' Arthur said to the druid. The druids were the priests of the old gods, Britain's gods. They were men of great power who once held sway over all Britain, of similar standing and importance to kings. Arthur had heard tell of their human sacrifices, their power, and the rumours of wizards and dark magic. The Romans had killed all but a few of the druids when the legions conquered Britain, but some remained upon their holy island of Ynys Môn, which some men called Anglesey, which was sacred to the old gods and their dying religion. Despite the growing Christian faith, all men respected and feared the power of the old gods, of the demons and spirits of the forests, lakes, rivers, crags, caves and springs. Even though their power and influence were diminished from ancient times, people still feared and respected the druids. Arthur called Kadvuz lord not because he was a king or commanded a great force of warriors, but out of respect.

'Another victory.' His voice creaked and cracked like an old timber door.

'Another war band stopped.'

'The gods reward you with battle-luck. Excalibur strikes our enemies down as though wielded by Andraste herself.'

'The men fight well, and we know our blade work.'

'You have worshippers of the nailed god in your company. Do you not?'

Arthur sighed. 'Some men who fight under my command are Christians, yes. But they are Britons and love our land as much as any worshipper of the old gods.'

'And yet their priests try to divide us, to drive the churls and simple folk away from our gods. They seek to overthrow our gods. They are a curse and should be driven from our land and thrown back into the sea.'

'I assume you haven't come to me unbidden from the forest to scold me about Christians?'

'No. I have not.' He frowned, bushy white eyebrows pinching over his hard eyes like storm clouds. 'I come from Ynys Môn, at Merlin's behest.'

'Merlin? I have not seen Merlin for over a year.'

'He has been busy, as have we all, travelling the length and breadth of Britain seeking to protect it from those would cast it asunder. Foreign gods assail us, not just the nailed god, but cruel and wicked Saxon gods. A war rages above and below our world, Lord Arthur, and we druids fight just as hard as you, not with sword and spear, but in the realm beyond our own.'

'What message do you bear from Merlin?'

'He bade me warn you that the northern kingdoms unite against you. That the northern kingdoms of Rheged, Lothian and Gododdin form an alliance to attack you and wrest the title of Pendragon away. They have powerful allies, the *gwyllion* Nimue who sits at King Urien's side in the Bear Fort connives and conjures against you.'

Arthur paced back and forth, his forehead creased, fists clenched.

'Do they march?'

'Not yet. But war looms. A fight amongst our own kingdoms which threatens everything you have fought for.'

'Damn those northern fools! We are so close to the victory we have always dreamed of. Within a season of reclaiming this entire island for our people. If we fight amongst ourselves, we open the door for the Saxons to spread further, to creep out of Lloegyr and reclaim the lands so recently returned to our people.'

'Just so. Enemies surround you, Arthur Pendragon, and Merlin calls to you.'

'I will heed his call. But first I must go home to Dumnonia and see to my responsibilities there.'

'Very well.' Kadvuz turned and swept his white cloak about him, striding back into the darkness with his great wolfhounds slinking beside him. 'Perhaps he will meet you there, for the need is dire. Our aims teeter on a knife-edge. War looms in the north, so prepare yourself.'

Arthur reached into his tent and grabbed the stone sceptre he had taken from King Ida in battle long ago. The cold stone helped Arthur think, its dome top felt like bone beneath his thumb. The sceptre seemed ancient to Arthur, as though kings of old had used it as a symbol of their power for countless generations, that some small piece of their wisdom lay trapped beneath its hard, chiselled exterior. In truth, he wasn't sure where the Saxon king of Bernicia had come across it. All Arthur knew was that it helped him see beyond the battlefields and the bickering over one god or another. If Merlin was right and the northern kingdoms were rising against him, then Arthur's rule was in peril, as was the future of Britain itself.

A war between the great kingdoms of Britain in the time before Arthur's birth had laid Britain low. In the days of Uther, Ambrosius, Urien, Letan Luyddoc and Cadwallon Longhand, Britons had fought each other, led to it by King Vortigern. The old kings of Britain had united to fight Vortigern, the Usurper of Deira, and the army of Saxon warriors he brought across the sea. They were the first to arrive on Britain's shores. Invited by Vortigern as he sought to use their brutality to subdue his enemies. Hengist and Horsa were the first seafarers to arrive, and their people had never ceased coming.

Arthur lay down beneath wool and furs and closed his eyes, listening to the victory celebrations, but all he could hear were the lamentations of conquered people, the screams of the wounded and cries of the displaced. His had been a life filled with war, blood and death, and now his greatest challenge would come from his own people.

3

Arthur's army disbanded. Its commanders led their men north, south and west to their distant homes. Lancelot, Arthur and Kai rode south before the marching column of black cloaks and Kai's two hundred men, once warriors of Rheged who had renounced their oaths to King Urien to follow Kai and fight for Arthur.

The moon waxed and waned as Arthur's war band journeyed into the barley and wheat fields of Britain's south-west. They marched past villages and farmsteads, dykes, hilltop settlements, coppiced woodland and kept to old Roman roads. Folk came out to bow and wave to the warriors, and they marvelled at Arthur astride Llamrei in his black cloak and coat of chain mail. They gaped at Excalibur, for few amongst the people of Britain had not heard Merlin's stories of how Arthur had pulled the blade from a stone to make himself Pendragon. Merlin and Nimue had spread such tales across the land in the days when they were lovers, before enmity had come between them like a disease. Merlin's deep cunning had filled the people's minds with tales of sorcery and ancient magic and prepared them for Arthur's rise. Those tales had bound folk to Arthur's legend, and after years of suffering and defeat, people had believed that they could defeat the Saxons, that a god-forged sword and a warrior favoured by Merlin could deliver victory.

Arthur embraced the legends and stories. He let them flow about him like a warm cloak. Once the stories had irked him, made him uncomfortable that Merlin crafted such tales to deceive people and make them believe Arthur was a great hero, a legendary figure, which Arthur the man struggled to live up to. But now he understood Merlin's cunning, understood that folk needed that belief. So he waved to the men and women who bowed to him at roadsides, the men who ploughed and sowed and the women who spun and wove. And when crowds grew large, Arthur drew Excalibur and let them marvel at her gleaming blade. Common folk reached out to touch his warriors' cloaks and offered them bread, mead and small talismans for luck. At night, men would slip away to find grateful maids and warm their beds, but Arthur's warriors always returned in the morning. They always came back to their warlord, the man to whom they had all sworn oaths of service.

On a warm, wet day where the sky was the colour of dirty boots, Arthur and his war band reached Durnovaria, once home to Uther Pendragon's summer court, and its fortress known as the Fist of Dumnonia.

'Home,' said Lancelot with a grin, as three girls leading a cart full of turves gazed up at his ruggedly handsome face.

'Home,' Arthur agreed. He had slept more nights in the field than he had in the Fist's warm bedroom and ate more meals out in the open than he had in its sprawling hall. It was far from Benoic, Lancelot's birthplace across the narrow sea, but his friend had lived and fought beside Arthur like a brother, and

Lancelot had spilled enough of his own and other men's blood to call Dumnonia home.

A ring of Roman stone walls circled the Fist, with a high stone gate with two arched entrances and stout oak doors. The walled part of the Fist could hold one hundred warriors and their families, but a sprawling settlement of wattle houses spread around the fortress on all sides and a cloud of dirty smoke sat above it. A ditch surrounded the walls, and the town contained the palace, barracks, feasting hall and dwellings within the walls, and then ramshackle houses of wattle, thatch and turf clung to the outside of the walls like limpets. That outer settlement sprawled beneath a cloud of dirty smoke with its smithies, brothels, seers, pigs, chickens, urchins and goats.

A tanner's yard on the edges of the settlement stank of stale piss, and the warriors grumbled at the stench as they approached the Fist's high gates. Those gates creaked open, pushed by two guards whose boots splashed in a rain puddle.

'Welcome home,' called a familiar voice as the three riders reined in before the gate. A big man strolled through the opening, hands on his hips and a green cloak thrown back over his broad shoulders.

'I hope you have the hearth fire burning, Malegant,' said Arthur, inclining his head in greeting. Malegant was long-faced with a short beard and his dark hair hung in two braids about the sides of his face, with the back of his head shaved in the Dumnonian fashion. He had once been the captain of Uther's warriors, a skilled warrior and a champion who now commanded the warriors Arthur left to guard the city and his queen.

'You picked a fine day for it.'

'The men are wetter than an otter's pocket,' Kai said, rain

dripping down his handsome face. 'Best get them into their homes instead of talking out here like washerwomen.'

'I've missed you too, Lord Kai. Come on in.'

'Right, lads,' Dewi called to the men. He turned to face the eager-eyed spearmen. He took off his wide-brimmed hat and let the rain pour from it before placing it back on his head. 'You can fall out. You are dismissed. Go home to your wives and may the sound of your humping drown out the sound of my wife's complaining.'

The men cheered, waving their spears, and then ran through the puddles and mud to disperse into the snarl of paths, alleys and lanes to find their homes. Malegant led the riders inside, where stewards took the horses so that Arthur and his companions could walk the rest of the way home. Malegant led them through the twist of cobbled pathways towards Arthur's hall. Faces stared out at Arthur from the limewashed buildings, topped with a patchwork of fresh golden thatch and older rotting thatch.

Rain pounded the cobbles and hammered against Arthur's metal helmet. People huddled beneath overhanging roofs to stay dry, and they bowed in deference as their high king and steward of Dumnonia passed. Arthur's hall loomed above the old city, a lofty building with high walls and a red-tiled roof patched here and there with brown clay tiles. Malegant led them along a sheltered walkway flanked by white pillars where ivy climbed across the cracked, finely chiselled stone.

They entered a wide hall, airy and clean, and Kai ran to warm his hands before the roaring hearth. As he always did, Arthur treaded lightly upon the scene etched into the floor by thousands of tiny tiles, fearful of his heavy boots breaking the faded but startlingly brilliant picture of fish leaping around a chariot. Tall windows and square holes cut into the white-washed walls showed glimpses of the bleak sky outside. Men and women in finely woven garments of red, green and blue came from the shadows to peer at Arthur as priests wove about them, whispering prayers and making the sign of the cross. Courtiers and too many priests, Arthur thought. Merlin would not approve. Guinevere craved a court full of bards and scops, of harps and flutes playing as the wealthy and well garbed discussed matters of court, philosophy, religion and courtly love.

Arthur's boots squelched on the old tiny Roman stones, leaving dirty brown mud stains despite his best efforts to tread lightly. A swarthy priest in a brown robe stood amongst a clutch of other sour-faced priests. They clasped the wooden and silver crosses at their necks and hissed prayers, which Arthur assumed were to ward off the evil of his pagan presence. He was the Pendragon and could run them out of the Fist should he wish or kill them with an order and a wave of his hand. But to do that was to anger their god, and the ever-increasing number of Christ worshippers throughout Britain's kingdoms.

The priests reminded Arthur of the times he had visited the grand hall when it had belonged to Uther. He had fought single combat there against Mynog the Boar and won, splashing the monstrous warrior's blood over the tiny-stone pictured floor. Then he had faced Uther's wrath and challenged the Pendragon to fight. Arthur shivered at the memory. Merlin and Nimue had been united beside Arthur that day, and the bishop and his priests had slithered away from Nimue's stone-encrusted teeth and *gwyllion*'s power. Uther had been a fearsome man, the high king for many years, a warrior of famous strength and cruelty who had led Britain in the days of the Great War, when his brother Ambrosius had wielded Excalibur, and the traitor Vortigern had first brought Saxon warriors to Britain's shores.

The hall's rear door creaked open and a bishop in a tall mitre strode through it, carrying a long white staff curved like a shepherd's crook. A woman followed, hair shining like burnished gold in the firelight. Her face was long and gentle with full lips, and her eyes were the green of a summer sea. She glanced at him and smiled, and Arthur could not keep the grin from his face or his cheeks from flushing with embarrassment, just as he did every time he saw her across a crowded room. She was his queen, once the princess of Cameliard, Guinevere, the most beautiful woman Arthur had ever seen.

Guinevere stood aside, and a man marched ahead of the queen and the bishop. He carried a brass-coloured trumpet and wore a long white cloth robe draped about his shoulders in the Roman fashion. The man's sandals flapped upon the stone floor, and he ascended Arthur's high platform upon which sat his throne. More people in fine robes filtered into the hall from behind Arthur. They bowed and filled the wide spaces between the feasting benches which were pushed to the sides of the vast open space.

'Do we have to do this every time?' Kai whispered, leaning in to Arthur's ear.

'I'm afraid so,' Arthur replied. He found the ceremony as tedious as his foster brother, but such displays and tradition were the price of power.

The trumpet blared, as loud and shrill as the carnyx in the enclosed hall.

'Welcome home, Arthur, steward of Dumnonia, Pendragon of Britain. The royal court rejoices and celebrates your return,' the trumpeter called, and every person in the hall bowed their head in reverence. Six warriors marched through the small door. The biggest of them carried the Roman imperial fasces, a long-handled axe tied about with wooden rods which had once symbolised the authority of old Rome but was now the symbol of the Pendragon's power. A command delivered by a man carrying the fasces was to be obeyed and recognised across Britain as Arthur's word. To defy it was to die. The warriors' boots stomped upon the tiles and filled the hall with their echo. They stopped, formed a column and lifted their heavy shields bearing the snarling dragon of Dumnonia.

'Queen Guinevere, and Bishop Serwan,' the trumpeter announced, and blared another shrill blast. He continued to speak as the bishop and the queen walked slowly to the high dais, but the sound was merely background noise beside Guinevere's startling beauty. She was like a red rose amongst warriors clad in steel, iron and leather as she glided between the royal guard and took her place in the chair next to Arthur's own.

'Welcome home,' Guinevere said, with a smile so bright it could dim the sun. Arthur's chest burned with longing. He wanted to run to the high platform and take her in his arms, to cover her face and slender neck with kisses. But men of power did not do such things.

'Thank you, my lady,' he said, his voice echoing around the high rafters. 'It is good to be home.'

'They tell me you defeated an army of Saxon raiders?'

'We did. It was a hard summer.'

'Praise God for your success!' called the bishop in a loud voice, and he raised two fingers. At least half the courtiers in the hall crossed themselves, and for a moment Arthur was alarmed to see so many Christians among them. That was something new, and Arthur wondered again at Kadvuz the druid's words, of his warning about the war between the old gods and the new.

'I am tired,' Arthur said. 'So are my men. I would like to wash and rest and speak to you in private.'

'The people long to hear of your exploits, my king,' said the bishop.

'Another day. We shall feast tomorrow, and all will be told at the right time.' Arthur spoke with a little too much steel in his voice, and the bishop's pudgy face flushed red.

'You heard the high king,' said Malegant, and he clapped his hands. 'Everybody leave the hall. There shall be a feast tomorrow in Lord Arthur's honour.'

An hour later, Arthur washed himself in a bowl of cool water. A steward had taken his armour and weapons away to be cleaned, and he wore just his trews as months of dried-in dirt and other men's blood drained from his body. A young woman took the bowl away and handed Arthur a jerkin which he used to dry the water from his body.

'Fresh scars?' said Guinevere, entering their chamber. She dismissed the girl with a wave of her hand and embraced Arthur. He breathed the fresh scent of her hair and held her close. He let his head dip and rest in the soft part of her neck beside her shoulder, and warmth spread through his chest like fire melting ice. Guinevere pulled away and traced her gentle fingers across the lurid red scars across his shoulders, neck and face. 'Soon you will be nothing but scar tissue. Then what will remain of Arthur?'

'Enemy blades are sharp,' he said. Her finger lingered on the long scar Uther had carved across his face.

'Look what they've done to you.' She spoke wistfully. 'I sometimes wonder how brave you must be to stand there as brutes like Uther and those Saxon beasts cut and chop at you. Most men would run away and hide at the prospect of such horror.'

'We won many glorious victories this year.' Arthur wanted to change the subject. He knew what it took to stand before the dangerous men, the killers, the champions, to tread where few men dared, but he did not wish to talk of war. 'Now, I am home.'

'Now you are home.' She kissed him, and Arthur could have stayed in that embrace for eternity.

'Gods, I missed you.'

'And I you. You leave me alone too long in this place.'

'This place?'

'Here in the Fist with that boy and his... handlers.'

'How is Prince Madoc?'

'He is Uther's son, and you are supposed to be his steward and protector, yet I am the one stuck here dealing with the humdrum matters of his education and care.'

'Really? And what have you taught the boy?'

Guinevere laughed at Arthur's teasing and lightly punched his chest. 'I meant I must oversee it. It is to me that his tutors complain.'

'I am sorry, my love. I am here now, and I will see the prince today. Does he behave?'

'He does. But he is a five-year-old boy, Arthur. Boys are rowdy. He has a little too much of his father in him.'

'Uther was a great warrior. It's good that the apple didn't fall far from the tree.'

'Maybe so. But being around him constantly is a reminder of our own... difficulties.'

'We have tried.' Arthur pulled Guinevere close again. 'We can try again now if you like.'

'We shall. You must have an heir. People talk. It has been five years since we married, and I am yet to be with child.'

'An heir to what? I have no kingdom. All that we have here is Madoc's, which we guard until he is ready to become king of Dumnonia.'

'You are the Pendragon, king of kings. Your child will inherit that title. This is expected of a wife. You fight and rule, your men respect you for that. It is my duty to keep your home, manage the court and its graspers and whisperers, and to bear you children. Would that I had been born a man, and all I had to do was wave a sword around for people to respect me.'

'There is a bit more to it than that.'

'Oh, I know. Camping out under the stars with your friends and riding your white stallion all over the place. Drinking ale and fending off every pretty maid in every town who bats her eyelashes at you?'

'There are no maids. None as beautiful as you, anyway. At least not this summer.'

'I knew it!' They laughed together and Arthur kissed her again.

Arthur and Guinevere spent the afternoon together in their chamber, and as evening approached, Arthur added a log to the fire at the room's western end.

'What's wrong with the Fist?' he asked, using another log to poke the fire back to life. They had dozed for an hour and the fire had died down.

'What do you mean?'

'Earlier you said that I had left you too long in this place. When you first arrived in Britain from Cameliard, you dreamed of Uther's hall and its finery.'

'I did, and there are fine things here. The best scops and poets, fine musicians and merchants bring the best cloth from across the narrow sea. But it stinks of Uther, of old furs, soil and horse.'

'Would you rather have gone north and married Urien? You could be at the Bear Fort at this very moment, his drool dripping on your face as rain and wind lash the place relentlessly all year round.'

'Don't be churlish. Of course I wouldn't rather be at the Bear Fort with that brute. But you are the Pendragon. You should have your own fortress, your own palace. A place that belongs to Arthur and Guinevere, not one that we keep like caretakers for a child who will turn us out the moment he becomes of age.'

'Madoc won't turn us out.' Arthur shook his head and went to a trestle table where stewards had left cold meats, cheese and ale. 'I'm hungry. Do you want something to eat?'

'He will turn us out. Arthur, leave the damned cheese and listen to me.'

Arthur put down the cheese and wooden cup of ale he had picked up as Guinevere was talking. 'I am listening.'

'He is the heir. Powerful people drip poison into the boy's ear. His cousins, aunts, landowners, merchants, weapons masters, they all have influence, and they are Dumnonians. You are not. I am not.'

'You believe these people turn Madoc against us?'

'Of course they do. You are Arthur ap Nowhere, born in Rheged but a man of no kingdom. I have heard the whispers when folk think I cannot hear. Merlin makes no secret of it. Every pig-boy and ploughman from here to Lothian knows you are the bastard son of Uther and Igraine. I am from Cameliard across the sea. We are not Dumnonians. But if you are Uther's son, then you are the heir, not Madoc.'

'That's enough talk for now.' Arthur's hand reached for the bronze disc he wore at his neck, a gift from the Lady Igraine as she lay dying, locked away in the grim starkness of the Bear Fort. 'I must dress. I have to visit the prince, and there are matters that require my attention.'

'Are you Uther's son?' Guinevere grabbed his wrists and made him look into her eyes.

'I don't know.'

'You don't know? Merlin seems to know, and he is the most powerful druid in Britain. He knows how to make contraptions that fling fire over fortress walls and how to make the sky go black in the middle of the day. He was there, in the Great War, when he and Uther broke the alliance between our kingdoms so that Uther could have Gorlois' wife. Uther wanted Igraine, wife of the king of Kernow, and Merlin made it possible. That was the end. Ambrosius died, the Saxons conquered our western kingdoms, and you are the child of that forbidden love. You are the rightful king of Dumnonia, Arthur.'

'Merlin says many things. I was raised by Ector, my spear-father. He told me...'

'For pity's sakes! What did he tell you?'

'That Uther was not my father and nor was Igraine my mother. I am the orphan child of a churl, taken by Merlin to take the place of Igraine's dead baby.'

Guinevere stormed away from him with her slender arms folded across her chest. 'So be that child. Be what Merlin tells every living soul you are.'

'He tells the tale, but it lacks legitimacy. I am not the heir.'

'Will you please listen to me, my love?'

Arthur went to her and held her again, but Guinevere looked away.

'I won't usurp Prince Madoc's throne.'

'Why not? All men usurp. All men betray.'

'I swore an oath to be his protector, and I will honour my word.'

'Break the oath. Nobody cares. Nobody but you.'

'I won't. My word and my honour are all I have.'

'Honour? What good will that do you when your sword arm grows weak, when the wars are over and your beard is grey.

Where shall we live then? What shall we eat? What good will your honour be then?'

'We shall build a home, a place of our own. A fortress where you can be comfortable and rule the kingdom beside me.'

'Really?' Her brow softened, and a smile played at the corners of her mouth, and Arthur gazed into her beautiful eyes.

'Truly. A fortress with a wide hall, stables, stone floors which shall be warm in winter and cool in summer.'

Guinevere stood on her tiptoes and kissed his cheek. 'And I can command its construction? It must be perfect.'

'You can lay every rock and timber yourself if you wish it. But it must be close to the River Cam. There is a fortress of the old people there, and I want a fortification within easy march of our enemies in the east. Our home can be as grand as you wish, but it must also be a fortress with a ditch, bank and palisade. I will rally my army there, within striking distance of Lloegyr.'

'We shall call it Camelot then, after the river, and it will be beautiful. A godly place.'

'A godly place?' The turn of phrase surprised Arthur, and he stepped back.

'A place blessed by the gods. A fine place.' Guinevere fussed at the sleeves of her dress.

'It will.'

'Perhaps once we have a home of our own, our luck will change, and we shall have our child. There is something I want you to consider, my love.'

'What is it?'

'We have tried for a child, and I have felt the quickening within me, but as yet the gods have not seen fit to bless us with a baby.'

'Our time will come. Shall we sit for a while, drink and rest? It has been a long year, and I have dreamed of resting beside you, just the two of us with no complications. No scouts reporting that the enemy is behind this hill or lurking in that forest. No problems to solve, how to cross this river or where to camp and find food. Just us. You and I, like normal people.'

Guinevere placed a hand upon his forearm, her nails brushing the tattooed death rings. 'But we are not normal people, are we? You are the Pendragon of Britain, and I am your queen.'

Arthur smiled and cuffed at his tired eyes. 'There is no surer way for a man to get his wife's attention than for him to put his feet up.'

She frowned and laughed with a shake of her head. 'You said our time will come. But what if it doesn't? What if we aren't doing the right things?'

'The right things? A man must petition his lord for access to another's water rights, or to cut more wood than is permitted from a coppiced wood. But any numbskull can father a child, and any slattern can bear one. Our time will come. Merlin seeks me, and when I see him, I will ask him to work his *seidr* in our favour.'

'Merlin seeks you? You have only just come home.'

'And I intend to stay here. To rest and recover. But trouble brews in the north, trouble that threatens to destroy everything I have fought for, everything we have worked for.'

Guinevere tutted and narrowed her eyes. 'Bishop Serwan says that if I pray to the Christian god, that he will make my womb fertile.'

'He wants you to pray to the nailed god, to the Christian god?'

'Yes, he says...'

'Those cursed priests.'

'He's a bishop.'

'Same thing. They shouldn't be at court. If Merlin finds out that you have been dallying with them...'

'Where is Merlin? Who has seen the great druid this last year or longer? The druids aren't the power they once were. How many even remain? Two, three? We must have a child, Arthur, and we can't cling to dying gods for too long. A woman's time does not last forever.'

'Be careful. Do not scorn the gods, or doubt Merlin's power. Your bishop can't give us what we seek. Merlin gave me the sword and made me what I am today. Without Merlin I'm...'

'Still Arthur. It's just a sword. What harm can it do to talk to the bishop? Just talk to him and see what he can do. For me, please, my love?' Guinevere kissed him again and Arthur could not refuse her. Every night on campaign he had dreamed of those lips and that smell. So he nodded and Guinevere was happy.

And the next day Merlin came.

4

Arthur woke early the next morning. He draped a heavy fox-fur cloak about his shoulders and left Guinevere dozing in bed. Sleep had come quick and deep, and Arthur already felt more refreshed than he had in months. His steps were light, feet snug in light leather shoes rather than heavy boots. Arthur was so used to living in his chain-mail armour that to walk without it was like floating on a cloud.

The sound of laughter drew Arthur to an open courtyard set between the smoke-grey stone and damp timber walls. He leant on a wall and, through the leaves of a field maple tree, watched Prince Madoc playing with another young boy. A steward watched them, a woman in a russet dress, a woollen mantle and a linen wimple covering her head. The boys ran about the grass, darting between birch trees turned soft yellow by the season, and purple, blue and white late-blooming flowers. Wind rustled through the trees, and Arthur thought of the days when he, Lunete and Kai had run wild in the forests around Caer Ligualid without a care in the world.

Arthur kicked off his shoes and smiled as his bare feet sunk into the damp grass, which showed the first hints of gold as the days grew shorter. He breathed in the earthy, fresh scent of the flowers and the slight stink of decay from fallen leaves. He picked a red berry from a holly bush and rolled it between his fingers. Arthur wondered where his foster sister Lunete was at that moment. She had married Theodric, a Saxon prince, after a Saxon war band had captured her during a forest raid. Lunete had professed love for her Saxon husband, and so now lived somewhere in distant Bernicia, in the far north-east where Theodric's father King Ida ruled from Dun Guaroy, his formidable fortress on a high, sea-lashed crag. She was happy, Arthur hoped. He missed Lunete, her wildness, how she would disobey Ector and then Arthur's spear-father would melt before her big brown eyes, forgive her just as he scolded Kai and Arthur for even the slightest of trouble.

'Lord Arthur,' said the steward. She bowed deeply and snapped Arthur from his memories. She snapped her fingers and urgently waved the boys towards her. They paused, glanced up at Arthur, and saw a tall man with a scarred face. They ran to the steward and gathered about her skirts.

Arthur tossed the berry into a clutch of tiny, pruned yew trees.

'I did not mean to disturb you, Prince Madoc,' he said. Arthur placed a hand on his chest and bowed to the boy, who cowered even further behind the steward's skirts. 'I am Arthur, your lord protector. You have nothing to fear from me, boy.'

'Come now,' said the woman, and tried to push Madoc from behind her dress. 'Be respectful and say hello to Lord Arthur.'

Arthur tried to smile, but gave up, aware how frightening his face with the long scar Uther had carved into it must seem to a small child. He wanted to bond with the boy, to make him understand their relationship and that he had nothing to fear. But he found talking to the boy as difficult as parlaying with an enemy on the battlefield. He stared up at a deep blue sky visible beneath the high stone and timber walls. Clouds the colour of fresh snow drifted lazily, their undersides tinged with grey.

'Come, sit.' Arthur walked slowly to a wooden bench set beside the pruned trees. He sat upon its surface crafted from sturdy oak, worn smooth by years of use. 'The sky was red this morning. Did you see it?'

'Yes,' said the boy as the woman urged him towards the bench. He sat beside Arthur and shuffled until he was as far away on the bench as possible.

'Have you heard the saying: red sky in the morning, shepherds' warning?'

'No.'

'No, lord,' the woman said, scolding the prince.

'It's alright,' Arthur said gently. 'The saying means if the sky is red early in the morning, it will rain sometime that day. They also say: red sky at night, shepherds' delight. That means that the next day will be a fine one.'

'Are you a great warrior?' asked the boy, eyes stuck on the death rings on Arthur's forearms.

'I do my best. Would you like to be a warrior?'

'I would. I will be the best fighter, like my father.'

'Then you will be a man to fear. A man of reputation. You are already growing into a fine boy.'

'I will be king one day.'

'I know. It's my responsibility to make sure that you are.'

'Do men fear you?'

'Some do, I suppose. But you need never be afraid of me. I

am often away, but I leave warriors here to protect you. If you are ever in danger, I will come and chase the wicked men away.'

'Are you my friend, then?'

'I am the best friend you will ever have.' Arthur leaned over and crooked a finger to beckon the prince closer. 'You will be king of Dumnonia one day, and everybody you meet wants something from you. Every lord, maid, tutor, cousin and friend wants your favour and they will try to convince you that their dreams and desires are to your advantage. The only person who wants nothing from you is me. All I want is for you to be well and to become king.'

'Are you king?'

'Sort of. But not like you. Now, I must go and talk to people who want something from me. There will be a line of them waiting to ask me to decide this, make a judgement on that. Then tonight there will be a feast. You can sit next to me at the high table, and I will have a gift for you. Would you like that?'

The prince nodded vigorously.

'Good,' Arthur said, and did his best to smile. 'I'll see you then.'

Arthur left Madoc in the courtyard, hoping that he had begun to bond with the young prince. He went to receive the scores of men he knew awaited to petition him over boundaries, blood feuds, inheritance disputes and any manner of problems which required his doom.

Later that night, the Fist bustled with stewards, courtiers, warriors, merchants, noblewomen and slaves, all in their best clothes as folk made their way to Arthur's hall to feast and celebrate his victories over the Saxons. Arthur sat at the high table with Guinevere on his left and Prince Madoc on his right. He took a drink of smooth-tasting mead, relieved that the pageantry of the fasces, trumpets, announcements and solemnity were over for the night.

Smoke rose from a roaring hearth and disappeared out of the roof's smoke hole as pork, beef and lamb roasted on dripping spits. Rushlights flickered on the walls, and along with the firelight they bathed the vast hall in a twitching, glowing half-light. It was forbidden to bring weapons into the hall, but warriors wore their mail and leather armour, and the wealthy wore gold and silver at their wrists and necks. Tapestries hung from the walls to hide the cold stone and dark timber. Arthur watched the people tear into hunks of meat and fresh bread, their faces flushed with the warmth of the fire and the taste of ale and mead. He glanced around at the hall and knew Guinevere was right. This place could never be his home. He ate and ruled in a dead man's palace.

'We should start work on Camelot right away,' he said, placing his hand over Guinevere's. 'Start planning now and be ready to start building in the spring.'

'Truly?' she replied, rewarding him with a smile to make his heart ache with longing.

'We can use the ancient earth ramparts beside the river, left there by our people before Rome came with her legions. I must find Merlin and try to solve the problems in the north. But you go with the fasces and the royal guard. Find craftsmen, builders, thatchers, stonemasons and labourers. Lancelot will go with you. In the spring, he will march with you to the River Cam with fifty men. You are in command of the palace and its comforts, but leave the fortress design to Lancelot, for it must be strong.'

'We shall have Roman pillars, a courtyard with a pool of water, and a bed with the finest linen and furs.'

'There is only one thing I ask. There must be a round table in the hall.'

'A feasting bench?'

'Of sorts, yes. Large enough to seat twelve men. Twelve champions and representatives of our kingdoms.'

'Why not just seat them on benches and you in your high seat? That's the way it's always done.'

'Because our kingdoms have fought one another endlessly since the Romans left. There are blood feuds and deep-rooted enmity between Powys, Gwynedd, Elmet, Rheged, Kernow and the rest. When they come to Camelot, each man must feel like an equal. There can be no slights taken, or insults given if every man, me included, sits at a round table as equals.'

'You warriors and your pride.' Guinevere took a sip of mead and shook her head in despair. 'I will make sure you have your round table. I might need to commandeer statues and pillars from the shires, the ones left by the Romans. Our home must be beautiful. When dignitaries visit, I want them to feel like they are in the presence of a consul or tribune.'

'Do what you must. But take Lancelot with you. Just in case a greedy war band, or masterless band of *bucellari* mercenaries fancies their chances at stealing your silver.'

A steward placed a massive joint of boar on the table before Arthur, and a wooden platter full of carved venison on the tables below. Wafts of thyme, rosemary and garlic made Arthur's stomach roll over with hunger as the stewards brought out stewed turnips, roasted goose, honey, butter and loaves of plaited bread still warm from the oven. Arthur tossed a chunk of meat to Cavall who lay beneath the table and Guinevere beckoned to a slave waiting in the shadows. The young man hurried forward with a chair. Guinevere slid her chair to one side, and the slave set the new chair between Arthur and the queen.

'What is this?' Arthur asked, though his heart sank because he knew the answer.

'Bishop Serwan will join us, so that the two of you can talk.'

'Not now, Guinevere. Another time.' Arthur would talk to the bishop, just to keep her happy, but seating the bishop beside Arthur gave him power.

'We cannot wait for this baby, Arthur. If you won't try every possibility, we might never have your heir.'

'Very well.'

Guinevere gestured to a table below the dais, and Bishop Serwan rose and clambered up to the high table. He walked slowly, strutting like a cock, smirking at rivals and men on the leading tables. His jowls shook as he climbed the stair and slumped down in the chair next to Arthur.

'You honour me, Lord Pendragon,' Serwan said, and inclined his head. 'Lord prince.' He repeated the gesture to Prince Madoc, who ignored him. The prince was otherwise occupied, feeding scraps from the table to the two great wolfhounds below.

'The number of priests in Durnovaria has increased whilst I have been away,' Arthur said, eating a slice of boar meat.

'We are fortunate that people flock to our Lord like moths to a torch flame.'

'I see many people now wear your nailed god's symbol. More kingdoms renounce the old gods in favour of the Christ.'

'It is a blessing. Many of my fellow bishops have been granted land to build churches.'

'What is the point of a church? The druids needed no buildings, and no silver to spread the word of the gods and do their work.'

'The druids are... shall we say... barbaric. They worship in caves and beside old trees. They sing to rivers and shout at the sea as if they could turn back the tide. My Lord Jesus is worshipped across the world, by Romans and folk in lands so distant we can barely imagine them, nor the beasts who dwell there. Lions, camels, and all sorts of fabulous creatures.'

'What is a lion?'

The bishop smiled nervously. 'Would that I knew, my lord. There are many mysteries in this world.'

'How is that your priests ask for silver and food, and the druids give all they own willingly to people wherever they go? They travel the roads and paths, healing the sick, birthing children, pulling teeth, casting charms and caring for the future of our lands. What do you do, bishop?'

'We are the link between the divine and the mortal. We pave the pathway to heaven with confession and forgiveness. Only by prayer and devotion can one be assured of a place in heaven. Our purpose is noble, and of vital importance unless you wish to spend the afterlife in an eternity of flame and suffering in the bowels of hell.'

'A man has his oaths and duty to keep him honest. I do not understand how scraping around on your knees and begging forgiveness paves the way to the afterlife.'

'These are complicated points, my lord, and ones that I would relish the chance to speak to you of in more detail. But perhaps in more peaceful surroundings.' Bishop Serwan flinched as one of Arthur's warriors belched so loud that the rafters shook. Men laughed and banged the tables, and they told tales of bravery from the wars against the Saxons.

'You have spent time with the queen whilst I was away?'

'I have been lucky in that regard, my lord, yes.'

'Uther tolerated you, but you must know that I support Merlin and the old gods.'

'I understand that, Lord Pendragon. But your lady wife has spoken to me of your... difficulties.'

'Difficulties?'

'Of your desire for an heir, which has not been forthcoming.'

'And?'

'And well, perhaps, the favour of God could help change that unfortunate predicament.'

A warrior stood up on a feasting bench and recounted a battle earlier that summer when Arthur's black cloaks had beaten back a force of King Aelle's Saxons.

'If you could consider praying...' the bishop continued until Arthur held up a finger of warning.

'Do not interrupt when the warriors speak,' Arthur said. 'I saw this man kill three Saxons to defend his friend's corpse on the battlefield. He has earned the right to speak by the blood he has shed for Britain. Can you say the same?'

The bishop slumped back in his chair and glanced at Guinevere for support. She remained silent, so the bishop fiddled with the jewelled rings on his fingers.

The warrior continued his tale, and tears rolled down his bearded cheeks as he remembered brave men fallen in battle to Saxon blades. The crowd in the hall fell silent and men drank to their lost spear-brothers, and suddenly the hall's great oak doors were flung open. They creaked on black iron hinges and a gust of wind blew into the hall and sent rushes scattering across the stone floor.

A figure appeared in the open space, a tall man wearing a black hooded robe. He carried a black staff with a fist-sized lump of polished amber at its top. The amber seemed to glow in the firelight like an egg-shaped drop of sun. The tall man slammed his staff down hard on the stone floor, and it was as though the very hall shook. He strode through the feasting benches, robes flowing around him as guards struggled to heave the great doors closed. The staff boomed as the man drove it onto the ground with every second step, and folk hurried to hide the silver crucifixes they wore about their necks. He reached the roaring fire and, with a sweep of his hand, he cast a powder into the flames to send a whoosh of sparkling smoke into the rafters.

Men gasped and women shrieked in fear as the tall man swept his great staff about the room as though he probed the vast space for signs of evil or wrongdoing. Folk cowered from him, leaning away, hiding their faces from his hooded gaze.

'Merlin,' Arthur whispered, and he rose to greet the most powerful druid in Britain.

Merlin pushed back his hood to reveal keen grey eyes in a face creased and weathered with age, though no man knew precisely how old the druid was. Ector, Arthur's foster father, had once said that Merlin was old even when he was a boy. Merlin was bald save for a ring of snow-white hair around his ears, which he wore in a long braid. Faded tattoos covered the old man's scalp, strange symbols, clawing beasts and writhing patterns. His beard was close cropped and beneath his black cloak he wore a long grey tunic.

'Welcome, Lord Merlin,' Arthur called, and opened his arms in greeting.

Merlin flashed a quick smile, revealing his astonishingly white teeth. 'Lord Pendragon, what strange company you keep of late.' He pointed his staff at Bishop Serwan, who squirmed in his seat as if he wanted the ground to swallow him up. 'I have never seen so many wretched things of the puny nailed god in one place. This must be what their rank heaven feels like. All we need are harpists and a god to pass judgement upon us, a god who lets his enemies crucify him.'

'Long have we awaited your return. Come, join us.'

'Long have I travelled to get here. Through much danger, I might add. But nothing on that long, dark road was as cutting to my being as the sight I see before me here in Durnovaria. These curs lay us low, Pendragon. They are like a blight in the wheat, or rats in the granary. They turn people from the true gods, the gods who forged your mighty sword, the gods who created the very land we stand upon.'

Arthur stepped down from the dais and strode towards Merlin. 'Come then, let us talk privately, you and I.'

'You have the manners of a soldier and the grace of a stunted weasel. High king or meanest churl, a man owes a druid hospitality, does he not?'

'Of course.' Arthur tilted his head in apology. He had sought to remove Merlin gently from the hall so that his men could enjoy their victory celebration without fear of the druid's wrath. The bishop's and his priests' discomfort were none of Arthur's concern. 'Please, sit and eat with me.'

Stewards set a feasting bench close to the fire and Arthur sat opposite Merlin as he ate a plate of venison, cheese, bread and honey, and washed it down with a horn of mead. He knew better than to interrupt the druid whilst he ate. The feast continued around them, but in hushed tones. There were no more speeches made, and no warriors stood up to remember fallen friends or boast about how many Saxons they would kill during next year's campaign.

After finishing, Merlin took a long pull at his mead and set the horn down hard on the table.

'Now,' said the druid. 'We need to talk.'

'Then walk with me on the battlements.'

'Are you sure you don't wish to bring your pet Christian along with you?'

'I am sure.'

'Perhaps you might need him to wipe your arse, or get you dressed for bedtime?'

'I am quite sure.'

'Then, good.' Merlin stood and grabbed his staff, his grey eyes as hard as granite. 'Because war is once again upon us. Not the war we wish to fight, but one we must fight if we are ever to secure our island for its people.'

5

Merlin followed Arthur out of the hall and up a set of wooden steps to the fighting platform, which ran the length of the fortress' palisade. It was wide enough for two men to walk side by side, and guards patrolled the high walls with lit braziers crackling every fifty paces to keep the men warm.

'The wind and the bees told me of your victories,' said Merlin, stopping to gaze out at a river turned to silver by moonlight, winding its way into the distance like a slithering dragon.

'We have penned the Saxons back to their strongholds,' said Arthur, pulling his cloak closer about his shoulders to keep out the stiff wind. 'Next spring we have a chance to crush them, to defeat them once and for all. They need men, and every crew which made landfall this year died beneath our blades. The Saxons cling on to what they have, but they are ripe for the taking, Merlin. All we must do is call the banners and throw them back into the narrow sea.'

'A fine speech. But I have come from the north, where your enemies work to cast your dreams of victory into a dunghill of ruin.'

'Kadvuz found me. He says the north rises against me.'

'It does. Urien rages against you, he mocks your titles, curses the *dux bellorum* and the Pendragon as a bastard whelp, a man of low birth masquerading as a king. Nimue drips poison into his ear, and she has brought Rheged, Gododdin and Lothian together in an alliance against you.'

'Why, when we are so close? Does Nimue not wish for Lloegyr's return?'

'She does, but more than that, she craves the return of Britain to the land it once was. A place devoted to the old gods. She is right, and I wish she and I were on the same side, for we want the same thing. But Nimue has not forgiven me for allowing the Christians to preside over your duel with Uther, for allowing them to control the great standing stones at Sorviodunum. She believes that you and I betrayed her and betrayed the gods by relinquishing the great stones to the nailed god.

'Nimue is maddened by the desire to return all of Britain's souls to Maponos, Neit, Arawn, Manawydan, Gwydion and Lleu Llaw. Once our gods grow strong again, the Saxon gods will tremble and fall before them. That is how we win this war. The gods will grant us victory if we can but bring souls to their worship. She is right about that. But I gave up Sorviodunum to the Christ worshippers so that you could have your victory over Uther. I did it for Britain. There was no other way.'

'I remember it well and you had no choice. Without becoming Pendragon, I could never have raised the army we needed to win at the River Dubglas. Have you sought Nimue, spoken to her? You were lovers once.'

'I have tried. But she is beyond rage.' Merlin gazed out into the night, and for the first time, Arthur saw emotion drag the druid's face down, sadness welling in his sharp eyes. 'I saw her once, but she flew into a rage and cast me out. I miss her,

Arthur, her wildness, her savage beauty, her cunning. She believed I betrayed the gods and that I am no longer in their favour. Nimue wants to build a new order of priestesses to become what the druids once were. She tries to teach Morgan the knowledge, but I do not believe she has the talent.'

'So Nimue connives against the both of us.'

'She does. She has the confidence of Morgan; the woman you sent to Urien in Guinevere's place to be his wife. Nimue raises Morgan's child, Mordred, to be the saviour of Britain. She believes you occupy his place, and every day they train that boy to fight and destroy you once he reaches manhood. Nimue and Morgan have sought the most skilled weapons masters and the wisest teachers. Owain ap Urien himself teaches the boy the cuts of the sword.'

Arthur glanced nervously about him. 'Do not speak of Morgan and that child.'

'He's your son. There's no hiding from it. Few know of your dark secret, and Urien is thankfully unaware. But there is evil there, Arthur. Nimue stokes the child and his mother with the power of the gods, and she has rallied three kingdoms to fight against you.'

Arthur slammed his fist down on the palisade. 'A curse on her. We are so close, Merlin. If I have to march north with an army, it will take an entire summer to defeat the northern kingdoms. The Saxons can strengthen during that time, form alliances, and rise against us. I cannot stop the ships arriving if I fight our own kingdoms in the north. Everything I have spent five years fighting for will be destroyed. Men have died to achieve what we have today. Good men, brave men like Balin, Anthun, Becan, and so many more.'

Nimue was an Irish woman, captured as a girl by Saxon pirates and raised as one of their own. Nimue was her Irish

name, and the Saxons called her Vivien. Raised in the secrets
and old knowledge deep within Ireland's mountains and black
pools. Irish druids taught her the secrets of their dark mountains, of dwarven smiths and elfish magic. The Saxons realised
her power, and they taught Nimue the ways of their gods, of
Woden, Thunor and the rest, but Nimue heard the gods of the
Britons in the trees, flames and rivers. Nimue listened to their
commands, and Arthur had seen her augur the fate of battle in
the guts of a goat and the blood of a raven. She spoke Saxon,
Irish, Roman Latin and the British tongue. Nimue knew the
nine spells of Woden, of Manawydan, Maponos, Arawn, and
had visited Annwn in a dream state, or so men said. Arthur
feared her power, and his stomach turned over as he remembered how cruelly he had dealt with Lady Morgan and his
bastard son, whom Urien now raised as his own.

'You must go north and face the renegade kingdoms,' said
Merlin. 'There is no choice.'

'I know it, but I don't like it. How can I fight the Saxons with
a northern army marching at my back?'

'You cannot. Nimue and Urien are as much a threat to
Britain as the Saxon battle-kings Aelle, Ida and Eormenric are.
They would cast us back to the way things were after the Great
War. Each kingdom standing alone, fighting each other, easy to
pick off by Saxon armies. If Urien and Nimue have their way,
our fight against the Saxons shall fail. Britain will be a Saxon
land within a generation. Lloegyr will stretch from the Thames
to the Humber and from Kernow to Pictland.'

'Urien plots against me because of Guinevere.' Arthur
winced at the cruel decision he had made. Blinded by his love
for Guinevere, Arthur had usurped an arrangement of marriage
made between Urien and Guinevere's father. Her father, King
Leodegrance of Cameliard, granted her hand in marriage to

Urien of Rheged, but Arthur had sent Morgan of Kernow north to marry him instead and quickly married Guinevere himself. He did not regret it, for he could not live knowing that Guinevere lay with another man, and he could never have delivered her into Urien's brutal hands. Arthur's hand rose to touch the bronze disc at his neck. He remembered how Igraine had suffered at Urien's hands. That could not be Guinevere's fate.

'He hates you for that.' Merlin's eyes darted to Igraine's disc. 'It was I who sent Igraine to Urien all those years ago, but it had to be so.' He stiffened and set his jaw; bushy eyebrows blown by the night wind. 'These are the hard decisions we men of power must take. But Urien also fears you because you are the Pendragon. Uther left him alone, so Urien loomed behind his great walls and his impenetrable fortress on its high crag and gave him no trouble. He won't bend the knee to you, Arthur, a man born of his own kingdom, foster son of his former champion, Ector. He wants you dead, and do not forget it.'

'If I march north with an army, there will be war with the northern kingdoms.'

'There will. A savage war, one that will rage until either you or the kings of Rheged, Gododdin and Lothian are dead.'

'We don't have time for it.' Arthur swallowed the urge to cry out with frustrated rage. How could Britain tear itself apart like this on the cusp of victory over the Saxons? He took a breath and mastered himself.

'And yet it must be done.'

Arthur's hand slipped to Ida's sceptre, which he wore tucked into his belt. He caressed the cold stone, seeking the wisdom of the battle-kings who had held it down the centuries. 'I shall go north with my black cloaks, and Kai's men.'

'That's close to seven hundred spearmen?'

'Aye. How many can Urien raise?'

'Perhaps a thousand, but only three or four hundred of them are warriors. The rest are the churls who owe him service whenever he calls. Farmers with spears and shields. That's the price of their landholdings in Rheged.'

'And Letan Luyddoc of Gododdin?'

'The same, perhaps less. Lothian too.'

'Why does King Letan side with Urien? His son Gawain and his champion Bors are at Dunpendrylaw. They are my friends. I rescued Gawain from Dun Guaroy! Have they forgotten that?'

'I went to the king's fortress at Dunpendrylaw last year and Letan has not forgotten. But Rheged is his neighbour. He finds himself trapped between Lothian and Rheged. It will be Gododdin that Urien attacks first if Letan comes out in support of you.'

'And Lothian?'

'King Lot would start a fight in an empty room. He sees only plunder and slaves in his alliance with Urien. But he'll come south with his wild highland warriors and cut a vicious swathe of suffering across our southern kingdoms.'

'If I can defeat Urien, then King Letan will join me.'

'He might. Prince Gawain and Bors have fought beside you before, as you say. They will support your position as Pendragon. But not if it means the end of Gododdin. I can go to Letan now, even as winter comes hard upon us.'

'I cannot call the banners again so soon after disbanding my army. To call the men of Powys, Gwent, Elmet, Gwynedd and Kernow might turn them against me. They have fought for too long without rest. The alliance I rule over as Pendragon stands on a knife-edge, Merlin. I simply cannot raise the men I need to fight Urien without risk of shattering Britain to ruin. I must go alone. With my black cloaks and Kai's men.'

'Urien hates Kai almost as much as he despises you. He was

Urien's oath man and betrayed that oath, bringing two hundred spearmen from Caer Ligualid to fight for you. By right, Urien can slay Kai the moment he sets eyes upon him, and no man would judge him for it. Kai broke his oath, but we know why he did it. Had he not, then we might well have lost the day at the Dubglas.'

'I'll march north with the men I have. It will have to be enough. We'll go now, even though it means marching through autumn into winter. We can forage for food as we go, though that will go hard on the people we take it from.'

'Beware Nimue and Owain. Owain is a great warrior, perhaps the champion of all Britain, and if you set foot in the Bear Fort, he will surely challenge you to single combat. Nimue will do all she can to cast you down.'

'You do not believe I could best Owain?'

'I did not say that.'

'I have the might of Excalibur; the sword I pulled from the stone to prove I am the rightful Pendragon.'

'Don't be so droll. The legends serve a purpose, as you well know. Part of you is still the fresh-faced pup I met beside the road, all alone and full of fear. The legend of the stone helped make you what you are. That was my doing, and don't forget it. Don't fight Owain if you can help it and keep away from Nimue. I shall go to Letan and see if I can convince the old fool to keep his warriors warm at home this winter. After that I shall go to Lothian and try to convince King Lot of what he must do, or not do, as the case may be.'

'Together we'll try to avert a war, so that in spring we can carry our spears against the Saxons.'

'Just so. There is one other kingdom we have not considered.'

'Demetia.'

'Demetia. Perched as it is like a snarling wolf's head at Britain's most westerly point.'

'Do you know King Morholt?'

'Don't be a fool. I know every king from here to Ireland and back to Benoic. Morholt and his wild Irishmen conquered Demetia when Ector was a boy. They are slavers and pirates from across the Irish Sea who won themselves a kingdom and have held on to it. They capture slaves, British folk, and send them west to their Irish cousins. Morholt hasn't a care for Britain, Lloegyr or our wars.'

'Then what does he care about?'

'Silver and women. Every year he takes a new young wife, and he must have whelped half a hundred children down the years. He is a simple man, but as cunning as a starving wolf.'

'Would he join our cause and fight for me?'

'Ha!' Merlin chuckled to himself, making a strange wheezing sound. 'Sometimes it still surprises me how empty the heads of warriors can be. He would rather dip his manhood into a smith's fire than fight for you. He might kill you, peel off your skin and make a hat out of you. Or he might come here and steal away your pretty wife, but he won't fight for you.'

'Even if we paid him in slaves and silver?'

'Do not contemplate such a thing. Selling folk, even Saxon folk, into slavery is no easy thing. It will rest heavy on your soul like a yoke. Better we try to win without Morholt and his pirates.'

'So north, then.'

'North it must be. If we survive that, I will come south and make sure the gods bless your new fortress.'

'What?' Arthur reeled with shock. 'How can you possibly know about that? Only Guinevere and I alone have discussed it.'

'Oh, I know all about your dream of Camelot, of your fountains, courtyards, luxurious bed and fine stone pillars. I am a druid, you fool. A mouse cannot fart in Britain without Merlin knowing of it. I have eyes and ears everywhere, and never forget it.'

'I need to replace my stewards.'

'At least you have picked a suitable location. The old folk knew where to build their fortresses. Strengthen it, make it defendable. I will come and make sure you don't make a pig's ear of it.'

Arthur held out his hand, and Merlin responded with a raised eyebrow, and Arthur withdrew his hand, smiling.

'I'll meet you in the north, then?'

'In the north. Where we must be cunning if we wish to save Britain from destroying itself.'

6

Guinevere complained that Arthur had to leave again so soon. He wanted nothing more than to spend a long winter with her, holding her beside warm fires and lying beneath comfortable furs, but the fire in Arthur's heart burned just as fiercely for Britain's fate as it did for Guinevere's love. Dumnonia's people complained when he commanded them to render up food and ale for the war band who would march north. Each year, every farm, fisherman, shepherd and landholder in Dumnonia rendered a tenth of their crops, livestock, eggs, milk and fish to the crown in return for King Madoc's, and therefore Arthur's, grant of land and for the protection offered by Dumnonia's army. It was that annual render that allowed the king to keep a standing army, and to feed the hungry mouths of every person at court. Arthur would take enough oatcakes, dried meat, cheese and honey to keep his men fed for four days, after which they would find supplies on the march. The complaints stopped when Arthur raised his voice and asked the landowners at court if they had ever seen a man scalped or gutted, or a woman defiled by Dumnonia's enemies. And that was the end of the discussion.

Arthur appointed a council of elders to run Dumnonia in his absence. They had done that work well enough during his long campaigns, and Arthur made each man swear fresh oaths to serve Prince Madoc truly, and to act in the best interests of the kingdom whenever they decided on disputes. Men could come to the council on two days per week, they could seek justice concerning things as small as disagreements over an ancient boundary, or rights of access to water for cows and sheep, their share of woodland to cut for firewood, and also seeking *sarheed*, the blood price, for murder or violence against a family member. In truth, Arthur had spent little time actually ruling Dumnonia since becoming its steward. He saw his role more as Britain's defender than Dumnonia's ruler. Arthur granted Guinevere's request for a place on the council, but he refused her request for Bishop Serwan to join her.

There were too many priests and bishops in Durnovaria already, and Guinevere spent too much time with Serwan for Arthur's liking. It was a delicate problem to remedy, because more and more people had converted to worship the nailed god. Not just churls and slaves, easy to influence by men who preached forgiveness of sins by a simple bath in an icy stream, but also wealthy and influential merchants and landholders. Serwan and his ilk promised a glorious afterlife and a life of peace compared to the violence and cruelty of the old gods. Many of those people still kept shrines to Bel, Maponos, Neit, Arawn and the many British gods. They saw the nailed god as another god in their pantheon, one who offered forgiveness and answers to their worries about death and the afterlife. But in Arthur's experience, Christ priests were ever hungry for silver and power and so Arthur preferred to keep Serwan at a distance, and not to grant him a position of influence in Dumnonia's ruling council.

On an autumn morning when frost touched the fields with a whisper of silver and a westerly wind blew damp brown leaves about Durnovaria's lanes and streets, Arthur led his men north to meet the rebels. He left two hundred men to protect the prince and the kingdom, and marched out with three hundred black-cloaked spearmen, and Kai's two hundred warriors. The former men of Rheged lived in a deep valley a half-day's march south of Durnovaria which had once belonged to one of Uther's champions. That man had died in battle, so Arthur granted the hall and its lands to Kai and his men, who took over the farms, mills, forests and pastures for their own, allowing the common folk to stay in return for their render.

Llamrei's iron-shod hooves clattered on the cobblestones, and Cavall darted about the great stallion's legs as the marching column left the city. Heavy boots and the click-clack of spears and shields filled the morning air, along with the rumble and squeak of the army's supply wagons drawn by donkeys who honked whenever Cavall came too close. Arthur rode at the head of the column with Kai and Lancelot, and half a dozen scouts ranged ahead on fast ponies, but the rest of the men marched on foot carrying their weapons, cloaks, blankets and as much food and drink as they could carry in their packs.

It took twenty days to march from the rolling valleys of Dumnonia to Rheged in the far north. They kept to old Roman roads wherever possible, following the straight lines first to Aquae Sulis with its baths and Roman buildings, then skirting around Powys and Elmet. Malegant, temporarily relieved of his command of Durnovaria's household troops so that Arthur could add his experience to the war band, marched with the column carrying the fasces, and a broad-shouldered warrior carried the Pendragon dragon banner, but Arthur avoided major towns and cities so as not to attract too much attention from kings, princes and warlords as he marched through their territory. Such visits required feasts and cordial formality and also questions from powerful men to which Arthur did not yet have the answers. Every king would already know of Urien's rebellion. Despite winter's onset, war stirred in the north and the rulers of Elmet, Powys, Gwynedd and the rest were rightly fearful of what that war meant for the borders and their people, but as yet Arthur could make no promises nor provide any commitments about what might happen in spring and where his famous black-cloaked warriors would fight.

The fasces demanded that folk render up supplies whenever Arthur asked, so his men reached the north with full bellies but worn boots and aching legs and shoulders. Throughout the long journey, riders came to look at Arthur's men from high peaks and distant hilltops. They were scouts alerted to warriors traipsing through the countryside seizing food, so even on rain-soaked days Arthur flew the dragon banner and made sure Malegant carried the fasces with his axe tied about by a bundle of rods upon his shoulder. Arthur had no doubt the lords of the kingdoms through which he passed knew of his presence, but it was Arthur's right as Pendragon to go wherever he pleased and so the scouts scuttled back to their lords with tales of warriors on the march in autumn, but that they were the Pendragon's warriors who posed no threat.

Arthur reached the Bear Fort after long, dreary marches through the forests and hills of northern Elmet into the wilder, crueller valleys and dales of southern Rheged. It was a land of sweeping heathers and steep cliffs, dark rocks and caves of which folk told tales of fetches, trolls and wood faeries who lurked in the darkness. People left elf-stones, food and charms for the hidden people, those ancient beings, to keep them from stealing children in the night and to keep their spirits quiet.

The warriors reached their destination on a grey chill morning with a wind so cold it stung the men's faces raw. The sky hung low, as if pressed towards the land by the weight of the gods above. Clouds twisted and turned about one another in hues of black, grey and snow-white and the men gathered cloaks about their shoulders and marched hunched over into the ear-whipping wind.

The Bear Fort loomed on its high promontory, glowering down at the river Eden, and Arthur followed the river's meander and up the steep-sided approach to King Urien's fortress. He had his men rest beside the river in full view of the fort and waited until half a dozen warriors cantered from the gate to look at Arthur's men from the high ground. Those men carried bright spears and shields bearing King Urien's bear sigil. Two warriors peeled off from the rest and galloped back to the fortress with news of the dragon banner and Arthur astride his white stallion.

The wind whipped in from the western sea and billowed around the hill to blow Arthur's hair away from his face.

'Wait here,' he said to his men. An icy drizzle seeped from the sky in a blustery fog to soak his cloak and armour so that Arthur shivered his way up the hill to the sharp, fang-like stakes of the Bear Fort's timber palisade. The Rheged warriors sat hunched over their saddles, pretending not to notice Arthur's approach, and when he reached them Arthur rode Llamrei around their horses, allowing Llamrei's whickering and stomping hooves to upset the other animals. The warriors frowned at him and fought with their reins to keep their mounts in check, and Arthur reined in before them.

'I am Arthur, Pendragon of Britain. Come to see King Urien,' he shouted to be heard above the howling wind.

'King Urien tires of meting out dooms to brigands and masterless men,' said a slack-faced Rheged warrior with heavy shoulders and a small, round face. 'He is at rest today. Come back tomorrow, and perhaps the king will see you then.'

'Lord.'

'Come back tomorrow and take your stinking band of thieving whoresons from my king's hill before we drive you out.' The warrior curled his lip and spat across his horse's neck.

'You will address me as lord. I have earned it, and I would have my right from you, soldier.' Arthur had not expected Urien to throw open his gates and receive him with flower petals scattered on the road and cheering maidens acclaiming his arrival. They were enemies. Arthur had deceived both Urien and Owain by sending Morgan to become Urien's latest wife instead of Guinevere. He had, however, not expected insults from one of Urien's warriors as rain seeped through his cloak and trickled down his armour like an ice-cold snake slithering down his back.

'Lord of what? Piss? I remember you when you were Ector's whelp from Caer Ligualid. Begone before I slap you about in front of your own men.'

'We shall fight then, you and I,' Arthur said, and placed a hand on Excalibur's hilt. 'Get down from your horse and arm yourself.'

'There's no need for that, lord,' said another of Urien's warriors. This man wore a torc at his neck and his forearms showed three death rings. 'We'll tell the king you are here and will send word if he will receive you.'

Arthur clenched his jaw. He considered simply riding past

the warriors and into the Bear Fort without King Urien's leave, then decided that would only make matters worse.

'Very well,' he said. He wheeled Llamrei around and cantered back to his men.

'That seemed to go well,' said Kai, as Arthur dropped from the saddle.

'Make camp here,' Arthur replied. 'I have a feeling they won't offer us guest friendship rights at the Bear Fort.'

'Do you still think there's a chance of peace?' asked Lancelot. The drizzle stopped, and he drew a hood back from his head and squinted up at the broiling sky.

'I will do my best to make peace with Urien.' Arthur took a piece of hard bread from Dewi as the warrior handed out a portion to every man in the war band. 'But if we can't have peace, then there must be another solution.'

'You've been around Guinevere's courtiers too much,' said Kai with a grin splitting his face. 'You're even sounding like one of them. What solution?'

'We'll see,' was all Arthur would say.

Urien kept Arthur waiting all day until eventually a solitary rider rode slowly down from the Bear Fort on a dappled mare.

'Lord Arthur,' he called from the hill. 'King Urien will see you now. Two men may accompany you. No more.'

'We'd better go, then,' Arthur said, gesturing for Lancelot and Kai to follow him.

'It might be better if I stay here,' said Kai. 'I broke my oath to King Urien, and he'd be within his rights to seize me.'

'You answered the Pendragon's call and broke your oath to do it. There was no crime in that. Besides, you're my brother, so I won't let him take you. Better for him to see you now and get it over with.'

'If you say so.' Kai blew out his cheeks. Arthur understood

his nervousness. Urien was a frightening man, and a powerful king. His enmity was not something to take lightly.

'I do. Dewi, keep the men ready. Don't line up in ranks, but keep spears and shields close.'

'Do you think they'll attack us, lord?' asked the captain.

'I'm not sure what to expect, but I don't want you caught lolling if hundreds of warriors come down from the Bear Fort screaming for your blood. So be ready.'

'Yes, lord.'

Arthur mounted Llamrei wearing his polished armour and his helmet complete with his feathers, and his long black cloak. Lancelot and Kai wore their own war finery, and they rode up the hill towards King Urien's hall following the messenger. The gate which bridged the gap across the fortress' ditch was down and Llamrei's hooves clattered on the dark wood as he whickered at the smell of civilisation after so long travelling in the wild.

The fortress stank of smoke, shit and damp thatch as Arthur rode into a wide courtyard surrounded by wattle houses, wet thatch and long-faced churls who gaped at Arthur's stallion and his war gear. He dismounted, and a guard came and helped Arthur with Llamrei's reins. They marched from the courtyard along a wide street flanked on each side by narrow buildings from which nosey townspeople peered through the gaps in closed window shutters. A chicken squawked and ran across the street in front of them, and a woman threw the stinking contents of her soil bucket out of a second-storey window.

They reached the hall to find a dozen of Urien's soldiers flanking the entrance in ranks, each one of them tall and broad, carrying a shield painted with Urien's bear and spears resting upon their shoulders. Those men made the entrance narrow, leaving Arthur barely enough room between them, so that he and his companions had to walk in single file. The soldiers stared at Arthur with hard eyes and curled lips, but he was just as tall and just as scarred as the worst of them, so he kept his back straight and met each man's gaze with defiance.

Arthur glanced up at the enormous bear's skull hanging above the hall door, and steeled himself, preparing to meet the famous king of Rheged, veteran of the Great War against the Saxons, feared king and a man who hated Arthur. A big-bellied man opened the hall door a crack, just wide enough for Arthur, Kai and Lancelot to sidle into. Inside, more Rheged warriors lined the entrance hall. Arthur stalked through the twin lines of warriors, the stink of their leather armour and ale-stinking breath thick in the air. They kept silent, and as Arthur's boots creaked on the hard-packed earthen floor, he met every hard stare and flat face, even though he wanted to turn and leave that fearsome place. His guts turned over, and he balled his fists to keep his hands from shaking. There were twenty men packed into that hallway, and at any moment they could close in and fall upon Arthur like an avalanche, cutting and slashing at him with their knives and spears.

'Your sword, lord,' said a short man with one ear missing. 'No blades permitted in the hall, you know that.'

Arthur drew Excalibur and his seax and handed them over.

'Careful with that,' Arthur said as the man grabbed the hilt. 'A god forged it. The sword might steal your soul.' He winked and enjoyed the look of fear in the man's eyes.

The roof of the Bear Fort's hall was high, and smoke-blackened. Rushlights flickered in iron crutches set high on support posts, which stretched from floor to rafters. Shields with Urien's bear sigil hung on the walls, along with the shields of enemies Urien and his warriors had slain in battle. Urien himself leaned forward in his high-backed throne, glowering and malevolent, like a great wolf before its pack. The skulls of five men killed by Urien himself adorned that throne, and the king ran a heavy hand down his braided iron-grey beard. A scar ran from the top of Urien's head down through his eye to his jaw. He was broad and thick-necked, with a round face and clever eyes. He looked gaunt and had lost weight since Arthur had last seen him. Shadows ringed his eyes and his skin had a pallid, grey hue.

Nimue came from behind Urien's throne, slinking like a great cat with her long talons and frightening appearance. She scowled at Arthur with her full-lipped, sharp-eyed face. Nimue had wide hips, and might have been beautiful, but for the black ash she wore smeared across the top half of her face so that her eyes were like dark, powerful pits. She covered the bottom half of her face with white paste, so that she looked like a demon of Annwn, and men feared her power. Nimue wore a necklace heavy with iron and stone charms fashioned into crude hammers, phalluses, spears and fish. Arthur had not seen her for five years, and strands of grey streaked her hair around the ears, and one great slash of it hung from her forehead. She thrust a hand in Arthur's direction and made the sign to ward off evil.

'Three turds have slid into my hall. An upstart, an oath-breaker, and a whoreson,' said Urien, his voice as dry and cracked as a riverbed in drought. 'I should have all three of you whipped for your impudence. I should take your heads and mount them on the door beside my bear. Or perhaps I'll make slaves of you, make you slop out my shit pail, or geld you and put you to work in my salt farm. I could sell you to King Marc of Kernow. He always needs miners to dig tin from beneath the moors.'

'King Urien,' Arthur said in greeting, and respectfully

bowed his head as though the king had not insulted him at all. Nimue hissed and Arthur ignored her.

'King Urien, what? Have you come to grovel and beg forgiveness for your deception? Have you, Kai, come to surrender yourself to my judgement for breaking your oath? Your father would be ashamed of you. This thing you follow isn't even your brother by blood. He's a bastard, a prancing pretender with a bright sword. What did Merlin make you do for that sword of yours? I never had him pegged as a boy-lover.'

'We come to make peace.'

Urien laughed and slammed his hands upon the arms of his chair. He laughed so hard that it heightened into a wracking cough which turned his face purple. 'Peace?' he spat. 'When has there ever been peace, you fool? When the gods walked amongst us and fairies washed their tits in the river?'

'You did not answer when I called the banners.'

'Why should I answer to you? Because you killed an old king? I hear Uther could barely lift his blade when you fought him.'

'Lord king, we are close to defeating the Saxons, within reach of driving them from Britain forever.'

'We? Who is this we you speak of? How dare you come into my hall speaking as though my people were your own, barking at me like some jumped-up midden-heap dog?'

'I am Arthur, Pendragon of Britain, steward of Dumnonia, and you will speak to me with respect,' Arthur shouted suddenly, and the guards on either side of Urien's throne jumped with surprise.

'Respect must be earned. Dumnonia is soft, her warriors made weak as kittens by their fertile soil and fat harvests. A whore could rule Dumnonia and no man there would object to it. You have a whore of your own now. You stole the woman I agreed to marry, that I arranged with her father in distant Cameliard to wed. How is your whore?'

'Careful,' Arthur warned, and Urien laughed and coughed raucously.

'Careful of what? You? You'd lick yourself clean if you could, turd of Arawn. You can keep your foreign whore. Lady Morgan of Kernow is both fair and willing, and I have a son, another heir. How many sons has your whore given you?'

'None,' said Nimue in her heavily accented voice. 'Nor will she. I've seen to it. Arthur is accursed. You gave up the great stones to the Christ worshippers and betrayed your own gods, the very gods who forged your sword and gave Merlin his power. You are a stain on this country, forsaken by the gods, cursed and despised. Your queen's womb is barren and foul, like rancid meat crawling with maggots and stinking of filth.'

Arthur shuddered at the thought of Nimue cursing Guinevere's womb. A picture of Nimue in a dark room invaded his mind, of her hunched over a cauldron or fire calling upon Arawn, or Bel, Maponos or Neit to curse Guinevere's body. That thought quickly turned to anger, and the dream of peace burned away like a dry leaf cast into a blazing furnace.

'I am the Pendragon of Britain!' Arthur roared, his voice echoing off the high rafters, and the guards about Urien took a step forward. 'You will both kneel and swear oaths to honour me as high king and answer when I call for you to bind your warriors to mine.' Arthur wasn't a king, had no desire to be one. He had become the Pendragon out of necessity, to call upon the warriors of every kingdom in Britain to fight against the Saxon enemy. Without that unification, Britain was doomed. Urien and Nimue had become Arthur's enemies. Hate dripped from them like poison and in the cruelty of their disrespect and curses Arthur realised that the pathway to peace with Rheged was impossible.

'I kneel to no man, bastard.' Urien stood, or rather, he tried to stand. Drool spilled from his mouth and his face turned as red as blood. He staggered, slumped back into his chair, and fell into a fit of wracking coughs.

'You will kneel, and so will your *gwyllion*.'

'Look at you, Arthur ap Nowhere,' said Nimue. 'You think you have power because you are Merlin's plaything? Where is Merlin? Where is the great druid? You are alone, and I will...'

'Silence! Enough of your hateful words! If you won't keel, then we'll fight. Will you stand against me, Urien, king of Rheged? Can you cross swords with me? We'll fight and the gods will show us who has the right of it.'

'I'll fight you,' came a voice from the shadows, and Prince Owain ap Urien, champion of Rheged, one of the most feared fighting men in all Britain, strode forward. He wore his long black hair loose about his strong, angular face. Death rings covered his forearms, and he fixed Arthur with a flat stare. A smile twitched the corner of his mouth, as though he had been waiting in the darkness behind the hall's great pillars just for this very moment, for Arthur to become goaded into a fight he could not win.

'If you are to fight in your father's stead, then so be it. We'll fight...'

'To the death,' Owain cut in.

'To the death.'

'We'll fight in the morning and when I win, Urien will be Pendragon of Britain and by the time the sun sets tomorrow, no one will remember the name Arthur ap Nowhere.'

'We'll fight now. Here. In your father's hall. If you win, Urien will be Pendragon. But if I win, then Rheged will recognise me as Pendragon and bind its warriors to my call.'

Owain glanced at his father, shocked that Arthur wanted to fight there and then rather than with the pageantry of a duel out in the open where every person in Rheged could see its champion kill the king of kings. Arthur had no time to waste. He needed this futile northern war over, so if there was to be a fight, then he wanted it now. Urien tried to talk, but all he could manage was a wheezing cough and so instead he waved a gnarled hand to show his agreement.

'Agreed,' said Owain.

'Swords, no shields,' said Arthur.

'Agreed.'

Owain waved to a guard and whispered to him, pointing at the hall and its feasting benches, giving the man orders to prepare the place and make space for him to fight.

'Have you lost your wits?' hissed Kai as he, Arthur and Lancelot withdrew to a corner of the hall.

'No,' Arthur replied, and took off his cloak. 'It must be this way.'

'What if you lose?'

'Then you'll probably die too. Badly.'

'Then don't lose.'

'Should I go to the men, lord?' asked Lancelot, his broad face grave.

'No. Just wait. But watch Urien's men, if they try to block the doors or pen us in, go for the weapons. Go to the steward there and have him bring Excalibur.'

Lancelot hurried to the steward, and Kai went to another to get Arthur something to drink before the fight.

'Hello, Lord Arthur,' said a quiet voice behind Arthur, a gentle woman's voice. Arthur turned and felt sick as Morgan stood before him, holding the hand of a five-year-old boy with dark hair and long limbs. Arthur gulped and gaped at the child, the boy who could only be Mordred.

'My lady,' Arthur said, inclining his head. She had the same big blue eyes he remembered, and golden hair tied up in an elaborately braided pile on top of her head. In the five years since Arthur had last seen Morgan, lines had begun to crease her forehead and there was a sadness in her once bright eyes, a dullness, and Arthur could only imagine what she had endured in her time as Urien's queen. Arthur remembered Igraine, how she had spent her last hours speaking kindly to Arthur when he had been a boy on the verge of manhood. How Igraine had suffered. She became the victim of Uther's love for her, of Uther and Merlin's scheme, which led to her husband King Gorlois' death. Britain's kings learned of the deception and there was outrage, just when Britain was on the cusp of victory against the Saxons during Merlin and Ambrosius Aurelianus' Great War. So Igraine had gone to Urien for the sake of peace, and had suffered a life of pain, cruelty and despair. Ambrosius had died anyway, and the Saxons took Lyndsey, Bernicia, Kent and much of Britain's south-east coast for their own.

'Don't you wish to say hello to Prince Mordred?' She looked down at the boy and back at Arthur. There was hate in her eyes, but her face remained serene.

'Prince Mordred, I am honoured to meet you.'

The boy shuffled back into his mother's skirts rather than look into Arthur's scarred face.

'Mordred, you must say hello. This is Arthur. He is the king of kings and a great warrior. He is also your... how shall we put it, Arthur?'

Arthur swallowed hard and glanced around in case Lancelot or Kai were within earshot.

'He is also,' she continued, 'your father...'s enemy. So perhaps we should hate him.'

'Hello,' said Mordred suddenly, and stuck out his tongue.

'I would wish you luck,' Morgan said, and Mordred hid behind her skirts again. 'But we should only speak with sincerity to guests. I hope Guinevere is making you happy.'

'Yes, lady,' Arthur stammered, relieved that the awkwardness would end as Morgan turned to walk away.

She paused and glanced over her shoulder. 'Beware, though, my old friend Guinevere has a burning fondness for strong, handsome men, like your friend over there.'

Morgan left, and Lancelot arrived with Excalibur and Kai with a flagon of ale. Arthur wiped sweat from his brow. He would rather fight ten champions than look into Morgan's eyes again. He was the creator of her fate, the man who had sent her to lie beneath Urien's great bulk as his calloused paws mauled her soft body. Worse than that, Arthur was Mordred's father, and his mother and Nimue were raising the boy to hate Arthur with a passionate fury.

'Are you ready?' asked Lancelot as he handed Arthur his sword.

'I have to be,' Arthur replied.

'Owain is a killer,' said Kai. 'You've seen him fight. He could be the finest and most dangerous warrior in all of Britain.'

'Can I beat him?'

Kai placed a hand on Arthur's shoulder and stared into his eyes. 'As you say, you have to. Or we shall all die this day.'

7

Benches scraped as slaves dragged them towards the hall's edges. People snuck quietly through the doors and took places in the shadows to watch Rheged's prince and champion fight the Pendragon of Britain. Arthur was born of Rheged. Many of the faces gaping at him in the hall's gloom were familiar, men who had fought alongside Ector, or faces he had seen in Caer Ligualid or at the Bear Fort. Warriors in fur and iron came to watch with professional interest; women in woollen dresses and knitted shawls with brooches at their breasts whispered behind their hands, pointing at Arthur and Owain.

Urien sat forward in his chair, slurping from an ale horn with his great head looking straight at Arthur. Nimue capered around Owain, shaking a sprig of holly drenched in one of her potions to give him the strength to be victorious. Mordred shot hateful looks in Arthur's direction and Arthur took deep breaths, steeling himself for what must happen next. For he must fight a dangerous man, a killer, a man who would fight with every ounce of strength in his body to rip Arthur's life away from him.

Owain stepped out from Nimue's blessing, though she continued to call after him in her native Irish tongue. She hopped from one leg to another, screeched and pointed two fingers in Arthur's direction. Arthur considered removing his armour and boots, to make himself lithe and quick, but the armour would protect him from any glancing slices and cuts from Owain's sword, so he kept it on. Fouled rushes covered the floor, and amongst them could be scraps of food and bone, and Arthur could not risk his barefoot standing on something sharp. Such a momentary distraction meant death when facing Owain's lethal speed.

Arthur drew Excalibur and gripped the hilt two handed. He closed his eyes and let the sword imbue him with its strength, with the power of the god who had forged it in the mists of time. He rolled his shoulders and swung the blade about him. Arthur dipped and crouched to stretch his legs and rolled his neck around sunwise twice. Owain too swept his sword about him, moving it in great circles, its gleaming blade flashing with astonishing speed. He was a head shorter than Arthur, but much thicker in the chest and across the shoulders.

'You should let me fight him in your stead,' said Lancelot.

'It has to be me,' Arthur replied. At that moment, and with all those hateful eyes watching him, Arthur wished his friend could fight in his place. Lancelot was a peerless warrior, big, fast and ruthless. Kai was a better swordsman than Arthur, and had been since they were boys. But destiny had brought Arthur to this point. He had fought Uther in the great stone circle, had fought Mynog the Boar and killed Saxon kings in battle. This was the world Arthur lived in and the price of being Pendragon. The path to peace always seemed to require supreme violence, seemed to force Arthur to face a brutal enemy and risk his life. The gods loved battle, blood, death and risk, and Arthur supposed he was beloved by Merlin and, therefore, by the gods. He let that thought kindle a fire inside him. *I am the gods' champion, Merlin's champion. I must be victorious.* And so he must, or it would be his life, Kai's, Lancelot's and every one of his warriors waiting below the Bear Fort's windswept crag.

'Fight!' Urien bellowed from his chair. 'Kill that upstart bastard. My son Owain's sword will deliver justice for Rheged!'

Owain bowed to his father and strode confidently to the centre of the hall. He pointed his sword at Arthur and beckoned him forward.

'Fight well, brother,' said Kai, and Arthur went to meet his enemy.

Urien's hall fell silent. No drums sounded, and nobody cheered. It was as though Arthur and Owain faced each other on a different plane, in a place between this world and the next in full sight of the gods of Britain. Arthur paced forward and brought his sword up to his face and then held it wide.

'Today we fight to settle a dispute,' Arthur shouted so that every person packed around the hall's edges could hear. 'If Owain wins, Urien will be the high king. If I win, Rheged will acknowledge me as Pendragon and send her warriors to fight for me whenever I call.'

'Enough talking, turd,' Owain snarled, and he came growling at Arthur, his sword slicing upwards in a murderous, silver-flashing arc.

Arthur threw himself backwards, but not in time to stop the sword's point from slicing across his chin. The very end of the blade nicked him, no more than a hair's breadth of cold steel, but it was enough to slice the skin open and for Arthur's blood to show red amongst the Bear Hall's smoky half-light.

'First blood,' Owain snarled, and he twirled his sword and stepped away. The crowd gasped at his speed and skill, and

Arthur knew he must be careful, must be faster than he had ever been before.

Arthur charged at Owain, lunging with his sword. Owain moved to parry the blow, but Arthur drew his sword back at the last minute and instead slashed the weapon towards Owain's neck. Owain ducked, twisted away and came up laughing.

'Is that it?' Owain said, shaking his head. 'How are you high king? A one-legged whore could best you with a broomstick.'

Arthur attacked again, this time hacking at Owain, lunging, slashing, but finding only air as Owain twisted away from him like a dancer. Arthur paused, breathing hard, beads of sweat on his forehead and dripping down his back. Owain was good. Better than any man Arthur had faced before. Too fast. Too strong.

'My turn,' Owain said. He came on, bouncing on the balls of his feet, darting forward like a snake and turning that lunge into an upward sweep of his sword that almost ripped Arthur's face open. He felt the blade pass before his eyes, the wind of its movement dry against the wet of his eyeballs. Owain drove his knee into Arthur's belly, knocking the wind from him. The sword came down in a slash to sweep Arthur's head from his shoulders, so he dropped to the ground and rolled away just in time. The blade stabbed down, and Arthur rolled again. 'Look how the king of kings rolls in piss and ale-stained floor rushes like a pig,' Owain called. He spread his arms wide and every person in the hall laughed.

'Get up!' Kai called. 'Get up and fight!'

Arthur flushed with embarrassment and clambered to his feet. He felt like a field churl fighting a champion, like a novice fighting a sword master. Owain came at him again, and Arthur parried his blows, banging two blows aside before Owain twisted his sword arm and sliced the blade across Arthur's forearm. He turned half one way, spun back the other, then whipped the blade across Arthur's shoulder. His chain mail took the blow, but it felt like a hammer thumping into the corded muscle. Owain dragged the sword back and turned the blade so that it sliced Arthur's skin open above his eyes.

Arthur reeled away. The cut was shallow, and stung like a whip, but head wounds bleed as fiercely as a death wound anywhere else on the body and blood sheeted down Arthur's face, running into his eyes and mouth. He tasted its iron and spat out a gobbet of his own lifeblood. Owain was killing him, and Arthur could feel not only his life, but the fate of Britain, slipping away.

'Kill him!' Nimue shrieked. 'I want his head and his manhood, geld him, cut him, kill him!'

'Arthur!' Lancelot roared. He dashed to Arthur and used his cloak to wipe the blood from his face whilst Arthur crouched beside a pillar. Owain came on in great strides, his eyes burning with glorious victory. Lancelot grabbed Arthur's face and shouted at him. 'You can't beat him like that. You see yourself as a lord, as honourable and good. But you are a brutal savage. Every fight you have ever won has been through ferocious will. You can't beat him sword to sword, but you are a beast, a brute and a killer. Use that. Use your savagery!'

Owain quickened his pace, and Lancelot darted away. Owain lifted his sword above his head, aiming to bring the blade down two handed and carve Arthur in two. But then time slowed and everything became clear. Lancelot was right, and Arthur let the beast inside him take over. He roared like a bear, let go of Excalibur and dived at Owain's legs. He wrapped his arms around Owain and drove him down towards the ground. The sword came down, but the blow fouled, and instead of its blade, the hilt thumped harmlessly into Arthur's back.

Owain fell heavily on his back, with Arthur clinging to his midriff. Arthur reached up and grabbed Owain's belt with his left hand, and with his right, he grabbed Owain's manhood and squeezed. With all the strength of a lifetime at war, of hefting sword, shield and spear every day, he twisted Owain's manhood like he was squeezing water from a washed shirt. Owain howled like a drowning fox and tried to twist away, but Arthur dragged himself up Owain's body like a creeping beast. Owain's sword flailed, but Arthur was too close for the weapon to strike. He twisted Owain's groin once more and then reached up for his face. Arthur's right hand scrambled at Owain's beard, found the corner of his wet mouth, and Arthur hooked his fingers in and ripped at the inside of Owain's cheek. Owain bucked and shouted, and Arthur ripped his mouth open at the corner like a hooked fish.

'Stand and fight!' Urien called, and then fell into another coughing fit. Arthur ignored the old king, felt Owain's blood between his fingers, and with his left hand he pinned Owain's sword arm. Owain's left hand clawed at Arthur, but he used his elbow to drive it away, reared up and smashed his forehead into Owain's face. Gristle and bone crunched beneath Arthur's forehead, so he lifted his head and pounded it three times into Owain's soft face. Bones broke, his nose turned to mush and Arthur realised he was roaring incoherently, his face washed with his own blood and now also Owain's. Owain's free hand clutched at Arthur's chest, bracing him so that Arthur could not headbutt him again. Arthur drove his thumb into Owain's left eye and gouged it like a boiled egg. He used his nail, cutting, driving into the jelly and scooping out filth. Owain screamed, a sound like nothing Arthur had heard before, a terrible noise which shook the Bear Fort's very foundations.

Arthur stood and slowly stalked to pick up Excalibur. He

dragged the blade's tip slowly across the floor, the scraping sound echoing in the high rafters. Owain curled up into a ball, whimpering in pain, clutching at the ruin of his face.

'Get up,' Arthur snarled.

Owain turned to him, his face an unrecognisable pulp of torn flesh, swelling and broken bones. His left eye was a mess of blue and purple goo, and his mouth flapped ragged and bloody.

'Fight him, my son, fight him!' Urien wailed. There was panic in his voice now. Panic and despair.

Owain rose, his entire body shaking in pain. He held his sword, and waved it at Arthur, blood and snot coming from his nose and mouth in bubbles. Arthur stepped in, batted Owain's sword aside with one strong sweep, and then brought the blade around in a flat arc. Excalibur tore open Owain's throat and sent a spray of blood through the shadows and hearth-fire smoke. Owain dropped dead, and without hesitation Arthur stepped over his twitching corpse.

People in the hall gasped, and a woman vomited at the horror of Owain's brutal death. Arthur pointed his sword at Urien, and the king of Rheged looked away.

'Look at me!' Arthur roared. Blood poured from the wound on his forehead so that he approached the king with a wet red face, eyes glaring like a death mask, Urien's son's blood still on his sword. Urien turned and gazed upon Arthur with trembling, teary eyes. 'Kneel.'

'Never,' Urien croaked, so Arthur leapt up onto his platform. The battle-fury was upon him, and Arthur felt no pity for the old brute. Urien's guards did not move to help their king. They sensed what must happen next and kept their places, spears at their shoulders and faces as white as ghosts. Arthur grabbed a fistful of Urien's tunic and cast him from the chair. His great bulk fell heavily and the once mighty king stared up at Arthur.

He coughed maniacally, clutching at his chest and throat, face changing from deep red to marble white.

'Swear your allegiance to me now, before your people,' Arthur shouted.

Urien gurgled, coughed and lay flat on his back. Froth appeared at his lips, and he voided his bowels, filling his hall with the rank stink of shit. Urien suddenly went still. Dead. No longer breathing. The king who had fought so valiantly in the Great War and who had ruled Rheged with an iron hand for decades lay dead at Arthur's feet, dying moments after his son and heir Owain ap Urien. Arthur walked slowly to Urien's corpse. His breath came long and deep, like a great stag in a deep forest. He put his boot on Urien's dead chest and lifted Excalibur, turning the blade carefully around every corner of the Bear Fort's hall.

'Your king and your champion are dead,' he said, voice hard, cruel and cold. 'I am Arthur Pendragon, your high king, and this is the price of defying me. King Urien sought to undermine our cause, to drive a blade into the alliance of British kingdoms and cast asunder all hope of a return to our island's former glory. Now he is dead. So you will all kneel now in his place.'

Arthur waited as the big growlers, the warriors in leather and iron, dropped to one knee, as did the courtiers in the fine tunics and warm cloaks. Everybody in the hall knelt, even Morgan dropped to her knees, though tears streamed down her face. All knelt but one.

'I'll not kneel to Merlin's plaything,' Nimue said, and marched from the hall.

'Let her go,' Arthur said when Lancelot moved to go after her. 'Lady Morgan, you kneel to no man. Rise, please.' The anger and the fury fled from Arthur like rain from fresh thatch and left him feeling drained. He sheathed Excalibur and used his sleeve to wipe the blood from his face. 'You needn't cry. You are the mother of Prince Mordred, who is now the sole heir to Rheged's throne. Mordred will be king here when he comes of age, and both you and he are under my protection. Lord Kai ap Ector of Caer Ligualid will rule Rheged until Prince Mordred is old enough to assume his crown.'

People in the hall whispered and gaped at Arthur, and Kai stared at him with a look of utter surprise upon his face.

'And Nimue?' asked Morgan, now standing with her shoulders back and Mordred held in her arms.

'Nimue can remain at the Bear Fort, should she wish. But I want no more trouble from this kingdom. Rheged's warriors will march whenever I call, and Kai will see to it that the kingdom is ruled fairly. If Nimue works against him, Lord Kai has my permission to put her to death. Is there any person here who disputes my authority?'

Nobody in the hall spoke. Arthur waited, staring at every face, aware that their king and prince lay dead before them.

'Then so it shall be,' Arthur said. 'What man here commands Rheged's army now that Owain ap Urien is dead?'

A large man with a shaven head came forward. He wore a bearskin about his shoulders over a coat of chain mail. 'I am Fferog,' he said. 'I am the captain of Rheged's warriors.'

'Then summon them. Call every man at arms to muster here at the Bear Fort within the week. Do it now. Every man, including you, will swear an oath of loyalty to Lord Kai.'

'Yes, lord,' Fferog said, and marched from the hall.

Arthur sat upon Urien's throne, his hands resting on the shining skull-adorned armrests. Morgan strode out of the hall and the people bowed their heads to Arthur and Kai and left in silence.

'You there,' Arthur called, and a pinch-faced serving man

scuttled forward with his hands clasped together and a fawning smile.

'Yes, Lord Arthur?'

'Clean up this mess.' Arthur gestured to the two corpses leaking blood across the hall floor. The servant bowed and beckoned for others to help him.

'Well, I certainly didn't see that coming,' said Kai as he approached the throne. He put one foot on the raised platform and wiped a hand down his beard. 'What am I going to do in this place?'

'Bring it to order,' said Arthur. 'Make sure Nimue causes no trouble. Stay here with your two hundred warriors, and if any of Urien's warlords grumble, put them down without mercy.'

'You are getting a taste for killing kings,' said Lancelot.

'Especially old ones,' Kai quipped.

Arthur removed his hands from the skull throne and grimaced at their yellow-white sheen. 'This place has an ill humour, Kai. Get a new throne and clear out the hall. Take down the shields and make the place your own. I did not come here to kill Owain, we will miss his sword in the battles to come. Urien's death was no fault of mine, but I am not sorry to see him gone. We'll wait for Fferog to summon the spearmen and then, Lancelot, you and I will march them and our black cloaks north to Gododdin. I will have peace between our kingdoms, even if I have to cut down every prince and king in the realm to do it.'

8

A week later, Fferog brought five hundred spearmen to muster at the Bear Fort on a day where frost covered the fields and meadows in a crisp, white blanket. Arthur spent the week arranging Urien and Owain's funeral balefires, which burned for three days in honour of the old king and his champion prince. They were days of melancholy which Arthur preferred to spend alone. He had killed two kings of Britain, and the fight against Owain had been so brutal that Arthur's hands shook for two days. He could not sleep after the fight. Thoughts of blood, pain and Urien's bloated form gurgling and choking on his own hall floor gave Arthur waking nightmares.

A healer woman sewed the wound on Arthur's forehead closed with a bone needle and clean thread, and the warriors and courtiers of Rheged avoided Arthur. They moved out of his way in corridors, and folk whispered behind their hands when he set the torch to the old king's funeral pyre. Nimue hid and Arthur left her alone, but Morgan paraded little Mordred in the hall and at the funeral celebrations so that all men could see Rheged's heir, and that Britain's high king supported him.

'I expected more,' Arthur said as he stared down at Fferog's men. Arthur stood on the Bear Fort's hill dressed in his war gear and wearing a fur cloak taken from Urien's chamber instead of his usual black cloak. Steam rose from his mouth in the still, chill air.

'It's only been a week,' Kai replied. He too wore a fur wrapped close about his shoulders to keep out the worst of the frost. 'Rheged is a large and rugged country. It would take another three weeks, at least, for messengers to summon men from the eastern hills and western coast.'

'Will you have enough men to keep the peace here?'

'There aren't rumours of any unrest yet. But we'll visit Urien's kinsmen and make sure nothing is fomenting in secret.'

'Good. Be hard with them. This is a hard country, and they respect nothing but ruthlessness. You might have to make an example of one or two if you find out they are gathering spears.'

'I had not expected you to name me regent, or steward, or whatever you want to call it.'

'Neither did I. I came here for peace, not to kill a king and his heir.'

'You are getting quite the reputation.'

'For killing kings? I know it. It's not what I wanted, but now Rheged is no longer our enemy. I wish it didn't always have to be battle and blood, but there was no other way.'

'What of Nimue? She will work against you, Arthur. Even now she will boil bats' wings, spiderwebs, mole claws and goose guts to cast a spell against your luck.'

Arthur pulled his cloak closer about him. 'What can I do? She is as skilled as a druid. They are above the laws of men. Killing a druid invites an eternity of suffering in the afterlife. My soul would become her plaything. Better leave her to

Merlin. I don't want her curses following me when I march to battle.'

'A woman can't be a druid. She's a *gwyllion*, a witch born in Ireland and raised by Saxons. I don't want to kill her either, but better to put her somewhere safe where I can keep an eye on her than have to fear what she might do in the darkness. I don't trust her. She hates you, and Merlin.'

'If you can find her, keep her locked up, then. But watch her, for she will bewitch any guard you put on her door. Better to have women guard her than men. When we are finished in the north, we'll let Merlin decide her fate.'

'A hardy-looking bunch,' said Lancelot, strolling down the hillside in his war gear and with his hair tied back at the nape of his neck. He blew into his hands and rubbed them together, casting a thoughtful eye over Rheged's warriors. Those men stood idly in loose ranks, clad in dark furs and scraps of iron and leather. They wore their hair and beards long, and each carried a spear, and a shield painted with Urien's symbol of the bear. 'When do we march?'

'Today,' Arthur replied. 'Dewi?' he called to the captain of the black cloaks. 'Have the stewards and slaves bring out supplies loaded into a wagon for the journey and have the black cloaks ready to march by midday. Hywel?' The Elmetian merce-nary trotted up to Arthur, wearing his Roman armour and a red cloak so faded that it was almost pink. Kai trudged back towards the Bear Fort to see to the countless tasks and dooms awaiting his decision in the king's hall, and Dewi hurried off to get the black cloaks ready to march.

'Yes, lord?' Hywel said, clasping his fist to his chest in the Roman fashion.

'You are in command of Fferog and these men of Rheged.'

'Me, lord? Thank you, lord!' A smile split the mercenary's face, and he stood to full attention.

'You've earned it. Don't let me down. Use Fferog as your second in command but keep them in good order and quash any rumours of unrest with a firm hand. But I don't want them brutalised. Men like simple orders and good discipline, they baulk at over-discipline. I want them to stand and fight if it comes to war with Gododdin and Lothian, not to flee our cause when the shield walls clash.'

'Yes, lord.' Hywel saluted again and set off down the hill towards Fferog and his warriors.

'Is he ready for command?' asked Lancelot.

'He's wanted it since the battle at the River Glein. But Dewi is my captain, so this is his chance. The rest of his mercenary band died at the Dubglas, so he's the last of them. Hywel fights well, and he's never let me down.'

'Then I will help him, and make sure these men of Rheged are ready to fight when the time comes.'

'It was the only way, wasn't it?' Arthur asked, now that nobody was in earshot. He didn't turn to look at Lancelot's broad face for fear of the judgement he might find in his friend's eyes. He watched instead as Hywel and Fferog inspected shields and spears and separated out men for scouting, vanguard and rearguard marching duties.

'Killing Owain?' Lancelot waved to a stable boy to bring their warhorses closer. 'Yes. Even if Urien had agreed to peace, he would not have kept his word. How could we fight in the south with an enemy conspiring against you in the north?'

'Aye.' Arthur shivered, the cold making his ears sting. 'This is no weather for men to march in, but we must strike quickly and quell this rebellion before it catches fire and grows.'

'Will Gododdin fight?'

'Merlin is there, so let's hope he has calmed King Letan Luyddoc's desire for war. Merlin believes Gododdin only refused to recognise me out of fear of Urien and Lothian. Gawain and Bors are friends, so this time let us hope we can resolve it without bloodshed.'

'And Lothian?'

'King Lot rules a wide, wild land, full of proud tribes. Rome built a wall to keep his people out of their empire. Merlin tells me that the men of Lothian fight like demons of Arawn, so let's hope we can avoid battle. To fight a bloody war in the mountains, forests and valleys up there will cost us men and time, and we can ill afford to lose either.'

'Well, best get to it, then.' Lancelot grinned and clapped Arthur on the shoulder, which bore a blueish-purple welt from Owain's sword. 'Maybe you can kill another king or two before we return home.'

'Bastard,' said Arthur, and Lancelot skipped away before Arthur's boot connected with his arse.

The combined force of three hundred black cloaks and five hundred warriors of Rheged marched north that day, leaving Kai waving from the battlements. A cold sun hung pale in the sky, and the moon appeared during daylight, ghostly and white, low in the sky like a great dead eye. Arthur rode Llamrei and Cavall bounded on ahead and he hoped the shadow moon was not a bad omen of what awaited him further north. They reached Gododdin after five days of slow progress through rain, sleet and paths bogged down with mud and wagon ruts filled with slop. It took a full morning for the men to heave the supply wagon out of one such hazard, and each night men kept fires ablaze for fear of dying of the cold whilst they slept. Warriors came to look at them from distant hilltops, and Arthur sent his scouts mounted on fast ponies to chase them away.

On the sixth day, Arthur reached the great hill fort of Dunpendrylaw, home of King Letan Luyddoc of Gododdin. The fort sat atop a huge, grass-covered mound which rose from the flatlands like a great hump. Dewi had a black cloak sound the carnyx to announce their arrival, and riders came thundering from the hill to line up before Arthur's small army.

'King Letan bids you welcome,' shouted a man with a tattooed face. He wore his hair long, and in typical Gododdin style he wore strips of dyed cloth woven into his locks, and a woollen tunic dyed red. The riders all carried shields bearing the stag sigil of Gododdin, and Arthur breathed a sigh of relief to receive so cordial a welcome. Arthur and Lancelot followed the warriors towards the battlements, and King Letan himself greeted them warmly at the front gates. He was grey-bearded, and his face lined with age, but he moved with the litheness and grace of a younger man. He clapped Arthur and Lancelot on the shoulder, thanked them for making the journey north and bade them enter his fortress, where Merlin waited with Prince Gawain and the monstrous figure of Bors, champion of Gododdin and Arthur's friend.

'You took your time,' Merlin barked, huddled beneath his cloak with a frown that could curdle milk.

'We encountered difficulties upon the road,' Arthur said, and Merlin's mouth moved silently as though he could not quite summon the right insult to toss in Arthur's direction.

'We had news of it,' Merlin finally managed. 'Urien and Owain are with the gods now.'

'Urien was a fine man, once,' said King Letan. 'I fought beside him in the Great War. Hard to find a braver warrior or better leader.'

'And he raided your cattle every summer and stole enough

fleeces from your flocks to clothe a thousand men,' Merlin quipped.

'Rheged recognises me as Pendragon,' Arthur said, fixing Letan with a hard stare. 'Her spearmen march beside me, united with the rest of Britain. Does Gododdin recognise the Pendragon?'

'I recognise you, Arthur, and your position as high king.' Letan bowed solemnly with a hand pressed to his breast. 'We can talk of such matters this evening whilst we eat,' he said with a warm smile. 'You are here now, and we can make right the wrongs of the past. I will send a man down to your warriors, and they shall all have a warm bed and full bellies before nightfall.'

Letan strolled off with Merlin, the two old men locked deep in quiet conversation.

'Where is Arthur?' shouted Bors in his booming voice. He was still the biggest man Arthur had ever seen. Bors was head and shoulders taller than any man in the gate, even Lancelot, and twice as broad across the shoulder. He wore a leather breastplate across his chest, and pieces of chain mail draped around his round shoulders and thick neck. The enormous man had a Saxon axe tucked into his belt, and a completely shaved head above a round, heavily scarred face. 'There you are! And Lancelot too!' Bors shouldered his way past Hywel and a dozen warriors and grabbed both Arthur and Lancelot, one in the crook of each of his hugely muscled arms. 'It does my heart good to see you both. We heard you got into a scrape down at the Bear Fort?'

'That's one way of putting it,' said Arthur, smiling and extricating himself from Bors' grip.

'I never liked Owain, anyway. His head was too far up his own arse.' Bors stepped forward and grabbed Arthur into a tight bear hug, lifting him from the ground and shaking him as a father might do to his son. 'I've missed you. You might be the bloody Pendragon, but to me, you're still Arthur.'

'Well met, Bors.' Arthur laughed, the fear of battle and weight of what awaited him at Gododdin falling away instantly.

'Remember when we stormed Dun Guaroy? Now that was a rare fight.'

'It was. So was the battle of the Glein. But we missed your axe last year when we fought the Saxons at the Dubglas.'

Bors scratched his beard and shook his head. 'Aye well. The less said about that, the better. But you're here now, and I want to hear all about the battles we've missed, and how you got the better of Owain. I never thought you had it in you.' Bors squeezed Arthur's biceps and chest. 'You have grown stronger since last we met.'

'Have I?' Arthur glanced down at himself.

'No, of course not. You're still a streak of piss even if all the kings of Britain bow and kiss your arse!' Bors erupted into raucous laughter, and it was impossible not to laugh with him. Arthur enjoyed his bawdiness after the grim tension of the Bear Fort.

'Arthur, I am pleased to see you again,' said Prince Gawain, tall and lean, wearing a bronze circlet on his brow. He grinned broadly and took Arthur's forearm in the warrior's grip. 'And Lancelot, welcome to Dunpendrylaw.'

Arthur's heart warmed to receive such a welcome. On the road north he had imagined a cold greeting, insults by sullen warriors and a hall full of enemies, just like his welcome at the Bear Fort. But Gododdin was exactly as it had been when Arthur had visited after rescuing Gawain and Guinevere from Dun Guaroy so many years ago. He felt genuine warmth in the smiles and light-hearted jokes, as was common between fighting men. Arthur walked with a lightness he had not felt since leaving Durnovaria, and as a slave handed him a horn of frothy ale, the horrors of his fight with Owain slipped away into distant memory.

King Letan's stewards showed Arthur and Lancelot to a room they could share, little more than a hut beside a stable, but it had a warm fire and two straw pallet beds, and was more prestigious than sleeping on the floor, or in the eaves of Letan's hall with the rest of the warriors. Arthur washed his face in a wooden bowl of cool water and brushed the travel stains from his boots and cloak. As daylight shifted to dusk in the late afternoon, a fist rapped on the hut door four times. Arthur opened it to find Merlin standing there, his keen grey eyes boring into Arthur's own with their usual cleverness and his amber-tipped staff in his hand.

'I need to find some bread to eat before King Letan's feast this evening. I can't wait all evening for food. Join me.'

It was not a question, so Arthur quickly cast his fur cloak about his shoulders and followed Merlin out into the blustery courtyard between Dunpendrylaw's stables, granaries and pigpens. They walked through lanes thick with mud, and a boy leading a goat hurried out of the way when he saw Merlin's tattooed head and druid's staff.

'The kitchens are this way,' Merlin said, pointing to the rear of King Letan's hall. 'I haven't eaten since this morning. I have been busy, Arthur. But then, so have you. Word came north faster than a crow on the wing, word of single combat and dead kings.'

'I tried to make peace,' Arthur said.

'Urien had no understanding of that word. He was a warlord, a king of war, a lover of battle and an old piece of toad gristle who stayed in this world too long. You did Britain a favour and I'm only sorry I wasn't there to see it. Is there dissent in Rheged?'

'I don't think so. I have left Kai there to rule until Prince Mordred comes of age to take the throne.'

'Prince Mordred, is it?'

'Yes. What of it?'

Merlin paused for a moment, stared at Arthur, laughed, and then carried on. 'What of the royal bastard's mother?'

'I do not think she will give Kai much trouble, as long as she and the boy are treated with honour and respect.'

'Just so.' Merlin ducked beneath a low door lintel and into a room made warm by a great clay oven burning at one end of a long wattle structure roofed with earth. Inside, six women kneaded dough with rough hands, and three men plaited soft dough into intricate patterns before the loaves went into the oven. Merlin gently moved one man aside with his staff. The man had his back to the door and was startled to see a druid stood before him. 'What news of Nimue?'

'She was at the Bear Fort, and she hates me almost as much as she hates you.'

'I had rather hoped that her anger might have softened. Was she furious?'

'Furious.'

'Did she attack you?'

'No, but she has placed a curse on Guinevere's womb, leaving my queen barren and without child.'

'Ah.'

'I could have killed her for that.'

'But you didn't.'

'No. What man kills a druid? She might be a woman, but she's as powerful as any druid.'

'Perhaps you are wiser than I gave you credit for. I can lift that curse, of course, but it would have been immeasurably more difficult had you killed Nimue. Where is she now?'

'Held secure at the Bear Fort until you go south to deal with her.'

'Hmm.' Merlin thought about that for a moment. A man with no teeth and flapping gums used a wide-bladed shovel to scoop a dozen loaves out of the oven. He set the golden-brown loaves down on the kitchen worktop and shovelled another dozen uncooked loaves into the oven. The smell of freshly baked bread made Arthur's stomach groan. Merlin picked one up and gingerly took a bite. He leant his staff against the counter and tossed the steaming loaf from one hand to the other and blew on his burning fingers. 'It's hot,' he said, blowing and rolling his lips around the bread in his mouth. He picked up another oven fresh loaf and passed it to Arthur, who took it hungrily and took a bite.

'I can taste honey,' Arthur said, and Merlin nodded appreciatively.

'I like Gododdin. It's so far north that we don't have to suffer the infernal presence of any Christ priests or sordid bishops. We are closer to the gods here, Arthur. Can you feel it?'

'I can,' Arthur lied. 'You are still in love with Nimue.' Arthur blew on his bread and took another bite, the soft, warm dough melting in his mouth.

'Love? What is love but the folly of weak men and simple-minded women? One does not love a woman like Nimue, nor could she ever love a man. She is wild, impossibly clever, cunning, and well versed in our gods, those of her native Ireland, and the Saxon gods. She is to be marvelled at and feared. But not loved. We all have our weaknesses, Arthur. Guinevere has power over you, and there's no denying it.'

'But you yearn for her.'

'Do you think you are talking to a pig handler or one of your dull-witted warriors? I haven't yearned for a woman since Ector was a child. Think on that before you ask me such absurd questions.'

'She can foment trouble in the north. She has power and speaks for the gods. Men will listen to the poison she spouts.'

'I shall deal with Nimue. You can put your gentle mind at rest. I see Owain gave you a parting gift?' Merlin pointed a bony finger at the scabbed gash on Arthur's forehead.

'He was not gentle.'

'No, I don't imagine he was. I am not sorry to see Urien gone from this world. He could have been... better, but chose a different path.'

'King Letan seems to have rolled over and let you tickle his belly. What happened to threats of war and Gododdin's failure to recognise my position?'

'Pressure from Urien. Gododdin is surrounded by Rheged on one side and Lothian on the other. How could Bors and Gawain march south but through Urien's lands? They could not leave Gododdin undefended for fear that Lot or Urien, or both, would attack and leave Dunpendrylaw in ashes. Letan acted prudently and in the interests of his people, so do not hold it against him. He is with us and was never against us by choice.'

'So he will send men south to join our fight against the Saxons?'

'Yes, yes. Of course he will. I didn't come all this way for nothing. There is, however, something we must do first.'

'Why do I get the feeling I am not going to like this?'

'The men of Gododdin cannot march with an enemy at their back, just as we could not have marched upon the Saxons with Urien snarling down from the north behind us. We must therefore help King Letan bring Lothian to heel.'

'That is not our fight, Merlin. Our fight lies in the south.'

'It does, but we shall need Bors and his warriors when the ice and snow melts, the swallows return, and Saxon war drums beat their war music.'

'We must go to war with Lothian?'

'Not war, as you mean it. That war could take years, a conflict of attrition fought across misty heathers and high mountain passes, of raid and ambush. No, we need a quick victory, to give King Lot a slap and bring him to heel.'

'How do we do that?'

'We surprise him, of course. By the gods, this is excellent bread,' Merlin called to the bakers, and they all bowed low to him. 'Truly, the gods have blessed you with skill. Now, do any of you or your families need my attention?' The bakers gathered about Merlin to ask him to pull a wife's tooth, and examine a child's clubbed foot. Arthur left him there and returned to his quarters and prepared for the evening feast. King Letan threw a lavish feast of mead, ale, bread, beef, pork, honey, steamed vegetables and poached fish caught fresh that day from Gododdin's winding rivers. Arthur sat beside Bors and Gawain at the high table, and it was an evening spent in the fine company of old friends. They told war stories, and King Letan's bard sang songs of the Great War, of Ambrosius, Merlin, Uther and their battles against Vortigern, Hengist and Horsa. Arthur drank and ate too much and woke the following morning with his head feeling like a warhorse had kicked it.

There was no time to nurse that sore head, however, for that morning they prepared to march north to war with King Lot and the wild warriors of Lothian.

9

Arthur marched north with his black cloaks, Hywel's five hundred Rheged spearmen and seven hundred Gododdin warriors who, at Merlin's request, Bors had mustered before Arthur's arrival. Those men camped, shivering in a wide meadow beside two great oak trees, and the warriors mustered from Gododdin's hills and woodlands cheered and clashed their shields when they saw Arthur's dragon banner and an army of warriors come to help them fight their old foes in Lothian. King Letan sent ten donkey wains loaded with food and ale for the army, and that food needed to feed the army on their journey north, for there was little foraging to be had in the stark northern hills.

Bors and Gawain rode with Arthur and Lancelot at the front of the army, whilst Merlin ranged ahead on foot, as was his wont. He preferred to walk alone, visiting villages and farm-steads to spend his nights with the simple folk of the kingdom. Merlin was as likely to spend a night on the floor of the meanest fishwife's hovel as he was a warlord's warm, comfortable hall. Merlin believed those roving journeys kept him close to the beating heart of Britain. He spoke to farmers of crop blight, or last year's harvest, talked with wise women and mothers of weaning babies, numbers of children born in each village, of potions, medicines and stories from the valleys and riverside villages. He checked on ancient trees and stone circles, prayed to gods in shadowed glades and deep, black pools. It was those ancient places, strange locations where people felt a sense of awe, where the hairs on the back of man's neck stand up, that Merlin said the gods had once walked and lived amongst the Britons in the halcyon days before the Romans came and tore it down with their legions and their knowledge of roads, marble, law and warfare. The Romans came with new knowledge, so that the people and gods of Britain were as children faced with people from the future, conquerors who changed the land forever.

The army marched through a thumping storm, and hailstones hammered against armour and helmets. They made camp beneath dripping boughs and on rain-soaked grassland and for days they trudged through roads and paths sodden with mud and running water. The army followed a winding lowland river heading for King Lot's fort at Bedegraine, where Lot's forefathers had ruled since before the Britons measured time.

'Do you see those bastards up there?' said Bors on the third day, which thankfully saw a break in the rain. It was a still day, dark and gloomy, where even the heavy, sullen clouds needed a rest from emptying their bellies. The river led the column into the bowels of a stretch of rolling, bare hills covered with brown, stiff heather and rocks lashed white by the elements where falcons soared above the stark bluffs and ridges. Bors pointed a meaty finger towards the northern heights, where six figures stood like wraiths in the distance. Cloaks flapped about them in the wind and their short spears caught the dull sun.

'I see them,' said Arthur, 'though we haven't seen a settlement for two days. Either we are close to Bedegraine, or they have horses hidden somewhere.'

'The men of Lothian do not ride. They run. They can run like wolves, run all day without tiring. That's how they raid, running barefoot like animals. They can run all morning, fight a battle, and then run all afternoon. The further we get now, the wilder the people. The Picts north of Lothian can run like horses, never tiring. Bastards have different blood in their veins.'

'Do they fight well?' asked Lancelot.

'They don't fight like we do. Lothians and Picts despise the shield wall and armour, preferring to fight as champions with axes, knives and throwing spears. They fight like feral beasts, with the strength of men who have addled minds, like the mad with no control and who seem to have strength beyond normal men.'

'If they are so fierce, why have they never taken Gododdin, or increased the size of their kingdom?'

Bors smiled. 'Luckily, there aren't many of them. They live in tribes beside the water or beneath high hills. Those tribes are constantly at war with each other. Feuds that go back generations, so long that the families and tribes have forgotten how their arguments and hatred for their neighbours began. The Picts are even more wild and savage than the Lothians. They howl down from the north with their faces and bodies painted blue. They attack Lothian, raid and plunder every spring and summer and then disappear back into their northern glens and mountains. Lothian's men are forever occupied in the north, and we should thank the gods for the Picts.'

'You talk as though you admire the Lothians?' said Arthur.

'Have you taken a dunt to the head? They smell like pig shit, are impossible to understand, and won't stand and fight like men. I hate the bastards!'

'Gawain?' Lancelot called to the prince, who rode beside Bors. 'What do you think of the Lothians?'

'They are very brave,' Gawain said.

Bors blew out his cheeks and waved a hand at Gawain. 'Gawain has never said a bad word about anybody in his life. He won't even curse Ida for keeping him imprisoned in Dun Guaroy. You could steal Prince Gawain's sword, and he would thank you and call you brother.'

'You have enough bluster for the rest of us, Bors,' Gawain said, and the rest of the riders laughed.

'Should we worry about the scouts?' Arthur asked, watching the men stood in silhouette against the sky.

'There isn't much you can do about them,' Bors replied. 'Even your scouts' fast ponies won't catch them. They'll be gone before your men can get close. Lot knows we are coming, make no mistake about that. I know Merlin spoke of a surprise, but it would be easier to surprise a wolf by pulling its tail.'

'How far are we from Bedegraine?'

'We'll be there tomorrow.'

Bors was right, for the next day Arthur's scouts returned on their ponies with word that the marching army would reach Bedegraine that afternoon. They found Merlin waiting beside a hazel tree, eating goat's cheese and a loaf of hard bread.

'What news of Lothian?' Arthur called, raising his hand in greeting.

'King Lot is ready for us,' said Merlin. 'He would not allow me to enter Bedegraine, which is an insult to the gods and the laws of our people. Never have I been so insulted. I am vexed, Arthur, vexed.'

Merlin would say no more and strode ahead of the column,

his staff's amber tip glowing and his cloak flowing about him. They reached Bedegraine on an afternoon where the clouds cleared to reveal a pale sky more white than blue. A doe ran from a dark pine forest, paused to look at Merlin, and then scampered away towards another clutch of rowan and ash trees.

'Bedegraine,' said Gawain as the river wound away to curve around a lowland plateau where a fortress of dark wood sat alone in a wide swathe of flatland. Bedegraine stood like a bleak sentinel in that place, as though there had once been a town or village around its walls, a city swept away to leave only the bare field and Lot's stark fortress. It was larger than Urien's Bear Fort, with high walls and buildings set within them. There was no thatch that Arthur could see, just low, dour buildings peeping above the parapet with their turf roofs old and sprouted with grass and weeds. Bedegraine was not a centre of life or living. No families could live there amid so much nothingness. It was a pure fort, containing only King Lot, his family, his hearth troop and their families, with enough room to house his warriors in times of war. Supplies came from Lot's vassals across Lothian, the render of common churls brought to Bedegraine so the king could keep his warriors fed.

The river curled around Bedegraine's eastern and northern edges, offering protection from those flanks. A stout wall sat beyond a ditch and bank. The bank was a deep brown colour, the shade of freshly dug soil, meaning that Lot had deepened his ditch and tossed the soil up to strengthen and heighten his bank. Twenty men waited on the plateau, all on foot.

'So much for a surprise,' said Lancelot, as Arthur called the army to halt.

'That's Lot, his three sons, his druid Peithan, and his champions,' said Merlin.

'Lot keeps his own druid?' asked Arthur.

'One does not keep a druid, thank you very much. Peithan roams Lothian and Pictland. That is his home. He represents Lot as I have chosen to represent you, though sometimes I wonder did I make the right decision.'

'Your support is a ray of sunshine, Lord Merlin.'

Bors laughed, and Merlin frowned. 'We'd better get this over with. Come on.'

Arthur stretched his back and urged Llamrei on to follow Merlin's lead. 'Stay, boy,' he called to Cavall, and the war dog sat on his haunches with his tail wagging in the short, coarse wild grass. Bors and Gawain rode with Arthur. Malegant carried the fasces and Dewi came for the black cloaks, along with a warrior who carried the Pendragon dragon banner on its high spear pole.

The men waiting for Arthur across the flatland all wore their hair shorn short and had smeared a ghastly white paste across their faces and heads so that they looked like dead men. They wore long cloaks wrapped about their bodies and carried short spears. A big man carried a crude triangular banner daubed with what Arthur thought could be an eagle or a falcon. Merlin marched in front of the leaders and a man strode out in front of the Lothian men. He dressed differently to the rest, with long, lank hair and a straggly beard which reached to his midriff, hung with bones and iron trinkets. Like Merlin, he carried a staff topped by a long, strange shard of smoky quartz the colour of a stormy sea.

'Stand aside, Peithan,' Merlin called across the rough field.

'Turn around and take your rabble of gentle southern milk-maids with you, Merlin,' Peithan shouted in a curiously high-pitched voice. 'Go back to your tilled fields and verdant valleys where men with soft hands rule weak people. Your lands are awash with Christians and Saxons. Lloegyr, men call it. Lost lands. Lost by you. You have failed the people in your care, so don't come up north strutting like a fox seeking a mate. You had power once, perhaps, but it wanes like a fart in the wind. Your people have lost. You are not the man you once were.'

'Mind your tongue. I remember when you were a whelp following Kadvuz around like a lost child.'

'Kadvuz taught me well, and I know as much of the knowledge as you or any other druid. The people here all worship the gods of Britain, our gods, the gods who created this land. Every man, woman and child from here to the far northern reaches worship only our gods. This is a blessed land, untouched and unfouled by enemy gods. Can you say the same, Merlin?'

'We come to talk to King Lot, not bandy words with a man who lives in a cave amongst bat shit, crabs and the bones of his own midden heap.'

'Enough,' called a man in a harsh voice. He was of average height, with a small, pursed mouth and bright blue eyes made even starker by the white paste daubed upon his face. 'They tell me Urien is dead. The old boar probably deserved it. So Letan sends his son and an army north to attack me. Just because Letan smiles and bows like a whore doesn't make him any better than me, or Urien, for that matter. Letan is a killer, just like the rest of us. Well. You shall all die in this place. Bors, I recognise you. You we'll keep alive. Like a pet hound. I'll geld you and put out your eyes, and when you beg for food, the children will laugh at you and wonder how feeble is the champion of Gododdin.' With a wave of his spear, King Lot turned and led his men back towards the fortress, without acknowledging Arthur, Merlin, the fasces or the dragon banner.

'What's happening?' asked Bors. Like Arthur, he had expected the usual exchange of insults and posturing. 'I didn't have time to respond. Bastard said he was going to cut my manhood off.'

'He's showing us he despises us,' said Merlin, gnashing at his beard.

'Lothian won't fight?'

'They'll fight, but when they choose to. Look at where we are.' Merlin gestured around at the barren flatlands and brown heights without a furrowed field in sight. 'Did you expect Lot to march out from behind his stout walls and ditch to fight us out here on the plain?'

'I suppose I did.' Bors shrugged and shifted the weight of the axe he wore strapped to his back.

'The fortress is here because it's impossible to lay siege to it,' Arthur said, more to himself than to the others. 'We could attack his walls and lose a third of our men in that ditch and climbing up that bank as they hurl spears, rocks and fire at us. Or we can pen them in and starve Lot out, but what would we eat and drink whilst we do it? If he knew we were coming, he could have hundreds of spearmen in there with enough food for a month. We have enough food for what, another two days?'

'Two,' said Lancelot. 'Perhaps four if we ration it carefully.'

'So, on the fifth day, we have to send men out ranging for supplies.'

'Lot will have warriors in every valley, farmstead, hilltop and village,' said Gawain. 'They'll kill your foraging parties one by one until this army becomes whittled to a starving, shrunken shadow of what we have today.'

'And that's when the bastard will attack,' added Bors. 'I don't want three or four of those little whoresons leaping at me with their axes when I haven't eaten for days. We'd be lucky to get back to Gododdin with our lives.'

'So why have we come?' Arthur said, growing angry with the

situation. Llamrei sensed his discomfort and whickered, stamping his great hooves. 'If we have no hope, then why have we marched north?'

'So that when you call for our warriors in the spring, which you will,' said Gawain, 'we do not go south and leave my father's kingdom undefended with Lot poised to strike at Gododdin like a snake.'

'Then we must have our battle, and have it quickly,' said Arthur. He dug his heels into Llamrei's flanks and clicked his tongue, sending the warhorse into a canter.

'Careful!' Merlin called.

Arthur rode Llamrei after the Lothian men, hooves throwing up clods of damp earth, Arthur's mind racing. He did not have the time to spend rotting in this barren land laying siege to Bedegraine, or to lose men in a stinking ditch, attempting to scale its dark timber walls, whilst Lot's wild warriors opened their throats and hearts with sharp spears. This northern rebellion had to end quickly, so that Arthur could return to the real war, the war with the Saxons.

'Back, usurper!' Peithan shouted, waving his staff at Arthur. 'Or I shall turn your guts into eels and your eyes to stone.'

'I am your Pendragon,' Arthur snarled, sawing on Llamrei's reins to keep the stallion steady. His blood was up, just like Arthur's, and Llamrei's forelegs scraped the earth and great steaming snorts blew from his nose. 'Merlin protects me from your *seidr*, druid.'

Peithan turned to see Merlin capering on the heather, his staff twisting, chanting words of power which Arthur could not hear, but that demonstration from the most powerful druid in Britain was enough to make Peithan cower. Peithan pulled a yellowed skull with scraps of dried flesh still clinging to the bone. He thrust the skull at Arthur and chanted his own curses, eyes rolling and voice undulating. Merlin chanted, twirling his staff and the army behind him fanned out, forming organised shield-wall ranks. They clashed spears against their iron-shod shields in time with Merlin's song, and the sound of it stirred even Arthur's heart.

Peithan wailed and hurried away from Merlin, waving his hands, terrified by the war din Merlin had summoned, seeking the protection of Bedegraine's palisade. King Lot and his men also hurried; all defiance fallen from their white-painted faces.

'King Lot of Lothian!' Arthur shouted, riding Llamrei into their path. 'There is no need to fight. We are not enemies. All you must do is swear an oath to recognise me as your Pendragon and swear not to attack Gododdin next year. Do that and we shall leave. You will not see me again. I give you my word.'

'I will swear no oath to Merlin's pet bastard, a dog of King Letan. Do not come to me with my enemies at your side and talk to me as though I am a boy fresh from his mother's tit! I was killing bastards like you before you crawled from your mother's loins.'

'One year of peace is all I ask of you.'

'The ally of my enemy is also my enemy. Get you gone, usurper!'

That word again. It cut at Arthur and surprised him. Had he usurped Uther's position, or Urien's throne? There was no time to consider such cutting accusations. Arthur drew Excalibur, heart racing, halfway to riding down King Lot and taking his head with a sweep of his sword. He stayed, sat back in the saddle. He had already killed two kings. To kill another like this would indeed make him a usurper, a killer of kings, rather than the man trying to achieve restoration and peace for Britain. So he watched Lot and his men scuttle across the wooden bridge and into the dark fortress. The gate came up on thick rope and there was no way to cross that ditch now but by assaulting the walls.

The army made camp in a forest half a morning's march from Bedegraine, and Arthur brooded beside his campfire. Merlin sat beside him with Gawain. Lancelot and Bors joined the men in a wrestling competition, thought up by Bors to keep the men entertained so far from home. Arthur ate a basic meal of dried beef and oatcakes, washed down with a ration of ale.

'We must attack tomorrow,' said Arthur, staring into the crackling flames. 'Midwinter approaches. Snow will cover these plains, and then in spring fresh ships will arrive from across the narrow sea.'

Merlin grumbled and nibbled at an oatcake. 'Samhain has passed us by,' he said, referring to the festival held across the land to signify the end of harvest season and the onset of the dark and cold of winter. 'I saw it celebrated last week on my journey north. All the harvests are gathered, and we are now in the dark half of the year. Men have brought flocks down from pastures to live close. Animals are inside houses for warmth, folk are fastening their window shutters closed and preparing for the short, bitter days. These are the days when we appease the gods with offerings. Food and ale left on woodlands' edge and outside houses for the hidden folk, the faeries and spirits. We must be back in Dumnonia before the festival of Imbolc. That is the beginning of spring, of green shoots and new hope.'

'And war season.'

'So it has always been. For a moment today, I thought you would ride Lot down outside his own home.'

'I should have.'

'Perhaps. What stayed your hand?'

'I have enough king's blood on my hands. What will people say of me if I kill another?'

'Why do you care what people say? What does the bear care if his prey wails about his ruthlessness?'

'I want to be... better than Urien and Uther.'

'Better how?'

'Just and honourable.'

'Pah! Such things are for women and bards' stories. You must restore Lloegyr to our people, by any means. By any means, I say! But much of what you say is true. We cannot linger here on the edge of Britain. Letan is right. He cannot send warriors south with an enemy at his rear. But we must end this now.'

'But how? We need all our men. Even if we marched for Dumnonia today, it would take weeks to reach home. There will be days we cannot march because of the roads, rain, snow, frost or lack of food. It seems like the land and our own people conspire against us. Are the gods truly with us, Merlin?'

'The gods are with us.' Merlin leant into Arthur and grabbed his hand. His skin was cold to the touch, and his grip was strong. He shook Arthur's hand, his grey eyes blazing. 'They are steeling us for the trials to come. Toughening you, Arthur, for the battles you must fight. Lothian is a challenge just like any other, laid before you to see if you have what it takes to go up against the Saxon gods, to do battle with Woden and Thuror. Defeat them, and the nailed god awaits you. Ambrosius failed. The gods put similar challenges in his path, and he crumbled and died. But what a man he was! What a warrior, brave, honourable and strong. The gods had their man of honour in Ambrosius, and now they need you.'

'I am a man of honour. Or I try to be.'

'How did you defeat Owain?'

Arthur stared into the campfire. 'Savagery.' He shuddered at the memory of Owain's eye, turned to mush beneath his thumb.

'That is what we need to win. Ruthlessness. The same brutal ruthlessness with which our enemies treat us. Had we been more brutally cruel when the Romans first landed their painted ships on our shores, we could have cast them out before the legions took hold. Had we been more savage with Vortigern when he brought the first Saxons here, there would be no Lloegyr. We have always been an island of tribes, fighting amongst ourselves like animals. We must be one, united under one leader. A man of ruthless determination who will stop at nothing to defeat Britain's enemies.'

'You believe I am that man?'

'You are. You must be. I am too old to seek another, and you will do it, Arthur, or we are truly lost.'

The weight of those words took Arthur's breath away. He was just a man who had been a boy in Caer Ligualid, then a spearman, and then a *comitatus*, a leader of a war band. Then he had become Pendragon. All those events had just happened, Arthur had planned none of it. He suddenly remembered the day he had tried to run away from Caer Ligualid as a young man. He had come within a hair's breadth of leaving Ector, Kai, Lunete and everything behind to make his own way in the world. Arthur wondered if things might have been better if he had run that day. Perhaps now he would serve as a simple spearman in a war band of Elmet, Gododdin, Gwent, Powys, or any of the kingdoms. He might have a wife and children, a simple life. But that was just a fool's dream. He was Arthur, chosen by Merlin to be Britain's saviour, and as he stared into Merlin's ancient grey eyes, he understood he must find the strength and ruthless cunning inside himself.

'So how to draw Lot out of his fortress? He won't make

peace. You saw him today. He is like a rabid dog. I must crush him, Merlin. Just like Urien. Just like Uther.'

'Crushed. It must be that way. Tomorrow, we poison the river and burn Bedegraine. When his people wail and his warriors run from their houses putting out the fires on their families' backs, Lot will march.'

Arthur shuddered at what must be done, at the price of it all. He thought of the Christ god, and how Christians believed that when a man died, their god weighed up the actions of his life. He looked back and decided if that person's good deeds outweighed his sins. What would that god make of Arthur's life? He curled up beneath his fur cloak, and could not sleep because faces plagued him, churning in his mind like a curse. Faces of the dead, like Mynog, Owain, Uther, Urien, Igraine, Ector, Octha and so many more. Mixed in with them came faces of accusation, Morgan, and Mordred, of Guinevere if she ever found out about Arthur's bastard son.

Too many sins. But he was Arthur Pendragon, and tomorrow the horror would begin, for winter was coming, Britain had to be saved and Arthur was beloved of hard, cruel gods of war, not the Christian god of peace.

10

_____

Merlin ordered every man in the army to empty their bowels into the river in the morning, so that one thousand five hundred men turned Bedegraine's river foul. Merlin himself stood over the water, chanting and capering about the riverbank and touching its flowing waters with his staff. Then, the druid sat beside the river and took a selection of small clay jars he carried about his person, and with them made a potion which he added to the river water. He also made a thick, foul-smelling black paste which he smeared upon every goose-feathered arrow the army had brought north. Three hundred men carried bows, mostly small war bows, and not the larger hunting bows which required monstrous strength to draw. Merlin lined them up before Bedegraine's ditch.

'Will they drink the water?' Arthur asked Merlin. His nose wrinkled as yet more soldiers relieved themselves into the river.

'In the south, we drink ale and mead because the water makes our stomachs sick,' Merlin replied. 'Up north they don't have the levels of wheat and barley as you do in Dumnonia, so they must drink the water. Their stomachs are used to it.'

'Do we poison their women and children to win the battle?'

Merlin pinched the bridge of his nose and took a pause. Then he said, 'Do you want to win this cursed fight quickly, or not? The women and children inside that fort would flay you alive and laugh as they do it. Don't be so squeamish. Making women and children ill for a few days is a small price to pay to draw out Lot's men and end this thing quickly. Agreed?'

'Agreed.' Arthur chose not to frustrate Merlin further by asking how many of those women and children would burn in the blaze the druid intended to rain upon Bedegraine's buildings.

'Take the main army to the cleft beyond that rise,' Merlin said, pointing to a bare hilltop topped with three great stones. 'At sunup, keep the men in the basin. No matter what you see or hear, do not advance. The fight will come to you.'

'What are you going to do?' Arthur asked.

Merlin sniffed the air. He bent and picked up a clump of rough grass and touched it to his lips. He stared at the sky, closed his eyes and spoke to himself silently, lips moving without sound. 'Just be ready. At sunup. Ready to fight, and stay deep in the lowlands, as deep as you can. Leave three hundred men with me, but before you leave, have each man build a tent and a fire to keep it warm. I want a lean-to, sail-cloth or leather tent erected for every man in the army. Leave a further fifty men there to keep every fire burning through the night.'

'You want an empty camp with fires?'

'That is precisely what I want. Leave the dragon banner here as well, where they can see it from the walls.'

Arthur questioned Merlin no further and set the army to work. They built the tents and shelters just as Merlin commanded, and Arthur had them constructed on the edge of where Bedegraine's flat plateau fell away into shallow lowlands between a network of high hills on either side of the river.

'I hope old Merlin knows what he's doing,' said Bors, scratching thoughtfully at his beard.

'Have you ever known him not to?'

'Fair enough.'

'Lord Arthur!' called Dewi, hurrying through the camp, followed by a man in a light jerkin and trews and a mud-spattered cloak about his shoulders. 'This scout returned from the north.'

'What is it?' Arthur asked.

The scout's mouth flapped open and closed, and he stared at Arthur and then back to Dewi. 'He won't bite you, just tell what you told me,' Dewi said.

'Yes, lord,' the young scout said, and swallowed hard. 'Lord Arthur.' He bowed his head and then stood straight. 'A force of Picts marches south.'

'How many?' Arthur asked.

'Four or five hundred, lord. It's hard to tell. They aren't in column, but spread out in groups of between five and twenty.'

'Lot must have allied with the Picts and called for them to march against us. When will they be here?'

'Tonight, or early tomorrow.'

'The gods help us when those wild bastards attack,' said Bors. 'They fight like fiends. It's like trying to trade blows with a boar or a monstrous cat. They won't stand still! I've never seen five hundred together in one place before. Lot must have promised them all the wealth in his kingdom.'

'Or a share of the plunder if they take Gododdin,' said Gawain.

'Let Merlin know,' Arthur said brusquely. The situation was

becoming worse by the minute. 'But tell him we stick to the plan.'

For the rest of that day, the men marched to the closest forest along the river, cut boughs and brought them back to Merlin. The druid barked and cajoled the warriors into building a huge fire outside Bedegraine's ditch. King Lot's men loosed arrows at them from the walls, so Arthur had to put a line of one hundred shields beside the ditch to protect the men building Merlin's great fire. As the sun began to set in late afternoon on a short winter day, Merlin lit that fire and it turned the sky red with its crackling glow. Arthur left him there, with the archers, the dragon banner and the empty camp, and marched the rest of his army into the damp, cold lowlands. He set the scouts and their fast ponies to patrol the northern marches with orders to ride back to him with news of when the Picts would arrive at Bedegraine's plain.

All the tents and equipment men used to make shelters were up on the high ground, where Hywel, Fferog and fifty warriors of Rheged were to tend fires all night.

'It's going to be a long night,' said Lancelot, sat beside his weapons with his cloak gathered about him.

'My arse is already freezing,' Bors complained. 'Can't we have even a small fire?'

'Merlin said no,' Arthur said. Cavall curled up beside him, and the men fed the dog scraps from their oatcakes.

'Sometimes I think he does things to punish us, or to amuse himself.'

'His mind works in ways we shall never understand,' said Gawain. 'We must trust him.'

The leaders huddled close together on the damp grass, as did the surrounding army. Men grumbled and shuffled, seeking some level of comfort as darkness turned the moor wet with dew. Men shared dried meat, whatever cheese they had left, oatcakes and skins of ale made warm by travel.

'Do you ever miss home, Lancelot?' Gawain asked after a time, to break the silence.

Lancelot thought about that for a moment, his powerful face staring up at the smattering of stars visible through the shifting, night-darkened clouds. 'My father, King Ban of Benoic, was a distant man. A good man, strong, a man to look up to. But I never truly knew him. In truth, I was closer to my weapons masters and my brothers than my father. My mother died some years ago, and she was a quiet woman who allowed her maids to raise her children. I miss the men who came across the sea with me, good men who have died one by one in the many battles we have fought in Britain. There is no closer bond than that between men who have fought and bled beside one another. A man who uses his shield to stop a blade meant for your own neck. I love you all, brothers, and I would gladly give my life for any of you. I know you would do the same for me, and that makes us closer than even the bond between man and wife.

'My eldest brother is my father's heir, my second brother is a priest and will one day be bishop of Benoic, my third brother trains to fight and is the spare to my father's heir. I, being the fourth son, came here following stories of Arthur and Merlin. I do not regret leaving, though sometimes I long for news of Benoic and its wars with the Franks and Saxons. I am here to make my name, so that when I am dead, people, I hope, will tell stories of Lancelot of the Lake, just as the bards will sing of Arthur, Bors, Kai, Gawain, Merlin, Malegant, Idnerth and the rest of the great warriors of our time.'

They all stared at Lancelot, the words stirring Arthur's heart. Arthur loved Ector, his spear-father, and he loved Lunete. He felt a heart-stopping passion for Guinevere, and her beauty never failed to take his breath away. But, as Lancelot said, blood bound these men to Arthur on another level; theirs was a brotherhood of blood. They shared that fragile existence between life and death. Each knew the battle-joy, the heightened sense of being in the maelstrom of battle brought on by the exhilaration of life-threatening danger. It was something only a warrior could understand, and its harsh paradox was that each of them would accept the other's death as a risk of war. Every man who took up a blade, who entered the warrior caste and rose above the common people, accepted that their fate would most likely be to die in battle. To die with another man's spear in his insides. A painful but glorious death, a death to claim the approval of the gods.

'Well said,' said Bors, clapping Lancelot heavily on the back. 'Our best is all we can do in this world. Fight well, obey our lords, try to write our names in the threads of destiny.'

'Threads of destiny?' said Gawain. 'Truly, I did not expect to hear such words come from your mouth, Bors of Gododdin.'

Bors grabbed Gawain, and they wrestled together, rolling between the rest of the group, who laughed as Bors playfully strangled his prince. They spoke of brave men who had died, of Ector, Balin of the Two Swords, Anthun and poor Becan, who had all met their ends in battle. One by one, men dozed and snored, steam rising from their open mouths as night settled in and the air grew colder. In the distance, fire arrows rose and fell like fiery birds flying into the sky, and as Bedegraine caught fire, the fortress cast the hills in a red glow like a summer sunrise.

Arthur tried to sleep. He lay with his eyes closed, but the screams and shouts of alarm from burning Bedegraine kept him awake. Arthur tried to console himself, knowing that those screams could well be the innocents of Durnovaria, of the Bear

Fort, Loidis, Dunpendrylaw or any British city should they fall to Saxon blades. King Lot had brought this suffering upon his people. If he had just recognised Arthur's position and sworn an oath not to attack Gododdin, then peace would reign over the north, and the people of Bedegraine would sleep soundly in their beds. Instead, the wives and children of Lot's warriors suffered. They drank foul water and fled from burning houses and, in the morning, battle would come. Just as Merlin hoped, Lot's champions, his men who prided themselves on their repu- tation, honour, individual prowess in battle, would surge from their burning fortress and seek vengeance. Arthur doubted Lot could hold them back, and part of him wondered if the Loth- ians would attack in the darkness. But fighting at night is a treacherous business where a commander has no control or view of how a battle unfolds. It would be morning, Arthur knew, a red morning, a morning of blood to settle the northern rebellion once and for all.

Across the hills, sunrise came in a pale sheen, like the colour of a blind man's eyes, creeping over the hills to gently push the darkness away. A thick fog lay about the sleeping army, so that the sunrise was all Arthur could see about him. Even his warriors appeared like hummocks lying in the soup- thick fog. Arthur sat up, his eyes gritty and bones weary from lack of sleep. Dew had made his cloak damp and his armour felt twice as heavy, its leather liner wet and cold against his skin. Cavall whined and sniffed the fog, so Arthur scratched his big head and whispered to him that everything would be alright.

'It's time,' Arthur said, nudging first Lancelot and then Bors awake.

'I can't see a bloody thing,' Bors complained, after swilling his mouth out with ale. 'It's like the sky has fallen in on us and we stand within a cloud.'

'What's that?' Lancelot said, pointing into the thick, wet fog.

A shape moved in the gloom, getting bigger, coming closer, and more than one soldier made the sign to ward off evil as if a hill-troll came to eat their bones in the twilight.

'It's Ced,' called a warrior. 'I'd recognise his skinny legs anywhere.'

It was indeed a man, running towards them at top speed. A man in a leather breastplate, his long face wide-eyed.

'Lord Arthur!' he called. He searched amongst the fog, trying to bat it away with his hands, breath coming in ragged gasps.

'Here, soldier. What is it?' Arthur said.

'Lord Merlin sent me. They are coming. The gates are open, and the Lothians are coming to fight.'

'Has battle joined?'

'Not yet, lord. They form up beyond the ditch. Merlin says to be ready, for he will lead them to you.'

'Well done.' Arthur took a sliver of silver from the pouch at his belt and tossed it to Ced, who grinned. 'Dewi?' Arthur called.

'Yes, lord?' said the captain, appearing with his spear and shield ready.

'Form the men up in four wide ranks. Keep within the fog until I order the carnyx to sound. Then we attack.'

Dewi banged his spear once on the ground. 'Yes, lord.'

'And Dewi?' Arthur said, just as his captain was about to hurry to carry out his orders. 'As soon as a scout returns, send him to me. We must know where the Picts are.'

'Did Merlin bring down this fog?' asked Bors, readying his huge Saxon war axe. 'There is a fell feeling about it.'

'The gods have sent it to hide us from our enemies,' said Arthur. 'Perhaps Merlin knew it would come, or perhaps he conjured it with his *seidr*. But the enemy will chase our men over that rise and charge into our shield wall. Then it's up to us to use that moment of surprise to kill them.'

'They'll believe we are still sleeping in camp,' said Gawain. 'With the campfires still burning. Lot plans to kill us before we stir from our beds.'

'And the Picts?' asked Lancelot, spear in one hand and his sword resting in its scabbard.

'We must hope they do not arrive before battle is joined. As it stands, we outnumber Lot three to one at least. But if the wild Picts come howling down from the northern hills, they could turn the battle.'

'And we'll all die here on this wet-arsed grass whilst those bloody Picts scalp us and send our souls screaming in the afterlife.'

'So fight hard,' said Arthur, 'and fight well. No mercy.'

Dewi jostled the men into wide ranks, urging them to keep quiet so that the only sound within the heavy winter fog was the clumsy clatter and bang of spears and shields, and the jangle of armour, belt buckles and cloak pins. Cavall stood beside Arthur in the front rank, lurking behind his legs as Lancelot waited to Arthur's right, and Malegant to his left.

'We are a long way from Durnovaria, lord,' said Malegant, the braids on either side of his long face shaking as he spoke.

'We are. But what we do here, we do for Dumnonia. Remember that,' Arthur replied.

Men roared from across the hill, the unmistakable sound of warriors charging, and the hairs stood up on the back of Arthur's neck. He carried a shield painted with the dragon sigil in one hand and a spear in the other. Excalibur rested in her fleece-lined red scabbard, but he could feel the blade as if it pulsed, singing to him for blood, wailing to be drawn and have her thirst slaked with the lifeblood of Arthur's enemies. Fferog and the men of Rheged were first over the rise, running in their fur and iron, charging towards the fog, Hywel unmistakable amongst them with his red cloak and Roman helmet with its red horsehair crest.

'Prepare to receive our own men,' Dewi shouted, and every man in the ranks took two steps to the right, to make channels for Hywel and his men to run into the fog.

Next came Merlin, cantering over the hill riding Llamrei, barely visible in the fog but for the amber tip of his staff and his flowing robes. Behind streamed the archers, running like madmen towards the fog. Hywel reached Arthur and stopped as Fferog and the rest of the contingent streamed through the gaps to take up positions in the rear.

'What news?' Arthur asked.

'They came from the gate,' Hywel said through gasps of breath. 'But as they formed up, more of them attacked from the flanks in the dawn half-light. They came from east and west to attack the camp, and we thought they would surround us.'

'Lot led them across the river during the night and came at you from your flanks?'

'Yes, lord. He must have, for those men came not from the fortress. They must have waited all night to fall upon our camp.'

'And instead found it empty.'

Hywel grinned. 'Yes, lord. Merlin led our retreat through the camp whilst they howled and stabbed at our tents and shelters.'

Lothians appeared on the ridge, hundreds of men with their short spears, axes and shields. Merlin disappeared into the fog, thumping up and down on Llamrei's back and waving his staff in the air.

'Sound the carnyx,' Arthur ordered, and banged his spear twice upon his shield. Dewi relayed the order and, a moment later, the shrill trumpet sounded like a metal dragon shrieking from the fog.

King Lot and his sons came on in the front rank and their warriors streamed behind him, tongues howling their undulating war cry. They could not yet see Arthur's shield wall in the fog, and as the sound of the carnyx died down, Arthur turned to his men and raised his spear.

'Who do you fight for?' he bellowed.

'Arthur! Arthur! Arthur!' roared back a thousand voices, and all tiredness fled from Arthur.

'On me!' he ordered, and marched forwards. Cavall barked, and the ranks of Britain's warriors came as one from the fog. Arthur set his jaw, exulting in the surprised expression on the Lothian warriors' faces as they saw an army marching towards them. Men came behind them waving their spears in warning, but it was too late. Those men must have realised by now that the camp where they thought to slaughter Arthur's warriors was empty. Lot and his princes followed men they believed to be fleeing in retreat, and warriors will always charge after a routed army. Only Arthur was not in rout. He was ready, and his warriors had come to kill.

They came from the mist like a ghost army, spears and shields ready, and Lot's men stopped one by one and gaped at Arthur's army. They were close, with their white-painted faces and long cloaks too close to flee all the way to their fortress now that they had run across the morning-wet moor in search of blood. Arthur drew back his arm and tossed his spear. It flew in a high arc and slammed into a Lothian warrior's chest.

King Lot and his sons waved their spears, cajoling their men, calling at them to attack. Bors was right, for they did not form an orderly shield wall but just charged in an unruly mass. The first of them leapt into Arthur's shield, trying to jump over the first rank, and they died as the second rankers pierced their throats, faces, chests and bowels with sharp spear points. King Lot himself charged with his men, howling like a wild animal, blue eyes twinkling within his white-painted face. He barked an order and his five hundred men drew back their arms and hurled their short spears.

They rose like a murderous flock of birds, arcing into the sky and then falling quickly, whipping through the air with a stinging sigh.

'Shields!' Dewi called, and every man lifted his shield.

A short spear thundered into Arthur's shield, almost knocking him backwards with its force. Men shrieked and grunted in pain as spears found gaps and slammed into soft flesh. A warrior behind Arthur fell to his knees, coughing gouts of dark blood with a short spear protruding from his gullet.

'Recover,' Dewi ordered.

Lot and his men had taken advantage of Arthur's lines raising their shields, and they howled and screamed like demons and crashed into Arthur's ranks. A wild-eyed warrior leapt low at Arthur, trying to come beneath his shield and tear out his groin with his axe. Arthur slammed his shield down hard and pinned the man. The axe came up and Arthur pushed his knee into the arm to deflect the blow. There was no time to draw Excalibur, so he whipped the seax from the small of his back and cut the Lothian warrior's throat. More enemies came, and Arthur fended them off with his shield and hacked at them with his seax. Bors swung his axe with such ferocity that he was almost as much of a danger to his own men as the enemy. He swept a Lothian man's head from his shoulders in a shocking display of strength, and blood sprayed bright in the mist.

A voice called to Arthur from behind, but he could not turn to hear it. His helmet covered his ears and enemies beat at his shield, axes trying to hook it down so other men could cut at his neck and face. The carnyx sounded three times in warning and Arthur killed the men attacking him with deft cuts of his seax. He risked a glance over his shoulder. The mist had cleared, burned off by the rising sun and on a northern hill he saw hundreds of wild warriors watching, waiting.

Arthur's stomach clenched. Four horses galloped from the mass of enemies assembled on the hillside, small, fast ponies with headless corpses strapped to their saddles. Corpses of Arthur scouts. The Picts had come, and they set off at a loping run, weaving wide around the battle and then charging down the hillside towards Arthur's flank. The Picts attacked, and Arthur desperately blocked Lothian axe blows with his shield. Wild and ferocious enemies surrounded him, and if he could not act quickly, then everything he had worked and fought for would die on a bloody moor in the distant north.

11

'Bors!' Arthur shouted above the ear-shattering crash of weapons and howls of the wounded and dying.

The huge champion of Gododdin glanced at Arthur, teeth bared, and face spattered by other men's blood. Arthur pointed his seax to the Picts who swarmed down the hillside like a diving murmuration of starlings.

'Bloody Picts,' Bors snarled.

'We need to bolster the flank. Lancelot, Bors and I will go. Gawain, Dewi, Hywel, and Malegant, hold the Lothians here.'

Arthur tore himself from the front rank and pushed his way back into his warriors. The Lothian men crowed as though his retreat from the front was a victory and the sense that they had forced the commander of the ghost men who had come from the fog imbued Lot's men with strength. Iron and wood crunched, and bones cracked. Men of Britain died fighting each other and that fact wounded Arthur worse than any blade. This was the wrong fight. Brave men died fighting their own country-men. Rage swelled, first as a ball of heat in Arthur's stomach, rising like fire up a parched tree to his chest, where it bloomed

into seething fury. Arthur dropped his shield, shoving men out
of his way with his shoulder. They moved around him like
water around a rock, warriors of Rheged and Gododdin and the
rear ranks of Arthur's black cloaks making way for their high
king. Bors was with him, shaking his axe and roaring at men to
get out of the way.

The Picts screeched like terrors, faces and bodies painted
with startlingly blue woad warpaint. They howled into Arthur's
flank like murderous bees, striking alone or in pairs, short
spears stabbing and cutting at Arthur's men and then darting
back into their own seething ranks which did not join battle,
but waited paces away from the fray, lashing out at weak points
along the line. A strange whirring sound filled Arthur's ears and
something whipped past his head too fast to see. A black cloak
grunted and fell with a thumb-sized rock embedded in his skull
where his eye once was.

'Slings,' Bors spat. 'Keep your head down. They can take the
eye out of a gnat from one hundred paces.'

More of the murderous rocks whipped across the flank, and
Arthur and Bors urged more men into that line of shields so
that they presented a stout wall to the Picts. Arthur's army
fought on two fronts, in the formation of a chevron, like an
arrowhead holding back furious assaults on two sides.

'Bors,' Arthur shouted over the whir of slingshots and the
din of battle. 'Take fifty men and hold the space between both
fronts.' Arthur pointed to the rear. 'If the Picts or the Lothians
get around the edges of either shield wall, we are all dead men.'

Bors set off, enormous axe in his hand as he bellowed at
men, dragging some by the scruff of the neck, filling the space
to the rear. Once Bors formed up there, Arthur's army would
look like the tip of a spear, a flat edge made by Bors, and then
the two shield-wall flanks forming the point. A warrior shrieked

beside him and hot blood splashed across Arthur's neck and armour. Another warrior gasped and shuddered with a sling-shot in his face, his mouth a terrifying mess of torn flesh and smashed teeth. Arthur had to act. Battle churned around him. Too many of his men suffered injuries and death wounds. If the fight was not resolved quickly, he would have to retreat, pursued across open country by murderous Picts and vengeful Lothians. That could not be. A Gododdin man howled in impossible agony as a Pict dragged him from the shield wall, grabbed a fistful of his hair and hacked his scalp away with a knife.

Arthur surged through the last ranks of his men, pushing through shields, spears and broad shoulders. He burst from the Pict-facing shield wall and stumbled as the resistance in front of him disappeared. Lancelot ordered more men to turn and face the Picts and make a fresh shield wall, standing touch-tight behind the front rank with spears held over those foremost men. The front rank knelt so that the front presented two shields, one low and one high, to the enemy. Sling stones thundered into that impenetrable wall like deathly hail. Arthur had lost all sense of order and discipline. He stepped forward off balance, into the open space between his men and the Picts, and righted himself just in time to see hundreds of wild warriors charging at him, faces painted blue, bare-chested and clutching brutal axes and knives. In one fluid motion, Arthur sheathed his seax and drew Excalibur. He held the blade in two hands and kissed the cold, shimmering blade, calling upon the gods who had forged it to imbue him with their strength.

Slingshots stopped as the enemy focused on Arthur. They came at him, a mass of blue-painted warriors howling, eyes rolling in their heads, such was their battle-madness. Arthur strode forward, sword still in two hands, and his sword flashed forward with strong-shouldered blows, each lunge and cut powerful and controlled. The Picts wore no armour, and so all Excalibur's sharp blade needed was the lightest touch to slice fearsome wounds upon their painted bodies. Axes and knives cut at him, but Arthur kept moving, parrying some, letting others bang against his chain mail, trusting his armour to absorb the blows. Weapons felt like punches as they thumped into his back and sides, but Excalibur moved like lightning, fast, sure and deadly, striking at the enemy with terrible precision. A man twisted away with his face slashed bloody, another fell with his stomach laid open, and a third tried to run when Arthur cut the fingers from his axe hand, but was blocked by his own men and then died with Arthur's sword in his heart.

A woman shrieked an undulating war cry and came at Arthur with wickedly curved knives in each fist. She leapt into the air and one knife clanged against Arthur's helmet. She landed close to him, spitting anger, and Arthur headbutted her, driving her down and stamping on her screaming face. They fell away from him then, hurrying backwards from the fearsome wounds and Arthur's implacable war skill. The Picts were small and wiry, all wild hair, beards, lean limbs and feral eyes.

A man stepped out from their ranks, wearing the white skull of a monstrous bear over his head. He carried two axes, pointed them both at Arthur, and roared at his warriors to attack. They came on in a mass of flailing weapons, and Arthur met them without fear in his heart. A blade cut deep into his thigh, but the pain was nothing compared to the terror he felt in his heart, the knowledge that too many of his men died to Lothian and Pictish blades. Men he needed to fight against the Saxons, men who lay dead now on a northern plain, far from Aelle, Ida and the other Saxon warlords waiting for him in Lloegyr.

Another blow rang on Arthur's helmet, and for a heartbeat the world went black. He tried to take a step, but his wounded leg buckled, and he dropped to one knee. A great cry went up from the Picts and another blow hammered into Arthur's back. He parried an axe with Excalibur, but hands grabbed his wrist and tried to wrestle the god-forged sword out of his grip. Arthur clenched his teeth, feeling death's shadow close, chilling, beckoning him to the afterlife, his mission to unify Britain and restore that which was lost disappearing beneath a Pictish onslaught. Just when all seemed lost, when Arthur was sure he was about to be overwhelmed by his enemies, a powerful force appeared beside him. A force so large it seemed to blot out the sun.

'Get up!' Lancelot growled as his sword cut the hand from the man grasping at Excalibur. 'Get up, damn you!'

Lancelot charged into the mass of blue warpaint, hate and war axes. He was head-and-shoulders taller than any Pictish warrior and they fell back from his shining mail, his monstrous physicality and his skill. Arthur roared like a beast and surged to his feet. He turned and lay his back against Lancelot's and together they moved, blades whirling, and the Picts fell back from them as Arthur and Lancelot carved them up like gods of war. Cavall barked and leapt from the shield wall, the great war dog bounding into the Picts. He leapt at a painted warrior and dragged him to the ground, fangs ripping at the enemy's arm. Arthur's leg and body ached dully, reminding him that wounds leaked blood there, but his rage kept him moving and kept Excalibur swinging.

The Picts fell back from them, and Lancelot cast his enormous arm around Arthur's midriff, holding him up. Arthur glanced along the battle line and the entire line of Picts had fallen back twenty paces, leaving a swathe of their dead where they had thrown themselves at Arthur's shield wall and died. A man faced him, the warrior with the bear's skull helmet.

'Challenge,' he barked in heavily accented, guttural Brythonic pointing both of his axes at Arthur, a gleam in his pale eyes. He wore his beard long and unkempt, and his face and body painted almost entirely with blue woad. A dozen women warriors stood about him, harsh-faced women with braided hair, knives in their hands and slingshots at their belts. The message was clear: the bear-man was their leader, and he challenged Arthur to fight and decide the day.

'If you die, your men go home,' Arthur said.

'If you die, your men throw down their arms and submit to me.'

Arthur swallowed and nodded acceptance.

'Let me fight him,' Lancelot said, but Arthur pushed his friend backwards.

'You saved my life. Go, take Bors and reinforce the Lothian flank. Keep Lot at bay.'

'If he kills you...'

'I know. Go.'

Arthur turned away from his friend. The risk was monumental, the lives of every man under Arthur's command at stake. But with Lothian and the wild Picts arrayed against him, there could be no other victory. The Picts could dog Arthur's every step south, picking off his men in ambush, night attacks, killing his foragers so that by the time he reached the safety of Gododdin his army would be cut to pieces. He had to kill the leader of the Picts so that his men, and his dream of Britain, could live. But if he lost, if his wounded leg failed him, or if one of those axes hacked Arthur's life away, then his men would become slaves to the Picts, laid open to their torture or sacrifice. It was an impossible decision, but that was why Arthur was Pendragon, to make decisions where other men would crumble and quake.

The bear-man raised his axes, and his warriors fell back to create space to fight. To Arthur's right, the battle with Lothian raged, and behind him Arthur felt the eyes of his men boring into him, watching him with desperate hope. He grimaced and limped forward. Arthur refused to look at his wounded leg. Blood seeped from the wound there, running down his thigh, calf, and into his boot. His head rang from the blow to his helmet and his body throbbed.

'The power of the gods is with you!' came Merlin's voice. Arthur turned, and Merlin rode Llamrei along the line of shields, his amber-tipped staff held aloft. 'Neit and Arawn give you power. You are the Pendragon!'

Arthur gripped Excalibur, feeling Merlin's power flow through the blade and into his arms. Llamrei's hooves pounded the battlefield, and such was the druid's reputation that the Picts cowered from him. Fear showed in the bear-man's eyes, and he licked his lips, axes dropping as he gazed upon Merlin, astride the great white stallion. Arthur charged, using the moment to strike, letting Excalibur absorb the pain in his leg and his desperate fatigue.

The bear-man came to meet him, axes swinging and teeth bared in the maw of his beard. He was a head shorter than Arthur, muscles long and taut on his slender frame. He wore grizzly scalps about his neck on a leather thong, blonde, brown and black hair with scraps of yellowed flesh clutching to the roots. Arthur feinted low and lunged high with Excalibur. The Pict misjudged the reach of Arthur's sword and drew too close with his deadly axes, so that all Arthur had to do was a flick of Excalibur into the painted man's gullet. He quivered there for a heartbeat, fear and knowing in his eyes and cold iron in his windpipe. Arthur turned his wrist and tore out the bear-man's throat. He pivoted at the waist, turned, whipping Excalibur around in a quick arc. Blade met skin, bone, ligament, and then emerged from the bear-man's neck. His painted, bear-skulled head toppled to the floor, and the Picts wailed as though it were the end of days.

'Behold!' Merlin called, and rode Llamrei across the kneeling ranks. He shook his staff and let Llamrei wheel around, stomping the battlefield. They cast their eyes down before the magnificent horse and the druid as though a god has descended upon a noble beast to walk amongst them as blood flowed and their leader died. 'Arthur Pendragon and Excalibur, sword of the gods! He is your king, the king of all kings! Your gods curse you for rising against him, beg their forgiveness, beg their forgiveness of your Pendragon!'

The Picts fell to their knees, gaping at Arthur and Merlin with terrified faces. Cavall came to Arthur's side, his mouth stained red with enemy blood.

'Who speaks for you?' Arthur called.

A woman rose from her feet, offering her knife to Arthur with both hands raised and head bowed. 'I am Ethne, of the Elk people,' she said. Her hair hung in long braids, her nose broken in some distant fight. She wore a skin across her body and leather leggings over calf-length boots. 'He was our chief, our lord.' She pointed at the headless man. 'We were his *targaid,* his shields.' She used the ancient word, the words the Picts shared with their Irish cousins across the sea. 'Now, we are yours.'

'Tell your people to fall back. You will fight no more this day. Have them go back to the highland villages but warn them that if they fight against me again, I will fill their country with fire and death.'

'Yes, Ard Rí, high king.' She bowed deeply, called to her people, and they backed away from the battle. Their once fearsome and furious war fury shook from them. Merlin rode about them, urging them back and calling to them in their own language.

'That was too close,' said Lancelot. His armour, hands and face mired with blood and filth. All about them lay the dead and the dying, and Arthur steeled himself for one more push.

'Find Bors,' he said. 'Swing about Lot's flank. Full attack.'

Lancelot hurried to the rear, and Arthur limped through the press of his men to the front line. He stepped across men clutching bloody wounds and corpses of black cloaks, Rheged and Gododdin warriors. Men moved out of Arthur's way, bowing their heads in reverence. They had seen Arthur fight the Picts and defeat their warlord and now they stood aside and let their *dux bellorum* face the Lothians.

By the time Arthur reached the front rank, the battle had broken away from a shield-wall clash. The Lothians already found themselves outflanked by Bors and Lancelot, and King Lot had formed two defensive shield walls, just as Arthur's men had done to face the Picts.

'Sound the carnyx,' Arthur said as he found Dewi, Hywel and Malegant at the front.

'We have them, lord,' said Hywel, his Roman armour dented and his short sword crusted with enemy blood.

'Yes, lord,' Dewi said, and went to find the trumpeter.

'Lord Arthur, please? They are there for the taking,' Hywel continued, but Arthur raised a hand to quieten the Elmet man.

'Enough blood,' Arthur said, having to tear the words from his exhausted body. 'Enough death.'

Arthur walked from the front rank and the Lothian men roared and shouted at him, shaking their spears and axes. King Lot stood in the second rank, a lurid cut upon his face and dead warriors all about him. The carnyx blared its long, shrill note and Arthur held Excalibur up by the blade, hilt raised high into the air to show that he wanted to parlay with the king of Lothian. All fighting ceased and the Lothian men shuffled backwards, shoulders slumping and cheeks blowing, relieved by the momentary respite.

'King Lot,' Arthur called. 'You are beaten. You have, what, three hundred men left who can fight?'

Lot stalked from his men, his armour and clothes ripped and his face pale and taut.

'My son is dead,' Lot said. He wiped blood from his face onto his forearm. He seemed dazed, his eyes vacant beneath the white paste now smeared with crimson.

'A lot of men have died this day.'

'He was a fine boy. Strong. Even-tempered.'

'Now he is dead.' Arthur spoke harshly, stepping towards Lot. 'We can finish this battle, if you wish. Your allies, the Picts, are cowed. I can order my men to charge and will kill every last one of you. It will cost me men to do it, but I will give the order as a lesson to others who attack their high king.'

'He had a young wife. And a little girl.'

Arthur sheathed Excalibur and pulled the stone sceptre from his belt. He banged its curved end into Lot's chest, hard, and the king snapped to attention and locked eyes with Arthur. 'If you do not surrender and kneel to me here, now, I will slaughter every Lothian man upon this battlefield. When that's done, I will loose my men upon Bedegraine without restraint. I will let them vent their anger and fury at the loss of their shield-brothers upon your people until not a soul remains in this gods-forsaken place. Lothian will be no more, a place of myth, a story told by mothers to frighten misbehaving children.' Arthur held King Lot's gaze, though he surprised himself with the threat.

King Lot's face twisted as he felt a pang of pain from his wounds. He nodded and dropped his weapons, and then knelt to Arthur. Arthur lowered the sceptre, and King Lot kissed its cold stone. 'I swear to be your man, you are Arthur, Pendragon of Britain and the men of Lothian will march whenever you call.' Lot spoke quietly, his pride and anger broken, leaving a shadow of the man who had stood before Arthur only a day before.

'Good. Now rise. We shall need food and ale, and my men will sleep under your roof this night whilst we treat our wounded. When we march, your second son will accompany me as surety of your oath.'

Lot opened his mouth, and it moved silently as though he half objected, and half understood what must be. Then he nodded.

'If you raise an army against me again,' Arthur warned, 'your son's life shall be forfeit, and I shall return with the warriors of every kingdom of Britain and turn your kingdom to ash.'

And so, the battle of Bedegraine was over. Arthur limped to the rear of his army, wounded leg throbbing, and waited until he was out of sight of both Lot and the Picts, and then he fell to the ground. Lancelot and Dewi dashed to him, and Hywel called for ale. Cavall whined and licked at Arthur's hand, and he fought to remain conscious.

'How many men did we lose?' he asked Dewi, and the stalwart captain bowed his head.

'We haven't counted yet, lord,' he said. 'But the fighting was fierce.'

'Aye.' Arthur sat and Hywel handed him a skin of ale which he drank from, the liquid washing the dust, mud and blood from his mouth. 'Too many have fallen.'

'Fetch Merlin,' Lancelot ordered, and Hywel hurried away.

'Did you mean that, your threat to Lot?' he asked, leaning into Arthur.

'No,' Arthur lied. The threat was necessary, and in truth, he had meant the words after stepping over the bloodied bodies of his men. It had been an unnecessary battle, a waste of life. Arthur wished he could close his ears to the sound of injured men wailing. It sounded as if Britain itself shrieked at him in mournful, woeful grief at the loss of so many men needed to fight the Saxons in spring. Men's blood leaked into the moor, and Arthur lay back and stared at the sky. Snow began to fall in fat, drifting flakes which landed cold and wet upon his face.

12

'What do they want?' Arthur asked, staring over Merlin's shoulder at the dozen Picts waiting for him across the hall.

Merlin cut the catgut thread with his knife and bound Arthur's leg wound tight with clean cloth.

'That will need cleaning daily. I will do it myself for the first few days. It's clean now, but if the spear, axe or whatever pierced your leg was filthy, you might lose that leg.' Merlin fussed at the pouches hidden in the folds of his tunic and cloak, and at the small leather bags hanging from his belt. He flicked his chin towards the Picts. 'They were the Pictish warlord's bodyguards, his sworn shields. You killed him. They are yours now.'

'I don't want them.'

'You have no choice. They are women, in case you hadn't noticed, given into their warlord's service by their fathers and sworn to fight to the death to protect him. That duty passes to whoever slays their lord in combat.'

'They didn't protect him very well in yesterday's battle.'

'That would be a good point, if you were discussing the matter with a child. You fought their leader in single combat.

The Picts are like the Irish, they have ancient rites that must be respected. They are sworn to you now. Keep them. They may come in useful. You need all the blades you can get.'

'How many men did we lose yesterday?'

'Too many. Your man Dewi has the final count.' Merlin examined the various bruises and cuts across Arthur's arms, head and torso. The cut across his scalp was almost healed, and Merlin smeared it with a foul-smelling ointment. 'You should really do better to avoid enemy blades.'

'Do you have any other pearls from your vaults of wisdom?' Arthur grimaced as Merlin pressed his thumb into a purple welt on Arthur's back.

'Yes. We can't linger at Bedegraine for long. We must march for Gododdin.'

'There are little enough supplies here, that's for sure. But the men are tired, and they need a few more days' rest. Let wounds heal a little, let the men recover their strength. Besides, there's snow on the ground.'

'There are too many men in this place,' Merlin snapped, and fixed Arthur with his grey eyes. 'Dawdle here, and before long, men's bowels will loosen, and they'll die of the shitting sickness. Is that what you want?'

'Obviously not.'

'Then heed my advice. I will travel ahead to Dunpendrylaw and have King Letan prepare provisions for your men. You can return to the south, stopping at every hall on the way. Secure their commitments for men to march in spring and use your position to keep your men fed.'

'Very well. What news of the south?'

'Nothing. Yet. As far as I know, no fresh ships have been mad enough to attempt crossing the narrow sea in winter, and the

Saxons are quiet. Preparing. I have another important matter to deal with.'

Merlin strode to a corner of King Lot's hall where a pitiful figure crouched against the wall, more like a collection of rags than a man. It quivered and covered its head with its arms as Merlin approached. The figure peered from between its hands. It was Peithan, Lot's druid. Merlin spoke to him in a strange, deep voice. Peithan rose, gazing into Merlin's eyes as if transfixed by them. His jaw hung slack, and he wavered, hanging upon Merlin's every word. When he was done, Merlin clattered Peithan once across the head with his staff, and Lot's druid collapsed to the floor again and fell into a deep sleep.

'He won't give us any more trouble,' Merlin called cheerfully. 'To Gododdin!' He swept out of the hall in a bustle of flowing cloak and tunic. The room seemed somehow darker after Merlin's departure.

Arthur sat back on King Lot's throne and waved the dozen Picts towards him. Despite a night having passed since the battle of Bedegraine, they still wore their woad paint and their war gear. The paint was cracked and creased, and their clothes torn and filthy from battle. They approached slowly, with downcast eyes. Each wore a sling at her belt, two curved knives, and a Pict war axe in a loop at their right hip.

'Ard Rí,' said the woman who had spoken to Arthur on the battlefield. She was short with blue eyes and flame-red hair tied in tight braids. Her broken nose made her face seemed slanted and she carried four dried scalps around her neck.

'I hope those came not from my men, Ethne?' Arthur said, pointing at her grisly necklace.

'They did not. We are your *targaid* now. Your shield. We were all raised to the blade from the time we could crawl. Each woman here fights as well as any two men.'

Arthur cuffed at his tired eyes. 'Then guard this hall whilst I inspect my wounded men.'

Ethne clapped a fist to her chest and each of them stamped their right foot twice down upon the ground. Arthur sighed. He wanted no part of their commitment to serve him. The Picts had almost destroyed him, and the thought of how close he had come to defeat made Arthur feel queasy. Using a spear for a walking stick, he stood up from the throne. Arthur groaned as he bent to pick up a cloth sack, which he slung over his shoulder. He limped slowly to the back of the hall, where forty of his men lay on straw pallets. It stank of blood and death, putrid and festering. Arthur found Dewi there. The captain knelt beside a pale-faced man, holding his hand whilst the man sweated and shook his head from side to side.

'Take off his cloak and breastplate?' Arthur said, wondering why Dewi and the men attending the wounded had not made the struggling man more comfortable.

'He's a black cloak,' Dewi said. 'Each of us is as proud to wear that cloak as a man would be to be the emperor of Rome. He won't take it off, wants to die in it.'

'What's your name, warrior?'

'Cenau,' the warrior managed through chattering teeth.

'You fought like a hero yesterday. I am proud to have fought beside you.'

The warrior smiled up at Arthur, and then he went still, dead eyes still staring into Arthur's own.

'He killed four Lothians yesterday,' said Dewi. 'Then one of the whoresons opened his belly with an axe.'

'How many did we lose?'

'Seventy dead. These forty injured, another two hundred injured, but not likely to die.'

'Seventy. So many.'

'It was a hard fight, lord.'

Arthur set the cloth sack down on the floor, reached into it, and took out a golden torc. It was a magnificent piece of craftmanship of coiled golden ropes with cruel beasts' faces at either end.

'This is for you, for your loyalty and bravery.' Arthur handed the torc to Dewi.

'I cannot accept it, lord, it is too grand for a simple soldier.'

'You've earned it. Wear it with pride or sell it when we get back to Durnovaria. It's yours to do with as you please.'

'Thank you, lord.'

'In this sack are the finest pieces from Lot's treasury. There's more over by the throne. Hand it all out to the men, to everyone who fought bravely. There are also some large golden plates, looks like Christian work looted in raids. Chop them up and make sure that every soldier receives a piece of hacked gold or silver.'

'Yes, lord.'

Arthur left him there and struggled, limping to the back of the hall. He opened a small rear door and entered a long room warmed by a hearth fire. King Lot sat beside his fire on a wooden chair, a heavyset woman beside him and a long-eared hound at their feet. Lot turned to Arthur and then stared back into the flames. A slave girl hurried to help Arthur, but he smiled and waved her away.

'I will march south tomorrow,' Arthur said.

'Yes. Tomorrow,' Lot replied, his voice low and distant.

'I'll take two hundred of your men with me.'

'Two hundred!' said the woman next to Lot. She scowled at Arthur and shook Lot's arm, but he paid her no attention and almost fell off his chair.

'What is your son's name?'

'His name was Ieuaf,' Lot said.

'The living son.' Arthur knew he sounded cruel, but he had little pity for the king of Lothian, who had caused so much bloodshed with his rebellion.

'Rhun,' said Lot's queen. 'My husband gave you his word, and we have already lost one son and heir. Can Rhun not stay here with his family?'

'No. I must leave certain that you will not rise again.'

'We will not. You have my husband, the king's, oath on it.'

Arthur's wounds sent a tremble of fatigue through his body, and he rubbed at his gritty, tired eyes. 'All this blood, all this death. You are safe here in the far north, safe from Saxon blades. Why did you not just recognise me as Pendragon? What difference is it to Lothian if Uther or Arthur is the Pendragon? Why rebel?' Arthur's wound sent a stab of pain shooting up his leg and he braced himself on the spear.

The queen waited for Lot to respond, but the king just gazed into the fire, slack-jawed and distant. 'The death of his son haunts my husband's mind,' she said. 'He was the son of the king's first wife. Rhun is my son. Born to us during a cold winter when snow covered the land. Just like this one. Ieauf was beloved by his father, a great warrior, proud and strong.'

'Now he is dead. It could have been avoided so easily.' Arthur shifted his position so he could look into Lot's face, grimacing at the pain in his leg. 'Are you satisfied now that Britain's soil is dunged with the blood of her sons?'

'Urien of Rheged sent a messenger to us,' said the queen after Lot remained silent. 'That messenger, she told us you were a demon-king. A bastard who had usurped Uther Pendragon's throne and now marched north to do the same to every king of Britain.'

'A woman?'

'Yes, a *gwyllion* with stones in her teeth, a hard woman with druid *seidr*. She stirred my lord husband with dark words. The witch told tales of Merlin and how he had become a servant of Arawn, and how the Lord of the Underworld has tasked Merlin with sending Britain's warriors to Annwn, to the underworld to fight for the dark god in his wars against his brother gods. She told of bloody wars in the south, and how Merlin's champion, Arthur, a bastard of no kingdom, wielded a sword forged in the otherworld, and with that sword he sent the souls of the land's finest warriors into Arawn's service. She sang to us, filled our ears with laments, of how Gododdin had always ridden roughshod over Lothian. How they considered us peasants, how King Letan Luyddoc of Gododdin was your pet. She bade us beware of Arthur ap Nowhere and Merlin, that we should join with Urien. She stirred my husband's heart and that of his champions with promises of vengeance over our old enemies across the hills. With Lothian and Rheged in alliance, Letan would find himself surrounded and have no choice but to succumb to our will. She said that, together, our three kingdoms could destroy you, and that Urien of Rheged would be Pendragon, and he would give Gododdin to Lothian, that Dunpendrylaw would burn and Gododdin would become one with Lothian under Lot's rule.'

'Nimue,' Arthur whispered.

'Yes! Nimue. That was her name. She was Irish and spoke the same tongue as the Picts. She came with a painted face, just like our warriors. How we hate Gododdin. For generations they have stolen from us, raided our herds, treated us like sheep shit on their boots. This was our chance to rise, for Lothian to become great, to secure victory over our old enemy.'

'Do you not raid Gododdin's herds?'

'Yes, but only in retaliation. They started it all.'

'When did they start it all?'

'Years ago.' The queen sat forwards; her mouth twisted in anger. 'In the time of our forefathers, always they have raided us, killing our sons and burning our farms. They are dogs! Murderers!'

Arthur shook his head at the folly of it all. 'Both Lothian and Gododdin have raided one another's sheep and cattle since the days when men first walked the dales and mountains of this land. You have been kings here since Rome left the great wall, just as Letan's forefathers forged Gododdin from the ruins of an abandoned Roman fort. Every kingdom on this island raids the other. Our warriors live for it. It is how they earn their death rings and their reputation. So it has always been, and so it will always be. You listened to Nimue, she poured honey into your ears with dreams of Gododdin's defeat and now you are ruined.'

'We are ruined.' The queen cast her head into her hands and sobbed. 'My poor Rhun. What will become of him?'

'He will have a place at my court and will have the comforts of a prince. He will have education and weapons instruction. But if you betray me, if Lothian so much as carries a spear into Gododdin lands, I will send you Rhun's head. Send men when I call. That is all I ask. Fight the Saxons instead of your neighbours, and you shall never have trouble with me.'

'What do we know of Saxons?'

'Nothing!' Arthur shouted. 'You know nothing of Saxons, Angles and Jutes. You talk of cattle and sheep raids as if you know something of war. You know nothing! Gododdin steals a few cows and a few of Lothian's warriors die every summer. The Saxons come to take everything from us. Everything! They come across the narrow sea not to steal our cows, but to destroy our people and cast us out of our own lands. Bernicia, Deira, Lyndsey and the entire south-east coast of Britain have already fallen. Lloegyr is now almost as large as lands still inhabited by Britons. Think yourself lucky you have only known cattle raids and not the fire and sword of men who would brave the horrors of the Whale Road to bring spears and men to our lands. They are brutal! Make no mistake, if I lose this fight and the Saxons defeat our armies, soon they will come here to your remote moors and your hilltop villages, and then all your womenfolk will become their wives and slaves, your children will bear Saxon names and when you are dead and your Saxon children are grown, nobody will remember that Britons lived here at all.'

'The *gwyllion* came, and the king listened. So we are at your mercy.'

'Have the prince ready to march tomorrow. In the spring, you will send three hundred Lothian spearmen south to me in Dumnonia.' Arthur turned and limped from the king's chamber, his heart heavy at what Nimue and Urien had cost Britain's defence.

It took two weeks to gather supplies in from the farmsteads and villages spread across Lothian's sweeping moors and highland fastnesses. Two weeks when Arthur had hoped to march the day after the battle of Bedegraine. He spent those days resting in King Lot's hall, healing his leg by the hearth fire and listening as the wounded died of the wound rot, even though Merlin and Peithan toiled day and night to save them. Of the forty seriously injured, the druids saved half, though they had to cut limbs from some and perform all-night, smoke-filled, sweating *seidr* prayers over others. Arthur's men constructed a huge death mound on the battlefield and burned the dead in a balefire which burned for three days even amongst snow, which continued to drift across the distant hills to blanket the moor in white. When it was over, they covered the ashes with soil and created a mound to mark the battle.

Lot spent his days staring into his bedroom chamber's fire and would speak to no one. Though young, Prince Rhun proved himself useful. He was a short young man of slim build with a thin face who carried no weapons and wore a simple woollen jerkin and trews. Rhun organised the gathering of supplies, and kept a tally of the wheat, barley, fish, eggs, chickens, milk and ale delivered from Lothian's countryside. He even sent back provisions, explaining to Arthur that the food would spoil on the road south before Arthur's men had time to eat it. The argument made sense and so Arthur allowed it, seeing no need to starve the innocent folk of Lothian for their king's ill judgement.

When the army finally marched out of Lothian, Arthur could ride Llamrei with his leg strapped up and healing well. King Lot and his queen waved to Rhun from Bedegraine's battlements, and he rode beside Arthur on a roan mare.

'Are there libraries in Durnovaria?' Rhun asked, after waving half-heartedly to his mother and father.

'The finest,' Arthur replied. 'With Roman and Greek scrolls, plays and comedies.'

'Truly? Will I be permitted to read them?'

'If that is what you wish. You do not fight?'

Rhun smiled. 'I do not share my father and brother's love for war. I am more suited to matters of the mind.'

'You sound like a priest. If you are more suited to matters of the mind, why did you not convince your father not to side with Urien?'

'He is the king, and he wanted to defeat Gododdin.' Rhun spoke simply, as if the matter was a foregone conclusion.

'If you want to read all those rolled-up parchments,' said Lancelot, who rode on Arthur's opposite flank, 'you'll need to learn Greek and Roman letters.'

'Are there any at court who can teach me?'

'You could ask Merlin. He speaks more languages than any man alive.'

'Truly?'

'I can hear you fools,' Merlin piped, catching up to them riding a chestnut gelding. 'Do you think I have the time to teach a princeling languages of which he has no need? They are nothing but dreary, drawn-out drivel anyway. Better to put yourself to use elsewhere. Like counting the render or helping Queen Guinevere build her Camelot. She will have need for men who can count and read. Building a fortress takes timber and stone. That timber must be cut, transported and trimmed to size. She will need wells for water, food, ale, barracks for warriors and houses for the stewards, bakers, potters, black-smiths, butchers and all their wives and children. Lanes and streets must be designed, measured and constructed. Where will the food come from and how will it be collected? Where will the grain be stored? Much and more to consider, manage and build, young prince. Put your mind to that, and forget about Marcus Aurelius, Socrates, Pliny, Aristotle and Virgil. Arthur, ride with me.' Merlin urged his mount into a canter and Arthur caught up with him so that they rode ahead of the long column of spearmen, donkey-drawn wagons and scouts mounted on fast ponies. Arthur's new Pict bodyguard marched behind the leading warriors, Bors, Lancelot and Gawain, who rode horses, whilst Dewi and Hywel marched on foot with the black cloaks, and the warriors of Rheged and Gododdin.

'Nimue was at Bedegraine last year,' Arthur said. He fished into the pack tied to his saddle and tossed a scrap of dried beef to Cavall, who walked beside Llamrei.

'I heard. She works against us. I had thought she had confined herself to poisoning Urien's mind. Not that he needed much pushing to become your enemy, of course. She has cost us men, and time.'

'I thought Nimue loved Britain, that her great desire was for the land to return to our people and the old gods?'

'It is. But her Britain. Not yours or mine. She believes us too tolerant of the nailed god. Which we are. But now is not the time to fight the Christ, we already have enough enemies in this world.'

'We should have taken her at the Bear Fort.'

'And done what? Kept her tied up like a hog awaiting the butcher's knife?'

'Stopped her.'

'She must be stopped; in that you are right. I will go to Nimue and try to contain her malevolence. But first I must go east and find Kadvuz. He had been amongst the borderlands these last months, in the badlands between Elmet, Bernicia and Deira. There must be a Saxon king of Lyndsey by now, unless Clappa of Deira or Ida or Bernicia have made it their own. Either way, we must know what our enemies have been up to before spring.'

Arthur glanced up at the cold sky. 'How long until birds and buds return?'

'Not long. It will be Yule when we reach Gododdin. Midwinter. Two turns of the moon later, the swallows and swifts will return, snowdrops bloom, and trees begin to show green through the frost.'

'It will take us one turn of the moon to march from Gododdin to Durnovaria.'

'Longer, perhaps. If the roads are full of snow and ice.'

'Which leaves only a few weeks' rest, to prepare and gather men before the Saxons' war drums beat from the east and new ships cross the narrow sea.' Arthur's chest tightened at the prospect of war season looming so soon after his return home. It was no time at all. No time to summon the warriors from every kingdom to fight beneath his dragon banner, no time to secure the badlands, the borders between British kingdoms and Lloegyr, which he had fought so hard to win with five years of hard fighting. 'There is never enough time to do things properly. We should build forts and stockades all across the frontier and man each with spearmen. We should have beacons across the mountains from north to south to give us warning that Saxons are on the march.'

'We had to come north. There was no choice. Foolish men and a jealous *gwyllion* forced it upon us.'

'Nimue, jealous?'

'Of course she's jealous. Of me, of you. Of the nailed god's increasing power. Of everyone and everything with the influence and power she craves.'

'Find her, Merlin, before she strikes again.'

'I shall do my best. And I will send word south to you of events in the east. Kadvuz will know what Ida and Clappa have cooked up over winter.'

Merlin rode eastwards and Arthur watched him go. He wanted to daydream of Guinevere, of a warm bed and long nights, but all he could think of were Saxon armies and where they might strike, and Llamrei's hoofbeats sounded like Saxon drums, torturing Arthur's mind with how, what, where and when. He wanted peace, to spend time with his queen and give her the baby she craved and deserved, but war waited forever on the horizon, calling to him, singing to him of glory and the destruction of his enemies.

13

Arthur spent three days at Dunpendrylaw. His men had marched across Britain in the harshest of seasons, and so he allowed them to celebrate the Yule midwinter festival with King Letan and his warriors. Gawain organised a camp for Arthur's war band outside Gododdin's royal stronghold, and Bors brought wains filled with barrels of ale, meat for roasting, spits, onions and garlic to roast over the fire and bards to keep the men entertained with song. Bors wrestled and roared with the warriors, rolling in the snow and ice, drinking enough ale to drown an ox, vomiting in bushes and then doing it all again. Arthur spent the celebration with Lancelot and Gawain in King Letan's hall, where they drank and feasted to the rebirth of the sun and winter solstice. They burned a ceremonial oak log to encourage the sun to warm and for the cold, dark winter days to lengthen. Bards plucked lyres and beat drums as they sang songs of the Great War, of Ambrosius, Uther, Igraine, Ector and of Vortigern. They did Arthur great honour and sang of his battles at the River Glein, and at the Dubglas. The men of Gododdin cheered when the bards sang of their heroics at the

Glein, and cast their eyes down, shamefaced, when the songs told of the Dubglas where they had not marched to support Arthur. After the three days, when the ale was gone and the men's faces became green with headaches and belly pains, Arthur marched his black cloaks and the men of Rheged south with promises from Gawain and Bors to join their warriors to his in the spring.

At the foot of the great mountains, which split northern Britain in two like the spine of a fallen god, Hywel broke off from the column and marched west to Rheged with his warriors, where he would join Kai for what remained of the winter weeks. Arthur warned Hywel to steer clear of Nimue and Morgan and their *seidr*, and the Roman warrior clapped a fist to his chest in salute and led his column into the dark forests of north-west Britain. It took the black cloaks four weeks to reach Dumnonia. They marched along roads and beside fields where slaves and churls bowed to the passing warriors. Children ran to them, touching their spears and weapons with wide eyes, and the men set those excited boys upon their shoulders so that the common folk laughed and clapped their hands. Arthur waved to the people, even donning his feather-plumed helmet at busier settlements. It was important for the people of Britain to be in awe of their warrior caste, for them to see the Pendragon in shining armour and war glory. It gave them confidence and belief that Britain had warriors of its own to combat the terrible stories of Saxon raids and burned villages. The fields stank of cattle shit hoarded all winter and spread over fields to prepare them for spring planting, and the people who waved did so with hands dirty and cracked by hard work.

'These are the people we fight for,' Arthur told his men. 'Honest folk. They put food in our bellies, and without them, this land would be nothing. Remember their faces and the laughing children when you stand in the shield wall. We are warriors. They render up one tenth of all they produce to us, and in turn, it is our duty to protect them. Never forget that. Remember the laughing children and doe-eyed milkmaids when you meet Saxon blades, for it is them you fight to protect.'

Arthur avoided Elmet once again to save time. Courtesy and the rules of guest friendship said that he should have spent a few days with King Gwallog and Idnerth, the Primus Pilum of Gwallog's Roman troops who still wore the plate armour and red cloaks of old Rome. But they were precious days. Spring raced towards him and from then until autumn, Arthur and his warriors would march against their enemies. With the few days and weeks left to him, Arthur would prefer to spend them with Guinevere, so he skirted Elmet and led his men across the border between Gwallog's kingdom and Powys, where King Brochvael ruled. Brochvael had supported Arthur at the battle of the Dubglas, sending his champion Einion and a war band of hardy warriors who had fought like bears. Arthur sent gifts of gold and silver to both Gwallog and Brochvael and told his messengers to carry news of the war in the north, and to remind both kings that Arthur had not summoned their warriors to fight against Rheged, Lothian and the Picts, so that they should be well rested when he called the muster for war in spring.

Arthur reached Dumnonia on a day when the sun shone bright, but the air was cold enough to make smoke plume from Llamrei's nostrils. Men wore cloaks pulled about their necks and shoulders and wore leather or felt helmet liners for warmth. Robins perched on bare branches and the land was shorn of colour by the changing season. Hardened warriors embraced each other like brothers when Dewi dismissed the black cloaks. They went with Arthur's thanks, and even though men had died and most marched with holes in their boots, and nursed injuries from battle in the north, they were happy with the silver and gold Arthur had taken from Lot's treasury. It was Arthur's job as their lord to furnish his men with rings and silver. They expected it; it was their pay, and their wives would expect something to show for so long spent away from home. The shards of hacksilver, and gold and silver cloak pins, brooches, rings and talismans, could be used to trade for clothes, food, spits, ceramic or clay jugs, cups and plates and any of a hundred items needed to keep a family home. Warriors gave Arthur their oaths, and risked their lives to fight under his command, and without reward of rings and silver, a warrior might consider their lord's duty unfulfilled and ask to be freed from his oath. Then a man could take his wife and children and seek a new lord who would better reward the warrior for his spear and his bravery. Ector had taught Arthur the ways of the warrior, and of leading men, so he was always careful to look after the warriors who fought under his command.

Dewi went home with orders to recruit fifty new black cloaks over the winter, to take the best of Dumnonia's spearmen and train them in Arthur's battle tactics before spring. Arthur's black cloaks were the finest warriors in all Britain. Veterans of large-scale battles, assaults upon stout strongholds, of hard marches, ambush and slaughter. Most of the cohort became Arthur's elite warriors in the days when Arthur and Balin of the Two Swords fought in the badlands between Britain and Lloegyr. They had fought for no king, just vengeful black cloaks roving the borders, punishing Saxon war bands. Many of that original war band had died in the endless wars, including Balin himself, who had died fighting his hated brother at the battle of the Dubglas. Every man who joined Arthur's black cloaks had to be proven in battle, an expert spearman with death rings to prove his prowess. Arthur's black cloaks always fought at the front and were fiercely loyal to the Pendragon. Shirkers and cowards could find only death in a welter of enemy blades if they donned the black cloak and could not live up to its standards.

Llamrei carried Arthur into a Durnovaria empty of queen, stewards and warriors. Prince Madoc was in the city with his maids, guards and tutors and Arthur spent two days there making sure the young prince was well and correctly cared for. He checked on the stores and render, and made quick decisions on any serious disputes which required his doom. Guinevere, Arthur learned, had departed for the River Cam and its earth-mound fortress of the old folk to begin work on Camelot. The people of Durnovaria shied away from Ethne and her *targaid* war band, who travelled without their woad warpaint but still cut fearsome figures. Few women went to war. Lunete had loved to hunt and ride and had constantly disobeyed Ector's orders and followed his men into battle. But that was rare. To see a dozen scarred women armed to teeth, marching with the Pendragon's war band with warrior's arrogance and pride was a sight to take people's breath away and Arthur knew that Ethne and her sisters would be the talk of Dumnonia with their scalp necklaces, curved knives, and their travel and weather worn leather clothes, scars, and braided hair which gave them a brutal, uncivilised appearance.

Arthur took time to decide on issues demanding his attention and ensured Prince Rhun had a room and access to Durnovaria's library. He ensured that his duty to Prince Madoc's welfare was complete, and then Arthur and Lancelot rode for the River Cam. Ethne and the *targaid* followed, running in their languid, loping gait, which they could keep up for hours without respite. They reached the banks of the River Cam and found an entire shanty town of people chopping, sawing, hammering, lifting and carrying wooden stakes up onto the hill where buildings made of freshly cut golden timber frames were already beginning to take shape. A long barge came upriver pulled by heavy-limbed horses, carrying dressed Roman stone taken from crumbled buildings in the east. People had built makeshift shacks and tents around the ancient earthworks to live in whilst they built Guinevere's dream stronghold, with all the Roman finery, tapestries, rugs and luxuries she could find. Arthur shuddered at the silver and gold each tradesman would require for so lengthy and ambitious an undertaking.

'It seems your queen waits for no man,' said Lancelot as he and Arthur gazed upon the expansive works from a nearby hillock.

'She does not,' Arthur replied with a shake of his head. 'Even when she was asked to wait for the spring, and for your guidance on how to build the fortifications.'

'Do you really want me to stay here and build this place when you march in spring?' Lancelot leaned forward in his saddle, arms crossed, gazing upon the chopping, lifting and carrying.

'You might be as good with the chisel as you are with the sword.' Arthur laughed at his friend's discomfort, imagining Lancelot's hulking frame sawing and shaping logs to make Camelot's stout palisade.

'Why do I feel like I will spend my year arguing with your wife while you wage war against the Saxons?'

'Guinevere has full control and autonomy over the palace and its furnishings. You handle the defences. There should not be a situation where the two of you are in dispute. Unless you wish to hang her tapestries over the palisade, or she wishes to build a ditch and bank beside her ladies' dressing area.'

'If life were that simple, my friend, every husband would

spend more time at home and every wife would have nothing to nag about.'

'A word of warning. Do not speak of nagging to Guinevere, or you might find yourself on the end of a tongue-lashing as sharp as any blade you have faced in the shield wall.'

'I do not doubt it. I'll be careful. There were women back home across the sea, you know.'

'I am sure there were. Shall we ride down and inspect progress? I am eager to see my lady wife.'

'Before we go, are you sure that you want me to remain here at Camelot for the entirety of campaigning season?'

Arthur smiled and shifted his position in the saddle. His wounded leg had healed, but there was pain deep inside the muscle, a dull, throbbing pain, and he still could not walk without a limp. Long days in the saddle left him sore and his leg screaming in pain, and he was looking forward to days of rest. He understood Lancelot's frustration, but his great friend, the man who had saved his life at the battle of Bedegraine, was the man he trusted most in the entire world. Lancelot and Kai were as brothers to him, brothers of the sword and of the heart. 'I need you here. Your mind and knowledge of battle and fortifications is better than my own, and I trust you to make Camelot as impregnable as the Bear Fort or Dun Guaroy. Which it must be, because we are close to the frontier here. Lloegyr is a two-day ride that way. Camelot must be here, because we must be able to muster an army to march into Lloegyr and meet the Saxon threat within days, not weeks or months. From here we can access the river by boat, Roman roads, be in the east, south or north before the Saxons can march from Lloegyr into any of our kingdoms.

'Camelot's closeness to Lloegyr serves well for attacking the enemy, but that is also its problem. I shall be away for most of the year fighting our enemies. The Saxons will attack, as they always do, and always will until we cast them back into the narrow sea. If they attack Camelot whilst I am with the army in the north or east, then I must have a stout commander here to protect Guinevere and the people here who are my responsibility.'

'You will leave men to guard Camelot?'

'Of course, and they will be under your command.'

'I am honoured to have your trust. No harm will come to Guinevere whilst I draw breath.'

'I know, and that is why it must be you.'

'Will Prince Madoc be here?'

'No, he will remain at Durnovaria, where he can be cared for and raised as Dumnonia's king. Camelot is my stronghold. My home. I am the steward of Dumnonia, and Madoc will be king there. Camelot is the home of the Pendragon, from where I can be high king and do what must be done for Britain without the affairs of Dumnonia and its succession to cloud my thoughts.'

'We must get the palisade up quickly. Once we have a wall, we can defend it, even whilst the rest of Camelot is under construction. Your forefathers used these earthen ramparts to fight the Romans. We can use them too. Each ridge is a ditch and bank of its own, and any attacker must descend and climb each one to reach the walls whilst we rain down hell upon their heads. So, we need spears, bows and sheaves of arrows ready alongside the walls. We can lay sharpened stakes in every ditch and firepit to light beneath attackers' feet.'

'See? I have nothing to fear. I would not like to assault a fortress defended by you, Lancelot of the Lake.'

They rode down towards the hive of activity and a steward took Llamrei and Lancelot's horses and found Cavall a large bone to chew on. Arthur left Lancelot with the builders, and he ambled through piles of sweet-smelling sawdust, and pits where men mixed the daub they would use to plaster over the thin wooden wattle strips of which Camelot's hall and buildings were to be built. Six men in leather aprons used long, oar-like spoons to stir a deep pit filled with wet soil, clay, sand and straw. Women crossed between the temporary shelters carrying baskets of clothes for washing, or wool to be woven out by distaffs. Folk bowed to Arthur as he passed, dressed as he was in his armour, his black cloak, with his plumed helmet under his arm.

The Picts attracted more attention than Arthur himself, with folk coming to peer at them, whispering behind their hands. One of the Picts growled at a group of children staring at them from behind a stack of wood, and the children ran away shrieking.

'I am safe here,' Arthur said to Ethne as they reached the lowest rung of grass-covered earthworks. A sunken lane led through the sequence of rising contours into the open area behind the rings of high earthen mounds. 'Find some food and rest your warriors.'

'We need no rest,' Ethne replied, in her usually laconic fashion. 'We are Picts.'

Arthur halted at the entrance to the fortress and turned to Ethne and her war band.

'I order you to find food, ale and rest,' he said. 'Report to me before nightfall.'

Ethne stared at him for a moment, lip curling slightly beneath the slanted mash of her broken nose. She thought about it, glancing around at the high earth mounds, the construction works and the flock of people busy at their tasks.

'Yes, Ard Rí,' she replied finally, and led her warriors out into the tangle of ropes, saws, barrels and tents. Arthur's new bodyguard had kept to themselves on the journey south. They ate and slept away from the black cloaks and asked for nothing. Arthur had grown to enjoy their stoic presence, they could fight, and had proved that in the battle of Bedegraine, and in the few fist fights which had broken out on the road south, as they always did among a war band on the march. Tempers frayed thin when groups of prideful warriors spent too much time together and Ethne's women had argued with black cloaks who had insulted them, or men who had made ill-advised comments about women being unfit for war. The Picts rewarded such comments with short, brutal justice and by the time the war band had reached Dumnonia, there was respect between the *targaid* and the black cloaks.

Arthur limped up the lane and was pleasantly surprised when he emerged from its shadows into the wide-open space at the fort's centre. A hall as long and wide as Urien's high seat in Rheged stood proudly amongst half-built houses, stables and pens. Its wattle and daub walls reached two storeys high, and half a dozen thatchers worked with bright gold straw mixed with reeds and rushes, cutting lengths with short scythes and covering thick oak beams with layers of dense, warm thatch. He marvelled at the progress made in so short a time. The craftsmen wore coarse wool clothes and frequently paused their work to blow on freezing hands. A woman stood at the centre of the open space, gesturing to the hall, talking with two older men in wide-brimmed hats and russet cloaks. She wore a green dress with a shawl about her shoulders, and she was like bright moonlight amongst the winter browns and greys all about her.

Warmth spread through Arthur's chest, and his breath caught in his throat. He slipped back into the shadows, just enjoying watching the love of his life. The cold sun caught her copper-gold hair, which she wore loose. Guinevere turned and her hair flicked to one side, revealing her long, slender neck. She was stunningly beautiful, and Arthur laughed silently to himself at how, even now, Guinevere took his breath away.

'Lord Arthur!' said a thick, honeyed voice, and everybody in the space turned to look. Arthur dropped his hand to the sceptre at his belt and dragged his thumb over the smooth, round head to calm himself. Bishop Serwan waddled towards him, jowls trembling, plump hands lifting the hem of his skirts to keep them out of the mud.

'Bishop,' Arthur said, unable to keep the frustration from his voice. It had been a moment to savour after so long away from home, a moment where a man gazed upon his wife and realised how lucky he was that such a woman rewarded him with her love. A moment spoiled now, snatched away like a leaf in the wind.

'Welcome to Camelot.'

'You have been busy.'

Arthur spied another building across Serwan's shoulder, this one completed. A timber structure almost as large as the main hall, and at its gable a cross stood high and proud, casting a long shadow across the fortifications.

'Quite.' Serwan turned to look upon his church like a proud father might gaze upon his newborn son. 'A house of God in Dumnonia. Praise be. The Lady Guinevere is a most gracious benefactor, and she truly walks in the light of the Lord.'

Those words, and the sight of that cross, sent a shiver down Arthur's spine, and he wondered how Merlin might react to see the nailed god's symbol at the heart of a fortress built by the old folk in the days when the gods roamed Britain. Guinevere caught Arthur's eye across the open space, and Arthur forgot his anger that Serwan seemed to have exerted yet more influence over his wife.

'Arthur!' Guinevere called, and clapped her hands. Arthur hurried to her, unable to hide his limp, or the grin from his face.

'When I left, this was but a dream,' Arthur said, taking her into his arms and pulling her into a tight embrace.

'And now we have a home. Our home. Camelot,' Guinevere said. She kissed him hard on the lips, and ran her long, lithe fingers through his hair. Then she pulled away and wrinkled her nose. 'You stink of horse, leather and wet dog.'

'The road south was long, and we had much trouble in the north.'

'I can see that.' Guinevere traced a finger across the long scar across his forehead, and her eyes flicked down to his leg. 'I must show you all that we have done, then you need to bathe. It's good to have you home. You look tired.'

'I am tired, and it's good to be home.'

Guinevere led Arthur into the newly built hall, and his muddy boots crunched on golden wood shavings. The smell of freshly cut wood filled Arthur's nose, and as he walked into the open gate, he marvelled at the wide-open space, where carpenters worked on feasting benches and carved intricate whorls and patterns on the roof-supporting pillars.

'Look at the back.' Guinevere pointed to the rear of the hall, and was so excited that she skipped once as she walked.

'I don't believe it,' Arthur replied. At the hall's rear, an old man with a bald head and arms covered in coarse black hair worked at a perfectly round table. It was large enough for twelve men to sit around, and the craftsmen had chiselled into it the sigils of each of Britain's great kingdoms, the dragon of Dumnonia, the bear of Rheged, the cross of Elmet, the stag of Gododdin and more. Arthur placed his hand on the wood and

found it warm and smooth to the touch. 'All can sit as equals.'
He closed his eyes and imagined the war leaders of every
kingdom sat around that round table, each of them united as
one nation against the Saxon threat. Arthur indulged himself,
and daydreamed of Bors, Kai, Idnerth, Einion, talking together
with him, discussing battle plans and strategy not just for the
coming summer, but for years to come, instead of fighting year
by year in reaction to Saxon movements. Arthur dreamed of
building a proper plan to defeat them, piece by piece, picking
off their weak leaders with an eventual glorious return of
Lloegyr to the Britons.

'Are you pleased?'

'It is magnificent.'

Guinevere clasped his hand and pulled him towards a small
oak door. 'One more surprise.' Through the door lay a long
corridor lit by small square holes in the high walls, so that light
shone through in shafts where dust motes danced. Doors lay on
either side of the corridor. 'These are quarters for our stewards,
and larders for food. Of course, there will be sleeping platforms
in the main hall for the warriors and such. But this room is
ours.' She opened the last door on the left, and Arthur stepped
into a large room with a wide, timber-framed bed, with a deep
straw mattress strewn with soft furs and woven blankets. A
hearth fire lay at the far corner, beside it tables with blue and
green glass cups and jars, and four white Roman pillars holding
up roof beams beneath the bright gold thatch. Open window
shutters let in light and rugs woven in bright colours covered
the floor.

'You have indeed been busy.'

'I have. This will be our home. A wonderful place of Roman
stone, filled with beautiful things where beautiful things can
happen.'

He held Guinevere, and they shared a long, loving kiss.

'I must wash and change.' Arthur pulled away from her, remembering his warrior's smell and the dirt of his clothes and armour.

Guinevere helped him take off his cloak, which had turned more grey than black after so long in the rain, snow and ice. She helped take off his heavy sword belt and to pull the chain-mail coat over his head. Guinevere called for a steward to fetch a bowl of water and a cloth, and Arthur stripped off his jerkin. He washed himself and Guinevere helped. He took off his trews, and she gasped at the jagged red scar upon Arthur's thigh. Her gentle fingers traced the wound, and then touched the other scars across his belly, chest, back, arms and face.

'Look at what they do to you,' she whispered. 'So much pain. I wonder, do the men in the fields and the women with their distaffs know how you suffer for their safety? Do they consider the blood, the fear, and the death our warriors give to keep them from Saxon slave shackles?'

'It does not matter if they know. What matters is that we do our duty.'

They held each other again and, as Arthur pulled away, he noticed a small silver crucifix hanging from a chain at Guinevere's neck. He pulled it out with his finger and Guinevere jerked away from him, tucking the Christian talisman behind her dress.

'Bishop Serwan has been kind to me. His god will bless us with a baby. With an heir.'

'He is certain of that?'

'He is.'

'Is that why his new church is as large as our hall?'

'What?' Guinevere scowled at him. 'What does that matter? He asked, and I agreed. The priests have such precious treasures. Gold, silver, bronze and ivory. God blesses them with riches because they are holy and heed God's word. Serwan gave me the blue and green glass cups you see there on the tables.'

'Where are the standing stone, the totems and places for folk to leave offerings to the old gods?'

'What have the old gods done for us but curse our land with endless war? When have they provided us with rich and rare gifts?'

There was fire in her eyes, so Arthur chose not to mention that he was only Pendragon because Merlin wished it and had given him the gift of Excalibur. 'It is not their god who provides the priests with gifts, it's the believers they take them from. Priests and bishops take from their worshippers and call it the will of God. Is Serwan's church the only price he and his god demands in return for our child?'

'Another small thing.' She waved her hand, as it was insignificant.

'Go on.' Arthur pulled on a light, fresh hemp shirt.

'We must both acknowledge God for him to bless us.'

'Acknowledge?'

'Oh, Arthur, don't play these silly games. You must pray as I pray. We must ask the Christian god for favour. Bishop Serwan will bless us, and Jesus will grant us his favour.'

'Jesus is God?'

'No. He is the son of God, and of the Blessed Virgin Mary.'

Arthur shook his head and took a drink of cool ale, not wishing to challenge Guinevere on the Christian mysteries, for she plainly was in no mood to be questioned. She was desperate for a child, and so was Arthur, and all he wanted was for her to be happy. 'Merlin will come soon. He will help, and you will be with child before we know it.'

'Merlin? Where is Merlin? How can he help us when he is not here?'

'I was with him, in the north.'

'And you asked him about our child?'

Arthur turned away. 'He will come.'

'Well, if he does not come before spring, you will be gone again, off marching and fighting until the leaves wither and turn brown, and I will be alone and childless. If Merlin does not miraculously appear before we celebrate Imbolc, then will you come with me to Bishop Serwan?'

Arthur tried to embrace Guinevere, but she pulled away.

'This is important, Arthur. If Merlin is not here by Imbolc, will you come to Bishop Serwan with me?'

'I will.' Arthur cared nothing for the fat bishop, but he wanted to give Guinevere happiness. He had dreamed of her for months in the damp, cold north. So he said what she wanted to hear and thought no more of how the church and the bishop went against everything Merlin believed in and how the high cross would anger the druid. Guinevere was happy, and for now that was enough.

14

Arthur had never been happier than in those weeks after his arrival at Camelot. He spent glorious days with Guinevere, planning and directing building works, their minds and energy locked together in the single pursuit of making Camelot beautiful and formidable. Arthur talked with carpenters, stonemasons, potters and labourers and even took a turn with adze and chisel. He enjoyed talking to experts in their professions about how to lay posts so that the wood would not rot, how to mix, cut and lay thatch, and of the various other intricacies particular to their crafts. All Arthur knew was the spear and how to march a force of men over high ground, how to traverse a river, travel through woodland, to kill, maim and destroy, and so he marvelled at men and women who used their skills to produce things, to build and provide a valuable service to their community. He walked the high earth mounds with Lancelot, and they spoke of the palisade and fighting platform, of how to construct the stairs leading from the fortress' internal space to the high defensive walls. Lancelot had decided not to use the highest earth ridge of the old earthen works as the key defensive position, it was too high and to build the platform for men to stand and fight upon would require a mound behind it, and that mound would be a monstrous undertaking. So, he used one of the lower ancient earth rings for the palisade, and the higher rings would provide elevated positions from which archers and spearmen could rain death down upon any attacking force from above.

Guinevere revelled in her responsibility, and her clear vision of Camelot's design continued to unfold within the old earthworks. Two weeks after Arthur's arrival, the hall was almost finished and its thatch completed so that a hearth fire could burn and its smoke escape through a round hole cut into the new roof. Guinevere wanted to hold the Imbolc festival in the great hall, the feast which lay between the winter solstice and the spring festival of Ostara. Bishop Serwan fussed and huffed at the prospect of what he called a pagan ritual as the hall's first celebration and asked instead that he consecrate the place with a sermon and a morning of prayer. Arthur refused and Serwan complained to Guinevere. He also complained to her of Ethne and the Picts, who spat at him every time he crossed their path. Guinevere took a dislike to Arthur's all-female bodyguard, calling them crude, ugly and coarse. She was right about all of those things, of course, but Arthur had grown to like the Picts' stoic severity and knew they would come in useful in the wars to come and so he bore Guinevere's complaints and said nothing to his loyal *targaid*.

Arthur's scouts ranged north and east on their fast ponies in search of news of the Saxons, but no reports came back to Camelot, and so Arthur indulged himself in the construction works and spent long nights with his beloved Guinevere. Plans for the Imbolc festival gathered pace, and on the morning of the festival, shepherds brought sheep heavy with lambs into the stronghold and people smiled and clapped to see the animals' full udders, for it was a sure sign of the sun's rebirth, longer days and hopes for bountiful harvests. Guinevere had stewards fill the hall with feasting benches and hundreds of candles adorned the benches and lintels.

The Imbolc festival was a raucous affair of too much mead and ale, with platters of boar, venison, duck, smoked fish, steamed vegetables, honey and freshly baked bread. Arthur spoke to the crowd and congratulated Guinevere and Lancelot for their achievements and hoped the fortress would be defendable before summer. They ate and drank, and the many candles shimmered and cast the hall in a warm glow to symbolise the return of the sun's warmth, and its light spreading later into the dark evenings.

Arthur sat on a high platform, with a throne Guinevere had commissioned to be carved from a single piece of oak. Guinevere sat on his left and Lancelot on his right. The feast was in full flow, with folk laughing and singing, red-faced and full of food and drink, when the newly hung doors crashed open and a bedraggled figure stumbled into the celebration. People inside the hall gasped as a thin man staggered on unsteady legs, propped up by two of Arthur's Picts. A hush fell over the room, and Arthur beckoned the man forward. He struggled, feet dragging in the floor rushes, mouth opening and closing and emitting only a throaty rasp. Arthur rose from his throne and hurried down to meet the man. Mud spattered his clothes, and his pale face bore a grave expression.

'He rode in on a lathered pony,' said Caoimhe, one of Ethne's warriors. 'He says he has news of the utmost importance.'

'I come from the north, lord,' said the scout, his voice a hoarse croak. 'I have ridden hard for more than a week.'

'Sit.' Arthur helped the scout to a quiet corner of the hall where he sat down and drank thirstily from a beaker of ale. Noise resumed around the hall as people returned to the food and chatter. Necks creaked and ears pricked to listen to what the man had striven so hard to bring to Arthur's ear. 'What news?'

'Ida of Bernicia died in the winter, lord. His son Theodric is now king. He has allied with Clappa of Deira and, over winter, they seized what was Cwichelm's kingdom of Lyndsey.'

'Then they now rule the entire east coast from Gododdin's borders to the fens in the south-east.'

'Yes, lord. Kadvuz himself bade me come to you. You killed King Cwichelm in the battle of the Dubglas, but his warriors rage and have willingly joined Clappa and Theodric. Kadvuz fears that Theodric and Clappa will march on Elmet before spring. Each of them rules a vast kingdom now, larger than Dumnonia.'

'Does Kadvuz suspect this, or know it for sure?'

'He says he has seen their warriors mustering. That the winter was mild across the narrow sea, and that already ships arrive with fresh, wild bands of Saxon, Angles and Jutish warriors. Theodric and his warrior queen ride white horses throughout the land, rallying their hordes to war. Despite frozen roads and dwindling winter food supplies, Kadvuz says war drums are already beating, and we must prepare because Theodric and Clappa can muster thousands of warriors. They ride across their kingdoms, rousing men with talks of conquest and plunder. Bernicia, Deira and Lyndsey are aflame with battle-lust. Forges burn bright with spearheads and men cut fresh ash for their spears.'

'Warrior queen.' Arthur spoke wistfully, his gaze locked on a flickering candle flame. Lunete was Theodric's wife, and now queen. Fierce, wild Lunete. 'Why does Kadvuz believe they march for Elmet?'

The scout shrugged. 'Who can say how the druids know such things, lord?'

'What news of Merlin?'

'None, lord. I saw only Kadvuz, and he was hard-pressed. Pursued by a band of Saxons and three of their own mad *seidr* men.'

'You have done well.' Arthur dug a hand into the leather pouch at his belt and produced two small, rusted coins bearing the hook-nosed face of a forgotten Roman emperor. Arthur pressed the coins into the scout's hand. 'Rest now.'

'War?' asked Lancelot. He wore a green wool jerkin beneath a green cloak, and his dark hair tied back from his broad, handsome face.

'War. The Saxons muster. Theodric and Clappa.'

'We could have killed them both at the Dubglas.'

'And perhaps we should have. We saved their lives to spare Lunete's.'

'But now your sister leads them as though she were a Saxon herself. She is our enemy now, just as much as they are.'

'The warp and weft of our lives is cruel and unexpected. Did you expect to be a warrior of Britain when you were a boy across the sea?'

'No, I did not. Fate brought me here. Just like fate took your sister to the Saxons.'

Arthur glanced at Guinevere, her shining hair and full lips glistening in the candlelight. He needed more time with her, just a few more weeks to play at being a husband, a little longer for the baby they both longed for to quicken inside of her.

'Call the banners,' Arthur said. Without thinking, he had drawn Ida's stone sceptre and gripped it hard in his right hand. 'Call them all. Every kingdom is to send their warriors and march here, to Dumnonia with all haste.'

'It will take Gododdin and Lothian weeks to muster their forces, gather supplies and reach Dumnonia.'

'What of it? We must do it now if we wish to be ready to fight in spring.'

'Why not gather our forces, those of Kernow, Gwynedd and Powys, and meet King Gwallog and the northern war bands at Elmet?'

'We meet here.' Arthur spoke more harshly than he intended, and he slid the sceptre back into his belt. 'What if the Saxons do not intend to march on Elmet? What if their target is Gododdin, or Dumnonia? We muster here, and then we march to meet the threat as one army.'

'Very well.'

'Call Dewi and have the black cloaks muster here at Camelot. Send out messengers to every farm and village to provide their render early. We need food and ale to feed thousands of warriors.'

'What shall we do whilst we wait for the army of Britain to arrive?'

I will rest with my wife, Arthur thought, and the corners of his mouth turned down with guilt. 'We shall prepare. You will stay at Camelot this year, my friend. Protect Guinevere and hold this fortress if the Saxons attack.'

'Are you sure?'

'I am. We will miss your sword, but if I am to march north, I must know my family and Prince Madoc are safe should Aelle or Eormenric stir themselves from the south. From here, you can protect the prince, who shall remain in Durnovaria along with Lot's son. To get to Prince Madoc, the Saxons must get past you. Who better to protect all I hold dear than the man who has saved my life, a man I can trust with everything I love in this world?'

* * *

Arthur woke the next morning with a sore head, and with Guinevere sat up in bed beside him, hair tousled and her bright eyes staring at him. Sunlight shone into their chamber through gaps in the wooden shutters and he groaned and closed his eyes.

'Imbolc is over,' she whispered, with one hand on her belly. 'Merlin has not come.'

Arthur sighed and reached for a drink, which he could not find. 'Merlin will come,' he said, voice croaky from too much mead.

'So you keep saying. We agreed that if he did not arrive by Imbolc, that you would allow Bishop Serwan to bless us, to help us, and listen to him speak of the Lord.'

Arthur groaned and ran his hands through his hair. 'Can it wait, my love?'

'It cannot!' Guinevere stood up from the bed and threw a fur cloak about her shoulders. With crossed arms, she went to stand by the window. 'You have called the banners to war, and soon you will be gone. I am still without child.'

'It will take weeks for the army to gather. We have time.'

'We do not! Do not be so dismissive. You men and your swords, spears and talk of glory. Did you ever, for one moment, consider what might happen to me if you die in battle, Arthur Pendragon? Last night when you drank and sang your war songs with the warriors and made boasts about how many

Saxons you shall all kill, did any of you mutton-headed fools give a care for your wives and children? Whilst you are off burnishing your reputations bright like gold, camping, marching and fighting with your friends and brothers in arms. Did you ever consider what becomes of Guinevere if the great Arthur falls in battle?

'I shall tell you what happens to me if you die. You are the steward of Dumnonia and the high king of Britain. But you have no kingdom. We have Camelot because you made it so, but where does it say that these lands belong to Arthur? Where are the boundaries of your lands? Which farms and villages will render up one tenth of their surplus to Arthur? Which forests, rivers, hedges, dykes and ditches form the edges of the lands owned by Arthur, which he shall bequeath to Guinevere should he tragically fall in battle? The very day news of your death arrives, the great lords of Dumnonia will appoint another steward to protect Prince Madoc and his kingdom. Perhaps a wealthy landowner will take on the role, perhaps Lancelot? Some ambitious man will assume that title gladly, and rule Dumnonia like a king until little Madoc is old enough to become king, or until some unfortunate accident or illness prevents him from living that long. Then, the steward can assume the throne. Who shall be Pendragon when Arthur falls? Marc of Kernow? Kai of Rheged? Gwallog of Elmet? One of them will fly your precious dragon banner and carry that silly bundle of rods about the country whilst men bow and scrape at his feet.

'What of Guinevere then? You have no heir. No legacy. Perhaps the new steward will force me to be his wife, or the new Pendragon? Perhaps I shall be married off to Morholt of Demetia or another fat, brutal warlord as part of a peace treaty. Perhaps they will send me back to my father in Cameliard to live out my days as a widow? They will pick at your land and pluck it away like feathers from a chicken for the pot. That, my dear husband, will be my fate. So, no, listening to Bishop Serwan cannot wait.'

'Very well. We shall see the bishop today.'

Guinevere was right, of course, and Arthur had not considered her delicate position. However, bearing an heir would secure her future. She would become the dowager queen and raise her son to the title of Pendragon and live a life of honour and prestige. She and the baby would need protecting, for their survival might depend on Lancelot or Kai protecting her and the child from greedy and ambitious men, but Guinevere would at least have a chance. So, Arthur supposed, the least he could do was listen to the fat bishop's musings about his one god and hope that Guinevere soon became heavy with child.

That afternoon Arthur sat in Bishop Serwan's church, and refused to kneel, as Serwan preached for almost an hour about miserable saints, how Jesus died for the sins of men, and how living in the Lord's light was the path to heaven. He read in Roman Latin which Arthur did not understand, and all the while Guinevere listened with her hands clasped in front of her chest and a solemn look upon her long face. Arthur's mind wandered, Serwan's sombre voice becoming an echo as Arthur pondered the problems of supply, strategy and trying to guess what dreams of blood and conquest Theodric and Clappa had crafted over the snow-filled winter.

When the sermon was over, Serwan made the sign of the cross and splashed Arthur with holy water, and in truth Arthur had not found the mass so bad. It had been a private affair, far from the judgemental, prying eyes of Camelot, and there had been no sacrifices or augury of the war to come. Just words, Roman babble, and a sprinkle of river water prayed over by a fat bishop. The nailed god was just another god to be respected and feared. There were many gods, so many that Arthur had lost count, Manawydan, Cernunnos, Arawn, Neit, Andraste, Rhiannon, Lleu Llaw, Maponos and so many more. So Arthur humoured Guinevere because her happiness warmed his heart. After that day he visited the church every morning, and after two weeks even began to hear sense in Serwan's tales of boys with slings, dreams, angels, floods and emperors incurring the wrath of God in a sea of sand.

In those weeks Dewi arrived with the black cloaks, each man furnished with a fresh night-black cloak, their spears set with fresh ash shafts and their leather breastplates clean and ready for war. They drilled shield-wall manoeuvres in the fields beyond Camelot, and the Pictish *targaid* joined in, using the flanks to hurl thumb-sized stones with incredible power from their whirring slings. Prince Tristan of Kernow arrived with three hundred spearmen from his father's small kingdom, and then grim Einion, champion of Powys, arrived with five hundred spearmen. Many of Einion's men bore the nailed god's cross painted upon their shields, and when Arthur asked the champion if King Brochvael the Fanged of Powys had renounced the old gods, he shrugged.

'He let the priests in because they gave him gold,' he said in his cracked, gravel-hard voice, and his eyes flickered to the church within Camelot and its high cross. 'Now they are everywhere, like crows, pecking and worrying at the common folk like a plague. I don't care which god they pray to as long as they fight like bastards.'

Which, Arthur supposed, was true enough. Bishop Serwan and his priests capered with delight to see warriors bearing the symbol of God. Men packed into Serwan's church every day to hear the word of God shouted from the altar, and Serwan flounced about Camelot as though he were a great lord. Green buds showed on reaching boughs. Swallows and swifts soared above Camelot's increasingly high, stout palisade, and Arthur prepared for war. On a warm day where men wore straw hats to keep the sun off their faces, Arthur went to church hand in hand with Guinevere. His bad leg felt stronger after weeks of rest, and he walked without a limp to the first pew and took his place as people filed in behind him. Men coughed and shifted, making space for yet more warriors, women and children to cram into Serwan's new church, which still smelled of freshly cut pine. Common folk came, as did those warriors of Powys who now worshipped the nailed god, and the Dumnonians Serwan had converted. Serwan bade the congregation pray in silence, and every head bowed to whisper their prayers to the Christian god.

Arthur bowed his own head and asked the nailed god to reward Guinevere with a baby, and no sooner had the thought entered his head than a loud barking startled him along with every other person in the church. Another dog barked, growling, snarling, and Arthur turned to see two great wolfhounds standing in the doorway, teeth bared, snapping and barking at every person in the church. A tall man appeared in the doorway, the sun behind him so that he stood in silhouette. He stepped forward, banging a long black staff upon the wooden floor, dogs stalking beside him, snapping their teeth and snarling so that the people in the church cowered and shuffled away from their anger. Arthur turned, and his stomach churned with shame. Kadvuz the druid had found him praying to the Christian god. He felt like a boy caught scrumping apples from a neighbour's orchard, or stealing bread from a baker's oven.

Kadvuz walked barefoot through the silent church, his wrinkled face drawn tight in horror, staring down his long nose at every person he passed, his cruel slash of a mouth twisted in anger. Every soul in the church dropped to their knees. One woman howled as though in pain and an old man wept and called out to the old gods to forgive him. The druid's presence imbued the congregation with fear, fear of their merciless and vindictive gods, their respect for the druids hammered into them down the generations since Britain first emerged from the primordial mists. Kadvuz wore a black tunic; mud and travel stains had turned the hem of his white cloak brown. He came to a halt and his eyes rested upon Arthur, and Kadvuz bent over as though punched in the gut. Arthur stood, guilt washing over him like a wave.

'This is a house of God!' Bishop Serwan shouted, emboldened by his god, his church and the perceived protection of its high cross.

Kadvuz closed his eyes and whistled once. His dogs bounded forward, snapping and snarling, hurtling towards the bishop, who cried out in fear and ran from the church, out through a back door like a frightened hare.

'Elmet is under siege,' Kadvuz said in a slow, booming voice, which contained none of his usual curt anger but was instead tinged with sadness, like the voice of an old man who is confused and cannot find his boots. Kadvuz stared at Arthur, and a single fat tear rolled down the druid's face. 'Elmet fights for its life, and you pray to the nailed god whilst its people suffer and die. You are the Pendragon, wielder of Excalibur that was once called Caledfwlch. Merlin trusted you, I trusted you.' Kadvuz swallowed and the lump in his thin throat bounced like a bucket dipping into a well. He gazed around at the gold plates and silver crosses on Serwan's altar. Kadvuz seemed to shrink, his back bent, and he leaned on his staff, looking suddenly like a frail grandfather rather than one of the most powerful and knowledgeable men in Britain. Arthur leapt from his pew and stood before the druid with his hands held out, half in supplication, and half wanting to help Kadvuz stand as tall and strong as he always had.

'Lord Kadvuz,' he said, 'come to the hall and rest.'

'Rest? Did you not hear what I said? Elmet is under siege by thousands of Saxon warriors. Theodric and Clappa have roused the entirety of eastern Lloegyr against King Gwallog. They have emptied their hole-in-the-ground hovels, they whet their spears and ask Woden and Thuror to bring them victory over our people and our very souls. Their war drums shake the very ground. They have spears, bows, war dogs and hate for our people and our ways. Gwallog took to the nailed god many years ago. He abandoned our gods and look what good it does him. Britons are dying, our people, your people. There is no time to rest.' Kadvuz roused himself and stood tall once again, age slipping from him, fierce eyes gouging into Arthur's own, his cruel mouth sneering. 'Look to the gods, Pendragon, look to the sword. Britain needs you.'

'Please, Lord Kadvuz, let us talk of these matters... elsewhere.'

Kadvuz grumbled, but he followed Arthur out of the church and across to the hall. Once inside, the druid accepted a wooden mug of ale and a plate of bread and cheese. His two wolfhounds followed and waited outside, where they leapt and growled playfully with Cavall.

'I was not worshipping their god,' Arthur said, sitting on a feasting bench facing the stern druid. 'I was...' He waited for Kadvuz to interrupt, to help him with the words he could not find, but the druid ate his cheese and never took his eyes from Arthur's. '...listening. Guinevere hopes for a child, and the Christian bishop promised that his god could help.'

'Help?'

'Help quicken a child within her.'

'Children? You speak of children?'

'That was why I was in the church. For Guinevere. I am trying to explain.' Kadvuz looked at Arthur as if he had lost his wits, and Arthur could not summon the words to continue with his excuses.

'You do not need to explain. I am not a fool. I saw you with my own eyes. I never thought to see such an insult to our ways in all my long years walking this land. Never, not since that cursed Roman dog Gaius Suetonius Paulinus marched his legions to our ancient sanctuary at Ynys Môn and destroyed our temple, not since he slaughtered most of our druids, have the gods faced such a sacrilege. We lost so much of our ancient knowledge on that fateful day long ago, the greatest of us, our links with the gods trampled beneath Roman sandals. Druids are forbidden from writing anything down; we pass down all our experience, knowledge of the land, the gods, and our history from mouth to mind, druid to druid. The Romans' destruction of our island temple and the killing of almost all the druids nearly annihilated the order. We lost so much. We stand on a similar precipice now. There are two battles raging across Britain, Pendragon, the battle for the land and a battle fought between our gods, the nailed god and the Saxon gods, a battle for our souls. Poor Merlin. Thank the gods it was I who witnessed today's horror and not him. Merlin would never believe it could be so. Our Pendragon bows to a new god, a god that is intolerant of all others. I have walked for an entire week to bring you news of Elmet's plight, and this is the welcome I find in Dumnonia. Have you abandoned us? Have you forsaken your ancestors?'

'I have not. I am as steadfast as ever. Look at the scars on my body. Look at me! There is no other man in Britain who has bled so much for our cause. Can there be any other soldier who has slain as many Saxons as I? Who has recovered as much of Lloegyr as I?'

'The fate of our people, and the fate of our gods, go hand in hand, Arthur Pendragon. You cannot have one if the other dies.'

'Can Elmet hold?' Arthur asked, desperate to hide his shame and change the subject. How could he argue his support for the old gods when Kadvuz had seen him in the nailed god's church?

'Not for long. Loidis and then Elmet must surely fall unless you march immediately. Gwallog appeals to you, Pendragon, his people await your armies. They stand upon Loidis' ramparts and search the hills, hoping to see the glint of your spears marching to save them. Many of them, men who forsook our gods for the Christian god, now cry out to Neit and Adraste for aid. I have been in the east. Ida the conqueror died, he who was one of the first Saxons to bring men and hate across the narrow sea. Ida's son laid his body in a longship and sent him out into the waves with his death ship aflame. Warriors lamented and a great wail went up as his body sank into the watery depths which once bore him to our land. Ida was old. You defeated and wounded him terribly and he never recovered his thirst for war. Theodric is young, king now, and like all young men, his great desire is to outshine his father's achievements.

'Ida was content to sit by his fire on Dun Guaroy's high crag and listen to his skalds tell tales of his former glories, and of the *Wealas* he had slain in battle. The day after Ida's death, Theodric began the war song. He gathers battle-chiefs about him, encourages champions from their harsh homeland to make the dangerous journey across the narrow sea. He promises them land, silver, glory and women and they will come, for such things stir the hearts of warriors like a fire. Some ships have already landed! War is upon us in the east, and it will come to Loidis first.

'We are the *Wealas,* their Saxon word for slave, and they wish to enslave us all and make our land theirs. Clappa has joined forces with Theodric and pledged his warriors to join this year's campaign. Clappa is old. You saw him at the Dubglas and your man had a blade at his throat and let him live. You showed mercy, then the Saxons show none. Clappa came to our shores with nothing and won for himself a kingdom. He killed and slaughtered, enslaved, burned, raped and cast our people out until he became king of Deira. I went to Deira, walked amongst his people in disguise, and his warriors speak of revenge against us for that defeat beside the River Dubglas. Clappa's last battle ended in humiliation and the old wolf wants to remedy that, for his reputation to burn as bright as it once did. So he binds his champions and his hordes to Theodric's. Thousands of them will march! The combined forces of Bernicia, Deira and Lyndsey aligned and bent on destroying Elmet and then the rest of Britain. How many of his Roman-clad warriors can Gwallog muster? Idnerth is among the greatest warriors in Britain. But they do not have enough warriors. Not nearly enough. He needs you, and he needs the Pendragon to gather every warrior in Britain to come to his aid.

'I had hoped to find you already marching, almost within Elmet's boundaries. Yet here you are. The nailed god keeps you here. He has your queen weakened and his bishop creeps into her ear like an insect. They have bound you to this Camelot you are building when you should be at war. Wake up! It is time to fight! We must meet the eastern threat quickly and brutally. Do you think Aelle and Eormenric in the south will spend another summer at peace? Do their warriors not yearn for rings and reputation? What will become of us if the southern Saxons attack at the same time as Theodric and Clappa? Think on it, Arthur, and how the nailed god makes you weak.'

Arthur could summon no response. He thought of arguing, of asking how it was in the Christian god's interest for the Saxons to defeat the Britons, for Arthur had never met a Saxon Christian. But much of what Kadvuz said was true, and the threat to Elmet and to the entire land was real. So Arthur just nodded his understanding.

Kadvuz rose and wiped the crumbs from his beard. 'I shall go north and hasten the muster from your northern kingdoms. Heed my words.' With that, he turned on his heel and left, leaving Arthur alone. Arthur could hear Saxon war drums thumping in his mind, smell the blood, almost see the men clad in fur and iron with their axes and their seaxes creeping across Lloegyr's hills to descend upon Elmet's borders like wolves.

Camelot, Guinevere, the child he craved, would all have to wait. War had come, armies marched from the east, and it was time for Excalibur. The weeks he had spent with Guinevere, building their dream of Camelot, had been some of the best of his life, but it was time to put aside Arthur the man of peace, to don his heavy chain-mail armour, black cloak and his closed-faced helmet with its black raven feathers. Britain needed its *dux bellorum*, and so two days later he marched out of Camelot at the head of his black cloaks, the spearmen of Dumnonia, and the men of Kernow and Powys.

Lancelot stayed to finish the fortress and guard Guinevere, and the high queen wept and would not speak to Arthur. She was angry, not because Arthur marched to war, for that was inevitable. Guinevere was angry because after Kadvuz's unexpected visit, Arthur had torn down Bishop Serwan's cross and changed the church into a barracks where Lancelot could house the two hundred spearmen left to guard Dumnonia's frontier. It was time for war, and the Christian god was no war god. It was time for the war god Neit, for swords, not prayers. So Arthur left Guinevere and hoped that the baby they both desired was growing within her.

15

Smoke filled the northern hills, smearing the horizon grey like a wolf pelt draped over its undulating ridges. Arthur rode Llamrei ahead of the army. Tristan and Einion also rode, whilst Dewi marched with the three hundred black cloaks. Ethne marched just behind Arthur with the *targaid*. The three hundred warriors of Kernow followed, then came five hundred Dumnonian spearmen, and the five hundred spearmen of Powys took up the rearguard. Arthur pushed them hard, reaching the borders of Elmet in two weeks, with enough supplies carried in wagons to keep Arthur's one and a half thousand men fed and in ale throughout the long days' marching. The first refugees appeared as Arthur reached the banks of the River Calder. Old men leading thin donkeys, weeping women with dirty-faced children, families with ashen faces and torn clothing trudged along the river's meander and told tales of Saxon war bands pillaging and burning across Elmet. They wept and tore their hair, distraught about cousins and aunties taken as slaves, of entire villages put to the seax, and of wild-faced men from across the narrow sea who showed neither pity nor mercy as they slaughtered women and children by the dozen.

Arthur had his men feed those desperate people from the army's provisions, and their tales of blood, rape and enslavement steeled the warriors for the fight to come. The army followed the river for another day, and Arthur's scouts rode ahead, returning to the column with ash-darkened faces and reports of horror at Elmet's great town of Loidis. By noon that day Arthur led his men into Loidis' valley and from a distance the warriors marvelled at hundreds of large crucifixes which lined the road into King Gwallog's stronghold. It was only when the army drew closer and Llamrei began to snort and tremble with fear that Arthur noticed corpses hung from each of those crosses. Men nailed by their hands and ankles, dead men with wounds in their bellies, one for each cross, set twenty paces apart. Men who had once been warriors and were now hung up by rusty nails, pale, naked corpses, stinking of rot with their eyes pecked out by crows.

A warrior behind Arthur vomited upon the road, and others cried out in terror. Arthur followed the road of horror, unable to look upon the corpses nailed on each side of the path, until he came to the smoking ashes of Loidis itself, the city he had once fought so hard to defend. All that remained were the ancient Roman walls, scarred and darkened by flame, and then black, crumpled timbers lying like a great, smoking skeleton within the old stone. Bodies cowered beneath the timbers, shrunken by fire so that they seemed as small as little children. Arthur found King Gwallog by the gate, bald, his body as white as a child's teeth, nailed to a cross with his insides hanging out. Arthur fought to hold back cries of rage and sorrow. Gwallog, who had supported Arthur in the early days, had sent Idnerth, his Primus Pilum, to fight beside Arthur in his first great battle at the River Glein when Arthur had struggled to find support from any of the great kingdoms. Gwallog had been a kind man, clever and respected by all who knew him. A proud man, honourable: hung up, nailed, stripped, left in dishonour by an enemy who despised him.

'Where are they?' Arthur said through gritted teeth.

'The survivors, lord?' Dewi replied. 'In the hills to the west, we believe.'

'The Saxons.'

'Our scouts seek them. They have retreated from the fires here, back to the east, where they have made camp. But we don't know for sure. The moors and mountains are large, so the scouts follow their trail and will return with news when they have it.'

'Get him down. Get them all down. They are Christians, so have the men bury them in their proper way.'

'Yes, lord.'

Arthur dismounted and handed Llamrei's reins to a young warrior. He walked alone around the walls, hand over his nose to keep out the stench of fire, and the hint of burned flesh on the wind, the last remnants of the innocents who had died and burned within the old city. Arthur remembered the city as it was, the cobbled streets and tall buildings, some built by the Romans themselves, and other houses crudely fashioned from the rubble of Rome's fallen grandeur. Timber and thatch had propped up and supplemented what had fallen under the weight of time. Straight dressed stone once joined with roughly hewn oak and pine posts and roof lintels, and buildings once topped with ceramic tiles had held sodden thatch or crudely cut wooden tiles, which rotted and leaked water into the ancient buildings. Gwallog's hall had been a huge Roman building, its stone rising three times the height of a man, each slab cut perfectly straight and laid one on top of the other. No man knew how they had cut such heavy stone, where they had quarried it, how they had moved the impossibly heavy blocks and eventually laid them atop one another. Now it was nothing. Destroyed by savages.

Time passed as Arthur walked, memories coming to him as thick as day-old stew. He shuddered at what it took to be him, of how alone he was with the decisions that cost or saved so many lives. There was blood on his hands, screaming children inside his head, pressure, and the weight of an entire nation resting upon his shoulders. The fight to save Loidis from Ida's fury had been brutal, won in the end by Merlin's mastery of the sun and moon, and his ability to build long-forgotten Roman war machines. If he closed his eyes, Arthur could almost hear the sounds of that battle, the crunch of Idnerth's Roman soldiers' boots marching in time, their strange spears and fantastic armour. He stopped, gathering himself as the emotion caught in his throat. Had he lingered too long in Camelot? He had, Arthur knew. Guinevere was too beautiful, their bed too warm, happiness and love enough to keep a man bound and content.

Loidis had stood five days ago, Arthur was sure. If he had marched two weeks earlier, if he had set out when that scout had ridden to Camelot on a lathered pony with news of Saxon war drums, he could have saved Gwallog and his people. Arthur felt sick, swallowed a lump of his own vomit. How many people had suffered and died so that he could live his dream of Camelot, fatherhood and marriage? He had marched along Elmet's borders twice that winter and had avoided King Gwallog's hall. He had missed a chance to enjoy the old king's company, of drinking with Idnerth and reminiscing about old fights and brave deeds. Gwallog had supported Arthur when few others would, and the guilt of avoiding his hall so that he could hurry home to his wife tore at Arthur's insides like a starving wolf.

Arthur reached for the sceptre he always carried in his belt, and he lifted it, staring into the harsh stone face carved into its tip. Saxon faces in a Saxon sceptre. Arthur could not hold in his rage, and he threw his head back and roared at the sky. He tossed the sceptre over the ruins and into the smoking ash. He had cut that long, stone symbol of kingship from Ida along with the hand that held it. It had brought Arthur moments of clarity, helped him to think, but now he could not bear to look at it. The sceptre was a Saxon thing, chiselled and hammered Arthur knew not where across the sea, but he felt the thing was ancient, imbued with the experience and brutality of dead Saxon kings. Arthur tossed it away as a sacrifice, as an offering to the god of war. Arthur gave Neit that stone symbol of Saxon kingship, and with it went the softness and warmth of the weeks he had spent in Guinevere's arms.

There must be a reckoning, vengeance for the people of Loidis, for its crucified warriors, for Gwallog and Idnerth. Arthur could march his men eastwards in pursuit of Theodric and Clappa. But to attack them was to die. They had thousands of wild warriors, but Arthur had only the warriors of Dumnonia, his two hundred black cloaks, Kernow's men and the spearmen of Powys. It was not enough. Blind rage was not the path to victory, no matter how much Arthur wanted to carry Excalibur against the men who had laid waste to Loidis. Only a fool would charge into the hills in pursuit of Theodric and Clappa. The Saxons could retreat towards their homes in the east, slinking over hills and through dales, waiting to find ground that suited their larger numbers and then slaughter

Arthur and his men as they blundered through pastures and wild briar. The Saxons always marched in war bands, small groups of men in ships' crews who foraged and looted for themselves, but always in touch with their leaders, a war horn's call away and ready to join up with the army when it was time for battle. What would become of Britain if Arthur led his warriors into a fatal Saxon ambush? Arthur had to use his head; he had to be the Pendragon. Vengeance would come, Arthur would make sure of it, but victory could only come with clarity of thought.

The hills about Loidis stood still, without a scrap of wind or rain. Clouds sat low and fat in the sky, touching the smoke columns as if the souls of the dead passed to the afterlife between the pillars of ash and the soft white clouds. Arthur looked out on those hills and thought of how the Saxons would celebrate their victory, drinking stolen ale and sharing out stolen silver. His response had to be measured. He needed Kai's men of Rheged, Bors and the warriors of Gododdin, the men of Lothian and the other kingdoms to join his army. He could not lay siege to Dun Guaroy in Bernicia, or to the fortresses of Deira and Lyndsey. That war could take years. It had to be a battle, a one-off decisive victory so that he could crush Theodric and Clappa's dreams of conquest before Aelle and Eormenric stirred from their southern fastnesses. Arthur stepped closer to the walls and laid his hand upon the cold, perfectly dressed stone. *I am sorry, Gwallog, Idnerth, and every soul who lost their lives in this place. I will avenge you, I swear it, or may my soul burn and toil in the depths of Annwn for eternity.* Arthur stood straighter, adjusted his black cloak and the neck of his chain-mail coat. Hundreds of eyes looked up, warriors, hard men, spearmen who hungered for the blood of the men who had sacked Loidis. Warriors loyal to him surrounded Arthur, but he was alone. The decision of when and where to march, when to attack, where to camp, how to interpret scouts' reports, all sat with him. The burden was heavy. Lives depended on his decisions. Not just the lives of his war band, but the lives of every soul in Britain. Arthur bore that weight, just as he bore the weight of his armour and weapons, with a warrior's strength and a king's resolve.

Arthur sent riders north to find Kai, Bors and Lothian's levy. He instructed Dewi to make camp beside the river a half-day's march away from Loidis' ruins, far enough away from the smell of the dead for men to eat and sleep. Arthur worked into the night, helping the men take down each cross and bury the man upon it. It was grim, bloody work. They dug vast graves and lay the slain gently down beneath the cold earth. When it was done, a dozen mounds like monstrous molehills spoiled Loidis' fields. For once, there was no bishop or priest to say the right Christian words over the burials, so Arthur had one large cross set upon each mound and hoped that the nailed god would appreciate the gesture and admit the dead to his heaven of harpists and singing angels.

They dug Gwallog his own grave with its own cross, and Arthur stayed by it long after his men retreated to their marching camp. They carried the rest of the bloodstained crosses with them and broke them up for firewood. Campfire flames licked at the darkness like demons when Arthur finally left Gwallog alone. Arthur could not have been sorrier, could not have wished harder for Gwallog to have a death more deserving of a king, or a man whose grandfather had worn the purple of Rome. Arthur left his sorrow and regret there with Gwallog's grave, and he hardened his heart to the cold brutality of war, to the ruthless savagery he must lay down upon his Saxon enemies.

Arthur used that time of silence to ponder his problems, to guess where and when the Saxons might strike next, and how to exact the revenge he and his men craved like drowning men crave air. Dewi had men erect Arthur's leather tent, so that by the time Arthur joined the warriors the tent was up, furs laid down to sleep on, and a small fire ringed with stones crackled at the tent's opening. Arthur slipped off his cloak and chain mail and was about to lie down to sleep when Malegant appeared by the fire with a bowl of food.

'It isn't much, lord,' Malegant said. 'Just the last of the cheese and piece of hard bread, I'm afraid.'

Arthur thanked him and took the food. He sat down and stretched his bad leg out. The journey north had brought back the pain and stiffness, and Arthur kneaded the scar as he ate.

'Ale, lord?' Malegant held out a skin of ale.

'Sit. Share it with me,' Arthur said.

Malegant sat beside Arthur and warmed his hands on the flames. 'Ale's a bit sour.'

'Aye.' Arthur swilled ale around his mouth and swallowed it, and Malegant was right. They sat together for a while, just sitting, watching the fire and listening to the men talk in hushed voices across the camp. There were no songs that night, no boasting, no wrestling or games of knucklebones after the horror of Loidis. Arthur passed the ale to Malegant, and the Dumnonian took a drink.

'They say the harvest will be good this year.'

'Really?'

'So they say. Lot of rain in Dumnonia last year.'

'Do you have a farm?'

'Yes, lord. My family's land. Two days west of Durnovaria. Good land. My father still lives there.'

'Do you have a family, Malegant?' The small talk was

refreshing. They were just two men, any men. The need to talk of Loidis and Elmet's ruin was obvious, but painful. Simple talk took some of the burden away. It made Arthur feel normal for a time.

'I do, lord. A wife and three girls.'

'No sons?'

'Not yet. Perhaps next year, if my wife is willing and we are lucky.'

'Dumnonia is a fine place to raise a family.'

'We are fortunate.' Malegant stared out into the night for a moment, clearly thinking of the families just like his who had suffered and died at Loidis. 'Prince Tristan camps with his men?'

'He does. He prefers it that way.'

'Those Kernow men are a breed apart, perched as they are at the end of the world.'

'They fight well.'

'They do, lord.' Malegant yawned. 'I think I'll turn in now, sleep well.' He smiled, his two long braids swinging around his long face as he stood.

'Malegant?' Arthur called to him as the warrior walked away. He turned. 'Thank you.'

'Every man needs company, lord. What will we do? For the people of Loidis, I mean. What will we do to the men who did... what they did?'

Arthur drained the last of the ale and wiped the drips from his beard. 'Kill them, Malegant. We'll find them, kill as many as we can, and chase the rest back to their stolen lands. Then, one day, I shall march upon their fortresses, their stockades, their homes, and teach them what it means to fear.'

Malegant nodded slowly, clasped a fist to his chest and disappeared into the night, and Arthur lay down to a sleep filled with King Gwallog's dead face, and the lines of crucified people, eyes pecked out and terrible. But in his dream, they scorned Arthur, accused him of forsaking them. Of wasting time in Bishop Serwan's church when he should have marched to war.

Arthur woke early and washed the nightmare-induced sweat from his body in the River Aire. He let the cool water take the pain from his leg and he sat deep so that the water washed over his head and emerged cleansed. Hoofbeats woke the rest of Arthur's camp, and Dewi brought a boy with short hair and trembling hands before Arthur as he dressed on the riverbank.

'This boy comes from the north, lord,' Dewi said.

'What news?' Arthur replied.

'Your scout reached us last night, lord,' said the boy in a frightened voice. 'So my Lord Bors sent me to ride through the night and tell you he will reach Loidis by midday today.'

'Any news of Lothian and Rheged?'

'They all march together, lord. A great host, more than a thousand men.'

'Find the boy something to eat, Dewi. Then strike camp and have the black cloaks ready to march. I will lead them out to find the enemy. The rest of the army waits here for Bors and Kai.'

Arthur rode Llamrei ahead of his three hundred black cloaks and the *targaid*. It was easy to follow the trail the Saxons left leading east from Loidis. Thousands of heavy boots left a dirty brown smear across the land as though a great serpent wound its way across the hills and dales, tossing aside debris as they retreated with their booty. They left broken shields, shivered spears, the bones of the food they ate, split boots and ruined cloaks. The dead also lined that filthy smear of churned grassland. Women's corpses lay discarded, captured British women subjected to torture and left to rot.

'We should at least cover their bodies,' Ethne said as they passed the third such body. 'Give them the dignity their captors denied them.'

'They stay as they lie,' Arthur ordered. 'We honour these women with vengeance, not with mere cloaks to hide their nakedness.' The men who followed would tend to the dead. Arthur's heart was beyond feeling. He had hardened it, made it the cold instrument it must be to face the men who had committed such atrocities against Gwallog's people. They followed the scar torn into Britain's land until it split into thinner tendrils of boot prints, long tentacles spreading out, reaching across the landscape. Arthur paused at that crossroads where the Saxon army had broken up into its constituent war bands, as chiefs and commanders led their men to forage, raid and scavenge for food in any villages lucky enough to evade their brutality when the army approached Loidis. Theodric and Clappa had loosed their men on Elmet's hinterland, and Arthur led his men into a country churned by boots, a hell world of desolation and death. The black cloaks reached a shallow incline set amongst three hummocks overlooking a sweeping plain where blots of smoke stained the land where villages had once stood.

'They camped here for a night,' said Ethne. She and the *targaid* picked their way through the detritus. She bent and held her hand close to the black, crusted remnants of a campfire. 'This fire warmed them only yesterday.'

'Some stayed longer,' called another Pict.

'Three war bands remained until this morning,' said a third. 'They have a wagon with them. Look, donkey shit.'

Arthur snarled. 'We can catch them. How many?'

'Hard to say,' said Ethne, slowly pacing through the tracks. She knelt and sniffed a pile of donkey droppings. 'The tracks have fouled one another.' She stood and dug her hand into a pouch fastened to her belt by a leather thong. The hand came out stained blue, and she dragged that hand down her face, smearing it with blue woad. 'We can find them. Just follow us.' She spoke so simply, as if it were a foregone conclusion that the *targaid* could find a war band with a half-day start on them.

'There could be hundreds of them,' Arthur warned.

Ethne frowned as though Arthur's words puzzled her. 'So?'

'Go then. We'll follow.'

Ethne barked at her warriors in their native tongue and without a moment's hesitation they set off running, twelve women loping over the hill with their languid, controlled gait. Arthur followed, Llamrei trotting at the head of three hundred black cloaks, who marched double time. They marched four normally paced steps, and then four hurried steps so that they kept pace with Arthur's warhorse. After a morning spent negotiating the highlands and ridges, they descended into the flatlands, crossing a babbling brook into a meadow where three cows lay dead on their side. The black cloaks sweated beneath their hard-baked leather breastplates and cloaks, and Llamrei needed a rest so that it was a relief when the sky quickly darkened and a straight, heavy rain emptied from the clouds in a relentless wash.

The war band slowed as Llamrei and the warriors picked their way through a gulley full of briar and thorny blackberry bushes, and Ethne appeared at the gulley's crest with her hands on her hips. She had run all morning and yet seemed as though she had simply returned from a morning stroll.

'We have them,' she called down to Arthur. 'They have divided into four war bands of fifty. Each has settled into a destroyed village for the day. They have mead, barrels of it.'

'Bastards want to spend the day drinking and celebrating

their victory,' said Dewi. He grabbed his cloak and wrung the excess water from it.

'It will cost them their lives,' Arthur said, and he led his men out of that gulley and towards an enemy who had wrought so much pain and destruction on a kingdom of Britain.

16

Fifty men lazed on milking stools, logs and empty barrels, or sat on fences, leaning through open doorways and window shutters as they drank rich, golden mead from horns and clay cups. They drank stolen mead from a barrel resting on their wagon and celebrated like lords outside dead men's homes. Bearded men in leather, iron and fur laughed and sang with drooping eyes and slurred voices, their spears, shields, seaxes and bows lying on the ground or resting against buildings from which they had dragged and either slaughtered, captured or enslaved the once peaceful inhabitants. A woman screamed from inside a single-storey home, a building half burned black, and half covered in old, grey thatch. The Saxons laughed at the woman's terror, and they ate meat roasting over an open fire they had made at the village crossroads. Doors and fence planks burned on their cook fire, and three weeping women in torn clothes and ash-smeared faces brought the men mead and cuts of meat whenever they demanded it.

'Bastards,' said Malegant, his knuckles showing white around the shaft of his spear. 'That could be my home. My family destroyed and enslaved. They are laughing at us, at these people.'

'They won't be laughing soon,' Arthur said, and glanced up at clearing storm clouds shot through with shafts of bright sunlight. The rain had stopped as Arthur and his black cloaks watched the Saxons from inside a stable on the village outskirts. They had followed Ethne and the *targaid* at double time, tracking wagon tracks along roads and dales until the sound of shouting and laughter led them to the first Saxon war band. Arthur leaned to his right where Ethne waited, sling in hand, face painted with blue woad. 'Where are the other two war bands?' he asked.

'Beyond that copse.' She pointed to a clutch of ash and elm trees to the north-east.

'Can they reach us quickly if they hear the skirmish?'

Ethne thought about that for a moment. She bobbed her head from side to side and then curled her lip. 'Yes, they could be here before the sun wanes. But that is more than enough time to take care of these drunken fools.'

Arthur winced as the sound of a woman shrieking peeled out from the half-burned house. 'Take your *targaid* around behind that milking shed.' He pointed to the long building, its wood silvered from years exposed to the elements. 'Loose your slings when you see my signal.'

'What signal?'

'You'll know when you see it.'

Ethne flashed a wicked smile and set off with her dozen Picts. They kept low, running south from the stable to a line of low hedges.

'Dewi?' Arthur said, and his captain appeared, helmeted and ready to fight. 'Take twenty men and slowly ease your way around to the north. When you hear the slings bite, show yourselves.'

Dewi nodded, counted out twenty men by touching their shoulders and led them slowly from the stable around to the north, following the land's contours to keep hidden from view. Arthur pulled on his helmet, the liner pressing down on his hair and the full-faced cheekpieces giving his breath a metallic ring inside his head. The woman screamed and the sound of her begging cut through Arthur like a blade. It reminded him suddenly of how Morgan must have sobbed beneath Urien's monstrous paws, just like Igraine before her. Wrapped up in that terrible sound, he heard the wails of all the women of Loidis, who had suffered whilst he delayed at Camelot. Arthur closed his eyes and saw all the crucified men, and Gwallog's pale, dishonoured body hammered to the cross by rusty nails. A king, and a good man, slaughtered by men stronger than him, men who longed for war and thirsted for battle. So now Arthur would give it to them.

'Wait until they come for me,' he said to Malegant in a voice as hard as granite. 'Then charge.'

'Then what, lord?'

Arthur turned and stalked towards the stable door. 'Kill them all.'

He left the stable with one hand resting on Excalibur's hilt. He wore his seax at the small of his back, his chain-mail armour and his black cloak about his shoulders. The crow-feather plume crested his helmet, and his boots splashed in rain puddles as Arthur marched across along the road leading to the village square. Llamrei waited in a ridge beyond the village, held there by a young black cloak to feed and brush the stallion. His hoofbeats would have given the black cloaks' approach away to the Saxons, so Arthur had left his warhorse out of earshot, along with Cavall who had lain down beside the horse, gnawing on a bone.

Arthur's heart rose and fell beneath the weight of his mail and his hand flexed around Excalibur's leather-wrapped hilt. The first Saxon saw him, a flat-faced man with narrow-set eyes and a greasy beard. He stood and pointed at Arthur, and the rest of the Saxons turned. They saw a lord of war in expensive mail, carrying an expensive sword. Only their kings and warlords could afford to go to war as Arthur did, for a man must possess either enough silver to buy the coat made of hundreds of inter-linked iron circles, and the sword which only the finest smiths could forge, or have the reputation to kill such a man and stop others from taking it from him. The Saxons stood slowly and reached for their spears, but most were out of reach, aban-doned, as they enjoyed the fruits of their murderous labour.

A short man with fox fur about his neck and wrists barked something at Arthur, but his mouth was full of meat and so the words came out garbled. He marched forwards, meat juice slop-ping into his beard, gesturing for Arthur to stop with one hand and waving to his men to arm themselves with the other. He wore a leather breastplate fastened with scraps of mail about the chest and shoulders and his long hair scraped back by a strip of cloth.

Arthur quickened his pace, closing the distance to the man in fox fur, who was clearly their leader. Arthur was amongst them now, amid fifty Saxons swaying as they watched him, minds fuddled with mead. They could surge at him, attack him with blades and cut him down in an instant. But Arthur cared nothing for the danger in that moment. All he cared about was vengeance for those who had suffered and died because these men and others like them wanted other men's land, women, silver and blood. The Saxon leader kept on walking, trying to swallow his food so that he could talk, holding up his palms so that Arthur would stop advancing. He was a Saxon used to fighting with spear and seax, not a swordsman, and so he did not know about distance, which in combat was everything. A man must know the distance at which he can effectively land a lunge, or a sweep of his sword, of how close he must be to parry, and how far he must step back to avoid his enemy's weapon. So he was too close when Arthur ripped Excalibur free of her red, fleece-lined scabbard, and the blade scraped on the scabbard's wooden throat. He was still too close as, in one fluid motion, Arthur drew the blade and used his wrist to whip it around, extending his arm, taking one long step forward, so that just a thumb's width of Excalibur's point tore through the leader's throat.

Blood welled at the Saxon leader's gullet. His eyes bulged, and he spat a mouthful of grey, half-chewed meat from his mouth. Arthur brought the blade around and held its hilt up to his face and kissed the cold, iron crosspiece. *Gods grant me revenge on these curs*, he whispered. *Make me fast and sure and I shall soak this soil with the blood of men who put your people to slaughter.* The Saxons gaped as their leader dropped to his knees, clutching at his slit throat. Dark blood seeped between his fingers and onto his fox fur and armour. Some hurried for their spears, others just watched, minds addled by mead as the Saxon toppled forward and died in the mud, his blood leaking to stain rain puddles crimson.

A whirring sound came from the village edge, and a Saxon's skull burst open with a horrifying crack like the sound of rotten wood snapping. The *targaid* let out their unnerving undulating war cry and more of their slingshot stones smacked into the fifty Saxon warriors. Men cried out as stones cracked ribs and knocked warriors unconscious. One man fell howling as his

knee burst apart like an overripe apple. Arthur set about the
enemy closest to him, cutting and slashing with Excalibur's
sharp blade. He opened a man's face, stabbed another through
the chest and ripped open a warrior's back as he tried to turn
and run.

Saxons found their spears and shields, scrambling and
calling to one another as yet more stones came hurtling into the
village with devastating accuracy. The carnyx blared its shrill,
metallic war song and two hundred black cloaks charged:
Dewi's picked men from one flank and the rest of the force from
the stable. A grizzled man with piercing blue eyes found his
courage and his weapons and came at Arthur shouting to
Woden. He stabbed his spear at Arthur, then feinted low and
slashed the point high. He was slow, and Arthur was lethally
fast. Arthur dodged the first attack, and parried the second,
twisting at the hip so that he barged the Saxon with his shoulder. His enemy staggered off balance and Arthur roared with
anger as he drove Excalibur's point into the small of the Saxon's
back. The sword punched through spine and guts, cutting right
through the Saxon as though he were made of soft dough.
Arthur ripped the blade free and turned to find another enemy
to kill.

Black cloaks charged into the fray, spears and shields
levelled, so they came in an unstoppable wall of stout wood and
sharpened steel. The Saxons cried out in fear. Twenty tried to
form a shield wall, but they were drunk and poorly led and died
when Dewi's men cut into them like vengeful war-demons.
More tried to flee, running into the tangle of houses, animal
pens, storage sheds and cow byres. The black cloaks went after
them, filling the village with death. Some of the Saxons tried to
run from the village, hurtling away from the vengeful Britons,
but they found twelve Picts waiting for them, warrior women

armed with axes and knives. Ethne's warriors tore into those fleeing men with brutal savagery, keening their war cries, swarming the Saxons with flashing knives and merciless brutality.

The fight was over in moments, two hundred Britons against fifty Saxons. Some of the enemy tried to kneel, throwing down their weapons in search of mercy, but found none. Malegant ducked into the half-burned house and came out carrying a blonde-haired woman wrapped in a woollen blanket. She hid her face against his chest and Malegant carried her to the wagon, where he lay her gently in the back. Another woman came howling from the house, her face taut with anger, dress torn and bloody, hair a tousled mess. She snatched up a seax and hacked into a kneeling Saxon, stabbing and bludgeoning him with the blade like a butcher. The black cloaks let her exact her vengeance until she collapsed in the mud, quivering and wailing like a madwoman. The Picts went to her, helping the woman to her feet and taking her to a stable to care for her injuries.

Arthur stood at the edge of the village. He removed his helmet and cleaned Excalibur's blade on a dead man's cloak, eyes fixed on the copse in the distance where ash and elm trees swayed in the breeze. He faced away from the slaughter. The sounds of begging Saxons made Arthur feel ill. There must be retribution for King Gwallog and Loidis, but Arthur took no pleasure in the sounds of suffering. It was one thing to kill a man in combat, but something else to cut down a man who begs for his life. So he waited until it was over, until the cries and sounds of hacking weapons ceased, and then he slipped Excalibur back into her scabbard.

'It's done, lord,' said Dewi, striding to Arthur across the blood-soaked village. 'All dead.'

'Now we find the next war band,' Arthur said.

'There isn't much sun left today, lord.'

'Then we shall fight in the dark. There are two more war bands within our reach, two bands of fifty men. Destroy them and we have weakened our enemies by one hundred and fifty spearmen today. We march. Prepare the men.'

Arthur sent the *targaid* ranging ahead to find the next war band, and they ran towards the copse in a long line, tireless and without complaint. Arthur marched at the head of his black cloaks, and they found the next war band feasting inside a long-house set between two slender rivers. Fifty of them sang and cheered inside a dead British lord's hall, eating his store of food and drinking his ale. The Picts killed any Saxon scouts set to watch the western approach, and Arthur had his black cloaks set fire to the hall's thatch. They kindled a flame using flint, steel and straw from a horse stable, lit broken fence panels and carried flame to the thatch and old wattle. It did not take long for the hall to catch light, for its thatch to cough stinking smoke into the sky. The Saxons came coughing and wheezing from the hall doors, and Arthur's black cloaks cut them down one by one.

The Saxons kicked the door closed once a score of their fellows met their doom in the gate, but the thatch bellowed green-tinged smoke, and flames leapt up the walls, eating at them, crackling, causing the timbers to groan and creak. The Saxons shouted. Some hurled spears through shutter windows which the black cloaks batted away with their shields, others peered out frantically from window holes, hoping by some miracle of Woden that their *Wealas* foe would disappear. But they did not. Arthur paced before the hall, Excalibur in his hand, impatient for the slaughter.

'Surround it,' he shouted above the fire's increasing roar.

'They'll come running with flames on their backs. When they do, they die.'

Dewi led the black cloaks in a circle around the hall and they waited, spears and shields ready. The *targaid* remained with Arthur, stood behind him with their axes and knives ready. A portion of thatch collapsed with a shower of sparks, and a gout of flames reached out from the roof like the flickering tongue of a serpent. The Saxons cried out with terror, and more of the roof collapsed as roof beams gave way and sent flaming thatch cascading down onto the Saxons who had settled in for an afternoon and evening of drink and celebration and now met the most fearsome of endings.

The hall doors suddenly crashed open, and a warrior hurtled from the dark space with fire eating at his greasy beard and his jerkin aflame. He ran with his arms flailing, making a sound like a screaming horse, and died with Malegant's spear in his chest.

'Here they come,' Arthur said. 'No mercy. Remember Loidis!'

'For Loidis!' the black cloaks called as one.

Two Saxons leapt from open window shutters, flames licking about their edges. They fell heavily and one tried to beat out the flames on his comrade's arms. Two of the *targaid* charged forward and killed the Saxons, hammering their axes down into the stricken men's skulls. The entire roof gave way with an ear-rending groan, and then collapsed with a great crash, filling the sky with embers and floating, flaming strands of rotten straw. The Saxons came from the hall like rats fleeing water. They ran like scalded cats from every door and window. Some dragged burning shipmates with them and others came screaming in terror.

Arthur strode into their midst and killed those horrified

Saxons with efficient cuts of his sword. Excalibur sang her war song, her shimmering blade cutting down the men who had so mercilessly butchered the people of Loidis. Arthur hewed at them until his shoulders and arms ached from the effort. Dead Saxons littered the space around the hall like a deathly carpet and when it was done, when every Saxon soul in that place was dead, the black cloaks sank to their knees with exhaustion.

It was grim work, death work, butcher's work, and Arthur found no battle-joy in it. The stink of fire and death soured his stomach, and he led his men away from the burning hall and its sickening stench.

'There's one more war band out there,' Arthur said, as he marched beside Dewi and Malegant.

'Sun's almost down,' Malegant said, frowning at the pink-tinged horizon.

'There's something out there,' called a black cloak, pointing his spear towards the east. 'Look. Iron.'

Arthur turned from the sunset to look out across the gently rolling dales. The River Aire flowed wide and then thinned to fast-moving rapids between high reeds and weeping willow trees. The dipping sun glinted off spear points and helmets, first one, then more so that the eastern riverbank twinkled like stars on a clear night.

'Saxons,' Arthur said.

'The third war band?' asked Malegant.

'There are more than fifty there. Ethne, take your *targaid* and run to the river. I want to know how many Saxons approach.'

Ethne set off at a run with her twelve Picts, and Arthur ruefully glanced over his shoulder at the tower of smoke swirling from the burning hall. He had been so eager to punish the Saxons and burn them just as they had the innocents at

Loidis, that he had not considered the beacon that fire sent out to the rest of Theodric and Cappa's war bands who were out foraging in the land around Loidis.

'It can't be the entire Saxon army,' said Dewi. 'Their war band would have spread far and wide by now. They can't all forage in the same valleys.'

'Get the men together. Form up in five ranks on me.'

Dewi urged the black cloaks into position, and the men murmured and shuffled, pointing to the north where another band of Saxons appeared, on Arthur's side of the river.

'How many can you see?' Arthur asked, squinting to count the spear points wavering against the darkening sky.

'Two score,' said Dewi, 'maybe more.'

Ethne came springing from the river, hair flowing behind her and weapons jangling at her belt.

'Too many Saxons to count,' she said, pointing back the way she had come. 'At least five long hundreds, maybe more.'

'Are any across the river?' Arthur asked.

'Not yet, but they march for the rapids. I can't tell how deep the water is there, but they will try to ford it. I've left the *targaid* there to harry them should they try the crossing.'

'Good.' Arthur ran a hand along his beard. He had three hundred men and faced a larger enemy to the east and a smaller one to the north. Arthur could retreat and march west towards Loidis where the rest of his army waited for Bors and Kai to join them with the northern levy, but Arthur could not be sure that more enemies had not circled about his flank in that direction to cut off his only route of escape. He could not attack the larger force. There were too many to fight. Neither could he attack the smaller force, because in the time it would take to slaughter those men, the larger army of Saxons would ford the river and hurry to reinforce their countrymen.

Arthur thought about advancing on the large army and holding them off as they tried to ford the river. He could make a shield wall and kill the Saxons as they clambered up the river-bank and make a great slaughter beside the River Aire. His black cloaks would slay twice their number at least before the larger force overwhelmed them and the smaller force whittled them down from the flank.

'Call back your *targaid*,' Arthur said to Ethne. 'We can't hold the river. Dewi, form the men into a marching column, and we'll retreat westwards.'

Arthur didn't want to retreat before the butchers of Loidis. It would imbue the Saxons with confidence to see their enemy run away from battle, and Arthur's warrior's pride pricked at him, urging him to stand and fight, to carry Excalibur against more of the men who had butchered King Gwallog and his people. Arthur was Pendragon, he was the high king respon-sible for bringing victory to Britain, and it took both cunning and bravery to win a war. The black cloaks whispered and grumbled as Arthur led them away from the burning hall. They wanted to charge, to cut at the Saxons, but it was Arthur's responsibility to make the hard decisions and so he ignored their sideways looks and rueful glances.

Ethne's Picts returned from the river and Arthur sent them ranging out to the west to scout for any Saxons trying to cut off their escape. Arthur marched in the column's rear with Male-gant whilst Dewi led them from the front. Every twenty paces, Arthur turned and watched the Saxons advance across the river. Their war drums sounded a rhythmic beat, and the enemy clashed spears against their shields. The smaller war band advanced, hurrying so that they marched parallel to the black cloaks, hurling insults and shaking their weapons to goad Arthur's men to fight. The black cloaks shouted insults across the grassland until Dewi growled at them to close their cheese pipes and hold their discipline.

'If we keep this up, we'll march into darkness,' said Malegant as he and Arthur turned again to keep an eye on the larger force at their rear.

'That's what I'm counting on,' said Arthur. 'They won't attack at night and come morning we'll have their tracks to follow to wherever that larger force makes camp. We'll have our fight tomorrow, and with our combined army, we'll soak Elmet's land with Saxon blood.'

Malegant grinned, and it all seemed so simple. A fast victory on a spring morning. Another triumph for Arthur against the hated Saxons, and vengeance for the crucified people of Loidis. But then Dewi shouted in alarm from the column's front. More shouts of surprise and fear followed, and Arthur's dreams turned to dust. A third Saxon war band appeared in the west, and the Picts returned from that direction, waving their arms in alarm. Arthur found himself surrounded and trapped between three enemy war bands.

17

'Five score at least, lord,' said Ethne, out of breath for once. Her Picts had come hurtling across the grassland to warn Arthur of the war band blocking their path of retreat. 'Spread out in two long ranks like beaters scouring a forest before a hunt.'

Spears wavered in the west like thin trees blown by the wind. Arthur turned to assess his surroundings. The larger war band was already crossing the river rapids and forming up on his side of the bank. Their war drums boomed, and three of their holy men capered before the warriors, thin men in furs shaking staffs and holding aloft yellowed skulls. The smaller war band continued to track Arthur's black cloaks, stopping now and then to hurl insults at the Britons. Some showed their bare white arses, and the rest of their warriors laughed and shook their spears.

'Too many to fight,' Arthur said to himself. 'Too many of us to die.' The sun's belly touched the western hills, casting the still-smoking hall in an eerie orange glow. He bent and tore a clump of coarse grass from beside his feet. Arthur smelled it, the peaty-wild smell of Britain. There were worse places to die, he supposed. He imagined how Gwallog and the people of Loidis had suffered as the Saxons hammered nails into the small, fragile bones of their wrists and ankles. He could almost hear their cries of pain in the wind. A long, painful death. They would have begged at the end, Arthur knew. When the pain became too much and the ravens perched on their shoulders, glaring with their twitching heads and obsidian eyes, waiting for the people to die so they could peck out their succulent eyes and tongues.

'It will be dark within the hour, lord,' said Malegant. 'Half-moon tonight, if I'm not mistaken, and cloudy. There won't be much light.'

'They'll still attack. Even in darkness. They want us dead. We've killed one hundred of their men, so they want vengeance just as much as we do.' Arthur sighed and slid the fingers of both hands behind the neck of his chain mail to release the weight around his throat. 'It never ends. They kill. We kill. They commit atrocities against our people, and we do the same against theirs. We demand revenge for those who suffered, then they do the same. We hate each other, a hate too hot to touch, like a blade fresh from the blacksmith's forge. Will there ever be an end to the bloodletting?'

'Not today there won't, lord,' said Dewi. 'I reckon there's about twelve hundred of the bastards surrounding us. That's a lot of blood.'

'We only have to kill six of them each,' said a bushy-bearded warrior with a glint in his eye, and the surrounding black cloaks laughed mirthlessly.

'A bit of light work before bed,' said another and exaggerated a loud yawn.

'Only six?' said a red-haired warrior. 'I could have six Saxons before breakfast.'

'That's what your mother used to say,' quipped another, and the rest of the black cloaks laughed raucously.

'Looks like we'll have to make a fight of it then, lads,' Arthur said when the dark humour had died down. It never failed to astound Arthur that warriors found humour in the direst of situations. The men teased each other mercilessly, every day and every night. They played tricks on one another, hiding boots, putting rabbit shit in men's helmets, pushing each other over when their backs were loaded with marching gear. But each one would gladly give his life to save another. Arthur had tried to explain it to Guinevere once, that bond between fighting men, but could not help her understand. It was friendship beyond love and respect. It was like a warm blanket, knowledge that made a man stronger when he understood with utter certainty that the surrounding warriors would throw their bodies in the way of a blade meant for his neck, and he would do the same for them. A true brotherhood, and it warmed Arthur's heart like a roaring fire on a cold winter night.

One and a half thousand Saxon warriors surrounded Arthur's black cloaks, enemies well armed and veterans of battles against the stout Roman armour wearing warriors of Elmet, and countless other skirmishes. They were hard men, men from across the sea, and there could be no way out for Arthur or his men. There were simply too many of them, too many spears, shields and seax blades. The fight could rage for hours, Arthur's men could fight like heroes from legends, but how long can a man stand and swing a weapon before he tires and slows? How long before a man who fights like a demon in the initial exchanges slows, as his muscles burn with fatigue? Spear shafts will shiver and break and shields shatter under the impact of enemy axes hacking at their boards and rivets. Wounded men will fall, weakened by loss of blood, and those men leave the next man in the shield wall open to attack. Arthur saw it play out in his head like a bard's story, saw his brave warriors fall one by one though they fought with unmatched skill and fury. A chill evening wind blew through Arthur's hair, kissing his neck with its soft breeze. It felt like Guinevere's gentle breath on his skin, tingling and welcome. Arthur pushed his helmet onto his head, setting his jaw, hardening his mind to the fact that he would never see his beautiful queen again. If he had left her with child, he would never see the baby born, never meet his son or daughter, denied the experience of their first step and words. He would never teach his son to hold a sword, or his daughter how to string and loose a bow, or watch her marry and become a woman.

There was no way out, and the Saxons had come to take everything from Arthur, his life, his future, his dreams. Everything he had worked for, everything he had become and would be, was about to end on a nameless northern moor. Arthur loosened his seax in its sheath at the small of his back and flexed his hand about Excalibur's hilt. If he had to die here, then he would make such a death, such a stand, that it would cost the Saxon horde dearly to take his life. If they were to snatch mighty Excalibur from his dying hand, then it would cost them hundreds of lives to do it. He would ruin their army, cut them, hack them and kill so many that Theodric and Clappa must retreat to their kingdoms deep on Lloegyr's edge to recover, unable to fight again that summer. Then, perhaps Bors and Kai would take the fight to them and use their greater numbers to crush those kingdoms' strength forever. Death surrounded him, but Arthur made his peace with it.

'The ground is boggy over yonder,' said Ethne, gesturing

beyond where the smaller war band who followed Arthur's black cloaks stood, still taunting the Britons. 'It rises behind them into a hummock, and around that higher ground there is bog water, foul and treacherous underfoot. We almost ran through it earlier today.'

'Then that's where we'll make our stand. We'll kill them as they struggle in the bog, and strike at them from above. How high is the hummock?'

'Not very. Waist-high, perhaps. Barely large enough for us all to stand on.'

'But to get there, we must get through those men. So we are going to charge them.'

'Charge them, lord?' asked Dewi, tilting his head like an old man who had lost his hearing.

'Charge them. Now. Form the boar's snout on me.'

'Yes!' Malegant growled with a glint in his eye. 'Bastards want to surround us? We'll make them work for their slaughter.'

'Boar's snout, on the high king,' Dewi barked, chivvying them with the butt of his spear. 'Leave anything you don't need for the fight. You don't need your bedroll, Kavi, nor your cooking spit. Leave everything but your weapons.'

Arthur drew Excalibur and took his position at the head of the attack formation. The boar's snout was a special shield-wall tactic used to break enemy formations. Arthur would form the tip of a wedge-shaped attack formation with two men formed up behind him, four behind them and then eight spreading out like a boar's tusk. The weight and ferocity of the attack must punch into an enemy shield wall or battle line and carve it in two. Once through the line, the attackers had not only shattered the enemy formation but the most dangerous fighters, the picked champions who fought in the front rank, had the chance to hew at the shirkers, the timid men of the enemy rear ranks. They were always the first to flee in any battle. The dangerous men fought at the front where reputations grew and men unafraid of blades and death sought to make their legends. Those at the back waited for the shield walls to break before they struck a blow. In Arthur's experience, few men died when the shields walls came together. It was tight work, pushing and shoving and stabbing over and under enemy shields, looking for a gap in which to slide a blade. It was when one shield broke that the slaughter began. When an army turned and ran, when shields dropped and backs turned was when even the shirkers charged forward to chop at fleeing men with their spears, axes and knives.

A rout always began with one man, one faint heart who had not the courage to stand with his comrades. One man who sensed battle shifting, who feared that his front rankers, the champions and finest warriors in his own army, were giving way. That man was always in the rear ranks, depending on braver men to do the knife work. Fear gnawed at him. He saw the big men in the enemy front ranks roaring, splashed with other men's blood, weapons rising and falling with merciless strength. That man could imagine such a blade cutting into his flesh, opening his throat, hurting him, causing him immeasurable pain. So he turned and ran. The warrior next to him saw that man running, shared the same fear, and so he followed, and then another, until dozens of men ran from the fury and horror of battle. As the rear rankers peeled away, so then did the rest, and in moments a shield wall was in rout and that was where men died.

'When we break them,' Arthur called to his men. 'Don't turn and kill them. Keep the charge going until we reach the hummock beyond. Keep going until you feel the bog beneath your boots. On the high ground, we make our stand. Are we ready?'

'Who do you fight for?' Dewi bellowed, clashing his spear against his shield.

'Arthur, Arthur, Arthur!' the black cloaks roared as one, and every man clashed their ash spear shafts against their iron-shod shields.

'Then let's see you do it,' Arthur growled when the noise had died down. '*Targaid*, run ahead and soften them up with your slings, then form up in the rear rank.'

'Yes, Ard Rí,' said Ethne, and her Picts took up position.

'On me!' Arthur shouted, and set off at a brisk marching pace. Dewi and Malegant took up the rank behind them, and the bravest champions amongst the black cloaks behind them. The *targaid* ran on ahead, pulling slings from their belts and the lethal stones from their pouches. The Saxon war band stopped their incessant taunting when they realised that the black cloaks advanced upon their position. They shuffled, spears wavering, looking to their leader for orders. They were fifty men, made brave by the larger numbers on their flanks, but those men were too far away to help them now, and Arthur grinned. Their leader faced the same decision Arthur had wrestled with but moments earlier. Should he stand and try to hold Arthur's men until the greater numbers reached him, and the slaughter could begin, or should he run? If the Saxon made a stand, then many of his warriors, and likely even he, would die. If he ran and lived, his fellow Saxons would curse him for a coward. That problem, that difficulty which all war leaders faced would eat at him like a worm in his mind. He must make a decision that would cost lives and pain, and no possibility would seem like the right one.

Fifty men milled about each other nervously in the Saxon

war band. Some formed a shield wall, others moved to the rear in case the order came to run, the rest looked to their leader and still he did not organise his men. The army by the river let out a great roar, and Arthur knew the commander there had given the order to charge. Arthur picked up the pace, shifting into a jog. His men followed his lead, keeping formation, belts, cloak pins and weapons jangling with every step. Ahead, slings whirred, and the first Saxon cried out in pain as a thumb-sized stone broke a bone or smashed open a skull. At twenty paces Arthur could make out their faces, beards, blue eyes, brown eyes, so much like the Britons themselves but for the animal fur they wore about their bodies. At fifteen paces he heard their frightened cries of alarm as more men fell to the Picts' slingshots.

The order came, a loud bark from within the milling mass of fifty Saxons. They hurried to form up into a shield wall, and Arthur's heart leapt with joy because it was too late. At ten paces Arthur broke into a flat run, Excalibur ready, muscles tense, mind tempered and ready to fight to the death. At five paces, he picked his target. Two large men carrying shields daubed with crude animal figures, their maws wide, calling to their shield comrades to tighten the shield wall. They saw a lord of war charging towards them, a tall man clad in the finest war gear, and all Arthur saw before him were the men who had crucified Gwallog. The *targaid* broke off their missile attack and without breaking stride they split into two lines, filtering around the sides of the boar's snout like birds changing direction in flight.

Arthur did not bother to strike at the first two men. He charged at them with full force, at a flat run with all of his strength and momentum pressed into the tense muscles of his shoulders, shoulders made strong by a lifetime hefting shield, spear and sword. He purposefully did not carry a shield, as the point at the head of the boar's snout arrowhead, he had to move fast. A shield would encumber him, become locked against the shields he must charge through. So Arthur ground his teeth, overcame the fear that gnawed at his heart to see Saxon killers waiting for him with spears levelled and shields ready. At three paces, Arthur held his breath.

A Saxon threw his spear, and it sang over Arthur's head, shaft wobbling in flight. Arthur's lips turned on themselves, his hand tightened around Excalibur's hilt, and then he hit them. Arthur's left shoulder hammered into a shield, the impact like a being kicked by a horse. He hit the rim and pain jarred his shoulder, shooting through his entire body, but he kept moving. The second shield caught his hip, but Arthur was through. Saxons shouted and roared around him, steel glinted and wild faces reared away from his fury. Arthur's power and momentum took him into the second rank, and the order for them to form had come too late. They had not laid their shields over one another, and Arthur barged into the gap between two shields in front of him.

Something hard hit Arthur's back, behind him blades chopped into wood, spear staves shattered like falling trees, shields broke and men screamed in pain as the black cloaks laid down their furious anger upon the Saxon war band who had so taunted them in their moment of peril. Arthur was in the third rank and the Saxons there lurched to get away from him, his heart sang with joy for he was almost through them, but then a spear stave tripped him, it swept his left leg away just as it was about to touch the grass, and Arthur felt the heat of panic in his chest. He went down, but tucked his shoulder and rolled. A spear point sliced against his chain mail and slid to sink into the ground.

Arthur came up snarling and swung Excalibur in a low arc and her sharp edge cut through a Saxon boot and the ankle beneath and a man shrieked in pain at his lost foot. He kept moving, twisting, stabbing his sword, though he could see nothing around him but legs, spears, boots and winingas leg wrappings. Arthur surged to his feet and stamped his foot down hard onto the screaming face of the man whose foot he had taken. A spear lunged at Arthur's face, but he parried it and opened the spearman's throat in a spray of hot blood. A shield barged into Arthur's back, pushing him forward and he turned with Excalibur raised to find Dewi and Malegant there, their weapons and faces spattered with enemy blood and their mouths twisted as they roared at Arthur to keep moving.

The Saxons ran from Arthur, and from the black cloaks who had successfully punched through their ragged formation. Arthur fought the urge to turn and hack into the rearmost men and continued on, forcing his legs to keep moving towards the hummock he could now see thirty paces away. The sound of combat clattered and banged behind him and men screamed at horrific injuries caused by spears, swords, axes, knives and seaxes. Arthur's boots splashed in foul, brackish bog water and the thick soil beneath sucked at his boots. He reached the hillock as the water reached his knees and fell onto the coarse grass and rolled onto his back.

The black cloaks followed, wading through the bog to flop exhausted onto the hillock. They left the Saxons devastated in their wake, fifty men reduced to a crawling mass of bloody destruction. Arthur saw six black cloaks dead amongst the enemy, and more limping towards safety. The *targaid* helped wounded men hurry through the water until the entire surviving black cloak force gathered on the grassy knoll, gasping for breath and relieved to be alive. They laughed and clapped one another on the shoulder at the sheer joy of escaping a force of men who had come to kill them.

'It's not over yet,' Arthur said, and stood staring out as the Saxon army formed up behind the defeated war band. They came from the river and from the west until hundreds of them marched towards the scene of Arthur's boar's snout charge. The war drums continued their song, urging the warriors on to the slaughter, which still lay within their grasp despite Arthur's victory. 'All we have done is make it harder for them, and made it easier for us to kill more of the whoresons before they kill us. I want every life they take to cost ten of theirs. I want us to fight so hard that every Saxon here will never forget what it meant to fight Arthur's black cloaks. I want their skalds to sing songs of our bravery, for news of our last stand to reach across the narrow sea, for mothers to tell their naughty children to behave or Arthur's black cloaks will take them in the night. So fight with every drop of strength in your bodies, brothers. When our spears break, we shall fight with knives. When our shields break, we shall parry their seaxes with our hands. When our knives break, we shall claw at them with our nails and bite them with our teeth. We are the black cloaks, the finest warriors in all the world, so let them see what it means to fight against us! Sound the carnyx!'

Arthur's men roared like wild animals. They shook their weapons and hollered at the darkening sky. The trumpeter raised the carnyx, its long, curved bronze tube rising above the spears so that its magnificent bronze wolf's head, mouth agape and snarling, glowered at the enemy. Its call came long and loud, shrill and metallic, like a beast from the underworld. The black cloaks formed up in a ring around the hummock, three circular ranks of shields and spears so that they could face an attack from any angle. The *targaid* took up position at the centre with their slings ready to loose at the enemy as they trudged through the bog. Arthur took up position in the first rank, as he always did, and now carried a shield taken from a wounded man who joined the rest of those who had suffered an injury during the charge, at the centre of the hummock.

The Saxons spread out in a wide half-moon about the knoll. They shouted and sang war songs in time with the beat of the drum and, all the while, the sun continued its descent, and darkness covered the land in its icy embrace. Arthur's men tightened straps, checked spear points and hefted shields, and the Saxon shield wall parted like an opening door. Two riders on white horses cantered through the space, a man armed with a sword and a woman with crow-black hair. Arthur took a step forward and his heart missed a beat. It was Lunete, his foster sister, and King Theodric of Bernicia. Theodric held his sword upside down to show that he wanted to talk, and Arthur left his shield on the hummock and walked out into the bog.

Theodric leapt lithely off his horse and helped Lunete climb down from her white mare, its coat shimmering like the moon in the twilight. Theodric looked so much like his father, King Ida, but younger. His flaxen hair shone like pale gold. He was handsome and of an age with Arthur, whom he fixed with his flint-like eyes. Lunete wore a circlet of silver around her crow-black hair, and her skin was milk-white. She wore a fitted coat of chain mail over a leather jerkin and offered Arthur no smile as she advanced with her husband.

'Sister,' Arthur said in greeting. He did not sheathe Excalibur, but kept the blade hanging at his side so that Theodric could see the blood smeared along its length.

'Arthur,' Lunete said curtly, a look of defiance in her eyes.

'King Theodric. I grieved when I heard news of your father's death. He was a great warrior.'

Theodric smiled at Arthur's wry tone. 'Thank you for that. He hated you. You killed my brother and took his hand. My father never recovered from that shame.'

'He should have spent more time practising his weapons if he was going to take my people's land.'

'Maybe so. But I will take you alive today, Pendragon. All your men shall die and you will live. Your death will be slow and painful, an offering to my father's soul where he awaits me in Valholl, Woden's great corpse hall.'

'We could fight now, if you wish? Just you and I here in front of your men. That would give you a real chance to avenge your father and brother. No need for fanfare or ritual, just you and I, here beneath the stars. Are you ready?'

'I think not. Look at all the men I have, whilst you have a mere three hundred of your famous black cloaks. Our skalds tell us you are the greatest swordsman who ever lived, that you kill men by the dozen and that lightning flies from your magic sword. Your screams will kill those stories.'

'Funny. I never had you pegged as a coward. Are you a coward?'

'Ignore him,' Lunete said, and placed a warning hand on her husband's arm. 'He tries to goad you. There is no need to fight him. He blundered into the bowels of our army with this paltry force and now he tries to claw a victory from the gaping jaws of defeat.'

'You look well, Lunete. Royalty suits you.'

She raised a long finger in warning. 'We grew together, Arthur, and were as brothers and sisters once. But that time was long ago. I am a queen now and a woman of my people. I rule beside my husband, together, as one. Though I loved you once, you are my enemy now.'

'Kai is well, in case you wondered. Urien died and Kai rules

Rheged until Prince Mordred is old enough to take up his throne.'

'This is no family reunion, or Yuletide feast. We come to kill you, Arthur, and your men.'

'You betray your people.' Lunete's coldness shocked Arthur, like a blow to the head, and he struggled to decide how to respond, so the words just poured from him.

'Betray a people who would have married me off to some fat old warlord somewhere? A people who saw me only as a prized cow to be sold off at auction to the highest bidder. Would my father have showed any care for my wishes in choosing the man I must marry? I think not. Would you have stepped in to save me from that fate, or my dear brother? When my husband's people captured me that day long ago, it was the best day of my life. A liberation! Look at me now, free, powerful, mother and wife of kings!'

'Wife to a coward who lets his wife talk in his stead.' Theodric flinched at Arthur's words and took a half-step forward until Lunete calmed him again. They spoke in Brythonic, not Saxon, but Theodric understood every word. 'I showed care for you that day at the River Dubglas, did I not? I set your defeated husband free, and allowed you to return to his side, did I not?'

'I am wife to a man confident and sure enough of his power to let his wife have a voice. Mark that, Arthur, and ask yourself if you would do the same?'

'You returned my wife to me that day,' Theodric said in his burring accent. 'So I will return that favour today. Pick your favourite man, the most valued amongst your warriors, and he can go free. Then, our debt to one another is paid.'

'And the rest?'

'The rest of your men must die, and you must suffer.'

'Then why are we talking here like fools? So that you can

call me a whoreson and I call you a coward? So that you can ride through your men on your fine white horse and look like the noble warrior? It's almost dark now, so we can have your fight in the shadows. Have you ever won a battle, lord king?'

Theodric smiled. 'Prepare yourselves, then.' He glanced up at the moon and the darkness and wrinkled his nose. 'The dark won't help you.'

'Just so. You'll find me in the front line, fighting beside my men. Where I always fight.'

Theodric laughed and shook his head. 'You Britons make me laugh. You think you are skilled fighters, such heroes. You are a conquered people! The Romans crushed you into submission and left you like lonely dogs, whimpering and cast back into the bleakness of time without rule or law. Now, we and our cousins from the Angle and Jutland come and make your land our own. Just like our little skirmish here, your people cling to scraps of land, creeping westwards year after year. It is just a matter of time before your land is a Saxon land.'

'I'll look for you on the field.' Arthur lifted his sword in salute. Theodric's words hurt more than any insult ever could. Last summer was the first year Arthur had pushed Lloegyr's borders eastwards; before that, the invading hordes had pushed Britains' kingdoms west, increasing Lloegyr piece by piece, and Theodric was right, if Arthur could not keep that tide back, then soon Britain would be no more. 'I still think of you, sister.'

Lunete smiled sadly. 'I think of you too, of how we played together in the fields and forest of Caer Ligualid. We were happy then.'

'We were.'

'But we were different people. That time is over. I still love you as the boy you once were, and the girl I once was. But such things are for children. The Lunete you once knew doesn't exist any more. She died on the day she was captured in the forest. Just as the Arthur I once knew died on the day Merlin gave him an enchanted sword. This is now, and we are on different sides.' She swept her arm around the massed ranks behind her. 'These are my people now. I have children, sons who will be kings one day. I fight for my people.'

'I would like to meet your children one day,' Arthur said with a sad smile. He forgot for a moment that over a thousand brutal warriors waited beyond her, men bent on tearing his war band to pieces. For a second they could have stood alone, just a brother and sister meeting after too long apart.

Lunete brought a hand to her mouth to hide her trembling chin. 'They would love you. And Kai. They are so like you both were. They have a look of my father, with Ector's eyes and strong face.'

Arthur lifted his head and glanced at the stars. 'Take care of your children and raise them well.'

'I will.' Lunete and Theodric turned to walk back to their horses, but Lunete stopped suddenly, and half turned back to Arthur. 'Do you remember that morning when you left home, when Kai and I found you and persuaded you to return?'

'I remember it well.' Before Merlin and Excalibur, before he had earned his first death ring, Arthur had wanted to run away and make his own way in the world. He had dreamed of becoming his own man and forging his reputation in another kingdom's war band, away from Rheged and the Caer.

'I wish you had gone. I wish things were different. But they are not. So, it must be death.'

Theodric ran and leapt onto his horse's back, hooking his leg over the saddle and sweeping himself onto it with a swish of golden hair and lithe limbs. A warrior tossed Theodric his spear, and the King of Bernicia raised it high and howled his war cry. A thousand warriors roared and clashed their weapons, and the war drums resumed their fearsome beat, *boom, boom, boom, ba boom, boom boom boom, ba boom.*

Arthur returned to the knoll with Excalibur in his fist.

'Did you talk them out of it?' asked Dewi with a wry grin.

'Afraid not. It's a fight to the death, lads. Prepare yourselves.'

18

'Sound the carnyx,' Arthur called, and the war trumpet screeched its terrible song out into the night. The sound made the black cloaks ready. It filled them with the pride for the cloaks they wore, and for the brothers they fought beside. They would need every drop of courage, pride, bravery and determination if they were to make this last stand against the enemy worth of song, and kill enough of Theodric's men to send their king and what remained of his horde back to their high crag in Bernicia.

The first wave of Saxons attacked the hummock on three sides. Men armed with spears and shields charged forward with wild abandon. Instead of attacking as one solid shield wall, they came on in a maddened charge, fuelled by the sight of the Saxon war band Arthur's men had slaughtered in their advance on the high ground.

'Shield wall!' Dewi shouted above the Saxon drums and their wild war cries. Arthur set himself, overlapping his shield with the warrior next to him, and the man to his left did the same so that they presented a solid ring of linden wood and iron to the enemy.

The first Saxons splashed into the bog, their boots sending up spray which shone like shards of silver in the moonlight. Then the familiar rhythmic whirring of the *targaid*'s slings began, and twelve of their lethal stones shot from the knoll to drop the first line of Saxons as though an invisible scythe cut them down, sending their bodies sprawling into the bog. Twelve more rocks flew before those men hit the water, and then another twelve, so in the time it takes a man to pull on his boots, a score of Saxons lay dead or dying in the brackish moor water.

'Come and die!' called Malegant.

'Keep it tight!' Dewi ordered. 'Keep the shield wall tight, no heroics. Keep it tight and let them die upon our spears.'

More stones flew from the Picts' slings and more charging Saxons fell, but not enough. Wide-eyed men with fur about their leather breastplates thrashed through the bog and reached the hummock with their spears and shields ready to kill. A wiry man with a flat nose threw his spear at Arthur, but he batted it away easily and the spearhead rang against the shield boss as it fell into the water. The flat-nosed man drew a seax from his belt, its blade spotted with rust, and died as the man behind Arthur thrust his spear forward and tore out his throat. It had begun, and Saxons attacked the black cloaks from all sides, weapons clanging, drums beating, men shouting, injured men screaming, all beneath the night-black sky.

Arthur stabbed down with Excalibur and her tip tore through a Saxon's thigh. A spear thumped against his shield, and then again. Arthur took the blows, his shield bashing against his shoulder with every strike. A black cloak's spear hovered by Arthur's ear, poised, waiting for the right time to strike. The Saxon who beat at Arthur's shield leapt high to slide his spear over the rim of Arthur's shield, and then the waiting spear point stabbed over Arthur's shoulder and into the Saxon's eye.

The Saxons not only had to wade through the bog, but they also now had dead and injured comrades to clamber over before they reached the knoll. Once there, they faced an enemy at waist height striking at them from above, where they had to stab upwards with their faces and shoulders exposed to the Britons' blades. A spear stabbed at Arthur's leg, but he brought his shield down hard and smashed its stave and slid Excalibur into the spearman's gullet and gave the sword a savage twist to spray the Saxons next to him with their comrade's blood.

The *targaid*'s slings fell silent as Ethne's Picts ran out of stones to hurl at the enemy, and so they joined the ranks, kneeling and striking with their curved knives between and beside the black cloaks' legs at the Saxons who fought at knee height. A spear came from the darkness, hurled from the massed Saxons, and it slammed into the black cloak next to Arthur, its point in his chest and its stave quivering as he coughed up a gout of blood. He fell forward, and the Saxons crowed with delight as they hacked into his fallen body.

'Arrows and spears!' Arthur warned his men as an arrow whistled over his head. The Saxons had lost men in that first furious charge, where Theodric had hoped to send his champions in a wild attack to kill Arthur's men quickly, but now he understood black cloaks did not die easily, and so he and Lunete began to use their heads. Arthur's men fought on the high ground, making it very difficult for his men to attack a solid shield wall from below. But that high ground could also make the black cloaks vulnerable, and Lunete and Theodric understood how to exploit that chance.

Arthur lifted his shield higher to protect his chest and face, as did every warrior on the knoll. In the charge they had held their shields low to block enemy strikes at their legs and midriffs. A wave of thrown spears flashed from the Saxon army, flying in arcs like murderous birds. Another black cloak grunted and fell and then arrows came with the spears and three more black cloaks fell, wounded, to be hacked to pieces by the Saxons below.

'Double rank!' Arthur shouted. 'Double rank!'

Dewi repeated the order and Arthur dropped to one knee, as did every warrior in the front rank. A shield came over his head from the second rank and covered the top of Arthur's shield. The same action fell into place around the hummock so that a wall of overlapped shields, two shields high, presented itself to the enemy. Thrown spears and loosed arrows hammered Arthur's shield, plunging into its boards, making it heavy. He winced as a spear point burst through his shield's boards and stopped a hand's breadth from his face, so close that he could smell its iron blade.

'Hold fast,' Arthur growled as yet more arrows and spears clattered into the black cloaks' shield wall. More men behind and around him groaned and cried out in pain. Arthur could see nothing beyond his shield and the one above him, but his black cloaks died, and there was nothing he could do to save them.

The arrows and spears stopped, and Arthur shifted his shield slightly to peer through the gap. The Saxons came on slowly, dragging corpses out of the water to give them a clearer march towards the knoll.

'Here they come,' Dewi growled.

'Top rank, withdraw,' Arthur ordered, and the shield above him gave way. Arthur stood and took the brief lull in fighting to look around him. A score of black cloaks had died during the missile assault, men Arthur knew, had marched with, eaten and drunk with. His men, his special force of black cloaks, men who had been with him in the old days, back when he and Balin of the Two Swords had nothing but their blades and their will to fight.

The Saxons' war drums beat without end, the sound rumbled inside Arthur's head, torturing him, banging in his ears and driving him mad. The enemy attacked, splashing through the bog and hacking at Arthur's men. Again they repelled them, shields blocking upward strikes and the rear ranks striking down at the Saxons' faces. Arthur lost all sense of time. Attack after attack came. For every Saxon who died or reeled away injured, another appeared to take his place. Arthur's arms, shoulders and back muscles burned with exhaustion and his battered shield suffered under the endless attack. Boards came loose, its iron rim lost its shape, and when a huge Saxon warrior hacked at it with an axe, the boards split until that Saxon died with Ethne's axe cutting off the top of his skull like a topped egg.

Black cloaks died, more fought injured. Arthur saw a young black cloak fight like a bear over the corpse of his dead friend until the Saxons pulled him into the water and he died in a welter of blades. So many brave deeds took place on that knoll and so many brave men died. Arthur took wounds to his legs and arms, but he fought on despite the blood. When his shield became useless, he battered at the enemy with it and then fought with just his sword alone. The Saxons seemed like a sea before him, drums booming, spears waving, guttural cries of hate rolling across the dark sky.

Theodric appeared on the edge of the bog, urging his men onwards with his spear held aloft whilst Lunete rode her white horse through the ranks, urging her warriors on to courageous deeds. Theodric locked eyes with Arthur, and Arthur beat his chest with Excalibur's hilt and then pointed the sword at the King of Bernicia. His mouth turned down with hate when he saw that challenge, and the king came on. A ring of enormous men came with him, Theodric's champions carrying axes in one hand and seaxes in the other. Every one of them wore a coat of mail and dwarfed the surrounding warriors in both height and breadth. They hurled the other Saxons aside, striding on to attack Arthur's tired, battered black cloaks.

Arthur steeled himself for the attack, and the black cloaks roared their defiance at the oncoming enemy. They came in a wild charge, splashing through the bog, and then threw themselves at the knoll. Arthur dodged an axe and opened a man's belly with a lunge. He twisted his wrists and sliced Excalibur's edge across the throat of the next Saxon. A woman shrieked over Arthur's shoulder and a *targaid* warrior dropped to her knees with an axe buried in her chest. Theodric himself came on, thrusting his spear at Arthur's men and showing his teeth when its tip drew blood from a black cloak's wound. The fight became desperate then. Not a black cloak had a shield unshattered, most of the spears shivered and broken so that they fought with knives, broken spear staves, seaxes or whatever they could find about their feet. Every man on the hummock fought injured, each of them smeared with blood and filth as they fought for their lives.

Excalibur took another man's life. A powerful hand grabbed his ankle and Arthur cut it away at the wrist. A knife stabbed at his stomach, but his chain mail absorbed the blow. A great cry went up to Arthur's right. He risked a glance in that direction to where Malegant fell to his knees with an axe in his thigh. A shaven-headed Saxon with tattoos covering his head dragged his axe free from Malegant's leg. He swung the weapon, Malegant parried it with his seax, but all his strength had deserted him, leaking out with the dark blood gushing from his leg. The Saxon's axe drove through Malegant's weapon, and the axe blade cut deep into Malegant's neck. The Saxon hauled Malegant from the hummock and the enemy roared with triumph to see one of the black cloaks' most valiant fighters pulled to his death.

'No!' Arthur called, all sense and control leaving him as Malegant died, leaving his children fatherless and Arthur without one of his trusted leaders. Arthur leapt from the knoll, landing in the bog water with Excalibur already lunging. He stabbed two men in rapid bursts, kicked them out of his way, all tiredness gone, strength born of rage flooding him with power. The tattooed warrior met Arthur, no fear on his broad face. His axe came up and Arthur chopped Excalibur down, shearing through its haft as if it were made of rotten wood. The tattooed man didn't flinch. He spun and cut at Arthur with his seax, and Arthur dodged the blow and crashed his elbow into the warrior's face. The Saxons fell back, eager to witness a moment of single combat between skilled champions. They clamoured in a tight circle, baying like wolves beneath the moonlight, the chill night air and exertion from battle causing steam to rise from their mouths and scalps like smoke.

The tattooed warrior feinted a low cut and slashed his seax at Arthur's face. As the weapon came up, he kicked out at Arthur's shin and the blow caused him to stagger, and the Saxon head-butted him full in the face. Arthur reeled, anger and pain swarming his senses. He shook his head to clear the stunned darkness, moving back into a defensive stance. The seax flashed at his face and Arthur parried it. The enemy drove his knee into Arthur's stomach and he moved away to soften the blow and avoid being winded. Arthur took a breath and steadied himself, gripping Excalibur in two hands. He held the blade before him and attacked. He cut down in strong, well-aimed cuts, moving with strength and speed. The tattooed man blocked one cut, but the next one banged into his chain-mail covered chest. He tried to cut at Arthur, but Arthur parried it and flicked the tip of Excalibur across his throat. It was not a deep enough cut to kill him, but enough to frighten him. The Saxons roared and one shoved Arthur in the back. Arthur leapt forward and reversed his grip on the sword's hilt, and stabbed the blade down. It surprised the tattooed man and Excalibur's tip stabbed through his foot and he howled in pain.

Arthur stepped in, yanking his sword free, driving the hilt beneath the Saxon's chin. His head flew back and when the enemy tried to right himself, Arthur crashed his helmeted forehead into the Saxon's nose with a crunch. He swayed, seax falling to his side, and Arthur took a small step back and cut Excalibur upwards from a low starting point so that the tip pierced the soft skin beneath the tattooed man's chin. Arthur pushed the blade with his two hands so that its point pushed through the Saxon's mouth, tongue, up into his brain until it punched through his skull.

The Saxons gasped as their champion twitched on Arthur's blade. He wrenched the blade free in a wash of terrifying dark blood and in one motion he pivoted at the waist and swung Excalibur around in a wide arc at the Saxons who had crowded too close to him. A sword is a fearsome weapon, long, sharp and capable of inflicting awful wounds. The very edge of Arthur's god-forged sword sliced across five different Saxon faces, laying open their skin like roasted pork. Theodric was one of those men and the surrounding Saxons shrieked in horror because Arthur had cut away their king's eye.

Theodric reeled away, clutching at his ruined face, and Arthur scrambled back onto the knoll and held his arms wide, Excalibur pointing at the starlit sky.

'Come and fight with Arthur!' he taunted the Saxons. 'You did not bring enough men! Come and die!' Spittle flew from his mouth, battle madness swamping his senses.

'Fire,' said Ethne, and at first Arthur did not heed her, unable to tear his eyes from the Saxons, who stared up at him with fear in their eyes. The feeling was intoxicating. A thousand Saxons were afraid of him, paralysed with fear by Arthur's battle prowess.

'More fire, and it's moving,' said a black cloak.

Lunete screeched like she was possessed, bullying her white horse through the ranks to get to her wounded husband. 'Kill them!' she cried. 'Kill them!'

The Saxons heaved forward like a crashing tidal wave, and Arthur believed his time had come. His men could not hold, not for much longer against so vast a force.

'It's men,' said a black cloak behind Arthur. 'Coming towards us.'

'With burning torches,' said a Pict.

'More bloody Saxons for us to kill then, isn't it?' said Dewi. 'Now, form up. We only have to kill another thousand of the turds.'

Arthur set his feet and brought Excalibur up for one last stand. A hundred of his black cloaks stood ready to fight. The rest were dead or lying wounded at the knoll's summit behind a ring of Arthur's warriors. Arthur was ready. He had killed a champion and wounded Theodric. His men had fought bravely and three times their number at least lay dead in the marsh. A valiant last stand, a fight enough to make a song to ring down through the ages, even if he would not live to see Lloegyr returned to its people.

The Saxons attacked Arthur's men with a renewed fury, throwing themselves at the hummock, clamouring over one another to strike a blow against Arthur and his black cloaks. Arthur's men held them, cutting and slashing with what remained of their weapons. The moving fires grew closer and greater in numbers, so many fires that they seemed like a moving mirror of the stars, covering the land in a sweeping, seething mass. Arthur fought beyond exhaustion, as did his men, fighting desperately for their lives and to slay as many of the Saxons as they could before meeting their own end.

A great cry went up from the Saxon army, a fearful collective scream of terror. A sound like the sea shook the night air above the noise of battle, and even in the darkness the edges of the Saxon army gave way, parting, collapsing as if brushed aside by the great hand of a god. The Saxons began to run and men heaved Theodric onto his horse and the king flashed a murderous look at Arthur, still clutching one hand to his ruined face.

'They are running,' called a black cloak, surprise in his voice.

'Bastards are shitting themselves, look at them!' said another.

Arthur could not believe his eyes, but his men were right. The Saxons were running, but not from Arthur's men, from the lights approaching from the west. From the west! Arthur threw his head back and laughed. The new force were not fresh Saxon warriors come to join the slaughter of Britain's high king, but Arthur's men, Britain's men. As the mass of torches grew closer, Arthur made out a bear-painted shield, and then the mighty stag of Gododdin. A gigantic man charged at the forefront, a man carrying an axe too big for any normal warrior to wield. Bors, champion of Gododdin, had come.

Theodric and Lunete rode away, and their Saxons followed, running away from the knoll with the same vigour with which they had attacked it. Arthur sank to his knees and half laughed, half wept at the sheer madness of it. The black cloaks and the *targaid* whooped for joy, and collapsed about Arthur, embracing one another, relieved at their survival when it had seemed certain they must die beneath a welter of Saxon blades. Arthur watched with joy as Bors, Hywel, Gawain and Kai led their warriors in a night-shrouded charge against the Saxons. He had not the strength to join them, though he desired nothing more than to slaughter every man in that enemy army in revenge for Loidis, and for Malegant's death.

Arthur lay back and stared at the moon, and thanked the gods for his luck, and for the gift of his and his men's lives. The sounds of battle roared in the distance as the black cloaks lay down spent. He had come close to death, within a dog's whisker of the afterlife, but his friends and allies had come, and now it was time to take the fight to the enemy.

19

'We heard that bloody awful trumpet of yours,' said Bors at dawn. He bent to wash the blood and gore from his axe in the river beside which the army gathered to rest and recover after a night of brutal fighting. 'At first I thought it was a cat drowning somewhere in the night. But then I remembered the sound of Arthur's infernal turdnax, carnshite, or whatever it is called.'

'Carnyx,' said Arthur, unable to keep the wry grin from his face.

'That's it. Carnyx. Anyway, I had already bedded three wenches before sunset, bested seven men in a wrestling tourney, eaten a side of roasted boar and drunk a full barrel of mead. It was a quiet night, and I'd nothing better to do, so I grabbed Kai, Gawain, Hywel and the lads and set off to see what all the noise was about.'

'A full barrel of mead?' Arthur asked, which was obviously enough to inebriate a dozen men.

'There was a drop left, enough to swill my mouth out in the morning.'

'Thank the gods you didn't overdo it then.'

Arthur held Bors' gaze for a moment, but the big man could hold his jest no longer, and they both burst out laughing. Bors and the army had fought all night, pushing Theodric's warriors to the river, killing them as they tried to cross, and chasing them down on the far banks. Bodies littered the moors, gulleys, hills and shallow valleys. Corpses floated face down in the river, caught in the reeds as ice-cold water flowed over flaxen hair and fur clothing. Arthur knuckled at his stinging eyes and rolled his sore shoulders.

'We would be dead if you had arrived an hour later,' he said.

'Night fighting is a treacherous business,' said Kai, 'but Theodric won't fight again for years. His army lies here, dead. Rebuilding will take him time.'

Arthur reached down into the fast-flowing water and let it wash over his hand, and then ran the wet down his face, the cool water refreshing as it removed some of the filth from his skin. 'Lunete was here.'

'I know. I saw.'

'She is as Saxon as Theodric now. Our sweet sister is gone. The woman who lives in her body is a Saxon queen.'

'Aye. She would have let her husband and his men cut you down on that blood-soaked hillock.'

'We shall build Malegant's balefire on that knoll. Afterwards, we'll set stones there, as a monument to him and the other black cloaks who gave their lives here on this field.'

'We'll do it before we leave.'

'I say rest the lads for a few hours,' said Bors. 'Then push east, follow the whoresons. We have them. We can slaughter every one of them before they reach Dun Guaroy and free Bernicia forever.'

'How many did we kill here?' Arthur asked.

'Too many to count. The dead are like ants. Hundreds of them. I think I've put my shoulder out killing so many.'

'How many men have we lost?'

'Half of your black cloaks are dead or too injured to fight again,' said Prince Gawain. 'But the rest of our losses are small. The Saxons were in flight. We lost perhaps fifty, maybe one hundred men.'

'You were at Loidis?'

'We were at Loidis. I never thought to see such cruelty and never hope to again.'

'We should pursue them. But what news of Clappa of Deira?'

'None,' said Kai. 'But rumour says he had an army just as large as Theodric's somewhere out here.'

'Clappa and Theodric were together at Loidis. Clappa can't be on this moorland. There are no tracks, and he would surely have heard last night's battle. The two armies split to forage for provisions. He can't be far. Perhaps he went towards the mountains in the north or followed the River Aire in search of fresh villages to plunder. We can't march until we know where Clappa is.'

'A pox on Clappa and his band of faint hearts,' said Bors, waving one of his monstrous paws dismissively. 'We can deal with them later. Finish Theodric off. Don't let him sneak back into his high fortress. Otherwise, we'll only have to fight the bastard again next year or the year after. Put him in the ground now. There will never be a better chance.'

'No, there won't.' Arthur stood and stretched his aching body. A dozen cuts, gashes and scrapes throbbed, in need of washing and treatment. He turned in a circle, staring out at each horizon on a morning where the sun came up fat and sombre. 'But just like in winter when I had to march my men north in the cold, wind and rain to bring Urien, Lothian and, forgive me for saying it, Gododdin to order. We cannot march into our foe's land and make war with an enemy at our backs.'

Bors frowned. 'Don't compare Gododdin men to Saxons.'

'My father had no choice but to side with Urien and Lot,' said Gawain. He stood next to Arthur and offered him some dried beef from a pouch at his belt. 'We had Lothian threatening from the north and Rheged from the south. There was no way we could march to join you. With our army gone, Lothian would have done to Dunpendrylaw what Theodric and Clappa did to Loidis. We did not ignore your call by choice.'

'I know, Bors and Gawain, you are the greatest of allies and the best friends a man could wish for. I meant our predicament is the same. If we march on Bernicia without knowing where Clappa is, without having eyes upon his army every day, then we risk finding ourselves in enemy territory with Theodric in front and Clappa behind.'

'Then we march quickly, kill the bastards before they reach Bernicia. Then find Clappa and kill his band of ragged bastards.'

Arthur put his hand on Bors' broad shoulder. 'You fought like ten men last night, Lord Bors, and thank you for saving my life and the life of my men. You are, I think, the greatest warrior in Britain.'

Bors pushed his shoulders back and tucked his thumbs in his belt. 'Thank you, lord.'

'Gather the warriors. They have roamed far in search of Saxon stragglers. Round them up and we can return to camp at Loidis to eat and rest.'

'The lads are out there finishing off any of the whoresons who are injured or are pretending to be. There won't be any Saxons left alive on this battlefield by midday. Those Picts of yours are murderous savages and no mistake. They've been amongst the enemy, keening a wicked dirge and scalping Saxons and making necklaces of dead men's hair.'

'The Picts helped keep us alive on that hummock. Yes, they are ferocious, but loyal. We are lucky to have them,' Arthur said, and he took Bors' forearm in the warrior's grip. Bors marched off with a sack in his fist, calling to men by name, tossing them arm rings and silver looted from dead Saxons. They laughed with him, called greetings to him in return, and the air lightened and seemed to lift wherever Bors stalked amongst the warriors. He pushed a man into the river and sent the warriors into raucous laughter, then hauled him out and gave him his own cloak to dry himself. He kicked one warrior up the arse and joined three others in a bawdy marching song.

'Kai?' Arthur said, and turned to his foster brother. 'Send scouts out searching for Clappa. We do not march until we know where his army lingers. I want to finish Theodric and Bernicia as much as Bors, but we cannot leave Clappa in the field.'

'I'll see to it now.'

'How much food do we have at Loidis?'

'Enough for a week. Maybe less.'

'Also organise foraging parties. Send them east into Lloegyr and take what we need from the Saxons. Theodric's men are desperate, so make sure no party goes out with less than three score warriors.'

Kai clapped a fist to his breast and marched off along the riverbank, leaving Arthur alone with Gawain.

'There will be another battle, then?' asked the prince of Gododdin. He was taller than Arthur, and lean with long limbs.

'There must be. Defeat Clappa, and then we can invade eastern Lloegyr.'

'Can we defeat them?'

'We have to. We can certainly crush Clappa now that we have beaten half of his and Theodric's army. But we must do it quickly, or he will simply retreat into Deira and Lyndsey and wait for a better time to attack, perhaps when our men have returned home for the harvest, or when we have run out of food and must disband our army.'

'Bors believes war is just about fighting, but he means no harm. He is steadfast and loyal.'

'I wish it were just about fighting, and Bors is certainly both of those things. People remember the fighting, the glory and the noble deeds. They shudder at the thought of the shield wall, of the blood, the injuries, the pain and the suffering. But battle is only one small part of war, one day amongst a hundred days of preparation. The reason the Saxons won so many battles and conquered so many of our kingdoms was because we were not prepared or united, and we did not understand the fundamentals of war. For example, do not march with an enemy in the rear, the necessity and difficulty of feeding thousands of men for weeks at a time, the availability of water and ale, locating the enemy and finding suitable and preferable ground to fight upon. These are the mundane matters a commander must consider, the elements that lead to victory, but you won't hear any bard sing of river crossings, high ground, of sides of bacon or sacks of oatcakes.'

'And thank the heavens for that small mercy. You are right, of course. Which is why you win battles.'

'I almost lost one today. I charged in, hunting an enemy driven by my thirst for vengeance, and men died.'

'We beat Theodric, and you took his eye; we won, and the Saxons lost.'

'King Theodric has more reason to hate me than any other

Saxon in Lloegyr. I fear my fight against him cannot end until one of us is dead.'

'Then let it be him, for we need our *dux bellorum.*'

'I must see to my wounds. Send word to me when we hear from Prince Tristan. He took his men of Kernow and followed Theodric and Lunete. I want to know what route they take and how far ahead of us they march.'

'Of course. Arthur?'

'Yes?'

'Get some rest.'

* * *

It took the rest of that day to see to the dead Britons and raise the funeral pyre upon the blood-drenched hummock where Arthur had made his last stand. The Britons stripped the Saxon dead of anything of value, and by the time the sun began to set, a pile of torcs, silver and gold arm rings, small coins, pieces of hack silver, seaxes, axes, shields, helmets, coats of mail and leather armour, cloaks, furs and a food that stank of too much garlic all lay beside the riverbank.

Arthur shared the spoils of war between each war band. He took nothing for himself but took a torc and a Saxon arm ring for each of the *targaid,* and a large share of the silver for his black cloaks. At dusk, in the moments before they would light the balefire, Arthur found Ethne and his Pictish bodyguard wading in a bend of the river.

'A little late to take a bath?' he called, and the Picts all bowed to him.

'We look for more stones, Ard Rí,' said a green-eyed woman with a fresh, deep red gash on her cheek. 'For our slings.'

'Every one of you fought like ten men today. Take these in

recognition of your courage.' Arthur handed each of them their battle prize. They bowed to Arthur again, and retreated into a huddle, inspecting their rewards, grinning with inordinate pride as they set the torcs about their necks.

'It was our duty, nothing more,' Ethne said. 'We are oathbound to protect you, to fight for you.'

'Well, you have my thanks. I could not ask for a finer guard.'

Arthur gathered with his remaining black cloaks around the knoll where they had fought so desperately, and the rest of the army came close to pay their respects as Dewi lit the balefire and sang the war song of Beli Mawr, and the surrounding warriors clashed their weapons together in time with his words.

Night covered the land when Arthur returned to the camp beyond the ruins of Loidis. He found his tent, stripped off his armour and weapons, and allowed a wise old woman to wash and treat his wounds. Dewi brought him a bowl of thin broth and some ale, and Arthur ate alone before laying down exhausted in his bed. No sooner had he closed his eyes when the sound of a man clearing his throat woke him from his half-sleep.

'What is it?' Arthur asked.

'Forgive me, lord,' said a familiar voice, and Arthur rolled over to see Hywel peering through the tent opening, clad in his Roman war finery. 'I did not wish to disturb you.'

'Hywel!' Arthur smiled and stifled a groan as he sat up. 'It is good to see you. How goes your command of Rheged's warriors?'

'Good, lord. Thank you, lord. They are stout fighters, and Fferog is a capable captain.'

'How can I help you?'

'Merlin is here. He waits for you in the ruins.'

'Merlin? Here?'

'Yes, lord.'

Arthur rose gingerly, muscles sore, wounds throbbing. Hywel helped him to pull on a light jerkin and fasten his black cloak about his shoulders with a cloak pin.

'Your helmet, lord.' Hywel picked it up and examined the black feathers, most of which were missing and the remaining ones broken.

'I'm afraid the plume suffered during battle.'

'Leave it with me. I will find new ones for you. There is no shortage of crows in Loidis and its fields. I don't think I have ever seen so many corpses.'

'You fought today?'

'Yes, lord. With Lord Kai, Fferog and our brave men of Rheged. We killed many Saxons, so many that my spear broke.'

'I am sorry, Hywel, for Loidis.'

'I was born here. Raised to be a warrior here. Idnerth himself trained me in the short sword and pilum spear.'

'Did you have family here, when the city fell?'

'No, thank God. My mother and father are long dead. I had a brother, but he died in battle many years ago. I once had a wife here, but when Idnerth and King Gwallog banished me, she became the wife of another.'

'What happened, Hywel, to make you leave your home?'

Hywel examined Arthur's helmet carefully whilst he considered that question. 'When I was young, I was not the man I am today. When we are young, we make poor decisions, we are lazy, and we think badly of our lot in life. We are jealous, we begrudge what others have, we think there is more out there, that something greater is being kept from us by those in charge, and we hate the privileged few. When we become older and wiser, we come to understand that it benefits a man to be content with his lot. To take pride in his vocation, his armour, his weapons and his craft. There is happiness in dedication, acceptance, friendship and respect. I wish I could go back and shake my younger self, to tell him what I have learned since. But I cannot. So I wear my *lorica segmentata* and my horsehair plume with pride, and regret the decisions I made. Let us leave it at that, lord, if you understand.'

'I understand. You are a fine warrior, Hywel, and I trust you with my life.'

Arthur left him with his helmet and went in search of Merlin, who came like a raven on the edge of a storm with news of armies, kings, war and blood.

20

Many of Arthur's warriors were already asleep after a night spent fighting and day dealing with the aftermath. Those who were awake saluted Arthur, standing and clasping fists to their chests. He returned the gesture, striding through campfires where men played knucklebones, told stories of incredible things they had witnessed during the fighting and remembered fallen brothers. Arthur reached the camp's edge and entered the darkness, crossing a ridge to where the ruins of Loidis loomed in the distance, burned timbers like great fingers clawing at the stars, Roman walls solid and black in the gloom, and Arthur shuddered at the *wyrd* of the place, where so many had died screaming. Arthur ground his teeth, wondering why Merlin came so late and made him leave his bed. Hywel could have brought the druid to Arthur's tent with whatever news he had brought from his travels across the wilds. Arthur entered the ruins, boots crunching on cinders, and he picked his way around the scorched, seared timbers strewn across the Roman cobbled road.

Shining eyes glinted at him from the ruins, a fox, badger or some other animal finding shelter where people once lived. He pulled his cloak tighter about him and followed the road alongside crumpled buildings, still rank with the smell of burned thatch and charred wood. Arthur caught sight of a light flickering up ahead, deep inside where Gwallog's splendid Roman palace had once stood. Arthur passed statues once of pure white marble, now stained brown, cracked and shattered by the intense heat as Loidis burned. He made his way through corridors where once tapestries and curtains hung, woven of the finest cloth to dazzle visitors to Gwallog's court. He stepped carefully through the space where the hall doors had once sat and into the open space where Gwallog once held court. The roof was gone, leaving the patterned floor strewn with debris.

A small fire burned where Gwallog's warriors and people had feasted, and a familiar old man cooked a skinned rabbit. Firelight flickered upon cracked pillars and snapped, blackened roof timbers. It was Merlin, sat with his back to Arthur on a fallen, smashed white pillar, turning his rabbit on a small iron spit.

'Tribunes of Rome once walked these halls,' said Merlin without turning. 'Governors and generals from the eternal city herself. Warriors from Gaul, Germania, Africa and Egypt stood where we are now. Men who straddled the world like gods built these halls and laid these floors, and men who live in holes in the ground cast it asunder.'

'I thought all druids hated the Romans?'

'We do. They put our religion to the sword, and what we know now is but a drop in the narrow sea compared to what my predecessors knew in the days before Caesar. I hate Rome, but I can still lament the loss of something beautiful, and Gwallog's palace was certainly that. Although he allowed the cursed

Christian rot into his kingdom, a fact which he most certainly regrets in the afterlife.'

'Unless he is in the Christ-heaven.'

'Ah, I had almost forgotten that you have discovered a fondness for the nailed god and the ridiculous notion of his virgin mother. You must be delighted that Gwallog is beside your god, plucking harps and singing songs amongst the clouds like a damned fool.'

'Their god is not my god.' Arthur's boots crunched on the tiny, warped stones which had once made up a vast picture on the palace floor. He faced Merlin, but the druid did not look up from his roasting rabbit.

'Not your god, you say, and yet there you were, praying in that abominable church you have allowed Serwan to build in Camelot. Our land suffers, the mountains weep, the rivers lament, our people die, and you have turned your back on the gods, on the gods who forged that sword you swing about with such pride, no less.'

'I have not turned my back on the gods. The Christ is just one more god. We already have many. What difference does one more make?'

'Do not take me for a fool!' Merlin bellowed. He shot up, standing to his full height. He became huge, filling the hall, eyes burning and making Arthur want to turn away in fear. 'Their god despises all others. He would see our gods banished and forgotten. He is the enemy of our gods.'

'I do not take you for a fool, Merlin. Please be calm. We have much to—'

'Calm? Calm, you say? Perhaps Gwallog should have been calm when the Saxons hammered nails into his wrists? Perhaps the women of Loidis should have calmed themselves as the

Saxons raped them over and over again whilst you prayed to Serwan and his one god?'

Arthur dragged a hand down his beard. As soon as the word calm had left his mouth, he knew it was a mistake. There is nothing worse one person can say to another during an argument than for them to calm down. It is like casting oil on a fire. 'Nobody regrets what happened here more than I. But the Saxons have paid for their savagery. Their dead fill the moors and their blood flows like a river. Enough of this, Merlin. I should not have allowed Serwan to build his church, and I should not have gone into that place with Guinevere. But it is done. Let that be an end to it.'

Merlin softened, his wrath shrinking. He bent and lifted the rabbit from the fire and peeled a sliver of meat away. Merlin blew on the steaming food and popped it into his mouth. He hopped from one foot to the other and blew out his cheeks.

'It's hot,' he said through the mouthful, as if that wasn't obvious. 'Would you like some?'

'No, thank you.'

'I love rabbit. And cheese. Do you have any cheese?'

'No.'

'That's a pity.' Merlin resumed his seat. 'I saw Nimue.'

'Is she still in Rheged?'

'She is. Kai does a good job there, and the kingdom prospers. Morgan raises Mordred, and she hates you. Nimue no longer lives at the Bear Fort, but has made her home in a cave, a deep, dark place by the sea where she keeps a gaggle of priestesses. I went to her there, and she tried to kill me. She hates us both, and I fear she will not stop until both of us are dead.'

'Does Nimue possess any power now that she is removed from both you and Morgan?'

Merlin grinned and wagged his roasted rabbit at Arthur. 'That is why you are the Pendragon. Why I gave you that sword. You see things other warriors don't. You, my dear boy, have a brain. Most warriors think with their groins or their spear arms, they think only of reputation, of charging into a fight, of slaughter and prestige. You see Britain as though it were laid out before you on a Roman *mappa*. You understand what it takes to move an army and to keep it in the field. You anticipate your enemy and know when to attack and when to wait. Rare enough skills. Rare indeed.'

'And Nimue?' Arthur reminded Merlin of the original point, flattered though he was by Merlin's words. They were words he needed to hear. Merlin's confidence in him reminded Arthur that he had, perhaps, achieved what few other men could since he had taken up Excalibur's blade.

'Ah yes, Nimue. She has power because she is all but a druid in her own right, except that a woman cannot be a druid, of course. But she has the knowledge. That gives her power, and she can wield that against us. She can draw influence, acquire silver, and with that, she can gather warriors to fight for her cause.'

'Can you stop her?'

'I have. For a time, at least. Do not ask me how, for these are matters known only between druids, and your feeble mind could not comprehend our battle.'

'Very well.' Arthur stifled a smile. Moments ago, Merlin had showered him with rare praise. Now he was feeble-minded once again. 'So we have removed Theodric and Nimue from our *mappa* of problems.'

'Which brings me to my next point. Believe or not, I did not traipse across the country to share rabbit with you in the ruins of King Gwallog's palace, young man. We have removed some problems. We pacified the north. Theodric, minus an eye, creeps back to Bernicia with your sister. I have tempered Nimue. All of this is true and welcome, but the south rises, Arthur. Whilst we fight in the north, Eormenric and Aelle stir. Their drums beat their warriors to war just as Theodric's and Clappa's. Kent and the lands of the south Saxons seethe with warriors. They will march north and west. Mark me, war comes now from the south.'

'A pox on them all!' Arthur clenched his fists and shouted up at the burned-out roof. 'When will it ever end? We have not yet secured our victory here. Clappa must be fought. We must press our advantage against Theodric, and now the south and south-east Saxons march against us. What are we to do?' Arthur could not help but show the emotion which tore at him like dragons' teeth. It was impossible. There were simply too many enemies to fight, but only one Arthur and one army of Britain.

'Aelle's warriors cast their envious eyes towards Dumnonia. They wring their hands, dreaming of its verdant pastures and lush meadows. They smell opportunity. They know we fight in the north, so what better time for them to attack than now?'

'We must march south with all haste. We must stop Aelle before he reaches Dumnonia, or Camelot, and Durnovaria will end up like Loidis.' A sudden vision of Guinevere crucified made Arthur grasp his head and shake out the unwanted picture from his mind.

'But as you say, our tasks in the north are not yet complete.'

'We cannot be in two places at once. If we split our forces, we shall lose both in the north and south and Britain will be no more. We must fight as one army and crush the Saxon kingdoms one by one. It is the only way.'

'And yet we face an enemy in the east, and two enemies in the south. This is not a problem you can solve with your sword. We must use our minds to defeat our enemies, our cunning.'

'You are the druid. What do you suggest?'

'The Saxons won't listen to me. They fear me and my power. That is true enough. Their holy men would heed me, and their kings might listen if I curse and threaten them. But the only thing they truly understand is the power of violence. You are the Pendragon of Britain, the man who can bring every spear of every kingdom to bear against your enemies. That, my dear empty-headed boy, is true power.'

Arthur scratched at a scab forming over one of the many cuts on his forearm. He paced the ruined floor, kicking pieces of crumbled masonry to skitter into the shadows. He did not have to defeat Aelle and Eormenric, he suddenly realised, just stop them from fighting whilst he finished off Theodric and Clappa. He could try to make peace, but what use is peace to a Saxon battle-king with a thousand warriors to keep happy with fighting, silver, women, glory and reputation? 'Tell me what you know of Aelle and Eormenric.'

Merlin grinned, and the firelight lit up the creases of his face so that Merlin seemed timeless, impossibly old and yet still quick of limb and nimble of mind.

'Eormenric is the son of Horsa, one of the very first Saxons to sail across the narrow sea and bring his warriors to Britain. Vortigern, the Usurper of Deira, invited them here. You know the story. Every soul in Britain knows the warp and weft of our downfall, the tragedy woven in blood by Vortigern in the Great War.

'Vortigern was brother to the king of Deira and hungered for its throne. To kill his brother the king and usurp its throne, Vortigern brought ships filled with fearsome Saxon warriors across the narrow sea. He knew them, for Vortigern had fought in Frankia and beyond for the Romans and brought mercenary Saxon war bands back with him from his forays across the sea.

Those first Saxons were Roman mercenaries, *bucellari*, and Vortigern brought them home to win a throne from his older brother, the king of Deira. Once Vortigern killed his brother and stole the throne, King Letan Luyddoc of Gododdin, Urien of Rheged and Uther of Dumnonia rose against Vortigern, expecting to put the usurper down quickly. But Vortigern brought more Saxons to our shores to swell his ranks, and their leaders were Hengist and Horsa, names you have heard of and fear.

'We did not know it at the time, so caught up were we in the fight against Vortigern, but those days saw the end of the age of British kings and kingdoms. Kingdoms born out of Rome's departure, built by blood and on the edge of brave men's swords. The war raged and Saxon ships came in ever greater numbers. Word flew on ravens' wings to their homelands in the Angle, Jutland and the Saxon heartland, of an island riven by war, a land lush and green, a paradise for men strong enough to seize it. And seize it they did. Vortigern usurped his brother and named himself king of Deira, and we almost defeated them.'

Merlin inhaled sharply at the memory and raised a trembling fist, but then it fell, and his chin dropped.

'Then the alliance fell apart,' he said, almost as a whisper too painful to give voice to. 'Ambrosius died. Gorlois died, and I brought his queen, Igraine, to Uther. There was outrage. The kings of Britain believed I was responsible for meddling in Gorlois' death to serve Uther's love for Igraine, and Uther gave up Igraine to become Pendragon. To buy the kings' support for Uther, I became an exile on Ynys Môn, Igraine went to Urien, and Uther became Pendragon. A truce was made. Saxon warlords became kings. Uther stopped fighting, enjoying his new title as Pendragon, king of kings. The alliance shattered and Saxons grew in power. The very Saxons Vortigern the

Cursed brought to our shores to fight in his army betrayed him and overwhelmed his kingdom. King Gwyrangon of Kent fell, Ida came, and now Saxons rule half of our island. Saxons are born here now, people of this land who speak a different language and worship different gods.

'Hengist and Horsa were the first. Brutal men who brought shield-wall fighting and its advanced tactics to our shores. Horsa killed King Gwyrangon of Kent and made it a Saxon kingdom. Eormenric is Horsa's son. He rules a wide swathe of land from Londinium and the River Thames estuary to the white cliffs on the east of our island's south coast. Aelle of the south Saxons came during Uther's reign. As you know, he rules the south coast from Kent to the badlands, the war-torn border between Dumnonia and his kingdom. I have met Aelle. He is both savage and cunning, a man who brought his people here from Jutland across the narrow sea and forged a kingdom for himself.'

'Both kings are dangerous. But different. Eormenric is the son of a great man, a conqueror and a man whom his people still revere. Horsa brought them land, wealth, pride, and a country of their own. Eormenric lives in his father's shadow. Above all things, he must wish to outshine his father's deeds, or at least to match them. How else can he do that but through war? He must expand Kent and conquer new lands.' Arthur turned to Merlin and smiled. 'His borders are all with other Saxon kingdoms, with Aelle and with Lyndsey. Clappa's land.'

'Just so. His champions and captains will forever compare him to his father, for whom they risked everything to come to Britain. Big boots to fill indeed. Eormenric makes his home in the old Roman city of Londinium, a trading city on the wide River Thames. It offers access by river to the narrow sea, and from there to Frankia, the north, south and all the lands of old Rome.'

'Aelle, on the other hand, is a self-made man. He must be old now. He is a king, and no doubt loved by his people whom he has made rich in land. His kingdom of the south Saxons does border Dumnonia, but we have had little trouble from him in recent years, beside the usual cattle raids he uses to keep his warriors busy. He must be content with what he has achieved, and enjoying the spoils of victory. So why does he march now?'

'Perhaps he has been goaded into it by his neighbour in Kent, or Aelle might lend his warriors to Eormenric's cause to give them the fighting and glory all simple warriors crave? Who can say?'

'Who can say without going there and finding out?'

'I am needed here. I must make sure Nimue keeps quiet and help heal your wounded.'

'I meant I would go and find out why Aelle's warriors march. It must be me, but I will not go alone. The army stays here to harry Clappa and Theodric, and I will ride hard for the south and parlay with Eormenric and then Aelle. Eormenric first to get a measure of the man, and see just how hungry he is for battle, then Aelle. Perhaps there can be another way, a way to make a temporary peace with one, or both of them.'

'Good. Now you are thinking like the Pendragon, that is where Uther failed. He could never rise beyond his instincts as a warlord, could never use his power and combine it with his mind.' Merlin stepped quickly towards Arthur and peered deep into his eyes, searching as though he could see into Arthur's very thoughts. 'You must wield your thought cage as you wield Excalibur. I fight these battles in my mind, over and over. Every battle, everywhere, every king, every enemy, every outcome, possibilities of defeat and victory endlessly swirling without certainty. You must do the same. You are beginning to do the same.'

'There is one other kingdom and one other king who has not sworn loyalty to me, a king we leave alone because of his barbarity. We do not talk of him out of fear of what might happen if that beast stirs from his lair, lying as it does on the edge of our island. Morholt of Demetia.'

'You cannot trust that Irish pirate and raider who calls himself a king. Beware of him.'

'He does not fight us. His men raid Powys and Gwent, but all kings raid one another. It has always been our way. Raiding is not war.'

'He is a killer, a slaver.'

'We are all killers, Merlin. Go to Morholt and make an alliance. He has daughters, does he not?'

'He does, and no sons. I do not like this, Arthur.'

'I care not!' Arthur shouted, and then mastered himself. 'You do not have to like it, but we cannot fight many wars with one army. I will go south, and you will go west to Demetia. The army stays here and harries Clappa. Kai can assume command in my absence. You are needed here, but this task carries greater importance. If we can bring Morholt's wild Irishmen to the war, maybe he can take his ships and sail around Kernow and Dumnonia and strike at the Saxons in their own lands, burn their homes for a change.'

'He will ask a high price. I warn you, do not play games with Morholt.'

'I am not the boy who took Excalibur from you so long ago, Merlin. I have become what you wished me to be. You see it, you know it to be true. You said it yourself: I am no Uther. You order me from my bed like I am some common errand boy bound to do your bidding. I am the Pendragon of Britain! I respect you, Merlin, and I always will, but that spear strikes both ways. Look at what I have sacrificed for your dreams!' Arthur threw back his cloak and tore open his jerkin, ripping it from neck to navel and stepping into the firelight better to show the scars on his face and body. 'There can be no half-measures any more. You speak of games? Games? We fight for the survival of Britain. Is this not what you desire? If we are to have victory over the Saxons, it will take more than battle. Did you yourself not say we must fight with our minds and our blades?'

'I did.' Merlin frowned and shook his head.

'Then do as I ask. Go to Morholt and I shall try to speak to our enemy kings in the south and hope they do not kill me.'

'They might take your head. Tread carefully.' Merlin's face took on a strange expression, glassy-eyed admiration and mouth trembling with fear. Arthur stood tall and let Merlin gaze upon the warlord he had created. Arthur was fearsome, every bit as savage, every bit as much of a killer as Aelle, Ida, Morholt, Horsa, Uther, Urien or any of them. Merlin opened his mouth to speak but held his tongue. He nodded understanding, and Arthur realised the look in Merlin's eyes was the look of a man who has kept a pet bear cub, nurtured it, fed it and encouraged it to its wild potential. It was the look of that man when the bear breaks free of its bonds with an almighty roar and descends upon the forest in all its majestic fury.

'Everybody wants my head. Give Morholt what he desires and loose his men on the Saxons.' Arthur reached for the comforting cold of Igraine's bronze disc at his neck. 'If there is to be war. Then let it rage across the island. War is all I have ever known. Now, every Saxon king and warrior shall feel its heat and taste its blood. Let the flames of war burn them all, and we shall see who is left standing at the end.'

21

Arthur reached Londinium in twelve days. He rode with Bors, the *targaid*, and Hywel carried the Roman fasces upon his shoulder. One hundred unwounded black cloaks provided an armed escort, and it had taken two days to find enough horses so that every man made the journey on horseback. The Pendragon dragon banner flew from a long spear and all along the road south folk came to gape and bow to the warriors who clattered along the Roman roads with grim faces and bright spears. Arthur rode at the head of the column on Llamrei, and Cavall had remained with Kai and the army in the north. The *targaid* scowled when they learned they would ride instead of run, but dutifully followed orders. They rode badly but never complained, even though their thighs and buttocks burned for the first seven days.

Summer washed Britain with balmy days, clear skies, foxgloves and blooming poppies. Butterflies danced around hedges thick with wild berries, whilst swifts and martins sang and flew in the treetops. The journey took them through the lawless borderlands between Britain and Lloegyr, but none of the masterless men, or *bucellari* war bands, gave the heavily armed riders any trouble. Scouts watched their progress along the road and Arthur allowed it. Bors wanted to pursue them, but Arthur did not require secrecy. He wanted Eormenric to know he was coming. The banner and fasces were unmistakable and so when the riders reached Londinium at midday on a day so hot that the road ahead simmered like steam from a boiling pot, Saxon warriors lined the road leading to the wide River Thames, but they did not bar Arthur's path.

'Doesn't look like they want to kill us then,' said Bors. 'We must be mad, like a herd of mice riding into cat-land.'

'Turn your shields upside down,' Arthur ordered. The gesture let the Saxons know they came in peace.

Warriors lined the road, hundreds of them in a long line with iron helmets and long spears held to attention. They glowered at Arthur with their braids and plaited beards, and he ignored them, keeping his eyes fixed on the river and the gate. The Thames flowed in a wide meander around the vast old city, a heady mix of Roman stone combined and repaired with brown wattle, faded timber and dreary thatch. They entered the city through its northern gate, which the Romans had called Porta Episcopi, its timber frame reinforced with iron bands and flanked by pitted stone walls. Llamrei's hooves clattered along the wooden plank bridge, and Arthur gulped as the structure shuddered beneath so many horses. Llamrei whickered, his eyes wide as he, like Arthur, feared that the bridge would collapse and send them all tumbling into the grey-brown river. The Thames flowed lazily, small waves rippling its surface as fat-bellied merchants' ships stacked with barrels and chests rowed side by side with sleeker fishing faerings with heavy nets gathered on short mast posts.

'A lot of the furry bastards, aren't there?' said Bors. He waved at the Saxon warriors like a father waving to his young daughter. Dozens of them packed into the city side of the bridge, every man clad in leather and fur and carrying either a spear or a Saxon war axe. The space was narrow, a little over twenty paces wide, and an archway led into the inner-city roads, smaller arches led along the walls to the left and right of the gate.

'Eormenric wants us to see how many men he has and how strong he is,' Arthur replied.

'I'm sure he's as mighty as Lleu Llaw himself. We don't look half bad ourselves, and at least we didn't get all dressed up for nothing.'

Bors wore his mail coat, as did Arthur. Every man in the company had polished their weapons and armour to a shine with river sand the day before reaching Londinium.

A Saxon grabbed Llamrei's reins and Arthur peered down at the blond-haired men.

'Horses stay,' the man said in heavily accented British. Llamrei scraped his hoof across the path and bobbed his head. The Saxon sawed at the reins and Arthur let go of them. Llamrei shuddered beneath Arthur, and then bit the Saxon's face with his stallion's teeth. The Saxon wheeled away with his nose a mess of blood and torn skin and Llamrei bucked, his shaggy fetlocks kicked out behind him and sent half a dozen Saxons flying backwards. The narrow space erupted into chaos with drawn blades and shouts of alarm. Arthur drew Excalibur and Bors his axe, and the black cloaks levelled their spears. Arthur grabbed Llamrei's reins with his left hand and brought the warhorse about so that the stallion's enormous body barged Saxons into the wall.

'Hold!' called a deep, booming voice. A man stalked from the shadows, head-and-shoulders taller than every other Saxon, his neck thicker than his head. His eyes were close-set and his mouth small, his features squashed into the centre of his wide head. He wore a wolfskin over his head and shoulders, the head and fangs draped over his skull, and he wore his long beard in two thick knots. 'Lord Arthur, welcome to Londinium.'

The Saxons bowed their heads and fell back before the new arrival. He raised his hands to show that he came in peace, and his forearms were like ham hocks. Arthur held Excalibur firm. Eormenric had meant to intimidate Arthur and his Britons with the show of force. Saxons saw all *Wealas* as weak, fit for nothing but slavery, and so Arthur had let Llamrei bully and hurt Eormenric's men. He could send messages just as well as the Saxon king of Kent. The Saxons glowered at Arthur and his men, seething with impotent fury.

'I am Hlothhere,' he continued, 'champion of Kent, and my king bids me escort you to his hall. But only you.'

'What about my men?'

'They will be safe. You have my oath, and King Eormenric's oath on it. We shall fetch them food and ale, as is proper for guests amongst our people.'

'Very well.' Arthur leapt from Llamrei's back and stroked the horse's long nose to calm him. 'One of my men will accompany me.' He glanced up at Bors, and the Gododdin man cocked his leg awkwardly over his horse's neck and slumped from its back. Rising to his full height, he surprised Hlothhere by meeting his gaze eye to eye.

'Come then, little man,' Bors said cheerfully, and clapped Hlothhere on the shoulder like they were old friends. 'I hope your ale is better than your welcome.'

Arthur handed Excalibur to Hywel and Bors gave his axe to a black cloak. Weapons were forbidden in any man's hall, and would certainly not be permitted into the king's presence. Arthur and Bors followed Hlothhere into the city, through a magnificent stone and marble building which had once been the Roman forum and the heart of Roman civic life. The pillars and friezes were impossibly detailed, stonework far in advanced of anything the crude Saxon or Briton craftsmen could manage. Weeds and patches of grass showed amongst the stone, and Saxon traders hawked their wares from ramshackle stands and barrows amongst the colonnades.

They walked alongside a Roman temple where goats brayed, and horse dung lay in stinking heaps on marble stones scattered amongst ruins patched by thatch and timber. The basilica stood half broken, with its grand arches still towering above a sagging Saxon-built longhouse built on to its side, the wattle and daub stained brown and green by weather and rot. Men sat on tables outside that building drinking ale from clay cups, and Arthur wondered if the Roman gods had died, or succumbed to the Saxon or Christian god. How else could the Romans have failed, when their buildings, which no man alive in Britain knew how to construct, stood like ghosts above primitive, rotting constructions of wood and mud?

Hlothhere led them through a tangle of winding streets which twisted and turned like a living thing, pulsing with grimy-faced Saxons, shouting, coughing, laughing from inside the maze of leaning, dreary buildings. Stalls lined the thoroughfares where merchants sold coarse woollen garments, pots of exotic spices and objects of glass, silver and gold brought from distant countries across the narrow sea and up the wide River Thames. Pigs snuffled through a marketplace, and one almost knocked Arthur over until Hlothhere kicked it away and gave the herder a clip around the ear. A pair of lean and sharp-eyed sheepdogs trotted beside a shepherd in a wide-brimmed hat.

The people of Londinium wore wool and linen, much like the Britons, but in different cuts and styles. The women wore two brooch pins at their breasts to hold up long dresses of earthy browns and greens and styled their fair hair in elaborate plaits woven into piles atop their heads. Men wore fur and wool, and russet cloaks held up with cloak pins forged in the shape of dragons, boars and horses' heads.

Eventually Hlothhere's path led Arthur and Bors out of the stinking city and into a raised, open space of high columns and white stone, at the centre of which stood a sprawling villa facing down onto the river, and beside the river a Saxon-built wooden hall extended the Roman building on two sides, making the structure larger than any king's hall Arthur had seen in Britain. Guards stood beside each tall column, and as Arthur marched along the Roman cobbled street, he noticed smoke rising from a hole in the Saxon part of the building and knew he approached Eormenric's court.

Heavy-set guards with long spears pulled open wide doors of oak inlaid with bronze whorls and depictions of running animals, and through those doors waited a long, narrow corridor made entirely of cold, pale marble, inside which two lines of Saxon warriors flanked the walls. Arthur stepped inside, and there was barely enough room for Arthur, Bors and Hlothhere to walk single file. Every warrior in the hall was a monster, thick-chested and tall, clad in hard-baked leather with fur at necks and wrists. They stank of sweat and stale leather, garlic and barley. The hall was less than five paces wide, and so the Saxon warriors were so close that Arthur's shoulders brushed against their muscled chests, and every warrior gave Arthur a hard-faced stare. Hlothhere went first, and after he passed, each warrior took a short step forward so that the space became even tighter. The air inside the corridor grew hot and thin, and Arthur had to barge his way through the enemy lines. He ignored them and fought back the natural fear of being in such an enclosed space, outnumbered and bullied by fearsome warriors who hated him. It would take mere heartbeats for them to cut Arthur and Bors down should they wish it, and before sundown Arthur's head might adorn one of London's bridges.

Arthur breathed a sigh of relief as he stepped out of the stifling corridor and into an airy, vast space set with colonnades and white stone paths, and pools of shimmering water. Bors grumbled under his breath and fussed with his armour. Sweat beaded up his broad brow. The Saxons had spoiled the clean Roman space with skulls set into crudely cut niches in the walls beside hung Saxon shields. They had draped full animal skins across pillars beside rushlights and at the end of it all, a man sat on a high-backed stone throne with one leg draped over the arm. He cleaned his fingernails with a short knife as though he were bored, as though his people had not gone out of their way to organise a hostile and intimidating welcome for Arthur and his men. An old man sat on a stone step beside the throne. He wore a fur cloak about his shoulders, and white hair hung thick like a pelt from his head. The old man's hands clutched a gnarled staff and shook uncontrollably, as did his head, causing the hanks of his hair to sway from side to side. The airy Roman atrium was larger than Camelot's newly built palace, and as Arthur, Bors and Hlothhere approached, their heavy boots stomped on stone floors meant for gentle sandals, and the sounds of each footstep echoed around the tiled ceiling.

'King Eormenric, son of Horsa. Lord of the Jutes and Saxons and king of Kent,' Hlothhere shouted, and held his hand out towards the man on the throne. 'My king, I present to you Arthur of Dumnonia.'

Arthur smiled at the not-so-subtle insult, but he declined to bow to his enemy. 'Lord Eormenric,' he said, and placed his hand over his chest in greeting.

'I have heard of you,' said Eormenric in accented British. He was young, his chin barely dusted with a thin, patchy beard. He wore his long golden hair tied back at the nape of his neck and a coat of chain mail, whose links included gold and silver so that it shone like a dragon's skin. The precious metals made the armour beautiful, but it was useless in battle. A spear or seax thrust with any strength behind the blow would shatter those links like a stone thrown into a frozen pond. 'They have given you the title of Pendragon.'

'I have been given nothing. I killed King Uther of Dumnonia in single combat and became the Pendragon of Britain.'

'He was old, as I understand it. But even so, congratulations on defeating him. It must have been… momentous.'

'You speak our language well.' Arthur had no wish to trade insults with a king he had spent precious time travelling across Britain to meet.

'When I was a boy, I had a *Wealas* nursemaid. She taught me your words. But you also speak our tongue, or so they say. My men tell me you won a victory over King Theodric of Bernicia?'

'I did. It was momentous.'

Eormenric wagged his knife at Arthur and sniggered. 'Well played.' He sat up, straightened in his throne and leaned forward. 'You must tell me about the battle. I long to fight in the shield wall. I have the skill for it, my men assure me. Perhaps we shall meet on the field one day.'

'I hope not.' Arthur glanced around the open space, surprised that Eormenric had not offered him and Bors any food or drink, as was the long-held custom of guest friendship which both Saxons and Britons adhered to. Eormenric was young, perhaps not even into his eighteenth year. He had high cheekbones and blue eyes, but his soft milky skin was unmarked by scars, and his hands looked small and slender resting upon his knees. 'Though I can imagine that you would make a fearsome foeman.'

Eormenric's eyes twinkled at that, and he slapped a hand on his thigh. The old man sat at his feet, leaned in and whispered something Arthur could not hear, and Eormenric's delight slipped away. He sat straight-backed and stern-faced. 'Why have you come to Londenwic?' He gave Londinium a Saxon version of its Roman name.

'We are kings, and our people have always been enemies. But I come to speak to a great man and seek peace between Dumnonia and Kent. War costs lives, and it makes our kingdoms poorer. If we can keep our warriors away from one another's borders, if we can put an end to the cattle and village raids, our kingdoms can profit. Replace our blades and war bands with trade and merchants, exchange silver, pelts, tin, furs, amber, grain, timber, jewellery, pots and iron instead of blood and good men's lives.'

The old man leaned into the young king again, and Eormenric kept his eyes fixed upon Arthur. 'Do you come to speak for Dumnonia alone?'

'I do. I am its lord and steward.'

Eormenric smiled and clapped his hands together, the sound startling in the quiet space. 'Woden forgive me. Where are my manners? I have not offered you any refreshments after your journey. We shall talk of these matters this evening, when you are properly rested, and my people will provide food and ale. You wish to talk more of these matters this evening, do you not?'

'You are most gracious, and yes, we should talk more.'

'But I am king of Kent, son of Horsa, not some market trader to be bargained with over the price of an amber necklace or a clay gourd. My time is precious, my ear is in demand. There must be a trial, a contest. If you succeed in that contest, then we shall talk of peace this evening. If not, then you can enjoy your refreshments and scuttle back to your *Wealas* shithole and your border skirmish with my northern cousins.'

Arthur had suspected such a challenge, as was ever the way with Saxon lords. He took a moment to master his anger and frustration at the impertinent young king and then forced a smile to his face. He had come to avert a war that could mean the end of his people forever, so he must endure the insults of a boy-king as a small price to pay. 'Of course. Name your challenge.'

'One of your party must wrestle Hlothhere here. No blades, of course, bare hands only. If my man wins, you will leave Londenwic with your tails between your legs. If you win, then we shall talk more of your proposal.'

Arthur turned to the baleful figure of Hlothhere, and the Saxon warrior returned his gaze impassively.

'I'll fight your man,' said Bors, and he stepped forward, flexing his huge hands open and closed.

'No!' Arthur hissed. 'It must be me.'

'Not whilst there is blood in my veins. This is my fight.'

'Very well,' Eormenric chirped cheerfully. 'I should warn you though, Hlothhere here has killed a dozen men in single combat and is the finest wrestler in all of Kent.'

'And I am Bors, champion of the men of Gododdin.' Bors took two long steps and squared up to Hlothhere, both men monstrously muscled, tall and broad.

'Excellent. I shall look forward to this evening's entertainment,' said Eormenric, and stood from his chair. It was only then Arthur noticed the king was tiny. Even across the atrium,

Arthur could tell that the top of Eormenric's head would only reach Arthur's chest.

'No,' Bors growled. 'You've tried to frighten us with your stinking Saxon bastards at the gate and in your hall. You insult the Pendragon. Now you want us to fight this monster. If it's a fight you want, let's have it now. Here.'

'Well... no...' Eormenric stuttered.

'Now!' Bors bellowed, and he threw off his cloak. 'Fight me now!' His face turned Roman purple, and his great shoulders bunched like boulders. He glowered at Hlothhere, and the Saxon looked to his king for guidance.

Eormenric shuffled his feet and bent to the old man beside him, and the ancient man stood and unfolded himself like a plant emerging from winter's chill to expand in the sun. He towered over Eormenric. Even though he was thin and bony, his frame dwarfed the young king. He croaked something in Saxon and his white hair shifted to reveal a white, scarred face with hard, flat planes and skin drawn taut across bones like cliffs. His eyes flickered, pale blue and covered with a film of white like a serpent. He was blind, but had once been a powerful man, a warrior, and the influence he had over Eormenric surprised Arthur.

'Then fight now,' Eormenric said petulantly.

Hlothhere shrugged and unslung the cloak from his shoulders. He pulled off his armour until he was stripped to the waist, and Bors did the same, but as Bors took off his mail and jerkin he paced back and forth, growling and talking to himself, shouting and stamping his feet. Hlothhere took up a position at the centre of the atrium between two circular pools, and Bors charged at him like a rutting stag. The two men crashed together with a thud, skin slapping, hands scratching and clawing for holds, muscles shifting like slabs of meat. Hlothhere hooked an ankle behind Bors' leg and threw the champion of Gododdin over his hip. Bors landed on his back and scrambled to his feet, but Hlothhere grabbed him around the waist and threw him down hard onto the stone floor.

Eormenric whooped for joy and clapped his hands, and Arthur could not bear to watch. This fight could mean the end of Britain, the destruction of its kingdoms and enslavement of its people, and he cursed himself for allowing Bors to fight the Saxon champion. But watching how easily Hlothhere tossed Bors about like he was a straw training sack, Arthur knew he could have never stood against the much larger man. Bors was the finest wrestler in Britain, and he had to find a way, for Arthur needed peace with the southern Saxons.

Bors tried to rise again and Hlothhere punched him hard in the face, the sound like a cleaver chopping onto a slab of beef. He rolled away and Hlothhere slammed an elbow into his back and raised his foot as though to stamp down and crush Bors' skull like a spider. Bors flipped onto his back and caught the foot and kicked out Hlothhere's standing leg so that the Saxon toppled to the floor. Bors leapt to his feet and shook his head. He stretched his torso from right to left and bent to touch his toes as if the beating he had suffered so far was little more than a warm-up. Hlothhere was all lean, defined muscle, his upper body the shape of a spearhead. Bors was solid bulk, like the stone pillars of Londinium. He was round and hard, no defined muscle showed in his wide frame, just rock-hard strength beneath a thick layer of skin. He was wide across the midriff, where Hlothhere was as narrow as a maid at the hips.

Hlothhere rose and crouched in a wrestler's stance, and he came on carefully, arms curled like crabs' claws. He dived low towards Bors' legs, and the Gododdin man leapt into him, driving a knee into Hlothhere's face. The Saxon slumped to his knees and Bors pounced on him. He grabbed the Saxon around the throat, and spun around, climbing onto his back with his knees tucked into Hlothhere's ribs like a rider on an untamed horse. Hlothhere tried to shake him off, blood pouring from his mashed nose, but Bors had a massive arm wrapped around his throat. They thrashed together, Hlothhere surging into a post so that Bors' back slammed into it, but the Gododdin man kept his grip. Hlothhere's face turned bright red, and then a shade of blue as Bors strangled the air out of him.

'Get him off!' Eormenric shrieked. 'Crush him!' He shouted in his Saxon tongue and stamped his foot.

Bors grinned, blood showing in his teeth and his eyes wide with mad fury. 'Gododdin!' he shouted, the cry long and loud, and with his free right hand he reached around and forced his fingers into Hlothhere's mouth, nails curling underneath his top teeth. Hlothhere thrashed and tried desperately to shake Bors off, and Bors bellowed like a charging bear, and he ripped his right hand backwards and tore Hlothhere's jaws apart with a terrible crunching, ripping sound. Lips tore and bone shattered, and when Bors tossed Hlothhere's lifeless body to the stone floor, his head was a flapping ruin. Bors turned on Eormenric and held up his bloody hands. 'Now we can talk.'

22

'I think there's still blood on the floor over there,' Bors said cheerfully that evening as they sat in the same atrium, but this time it was filled with feasting benches thronged with the great men of Kent.

'I think I'll have nightmares about what you did to Hloth-here's head,' Arthur replied, and pushed away a joint of venison a slave had placed on his plate. Instead, he took a piece of bread and dipped it in honey.

'Bastard wanted a fight, and that's what he got. He said nothing about any rules. All that horseshit with their men in the corridor and at the gates? They're lucky I didn't pull every one of their bloody heads off.'

Arthur and Bors sat alone, and Arthur hoped that his men and the *targaid* were safe and waiting for him by the city gates. It was early evening, and the mood inside Eormenric's villa was sombre. Saxon warriors spoke in hushed voices as they ate beside merchants wearing rich cloth coloured in bright greens and blues. Of the king himself there was as yet no sign, save for a large box covered by sailcloth beside his empty throne. The feast went on, and Arthur ate sparingly. He had no desire to eat. All he wanted was to agree a peace with the young king and then leave, and so it was a relief when King Eormenric finally emerged from behind a wide tapestry and took his throne. He wore a green cloak over his fine armour and a circle of gold upon his brow. The old man came shuffling behind him, using his staff to tap the floor and find his way to sit beside Eormenric's throne.

A slave announced the king's arrival, and a war horn blared in his honour. All the men in the atrium rose and offered a deep bow, and Arthur and Bors also stood as a mark of respect, but they did not offer the Saxon king a bow.

'Lord Arthur,' Eormenric called, after he had waved his men back to their seats. 'We can talk now, if it pleases you.' He waved Arthur towards him, a lazy, careless and disrespectful gesture.

'Mind your temper,' Bors whispered as Arthur rose to his feet. 'Remember why we are here.'

Arthur approached the king and could not help staring at the wizened old man whose blind eyes followed Arthur, his head twitching and shaking. Criss-crossed scars covered his forearms, scored across blue veins and thin skin. Eormenric had stormed off in a childish temper following Bors' victory. The old man had stamped his staff three times on the stone floor to call a gang of slaves who hurriedly dragged away Hlothhere's corpse. One slave had vomited at the horror of what remained of Hlothhere's head, and all the while the old man watched Arthur through his pale, blind eyes. The ancient one had power and influence over Eormenric. That much was plain. But Arthur wasn't sure if he was a Saxon holy man, or something else.

'Are you ready to talk, King Eormenric?' Arthur asked.

The king waved to a slave who hurriedly brought him a

horn of ale. He snatched it from her hand, and some of the froth slopped onto his boot. Eormenric slapped her hard across the face and turned to Arthur. 'What can you expect from a *Wealas* whore?' he said. 'Perhaps I'll have the skin flogged from her back later. Or let my guards tup her, all twelve of them. What do you think?'

'I wish to talk to you about striking an agreement between our kingdoms.' Arthur fought to keep the loathing from his face.

'Oh yes. I had almost forgotten. We shall get to that. All in good time. First, I want to introduce you to my pet.' He pointed to the box beside his throne and then called to another slave. The man grabbed the sailcloth and dragged it away to reveal a wooden cage. The men in the hall cheered when the cloth came away. They laughed and jeered, and Arthur had to bend at the hip to see what lay inside. He expected to see some sort of exotic animal and was surprised to find a man inside, an old man, the top of his head bald and long, unkempt hanks of grey hair growing from the base and sides of his skull. He had a filthy matted beard crawling with lice and was completely naked, only coarse white body hair covering his chest, arms and legs.

Arthur involuntarily covered his nose with his hand at the stink of the man, who looked as though he had not bathed for twenty years. The figure cackled, revealing a set of broken brown teeth, and his eyes blazed with the look of the mad.

'This my pet,' Eormenric said triumphantly, which puzzled Arthur, for the man was clearly insane and so old as to be close to death. 'Vortigern, say hello to a fellow *Wealas* king.'

The figure in the box turned in a circle and showed Arthur his bony arse, sending the men in the atrium into fits of laughter.

'Vortigern?' Arthur said, unable to believe that inside Eormenric's cage sat the despised former king of Deira, the usurper, the man responsible for inviting the Saxons to Britain and starting the Great War.

'Yes, Vortigern,' Eormenric said, and he grinned, savouring the look of horror on Arthur's face. 'He has been our guest here for many years. Though he can be troublesome. He has a fondness for throwing his own shit around. Hard to believe he was once a great man amongst your people. He amuses us, a fool who capers and rolls for scraps of food like a dog.'

Arthur was too stunned to speak. Vortigern turned again in his cage, babbled incoherently and spat at Arthur. Men at the benches threw bones and scraps of meat at the former king, which he gathered up and sucked noisily.

'How?' Arthur managed, still struggling to gather his thoughts.

'My father, Horsa, took him prisoner when he conquered these lands, and he has been in chains ever since. A fitting symbol of your entire people, don't you think?'

'Then Vortigern has found the fate he forged for himself when he brought your people across the narrow sea.'

'Almost like something from a skald's story, isn't it?' Eormenric stood and knelt by the cage. He made silly faces which old King Vortigern mirrored. Eormenric waved him forward and when Vortigern came within reach, Eormenric punched him in the face and the crowd hooted with laughter. Eormenric stood and yawned extravagantly. 'It's been a long day. I think I shall retire.'

'But lord king, we must talk of...' Arthur began, until Eormenric raised a single finger to silence him as though Arthur was a troublesome child.

'No more talk tonight. In the morning, we shall continue our conversation. Sleep well.' He walked away from his throne without stopping to hear Arthur's words and left the atrium in a sweep of flowing cloak and flashing chain mail.

Eormenric did not return to the feast, and Arthur spent the rest of the night sat beside Bors, both men stunned at the shocking fate of the once feared and powerful King Vortigern. Arthur fumed silently, pushing food around his plate with an eating knife.

'He's taking you for a fool,' Bors had said upon Arthur's return, but said no more when he saw the look on Arthur's face. Arthur was in the middle of a war and did not know how Kai pressed the fight against Theodric and Clappa. Arthur's army could lie in ruins on a distant battlefield, or a Saxon king could be dead and swathes of land returned to British rule. The sense of wasted time burned Arthur, making his skin crawl and itch with impatience. He thought of leaving immediately, but with guards at every door in the atrium, Arthur suspected they would stop him and force his return. They did not offer Arthur and Bors the courtesy of sleeping quarters, and so they lay down to sleep beside their feasting bench, as was the custom, and just as common warriors did in Eormenric's atrium and in halls across the land. Arthur lay down beneath his cloak and closed his eyes as his mind worked over the puzzle of how he could make peace with a young king full of pride and arrogance.

Men snored as they slept all around him, but sleep would not come for Arthur. Bors had fallen asleep instantly and his heavy breathing was enough to keep Arthur awake, even if his myriad problems weren't enough to keep him from the dream-world. Arthur turned and felt something small hit him on the shoulder. He ignored it and closed his eyes again, and then something struck his head. Arthur sat up and saw a small bone lying next to him. Something hissed in the darkness, and then hissed again. Arthur stood and tiptoed carefully towards the sound, edging slowly across the atrium made dark now that slaves had blown out the rushlights and torches.

'Come closer,' whispered a voice in Arthur's tongue. 'Here. Come.'

Arthur followed the voice and stopped when he realised it was Vortigern calling to him from within his cage.

'Are you really him?' Arthur asked as he knelt beside the stinking, pitiful figure.

'Once, yes. Now?' He cackled and then clapped a filthy, broken-nailed hand to his lips. His face was as wrinkled as a winter leaf, and he was skeletally thin. Faded death-ring tattoos circled his forearms, and he twitched and itched, head bobbing and mouth drooling. There was a sadness in his deep-set eyes and in the downturned curl of his lips. 'Are you truly the Pendragon?'

'I am.'

'What of Uther?'

'I killed him.'

Vortigern shuddered. 'And Merlin?'

'Merlin thrives. We strive to recover that which was lost.'

'So much was lost.' Vortigern grabbed the wooden bars of his cage and placed his head between them, staring hard into Arthur's eyes. 'I came close and lost everything. Then...' He wept, fat tears rolling down his gaunt cheeks, his frail body shaking like a feather in the wind.

'What do you want? You are the father of our doom. How could you bring the Saxons to our home?'

'Pah! Don't be a fool. Merlin has filled your head with turds. Many kings brought war bands from across the sea to fight for them in those days. They call me a usurper, but that throne was mine! My brother was a bastard, and I wanted what was mine. But Hengist and Horsa betrayed me and then...'

'Now you sit in a cage, and Horsa's son rules Kent.'

'Eormenric? He is a simpleton, a cur! Horsa still rules Kent. Don't let Eormenric's display of kingship trick you. He is a stunted weasel, an unwanted turd in the ale barrel. Horsa still rules!'

Arthur sighed. 'Then who is the man who sits on the throne? Why are you bothering me?' He had no desire to talk to a man driven mad by humiliation and torture, a traitor who had ruined Britain and caused so much death and suffering.

'Eormenric sits on the throne, but Horsa is the old blind man beside him. Horsa rules! The Saxons would never allow a blind cripple to rule them, but nor will they accept Eormenric's rule when the old warlord finally dies.'

'Will Horsa make peace with Dumnonia?'

'I sit beside them both every day, as I have for decades! They think me mad, and perhaps I am! But I listen. And I know.'

'What do you know?'

'They cling on to power. Weakened. Horsa won't last much longer, and his son is an empty-headed weakling. Eormenric boasts of war, but he would not leave Londinium for fear another of his champions would kill old Horsa and take his place. But he won't make peace, not ever! How would that look to the warriors who covet his throne?'

'I am wasting my time here?'

'Yes! Go to Aelle. He is the warrior, but he is old. He will make peace, but at a price. You must pay whatever he asks, though it will be a great sum. Enough to keep his warriors rich in silver for a year or more. Kent will eat itself when Horsa dies, and until then they will boast and talk of war, but its armies will do no more than raid.'

'What if you are wrong?'

'I was wrong before. Trust me now, I beg you.' More tears dripped down his face. 'Let this be my redemption.'

'Only the gods can give you that, Vortigern.'

'I counsel you wisely, young Pendragon. Heed my advice and do me one favour in return?'

'What is it?' Arthur frowned, expecting the old man to ask Arthur to set him free and carry him away.

'Give me your eating knife and allow me to end my suffering. Let me open my veins so that the cursed misery of my life can end.'

Arthur glanced around the hall. The gate guards all slept, as did every warrior in the hall, curled up beneath their cloaks in the floor rushes. He had wasted enough time in Kent with his blind king and his puppet son. Arthur slipped the eating knife from his belt and handed it to Vortigern.

'May the gods have mercy on your soul, for the people of Britain will never forgive you.'

Arthur left Vortigern in his cage, and the old usurper sighed with relief as he opened his veins and welcomed death's relief. Arthur crossed the sleeping warriors and woke Bors, which took increasingly violent shakes of the big man's shoulder. Bors finally woke and Arthur led him out of the atrium, through the marble hall and out into Londinium's winding streets. Bors asked no questions as they crept along the cobbles, and no guards patrolled the streets at night, so Arthur moved unnoticed through the jumble of Roman stone and Saxon wattle and daub. They found Hywel and the *targaid* in a stable by the river gate, sleeping beside their horses' stalls. Bors and Arthur woke the warriors, and they saddled their horses quietly in the darkness.

Four river-gate guards died with slingshot stones in their

skulls and Arthur and his war band left Londinium by the same gate through which they had entered. They rode over the wooden bridge and the Thames' black waters and then out into the night-shrouded land beyond. Riding at night is a treacherous business, but Arthur led them slowly along the Roman road, eager to put as much distance between them and any men Eormenric might send in pursuit. The war band left Kent and headed south-west towards Aelle's lands of the south Saxons.

Arthur rode with a head full of Vortigern's captivity, Kent's weak young king, and what that meant for Britain's future. His army remained in the north, locked in the fight to keep Theodric pegged back in Bernicia and to find and destroy Clappa's army. Arthur's riders entered Aelle's lands after a week in the saddle, and Arthur sent Ethne and her Picts ranging ahead of the column to scout the lay of the land, its roads, and to return with reports of settlements, armed men and other information to inform Arthur of how best to approach the enemy king. Arthur knew Aelle lived within the Roman fortress at Noviomagus Reginorum close to the south coast, but to get there meant hard riding through a country thick with enemy warriors and war bands.

The *targaid* returned as evening drew in on their first ranging south. Arthur met with Ethne as his men made camp beside a vast oak tree. She left her horse with a black cloak and hurriedly leapt over the thick roots.

'The Saxon king comes to you, lord,' she said, out of breath for once. The scouts' horses all showed white lather upon their flanks and the riders bent to take a drink and recover.

'Aelle comes here?'

'Aye, lord. He knows of your arrival in his kingdom, and King Aelle rides to meet you.'

'With how many men?'

'A force to match your own, though he does not wish to fight.'

'Did you speak with him?'

'No, Ard Rí. A man met us on the road bearing Aelle's royal torc and flying his standard. We rode all afternoon to bring you the news.'

'You did well. Rest now and recover. When will he reach us?'

'On the morrow, lord.'

Arthur and his warriors woke early and waited on the Roman Port Way road. Arthur had them form up in five ranks with the *targaid* behind him. Hywel and Bors stood beside Arthur, and Hywel carried the fasces, whilst a black cloak in the rear ranks carried the dragon banner. Six riders cantered on the road and stared at Arthur's men, before galloping away south, and at mid-morning King Aelle himself arrived on a black stallion as big as Llamrei, and with him came two hundred Saxon warriors carrying shields, spears, axes and seaxes.

'These Saxon bastards love a bit of intimidation,' said Bors, squinting down the road at the larger enemy force, the memory of Londinium still fresh in his head. 'Aelle comes with twice our number at his back.'

'They do,' Arthur replied. 'But be thankful he didn't bring an army to slaughter us.'

'He still might.' Bors turned to Arthur and winked, and Arthur could not help but laugh at the madness of it all, of being in a second enemy's land so soon after braving Londinium.

Aelle needed two men to help him climb from his horse. He wore a red cloak trimmed with white fur and a thick gold torc coiled about his neck. Aelle walked towards Arthur, using a spear as a walking stick to brace a stiff left leg. His hair, a mix of flax and silver-coloured strands, fell down his back in a thick braid and he wore his beard close cropped to his angular jaw. Arthur walked forward to meet him, and the Saxon king's blue eyes flicked down and noticed Arthur's own limp. The pain in Arthur's leg had grown worse after so many days in the saddle and he could not bend his leg without pain stabbing down his thigh and into his knee. The Saxon king came alone, leaving his men milling on their horses behind him, and so Arthur walked alone from his own war band and raised a hand in greeting.

'You are in my land,' Aelle said in Saxon.

'I am Arthur. Come to talk with you, Aelle, king of the south Saxons.'

'I know who you are.' He pointed at Arthur's leg and then gestured at his scarred face. 'You bear the marks of war just as I, though you are a much younger man. Come sit with me. We shall eat, and you can tell me why you risk your life coming into my kingdom.'

Arthur and Aelle sat on a fallen tree trunk beside the road, and Aelle's men brought them blood sausage and black bread, and Hywel brought a skin of ale and a handful of oatcakes which the two kings ate in silence until their men withdrew and left them alone.

'I come to talk, not to make threats or exchange insults,' Arthur said, wiping crumbs from his beard.

'That's a pity. I have some good insults prepared for you. So, Pendragon, tell me why I shouldn't kill you and rid myself of a capable enemy?'

'I want to strike a truce between our kingdoms, a peace to allow our people to flourish and for our spearmen to rest.'

'Your spearmen are fighting in the north. Dumnonia is unprotected. Perhaps I should take my men west and capture the stronghold you are building inside the fortress of the

ancient ones? Or I could sack Durnovaria? I could take
Dumnonia and make it my land.'

'You could try. But how many battles have your people won
since I became Pendragon?'

Aelle laughed. He had a small, flat nose and flinty eyes set
above a square jaw and had two fingers missing from his left
hand. 'Few enough. But Dumnonia is weak, and you don't have
the men to protect it.'

'If you attack Dumnonia, I will bring the warriors of every
kingdom in Britain south and we shall descend upon you with
so many spears that our army will drink your rivers dry. We
shall raze every one of your towns and sow their ruins with salt.
I give you my solemn oath on that, King Aelle. Attack
Dumnonia now, and every warrior in your army will perish, I
will make slaves of your people, and men will shudder when
they hear the fate of King Aelle of the south Saxons.'

'I thought you did not come to threaten me?'

Arthur leaned back and let the hardness fall from his face.
'You started it.'

Aelle smiled ruefully, nodded and fumbled for a shred of
food stuck in his teeth with his tongue. 'So, you come with an
offer?'

'I come to offer you peace.'

'I am a leader of warriors, just like you. We must keep our
men happy with silver and glory, Arthur Pendragon. If my
spearmen shall have no glory, how shall I keep them happy and
loyal? What use is peace to me?'

'I will pay you silver to keep your men satisfied.'

'Of course you will. Is it a coincidence that you arrive in my
kingdom just as a fleet or Irish pirates raid my coastline?'

'Yes,' Arthur lied. Merlin had persuaded Morholt of
Demetia to bring his ships and his Irish warriors to raid Aelle's

and Eormenric's coastal towns. Arthur hid the satisfaction from his face and tried not to wonder what price the Irish warlord had demanded from the druid.

'I came here years ago with three ships and men to crew them. My father's father built those ships. He cut their keels from single oak trunks, he laid their clinker-built hulls, and cut their oars from stout ash. I came here because other men invaded our lands, stronger men with larger armies, men displaced from their own lands as the Roman Empire shrank and the legions scuttled back to their eastern heartland. So we came across the sea, and I lost one ship in the crossing. Seventy men died that day, screaming in the howling storm as waves like mountains dragged them down to a death without honour. The rest of us made landfall, and I carved out a kingdom over other men's bones, drenched this island in blood, and with these hands I made myself a king.' Aelle opened his large hands, and he stared down at the callouses and missing fingers. 'I am older now, and have slaked my thirst for blood a dozen times over. The young crave reputation, silver and women. I have all of those things, so now I crave something else. I want a kingdom for my sons to inherit, which my grandsons can grow up in and thrive. Can you understand that?'

'I can. I want the same thing.'

'But it is an old warrior's dream, a folly, the longings of a man who has lived a life too long in the shield wall. For you and I know that there can never be peace in this world. Not as long as there are men in it, and spears in it, and silver and grand halls, ships, ale, women, swords, armour, helmets and songs of heroes. Such things call to us. They sing to our young hearts, and we march with sharp blades and vicious intent. There will always be war, and we must all prepare for it or suffer its horrors. I have pirates off my coast burning and enslaving my people, and my men tell me young King Eormenric bangs the war drum to keep his men happy, and I am no friend of Kent. I could march my warriors into Kent and rip a swathe of ripe land from the pup-king's grasp. So perhaps we can have peace, you and I, Arthur Pendragon, but only for two summers, and only if the price is right. Then it must begin again.'

'Name your price, and there shall be peace between our kingdoms.'

'Three thousand Roman pounds of silver.'

Arthur almost fell off the tree trunk. 'Has any man ever seen such a sum?'

'Peace is an expensive business.'

'Five hundred pounds, and three wagons of tin from Kernow.'

Arthur and Aelle haggled and bartered like merchants at a riverside fair, and Arthur finally agreed that one thousand five hundred Roman pounds was the price, and that he would deliver it in two halves, one to be paid that summer, and the next the following spring.

'Can you find such a sum?' Bors asked after roaring with laughter so hard that he almost pissed in his trews.

'I must. But now we have peace in the south. Eormenric is too petrified of his own warlords to leave Kent, and Aelle will not attack us. So we ride hard north and back to war. We shall crush Clappa and Theodric, Bors. We shall recover their lands and win a victory to make the rest of Lloegyr shudder in fear.'

23

Twenty days later, Arthur found his army camped outside Dun Guaroy's high crag on Bernicia's wave-battered coast. Arthur had followed Dere Street north until his scouts found scars left upon the land by the army of Britain. The army had made camp around a captured village, so that leather and sailcloth tents spread out around a clutch of wattle houses topped with earth, and the covered pit dwellings of Saxon churls. Arthur rode Llamrei through gathered warriors of Gododdin, Rheged, Gwent, Gwynedd, Powys and Dumnonia and, as he rode, a cheer spread through the camp. It started as a few men on the camp's periphery, calling a greeting and raising their spears in salute, and grew like a wave washing through camp until a thousand men shouted his name and clashed their weapons together. The din lifted Arthur, and he rode as though flying on a cloud. He waved to them, drew Excalibur and held the mighty blade aloft, and the warriors of Britain roared their acclamation to see their Pendragon returned to lead them to victory.

Arthur found Kai, Tristan and the rest of leaders stood on the beach, its sand left dark and heavy by the retreating tide. He left Llamrei with a soldier and walked across the beach, holding his cloak to stop the sea wind whipping it around his feet.

Kai smiled broadly and raised his hand in greeting. 'It's about time,' he quipped, shouting to be heard above the gale. 'I thought Eormenric had taken your head.'

'I have it still.' Arthur shook each of the wrists in the warrior's grip. 'What news of Clappa?'

'Four hundred men screen his army and prevent them from returning to Deira. So Clappa's army remains in the field, foraging what scant food remains in border villages. They are hungry, and angry. Einion of Powys leads the four hundred with orders not to engage the enemy, but to burn grain and harry Clappa's foragers. Einion has burned river bridges and ambushes Clappa at fords and mountain passes.'

'How many men remain in Clappa's force?'

'Fifteen hundred, we think. Though he has called up the men of Lyndsey, so he could have close to two thousand.'

'And Theodric?'

'Inside there.' Kai pointed to Dun Guaroy. 'And we all know how strong that place is. Do we have to worry about the south?'

'There will be no attacks from Kent or the south Saxons this year.'

'I can only imagine what you had to do to bring Eormenric and Aelle to agreement.'

'There is much and more to tell, but now is not the time.' The tale of Bors' fight against Hlothhere, and of the terrible fate of Vortigern the Usurper, were tales best told beside a hearth fire. 'We need to bring Theodric to heel. He is beaten, and he knows it. Then we destroy Clappa.'

'The men are restless,' said Tristan. 'They have been away from home for too long. Fields need work, animals need tending. We cannot make war forever.'

'We won't need to. Press home our victory over Bernicia, then destroy Clappa. Once that's done, the men can march for home. You have my word. We shall leave the northern Saxons unable to fight for years, and the southern Saxons won't trouble us until at least next summer. Crush them now, and then next year we destroy them.'

'How are we going to get Theodric out of that?' Kai pointed across the bay to where Dun Guaroy perched on its high precipice.

Arthur had once infiltrated that strongest of fortifications and rescued Guinevere and Gawain from King Ida's grasp. The memory of that fight, of the blood and suffering, sent a shiver across Arthur's shoulders. Its sharp timbers rose like monster's teeth atop a humpbacked crag in a wide tidal bay. The crag loomed dark and foreboding across the rolling grey sea, with sharp cliffs and sheer sides leading down to crashing white-capped waves, and a sloping, grass-covered hillside on the land-ward side. A bleak, dark wooden hall topped the crag, all sharp edges and threat. Its thatch was a dark brown, and the palisade, which was still under construction when Arthur last saw it, was now finished. The new fortifications were jagged and sharp, like blades buried into the rock and pointing to the sky in defiance of the men from whom the Saxons had ripped the land. Those new timbers shone yellow like gold, stark against the dull greys and browns of the older buildings. Gulls swooped over the dunes, gliding on the breeze, and the smell of the sea was thick in Arthur's nose.

'Theodric knows we are here, but he also knows we can't assault him or besiege him. A siege by land is useless when he has the sea and ships to fish it and bring in supplies,' Arthur said, talking to himself as much as the others. 'He can't march out to fight us, not after the defeat he has already suffered.'

'If Merlin were here, we could ask him to block out the sun and build more of his druid's *seidr* war machines,' said Bors, who had joined the group. The others grinned, but kept their eyes fixed on Arthur.

'Merlin is not here. Though we owe him once again. He went to Morholt of Demetia and persuaded him to take his ships against Aelle and Eormenric. So we must draw Theodric out and come to terms.'

'Terms?' asked Tristan. 'We gave Theodric his life after the Dubglas, and he rose against us again. If we do not take his head now, we leave an enemy at our backs. We cannot fight the same enemies year after year. There must be a conclusive victory.'

'There must. But we must pick the battles we can win. Cripple Theodric now, and we destroy Clappa whilst he remains in the field. Wipe Deira out, as we did Lyndsey. Another Saxon kingdom defeated. We leave Bernicia isolated and Lloegyr spilt into two, the southern kingdoms and then Bernicia alone, hundreds of Roman miles north, isolated and without allies. Next year we take Dun Guaroy and destroy the Saxons' last stronghold in Bernicia, but I shudder at what it will cost us to take it. After that, it's Kent and Aelle and then Britain shall finally be restored to its people.'

They stared at Arthur for a moment, their minds working to understand the gravity of his words. He spoke of an ultimate victory they had never dreamed possible, and now Arthur showed them the way. A measured plan, realistic and possible.

Arthur held each of their gazes, one at a time, allowing them to drink in the certainty and steel of his conviction. 'Order the army out. I want every scrap of land about Dun Guaroy razed. Every man killed, and every Saxon woman and child left outside its walls. Destroy Bernicia, burn it, kill every goat, cow, sheep and pig. All I want to see of Bernicia is smoke and ruin, and all I want to hear is the lamentation of Theodric's people.'

For a week, Arthur's army put Bernicia to the sword. Every day Arthur waited on the beach outside Dun Guaroy in full armour, Hywel beside him carrying the fasces, and the black cloaks at his back with the mighty dragon banner flying, snarling and clawing with its woven teeth and claws a constant reminder to King Theodric of exactly who destroyed his kingdom. Blue skies and sunlight made the sea blue and calm, but inland smoke burned from so many fires that towers of ash and filthy grey clouds turned Bernicia into the underworld of the Saxon religion.

On the eighth day, a thin rain drifted in from the sea and at midday on the ebb tide, a company of twenty riders picked their way down Dun Guaroy's promontory and rode slowly along the beach until they halted before Arthur and his black cloaks. Lunete and Theodric rode their white horses, and the rest of the warriors came with their shields and spears held upside down to show that they came in peace. Arthur put on his crow-feather plumed helmet and marched out alone to meet them in his war glory.

'We come to talk,' Lunete called from the back of her beautiful white stallion.

'You come to ask for peace, and you come to talk because you can come no other way,' Arthur said. 'Get off your horses and come and stand before me.' Arthur pushed his shoulders back and held his chin high. He was not the supplicant he had been in Londinium and with Aelle; here he was a conqueror, a ruthless warlord with the army of Britain at his back.

Lunete turned to Theodric, who wore a thick strip of linen about the ruin of his eye and face. Theodric bowed his head and climbed down from his horse, and Lunete followed. Arthur waited patiently whilst they walked to stand before him.

'There must be peace,' Lunete said, brushing her black hair away from her face. The rain plastered her hair to her head, and she seemed pale, her big eyes sunken.

'Can you speak for yourself?' Arthur asked Theodric, and the king's one eye blazed with fury.

'I can,' he said through gritted teeth.

'Then what say you?'

'We ask for peace.'

'You ask, or you beg?'

'We ask, Arthur. Do not be like this,' Lunete said.

'Like this?' Arthur laughed. 'Look at your kingdom.' He cast his arm towards the towers of smoke. 'I destroyed your army, and now I lay waste to your kingdom. Perhaps I should kill you here on this beach and have my supper in your hall?'

'We come to parlay in good faith. You are a man of honour.'

'Am I?' Arthur's fingers twitched. With one sweep of his sword, he could slay Theodric and end Bernicia forever. But he was Arthur, and what is a man without his honour? Kill Theodric now and every enemy would know never to trust his oath or risk meeting him face to face. So Arthur closed his fist and let honour keep his anger at bay.

'Please, Arthur. Listen to what we have to say. Listen, if I ever meant anything to you, if you even hold one fond memory of our lives in the Caer.'

'Our old lives did not seem to matter too much to you when I stood alone and outnumbered before your army. You would have killed me and my men. I am the man who fights alone, who fought Uther and Owain in single combat. I am the man who rides into enemy kingdoms and who stares down enemy armies on the battlefield. I am the man who defeated Bernicia. I am Arthur, but not the Arthur you once knew. You tried to butcher me, and many of my men died before your fury. So reap it, Lunete, reap the field of destruction you have sowed. Reap it!'

Lunete bowed her head, shamed by the truth of Arthur's words. Theodric stepped in front of his queen.

'I will give you my oath that we will not march beyond our borders,' he said, mouth curled in disgust at his dishonour.

'Your oath? It will take rather more than that. All your lands beyond this bay are now mine. I cede them to Gododdin to be ruled by King Letan as he sees fit. You will kneel to me and acknowledge me as your high king. You have trade from the sea, and silver in your high fortress, so you will pay me a sum of one thousand Roman pounds of silver, and each of your warriors will leave their spears, shields and seaxes on this beach.'

'One thousand pounds?' Theodric spluttered. 'An impossible sum!'

'Make it possible. Bring out all your treasures, all your weapons. Sell your slaves and your ships and bring me what I demand. This is your war. You are the aggressors and now you are defeated,' Arthur shouted, fists clenched, face as hard as the jagged cliffs.

'But you swear that the attacks on our lands will stop.'

'I will swear nothing! Kneel before me now and beg for mercy. Kneel before the people of Britain. You are defeated, shamed, humiliated. Kneel now, and you may keep your lives.'

Theodric sagged. All pride and fight fled from him like birds in winter. He dropped to his knees in the sand, and the warriors behind him did the same. Only Lunete remained standing, tears rolling down her white cheeks, and then she too knelt before Arthur. Arthur stood triumphant over them, and made every enemy on that beach kiss the axe and rods of his imperial fasces, the Roman symbol of his power. They swore to recognise

Arthur as Pendragon, and to provide the sum demanded, a sum taken from Saxons to pay most of Aelle's price of peace.

As the Saxons retreated to their high fastness, Lunete called to Arthur, but he turned his back. She had chosen her side, and Arthur's heart was cold to pity. Arthur left Dun Guaroy three days later with wagons laden with Saxon spears, shields, seaxes and iron-riveted chests full of silver coins, gold brooches, cloak pins, candlesticks, plates and rings, most of which he knew had been stolen from Britons during Ida's conquest of Bernicia during the Great War. Arthur left Bernicia in ruins and its king broken, and marched two thousand men south in search of Clappa, of battle, and the destruction of the Saxon kingdom of Deira.

24

Arthur marched the army south along the Roman road into Saxon Deira, the kingdom which spanned the space between the River Humber and the River Tees. Einion's war band had kept Clappa's army away from his fortifications at the old Roman towns of Derventio and Eboracum, each with stout Roman walls reinforced by ditch, bank and wooden palisade. Scouts found Einion and his warriors outside the forest of Celidan, and heard news that Clappa and his men camped deep inside the dense woodland, and had been there for a week since the news arrived of Arthur's scouring of Bernicia.

'They are starving, lord,' said Einion as the army's leaders stared down at the vast canopy from an escarpment above an abandoned clay pottery whose vast ovens and clay pits stood empty. The Saxon churls had fled the area before Arthur's advance, retreating east towards the safety of fortified towns, leaving the land a ghostly place of cows lowing with bellies full of milk, untended fields and villages where pigs snuffled in houses and chickens roosted in open window shutters.

'Well done,' said Arthur, and Einion's grim, weathered face

cracked into a half-smile as the champion of Powys allowed himself a moment of pride. 'How many warriors are in the forest?'

'Two thousand, we think. Hard to count the bastards. They march in small war bands. That was how we kept them back. If they'd come together as one army, we'd have stood no chance.'

'But they are together now?'

'Aye. All the rats in one place. They had to. They're eating roots and leaves in there, lord. Bastards look like fetches, like dead men wearing other men's armour.'

'Then now is the time to fight them. We have equal numbers, but we are strong, well fed and ready to fight.'

'They are dug in though, lord. Clappa has gathered briars and thorn bushes to make a waist-high wall, and they've dug pits and set traps in the trees. One of my lads fell in a pit with sharpened stakes at the bottom. One went into his groin, took him a day to bleed out. We couldn't pull him off the bloody thing.'

'They'll pay for that, for everything. Don't worry.'

'I'm not. You are here now.'

Arthur clapped him warmly on the shoulder and went to his four hundred warriors, thanking them. They told him stories of wild fights on riverbanks, of night attacks, of brave deeds, and Arthur listened, congratulating men he recognised by name, and clasping the forearms of others in respect. They had made a battle possible, a chance to destroy a Saxon kingdom and slaughter King Clappa and his Saxon horde, and to restore Deira to British rule.

'Fighting in a forest is a dirty business,' said Bors that night as he, Arthur and Kai shared a skin of mead. 'Too many surprises. You can't see what's coming on your flanks. Archers hide in trees, and the enemy can dig traps and hide them with leaves. I don't like it.'

'You've fought in the forests around Gododdin your entire life?' said Kai.

'I know. Doesn't mean I have to like it, though. Better to have the battle on a big, open field. Shield wall against shield wall. Proper battle.'

'I don't think Clappa will be so obliging,' said Arthur. 'His men are hungry and weak. He doesn't want a battle.'

'So, it's going to be a fight in the forest?'

'It will. And it will be tomorrow.'

'Tomorrow we should send men ranging into the trees. We need to know every pond, every gulley, every clearing. We need to find where there is high ground, brooks, rivers, rocks and anything else Clappa can use against us.'

'Then that is what we shall do,' Arthur agreed. 'We are between them and what they cherish most. Their homes, their wives and children. That makes Clappa's men fearful. If I could, I would avoid fighting in the forest, because everything you say is true, Bors. But there must be a fight, and we must win. They might advance out of the trees to fight us if we burn and ravage their homes, but we do not have time to wait them out. We can perhaps feed our army for another week, and the warriors are eager to return to their homes and farms. If we keep this army in the field too much longer, there will be no harvest and no food for winter. We must have our fight and our victory now.'

The following day, Bors sent scouts deep into the forest. Two hundred men armed with bows went into the forest on foot, ranging deep into the tangle of oak, ash, beech, hazel, birch and alder. Arthur sent his black cloaks riding east with orders to find as many reaping hooks and lengths of rope as possible, and they returned at midday as the first of Bors' rangers returned from the woodland. Thirty men died in the trees, picked off by Clappa's men and their traps. The scouts wove a tapestry of guarded pathways, treacherous gulleys, death pits and men huddled between the boughs, coughing and drinking from a murky stream.

'Did you count the men behind Clappa's fence of briar and thorns?' Arthur asked.

'Impossible to say, lord,' said a short man with a pointed beard. 'How can we count them between the trees?'

Arthur turned to Bors and Kai. 'We attack now. Ready the men.'

Warriors formed up in ranks of fifty, and Arthur stared into the gloom beneath the branches. He should wait. He needed more time. Arthur knew he should fully scout the woodland and its surroundings, but why wait when his enemy was trapped, weak and hungry? He mounted Llamrei and cantered ahead of the spearmen to join a line of two dozen horsemen, each of which carried a reaping hook fixed to a length of twisted hemp rope. Arthur drew Excalibur and led the riders into the forest, careful to keep to the tracks and deer paths pointed out by his scouts.

The air grew close within the trees, and Arthur kept Llamrei at a trot. He searched every gap, every break in the woodland for any sign of surprise or ambush, allowing Bors' scouts to ride ahead and point out where Clappa's traps lay beneath leaf mulch and fallen branches. Trees creaked and groaned around him, and Llamrei whickered and shook his head at the bad ground underfoot. Arthur's spearmen remained on the forest's edge, waiting for his signal to attack, and he waved the riders on with Excalibur's shining blade. The scouts reined in and pointed to a glade visible through a clutch of hazel trunks. Arthur saw the fence, little more than a waist-high gathering of bushes, but the thorns and briar made enough of an obstacle to make it defensible, and so Arthur waved up his riders with their rope and hooks.

Arthur raised Excalibur to signal the attack, and just as he was about to point her blade at the enemy fortification, an arrow whistled through the foliage and took the lead scout between the shoulders. Another flashed so close to Arthur's face that he felt the wind of its passing.

'Now!' Arthur ordered. 'Do it now!'

His riders urged their mounts into the clearing, but arrows came like a deathly hail. One struck the tree beside him and Llamrei scraped the mulch with his foreleg. Riders fell and horses reared with arrows in the necks and rumps. But most of Arthur's men made it through. They tossed their hooks into the briar and fixed hemp ropes to their saddles. Faces appeared behind the makeshift fence, gaunt faces with desperate eyes shaking spears and axes and shouting alarm to their fellows. Arthur led his horsemen, cantering away from Clappa's camp and behind them, the reaping hooks dragged away the thorn and brush fortifications to leave Clappa's warriors unprotected.

More arrows flew from deep in the forest and Arthur had to duck close to Llamrei's neck to avoid their flight. Six of his men fell from their mounts, and three horses toppled over as dozens of arrows flew through the trees. It was an ambush of missile fire. They had let Arthur's horsemen pass and now meant to slaughter them as they tried to escape the forest. Arthur whispered into Llamrei's ear and urged his stallion onward, his heart racing, fearful that death would take him in the forest before he secured the destruction of Clappa and the Deiran Saxons. Llamrei reared and Arthur clung to the reins. An arrow slapped into the stallion's flank and another into his chest and Arthur cried out with sorrow. Llamrei thundered towards the forest's edge and behind Arthur came only four riders who had survived the murderous arrow attack.

Arthur reached his warriors and leapt from the saddle. He flung his arms around his faithful stallion's neck and pressed his face into the muscle. 'Forgive me, old friend,' he said to the horse, his hands coming away bloody and his heart wrenched with sorrow. Arthur reluctantly handed his reins to a warrior. 'Take him to the rear and see to his wounds,' Arthur ordered.

Cavall ran to Arthur and bounded around his legs. He bent and stroked the war dog and sent him off to watch over Llamrei.

'Attack!' Arthur bellowed to his spearmen. 'Men of Britain, brave warriors of Gwynedd, Dumnonia, Powys, Gwent, Rheged, Dumnonia, Gododdin and Lothian! Our enemy awaits in those trees! Fear not their arrows. Within those trees are Saxons and their king, men who made our people suffer for years. Now is our time! Now we shall put them to the slaughter. We shall fill this forest with their dead and return lost lands to our people!'

The army raised their spears and cheered, clashing weapons.

'Who do you fight for?' Hywel bellowed.

'Arthur! Arthur! Arthur!' replied two thousand men, and Arthur led them into the trees. He sheathed Excalibur and took a shield and spear from Hywel. Ethne and her fierce *targaid* formed up behind him, and the black cloaks stretched out on either flank. The forest was too thick for shield-wall fighting, and so the Britons marched in ragged ranks, keeping with their countrymen and led by their champions.

Arthur raised his shield as the first arrows came, thudding into its boards like hammer blows.

'Ethne?' Arthur said, and the Pict warrior appeared at his side. 'Take your *targaid* and your slings and hunt those archers. I want them dead.'

'Yes, lord,' she said, with a wolfish grin. Ethne and her Picts had daubed their faces and bodies with blue woad warpaint, and they loped into the trees like wolves, slings whirring, and before long the first of Clappa's archers sang out in pain.

Arthur continued the advance, arrows thumping into the ranks as men behind him screamed and grunted as arrows found soft flesh behind hard shields. He stalked through the trees, angered by enemy archers and the toll their arrows took upon his men, but he reached the clearing, and the missiles stopped. Arthur stood in the space where trees gave way to clear ground and Clappa's men stood in the gap ripped into his defences by Arthur's riders. The faces staring back at Arthur seemed hollow, desperate and primitive, all bared teeth and deep-set eyes, unkempt hair and shining blades. These were men with nowhere to go, no retreat, men who had marched out of their homes in spring with a dream of victory and plunder, who had destroyed Elmet and Loidis and now found themselves backed into a corner in a fight for their very lives. Each wild-eyed stare told Arthur that Clappa's men knew their homes and families, their wives and children, would suffer unless they won this battle. The Britons would show little mercy to those who had enslaved their people.

'Shield wall!' Arthur ordered. 'Sound the carnyx!' Hywel blew the shrill war horn, and Arthur's army formed up in narrow ranks, thirty shields across, wide enough to charge into the gap torn into the briar fence. Arthur had explained his plan to the captains and champions before battle, and now they hurried into formation. The far left and right flanks faced out towards the forest with shields ready to absorb missiles from the trees and as Arthur led the charge from the front, arrows came from the trees again, fewer than before, but the sound of his men's shouts of pain encouraged him to the violence he must lay down to secure victory for his people.

Arthur charged in the first rank, a walking charge with spear held firm in a solid wall and his spear levelled for attack. The Saxon shield wall howled their anger and shook their spears and Arthur met them shield on shield as the crack and bang of iron and wood filled the forest with the terrible din of war. The man opposite Arthur gave way when Arthur barged him backwards, a man so thin that his arms seemed like twigs. Arthur killed him with a spear thrust to the neck and led his men onwards. The Britons filled the opening in the briar fence and the Saxons before them gave way like melting ice. It all seemed so easy, too easy, Arthur thought, and just as that warning entered his thought cage, Saxon war drums boomed in the distance. The sound came not from Clappa's camp, but from the flanks, and Arthur realised with terror that he had marched headlong into a trap. His stomach dropped, heat burned his chest, and he removed his helmet to search through the trees for a sign of the enemy.

Thousands of Saxons hurtled through the trees, howling and shaking their spears and seaxes. They came from both flanks, and Arthur's army panicked. Half of his men were inside the briar fence and the enemy who had faced his shield wall took ten steps back and screamed their defiance at him. Arthur realised there were mere hundreds inside the camp, and the greater force had lain in wait for Arthur's attack, so that now the briar fence became a trap for his own men. He turned and tried to call out orders, but his warriors panicked. The men outside the fence turned to face the enemy but found themselves outnumbered as half of Arthur's force banged and pushed against each other to get out of the narrow gap in the fence and join the fight.

What Arthur had believed was a march to a victory over a starving, beaten army became a fight to death against Saxon warriors with everything to lose. Men who would fight until their last drop of blood to survive. The Saxons inside the camp charged, and Arthur found himself attacked on three sides by a furious and cunning enemy. Clappa had outwitted him, tricked him, played on Arthur's hubris and now charged to drive home the kill with vengeful savagery.

25

A Saxon in dishevelled, lank fur roared across the camp and Arthur threw his spear, taking the man in the chest. He drew Excalibur and looked about him desperately as his men fought for their lives. All sense of discipline and order had vanished, every man fought for himself: the men inside the fence trying to push and fight their way out; the warriors outside battling to fend off an enemy who fought with the element of surprise fuelling their blades with strength.

Thoughts swirled in Arthur's mind. How had his scouts missed the massing enemy in the trees? An easy mistake to make, he supposed, in the vastness and gloom beneath the high canopy. War was trickery and surprise before the blood and death. It was understanding the enemy, and the lands on which a battle would be fought. It was hills, rivers, woods, cliffs, and using those features to lure an enemy to fight on ground of your choosing. Arthur had surprised and slaughtered his enemies countless times, but now Clappa had done the same to him, and the lives of Arthur's men hung in the balance, depending utterly on Arthur's ability to change the battle, to command them and lead them out of Clappa's trap.

'Kill the men inside the fence,' Arthur shouted to his men. 'Black cloaks on me. Kill these men first!' Arthur charged into the camp, understanding that he had to act; to stand there bemused and stuttering was to die. So Arthur went on the attack. He blocked a Saxon spear with his shield and opened the man's throat with a sweep of Excalibur's blade. Black cloaks charged into the Saxons, throwing the starving men down, cutting at them with spears, axes and seaxes. The *targaid* hurled themselves over the briars and thorns, undulating their terrifying war cry, they surged around Arthur, slings loosing stones into the enemy ranks. A Saxon leapt at Arthur and Ethne met him, cracking her curved knife across his skull with a sickening crunch, and without pause she set off again into the fray.

The enemy inside the camp died as his black cloaks battered and slashed them to ruin, and Arthur turned to the battle outside the fence. He pushed his way through the press of men and found Kai hollering at the warriors of Rheged to form a new shield wall as the Saxons slaughtered the disorganised men of Kernow and Gwent in the front rank.

'We must retreat,' Gawain said, grasping Arthur by the shoulder. 'Retreat and form up again.'

'Stand and fight,' Arthur growled.

'If we stand here, we shall all die. Is that what you want? Bury your pride, admit that Clappa tricked us, reform and then attack. They are cutting us to pieces!'

Time slowed as Arthur watched blood spill, and men die beneath Saxon blades. The front rankers tried to run, but the men behind them pushed them with their shields so that nobody attacked the Saxons, and spears, seaxes and axes tore

into shoulders, skulls, necks and chests and made the air thick
with the stink of blood and voided bowels. Einion of Powys
bullied his way to the front and cut two men down before a
Saxon stabbed a spear into his chest with such venom that the
point burst through the back of Einion's chain mail.

'No,' Arthur said to himself. 'Not like this. Not when we are
so close. It cannot end like this.' He watched six more men cut
down, turned to see the same slaughter unfold on the opposite
flank. 'Retreat,' he ordered, ripping the words from himself
despite his desire to stand and fight back. 'Retreat to the forest's
edge.'

The order went up and men ran. Bors, Gawain, Kai, Orin,
Tristan and Hywel tried to stem the panic, but it was too late.
Arthur grabbed men and shouted at them to retreat in disci-
plined order, but they could not hear him, so traumatised were
they by the Saxon ambush. Arthur's black cloaks, the men of
Rheged and Gododdin, formed up and retreated, stalking backwards through the undergrowth so that they presented a solid
shield wall towards the enemy. The Saxons continued to attack,
war drums booming, faces spattered with Arthur's men's blood.

A warrior bullied his way into the Saxon front rank, a wiry
old warrior with a lined, gaunt face, a grizzled beard and a thick
silver chain looped twice about his neck. He carried a sword in
his hand and wore a coat of shining mail. King Clappa come to
glory in his ruthless victory.

'We meet again, *Wealas*,' Clappa spat. 'I want your head,
Arthur ap Nowhere. I am going to piss in your dead throat. Your
wives will be our whores and your children our slaves. I have
you! Are you ready to die, turd of the underworld?'

Arthur ignored him, too shaken by the battle's outcome to
speak to an enemy he had sought to destroy and now found himself

retreating from. The Saxons bayed like wolves, following Arthur's retreat in a seething mass of iron, fur and blood-slick blades. Arthur held Excalibur before him and placed one foot behind the other, backing off carefully, waiting for the enemy to descend upon him.

'The gods help us!' a warrior cried out behind Arthur. 'They are behind us.'

Arthur turned, the impossibility of another counterattack draining him of strength. Surrounded by Saxons, all dreams of Britain, of Guinevere and Camelot turned to ashes in front of his eyes. Guinevere's face came to him in that moment, her breathtaking beauty, the warm touch of her skin. Clappa's cunning would rip Arthur from his love forever, leaving his ruined corpse to rot amongst the leaves and filth of the forest floor whilst Clappa paraded his head around Lloegyr as a victory trophy.

'It's true,' said Bors, pushing through the throng. 'Five hundred of them block our retreat.'

'Take Kai, the men of the Gododdin and Rheged, and kill those men, Bors. We can't die here. Not like this.'

'If we can't break out...'

'I know it. I'll hold them here.'

Bors strode off, bellowing orders and dragging men with him. Arthur set himself again to face Clappa's horde with his black cloaks, and the *targaid* gathered about him. Clappa roared at his men to charge, and they came through the trees like demons, their thin faces bent on death and destruction. Arthur caught a spear thrust upon his shield and lay about him with Excalibur. He stepped out of the shield wall and cut into the enemy. If he was going to die, then he would die fighting. He ducked beneath a knife and cut the legs from his attacker, rose and sliced Excalibur across a man's throat. A *targaid* warrior died with a seax in her belly, and another when a spear opened her throat.

Clappa waited behind his men, eyes fixed on Arthur as more Saxons came and Arthur met them. His shield broke, smashed as a Saxon battered it with a double-bladed war axe until Ethne ripped open his groin with one of her knives. Arthur tossed the ruined shield aside and fought with two hands wrapped around Excalibur's hilt. A black cloak died with two spears in his chest, and Arthur killed a bald-headed man with his sword. Battle raged, blood flowed, men died and, all the time, the Saxons attacked with renewed fury. Arthur fought in the front and so could not see how his men fared on the flanks and rear. All he could do was fight for his own life and those of the men around him. His boots trod on filth mashed into the leaf mulch. Other men's blood and offal turned the forest into a horror of death beneath the ancient trees.

The Saxons' war drums thudded relentlessly and for every enemy Arthur killed, another sprang to take his place. A man with drooping moustaches knocked Excalibur from Arthur's hand and was about to open his throat when a *targaid* warrior cut him down with her wicked knife. Arthur bent to pick up his sword, and Clappa saw his chance. The king of Deira charged forward with his sword raised and Arthur knelt, raised Excalibur and parried the blow with a loud clang, which sent a shock down Arthur's arm. Clappa drew his sword arm back to strike again and stopped. He took a step back and Arthur stood. The Saxons suddenly gave way as if blown by a god's breath and their war drums stopped. They shouted and cried out in alarm, eyes wide and lips drawn back in terror.

'*Seidr*!' they called in their native language. 'Fetches! The dead come for us!'

Arthur peered over their heads, desperate to see what had

put such fear into an enemy on the verge of a glorious victory. Then he gasped, for marching through the dense trees came ranks of Roman legionaries. Their bright helmets gleamed in the shadowy boughs with their red, bristling horsehair plumes appearing and then disappearing between the oak, ash and elm. Their iron-tipped pilum spears caught shafts of light, and their red cloaks and painted oval shields came from the gloom like a mighty legion of old, like a ghost army marching through the forest towards Clappa's Saxons.

The Romans advanced into a clearing, and Arthur laughed for joy. He raised Excalibur up high and roared unbridled delight at the heavens, for the man leading the Roman ranks was Idnerth, Primus Pilum of Loidis, a friend Arthur believed had perished in the horror of Loidis, and beside him strode Merlin, staff in hand, chanting to the gods, filling enemy hearts with dread. Idnerth came on, his red plume running crosswise to his helmet. He barked an order and his men launched their pilum spears. Those spears with their long, thin shafts of half-ash and half-iron hammered into the Saxons with deadly force.

'*Venus Victrix!*' Hywel called, weeping with unbridled delight and relief to see his countrymen marching through the trees, arriving unlooked for to send the Saxons into terrified flight.

'Attack!' Arthur called, and he charged at the stunned enemy. As Idnerth's men came closer Arthur realised it was not a full-strength legion, but only two score men, some limping, others painfully thin, survivors from Loidis come to wreak their vengeance on the hated enemy. The dense forest and clamour of battle made their numbers seem greater, but if Arthur could now see how few men Merlin and Idnerth brought to battle then it could be moments before the Saxons saw it too. Arthur barged one Saxon with his shoulder, cut another down with his sword and in one fluid movement twisted at the hip and cut the head from a Saxon's shoulders. Clappa had come so close to a stunning victory, but Idnerth's arrival gave Arthur a precious chance, a sliver of opportunity to grip the Saxons' momentary fear and shake it into a chance to live, to fight for Britain, to win and return to his love, to his Camelot, and destroy Clappa on the cusp of the Saxon king's greatest triumph.

Arthur waded into the fray, smashing enemies aside until he came face to face again with the Saxon king of Deira. Clappa fell shrieking away from Arthur's fury, still shocked at the sight of Merlin and Idnerth, not yet understanding that those few Romans could not turn the tide of battle if his men stood firm. Clappa raised his sword, but Arthur batted it aside. Clappa, king of Deira, closed his eyes and screamed like a frightened child as Arthur bore down on him with all his vengeful fury. Excalibur stabbed deep into Clappa's Saxon heart and Arthur twisted the blade, ripping and tearing at the enemy king until he flopped dead in the undergrowth and his warriors howled in horror to see their leader slain.

Black cloaks hacked and cut at the stunned enemy. Bors, Gawain and Kai led them, screaming, charging, slathered in the blood and filth of battle. That fury, the death of their king and the shocking Roman charge sent the Saxons into a rout. The Britons pursued them with unbridled battle-madness, the relief of survival on the brink of destruction imbuing their arms with vengeful strength. They swarmed past Arthur like a flock of monstrous birds, seething, slashing and cutting at the Saxons. Arthur ran to Idnerth and could not restrain himself. He flung his arms around the tall commander and laughed with sheer joy.

'I thought you were dead,' Arthur said.

'So did I,' Idnerth replied, as stoic as always. 'Then Merlin found us.'

The slaughter in the forest of Celidan continued until nightfall. The Britons who had come so close to destruction offered the enemy no mercy, and Arthur left his men to their savagery. Arthur went to Llamrei and was relieved to see his horse still standing as men treated his arrow wounds. Arthur found Merlin talking to Bors at the forest's edge, and when he approached, Merlin greeted him with a raised eyebrow.

'I came just in time,' Merlin said, like he was scolding a child. 'It is becoming a habit.'

'You did, and thank the gods for it. Idnerth?'

'I found him high in the mountains with his few remaining legionaries, all of them wounded and suffering from the shock and horror of Loidis' fall. They retreated there after the brief fight on the city walls to heal their wounds. Idnerth fought in the hills against roaming Saxon war bands, but dared not bring his men down from the heights in case they fell afoul of the larger Saxon force. Only two score of his men survived. That is all that remains of Elmet and the proud men of Loidis. Not enough to mount a counterattack against the Saxons, but men ready to strike a blow despite their wounds.'

'Two score seemed like two thousand in the trees.'

'I had rather hoped that it would. The forest was on our side, the heavy trunks and ancient trees shadowed our advance and made our numbers seem like hundreds, rather than dozens. I must confess that Idnerth and I didn't simply appear in the forest when you needed us most. We saw your army arrive, and we saw Clappa send his men out into Celidan's furthest reaches to avoid your scouts. So we waited and came to join the fight just when Idnerth thought we could turn the tide. A close-run thing, but Clappa is dead, Bernicia is destroyed, and we should rejoice in those victories. You were successful in the south. I should congratulate you on that.'

'Truly?'

'No. You could not have done it had I not persuaded Morholt to take his ships south. There was a price to be paid for the Irishman's warriors. Morholt requires husbands for his daughters, royal husbands. So I promised Morholt that his eldest daughter would marry King Marc of Kernow before winter.'

'Does King Marc know of it?'

'Not yet. Though the girl is a beauty. Iseult is her name, and I do not believe the king of Kernow, who is as famous for his number of wives as he is for the tin beneath his kingdom, will refuse such a prize.'

Arthur laughed at Merlin's haughty look of triumph, and he dragged the druid into an embrace. Merlin allowed it for a moment and then pushed Arthur away.

'Show some decorum, please. Think of the men.'

'Forgive me. We won. Deira is no more and all that remains of Bernicia is Theodric's coastal stronghold.'

'We have won the north. Lloegyr shrinks and Britain grows. A victory, a triumph indeed. You are our *dux bellorum*, the only man ruthless and brutal enough to do that which must be done for our people. Kings have died this year, the war changes, power shifts and a new Britain emerges from the blood and flames.' Merlin allowed himself a smile, winked at Arthur, and strode off into the forest, leaving Arthur to celebrate with his men.

Many had died, but Arthur's dream of a unified Britain emerged from the smoke and shadows, taking shape amongst victorious battles, the howl of the carnyx and the thrum of Saxon war drums. As Arthur congratulated his champions, and clasped the forearms of his victorious warriors, he longed to see Guinevere, to return to Camelot, and he hoped that Lancelot had taken good care of his queen, for it was all for nothing without her.

* * *

MORE FROM PETER GIBBONS

The next book in The Chronicles of Arthur series from Peter Gibbons is available to order now here:

https://mybook.to/ChroniclesArthur4

GLOSSARY

Annwn – Celtic underworld.
Bard – Professional storyteller in Celtic culture.
Caer Ligualid – Roman city in what is now Carlisle, Cumbria.
Cameliard – Brythonic kingdom in Brittany.
Civitas – Roman towns based on pre-existing Brythonic territories, with streets and imposing administrative buildings like forums and recreational buildings like amphitheatres and baths.
Druid – High-ranking priest or shaman in Celtic culture.
Excalibur – Arthur's legendary sword.
Fasces – Roman symbol of power, an axe wrapped in rods, used to symbolise a Roman magistrate's civil and military power.
Fetch – Ancient word to describe a ghost or apparition.
Gwyllion – Welsh word for a witch or spirit.
Lorica segmentata – Type of Roman armour with overlapping plates riveted to leather straps.
Pilum – Roman spear.
Scop – Poet.

Seidr – Ancient word for magic.

Volva – Seeress or witch.

Wealas – Saxon word for Britons, which also means slaves.

Ynys Môn – Island of Anglesey.

HISTORICAL NOTE

Camelot is the third book in this Arthurian series, a follow-up to *Excalibur* and *Pendragon*. We began the series with Arthur finding his way in a crumbling Britain, born into a country cast into darkness following the Roman departure in the first decade of the fifth century after four hundred years of rule. *Pendragon* saw Arthur develop into a warrior and leader of men and ultimately become high king of Britain. *Camelot* continues Arthur's journey, his story woven of Arthurian myths and legends and taking inspiration from the early texts, such as 'Y Gododdin', an elegy for warriors of the Gododdin tribe from a region in south-east Scotland, Bede, the *Historia Brittonum* (History of the Britons) written by Nennius, and the medieval work of Geoffrey of Monmouth and Chrétien de Troyes.

A big influence on the series is Nennius' work, and he wrote his *Historia Brittonum,* a history recounting the founding of Britain and a history of its kings, sometime in the ninth century. Nennius gives Arthur the Roman title *dux bellorum*, or lord of war, and provides the details of Arthur's twelve battles. Those twelve battles provide the backbone for this series, for example the battle of the River Glein which featured in *Excalibur*, and the two battles at the River Dubglas featured in *Pendragon*. In *Camelot* we have the battle of Bedegraine, and the battle at the forest of Celidan. There is significant debate between historians on the actual location for Arthur's battles because the locations mentioned in the *Historia Brittonum* do not match current place names. The battle of Bedegraine also features in the early French work *Merlin* and is an important event in Thomas Malory's *Le Morte d'Arthur*, where Arthur secures undisputed kingship. The battle of Celidan features in Nennius' list, the forest also named Cat Coit Celidon, and has been placed in different locations from southern Scotland to south-east England, and in Camelot the battle sees Arthur put an end to King Clappa and the Saxon kingdom of Deira, for now.

Camelot is well known as the legendary centre of King Arthur's realm. There is no mention of Camelot in the oldest works, and it is first mentioned in Chrétien de Troyes' twelfth-century chivalric poem *Lancelot*. In some of the medieval texts Arthur holds court at Caerleon, but by the time of later texts Arthur is firmly rooted at Camelot which Malory, for example, locates at Winchester. Camelot is clearly a legendary place, but historians such as John Leland have identified it at Cadbury Castle, a hill fort in Somerset with twelve hundred yards of perimeter surrounding an eighteen-acre enclosure and rising about two hundred and fifty feet above the surrounding countryside. It was refortified in the Arthurian era and was occupied by a powerful leader and his followers, and so I have made that hill fort the location of Arthur's famous stronghold in this novel.

Uther Pendragon first appears in the old Welsh poems but was given more prominence by Geoffrey of Monmouth in the twelfth century in his *Historia Regum Britanniae* (History of the

Kings of Britain), and Geoffrey's account of the character was used in most later Arthurian tales. He is the brother of Aurelius Ambrosius, and Geoffrey also recounts Uther's passion for Igraine and Merlin's interference in her marriage to Gorlois. Uther features heavily in this series, and it is of course from Uther that Arthur seizes the title of Pendragon, high dragon, or high king of Britain.

In this book we also see Mordred growing under Morgan and Nimue's care, and we shall see more of Mordred in the next novel as we lead up to the terrible events at the battle of Camlann. Arthur's twelve battles are far from finished, and he must march again to defend Britain against the encroaching Saxon threat.

ACKNOWLEDGEMENTS

With thanks and gratitude to Caroline, Ross, Candida and the fantastic team at Boldwood Books.

ABOUT THE AUTHOR

Peter Gibbons is a financial advisor and author of the highly acclaimed Viking Blood and Blade trilogy. He originates from Liverpool and now lives with his family in County Kildare.

Sign up to Peter Gibbons' mailing list for news, competitions and updates on future books.

Visit Peter's website: www.petermgibbons.com

Follow Peter on social media here:

facebook.com/petergibbonsauthor

x.com/AuthorGibbons

instagram.com/petermgibbons

bookbub.com/authors/peter-gibbons

ALSO BY PETER GIBBONS

The Saxon Warrior Series

Warrior and Protector

Storm of War

Brothers of the Sword

Sword of Vengeance

The Chronicles of Arthur

Excalibur

Pendragon

Camelot

WARRIOR CHRONICLES

WELCOME TO THE CLAN ✕

THE HOME OF
BESTSELLING HISTORICAL
ADVENTURE FICTION!

WARNING:
MAY CONTAIN VIKINGS!

SIGN UP TO OUR
NEWSLETTER

BIT.LY/WARRIORCHRONICLES

Boldwood

Boldwood Books is an award-winning fiction publishing company seeking out the best stories from around the world.

Find out more at www.boldwoodbooks.com

Join our reader community for brilliant books, competitions and offers!

Follow us
@BoldwoodBooks
@TheBoldBookClub

Sign up to our weekly deals newsletter

https://bit.ly/BoldwoodBNewsletter

Made in the USA
Middletown, DE
18 September 2025